SACRED GROUND

MERCEDES LACKEY

TOR

A TOM DOHERTY ASSOCIATES BOOK
NEW YORK

This is a work of fiction. All of the characters, organizations, and events portrayed in this novel are either products of the author's imagination or are used fictitiously.

SACRED GROUND

Copyright © 1994 by Mercedes Lackey

A Tor Book
Published by Tom Doherty Associates
175 Fifth Avenue
New York, NY 10010

www.tor-forge.com

Tor® is a registered trademark of Macmillan Publishing Group, LLC.

ISBN 978-0-7653-9348-7

Our books may be purchased in bulk for promotional, educational, or business use. Please contact your local bookseller or the Macmillan Corporate and Premium Sales Department at 1-800-221-7945, extension 5442, or by e-mail at MacmillanSpecialMarkets@macmillan.com.

First Edition: March 1994
Second Mass Market Edition: May 2017

Printed in the United States of America

0 9 8 7 6 5 4 3 2 1

To those who were here first
Mitaque oyasin

CHAPTER ONE

SHE POURED A dipperful of water over the hot rocks in the heaterbox, and steam hissed up in sudden clouds, saturating the dimly lit sauna with moisture. The smoke of cedar and sweetgrass joined the steam, the humidity making both scents so vivid she tasted them in the back of her throat.

She sat down cross-legged on the wooden floor, boards that had been sanded as smooth as satin underneath her bare thighs. It didn't matter to her—or more importantly, to Grandfather—that this sweatlodge was really a commercially made portable sauna; that the rocks were heated by electricity and not in a fire; that the sweetgrass and cedar smoke were from incense bought at an esoteric bookstore in Tulsa. Or even that the sweatlodge as a place for meditation was more common among the Lakotah Sioux than the Osage; Grandfather had borrowed judiciously from other nations to remake the ways of the Little Old Men into something that worked again. *The destination is what matters,* he had told her a thousand times, *and the path you take to get there. Not whether your ritual clothing is of tradecloth or buckskin, the water you drink from a stream or a spring— or even the kitchen tap. Sometimes ancient ways are not particularly wise, just old.*

So they had this contrivance of the *I'n-Shta-Heh*, the "Heavy Eyebrows," installed in what had been the useless half-bath at the back of the house she and Grandfather shared. Most of the time it served as nothing more esoteric than anyone else's sauna, useful for aching muscles and staving off colds.

Sometimes it served purposes the *I'n-Shta-Heh* who built it would never have dreamed of.

She closed her eyes, sweat salty on her upper lip, and stripped off the layers of her working self the way she had stripped the layers of her working clothing before she had taken her ritual bath and entered the now-sanctified wooden box. There were layers to *who* she was, like an onion, each layer both hiding the one beneath and keeping the one beneath from reaching outward.

Jennifer Talldeer. The face that the white world saw; ironic name for a woman a shade less than five feet in height. Doubly ironic considering how tall Osage men and women tended to be. *Your mother's genes,* was what her father said, when she asked him why she was the runt of the litter. *That sneaky Cherokee blood. You know how they are.* With no acrimony; no one in her family believed in refighting old battles. Her mother had just smiled.

Private Investigator, degree in criminology. Nice little house, nice little neighborhood, nice little mortgage, in one of the older parts of Tulsa. Nice old neighbors, who thought it charming of her to take in her aged and "infirm" (ha!) grandfather. That persona was the first to go, washed away in the steam.

Next, the woman who danced at the powwows, engaged in her little hobby of rescuing sacred objects from profane hands; another mask, just one a little closer to the truth, a little deeper to the bone. A woman who bore two names, one for the earth-people and one for the sky-people, although it was the latter she used. *Hu-lah-to-me*, Good Eagle Woman, daughter of *Hu-lah-shu-tsy*, Red Eagle. Good Eagle was not registered on either side of her family, Osage or Cherokee, but she and her family had more right to call themselves Native American than plenty who were registered and could speak of no more than a single grandparent of the full blood.

Fly away, Good Eagle. Gone; there wasn't much there anyway. Jennifer was what she *did*; Good Eagle was simply an intermediary between what she did and what she was.

Last layer; what she *was*.

The third Osage name, a name that was learned and not given. Kestrel-Hunts-Alone.

Not a "normal" name for a woman.

Kestrel, pupil of a man with three names, her grandfather. His Heavy Eyebrows name, Frank Talldeer. His second, *quite* out of keeping with the *Tzi-Sho*, and a name embodying contradiction, *Ka-ha-ska*, White Crow. And his third—embodying even more contradiction than the first—*Ka-ha-me-o-pah*, Mooncrow; crows do not fly at night, nor are they associated with the moon, and those birds that do fly at night are generally the enemies of crows. The power of the Osage centered on the sun, not the moon; a man of power should have had a sun-name, like her father's. Contradiction piled on contradiction. . . .

Shamanic apprentice to her grandfather, her spirit-name was taken from her spirit-animal, student as she was in the teaching of one of the Little Old Men of the *Ni-U-Ko'n-Ska*, the Children of the Middle Waters, whom the Heavy Eyebrows and Long Knives called "Osage." By birth and by spirit, she was gentle *Tzi-Sho* gens, the peacemakers, and here lay the irony, for not only was Mooncrow teaching her the peaceful medicine of *Tzi-Sho*, he was teaching her the medicine of the warriors, the Earth People, the *Hunkah*.

And, as if that were not enough, he was teaching her the special medicines reserved for each of the clans! For that, she had thought, one had to be a Medicine Chief and not simply a shaman. Grandfather had never once come out and said that he was—

Then again, maybe he was simply living up to his contrary nature. *He* wasn't registered, either; nor were any of his forefathers. And he wouldn't use any of the Peyote rituals that had crept into, and indeed supplanted, most of the Osage ways; they were like kudzu or mimosa in the red-clay soil—not native, but once there, impossible to get rid of. He had certainly been teaching her things no tradition she knew of called for; he had adopted the Lakotah sacred pipe; and he was passing to her the medicines of virtually every Osage clan from Bear to Otter to Eagle, things she thought were kept as clan secrets.

That *would* be like him; the man who cheerfully used an electric sauna for a sweatlodge, who prepared sacred tobacco in a fruit-dryer bought at an ex-hippie's yard sale, who purchased his cornmeal for ceremonies at the big chain grocery—

Who taught a woman Warrior's Medicine.

Kestrel realized where her thoughts were leading her, and resolutely brought her concentration back where it belonged. This Seeking was not about Mooncrow, but about herself. About her progress, or rather, lack of progress.

There was something holding her back, and she did not know what it was. Mooncrow would not tell her, saying only that if there really was something holding up her progress, she already knew what it was; typical contrary reasoning. She wondered where he'd gotten that particular mind-set; it wasn't typical for Osage Medicine. And it certainly made life difficult for his student. She could have used a teacher less like Coyote and Crow, and more like Buffalo and Eagle. Simpler instruction, fewer tricks; more straightforward direction, fewer riddles.

He's doing it to me again. Making her annoyed, taking her thoughts off the path. To be honest, making her *angry.* He had chosen to teach her, and *how* he taught her was his choice, not hers. It was her duty, her privilege, to learn. If she were failing somewhere, it was up to her to find out where and why, and correct it. Only then would she earn her medicine-pipe.

She let her temper cool, poured another dipperful of water on the rocks, saw that the cedar still burned, and started over, determined that Mooncrow and his contrary ways would not distract her again. He was "just doing that," like the buffalo, who did what they pleased, when and where they pleased, and if it seemed out-of-season, who would dare to stop them? Steam wreathed her, heat and semidarkness held her, and this time she slipped away from herself to fly among the other worlds, among the other Peoples of Water, Earth, and Sky.

It was in the Sky she found herself, a sky blue and cloudless to the east, dark and cloudy to the west, with Grandfather Sun on her back and wings, and the heat of thermals off the prairie below bearing her up. She flew above the meeting of forest and prairie, with the oaks and redbud, cottonwood and willow stretching into the east, and an endless sea of tallgrass to the west.

If she had worn human shape, there would have been the hot, dry scent of grasses carried by the thermal she rode, but raptors have no sense of smell, and all that came to her through her nares was the heavy, drowsy heat.

She flew in the shape of her Spirit-Animal, the kestrel of her name. A good shape, one suited to swift travel, although if she had hopped like Toad or crawled like Turtle, the results would have been the same—those she needed to have counsel of would have found her, if she had not been able to travel swiftly enough to find them. That was the way it was; the *Wah-K'on-Tah* saw to it, in whatever ways it suited the Great Mystery to work. If, however, she chose to perch and wait—she would never find those wise counselors. And it wasn't a good idea to tempt other, smaller mysteries into action against her by being lazy.

So she flew, low over tallgrass prairie, until movement below sent her up to hover as only kestrel, of all the falcons, could.

Rabbit looked up at her from the shadows at the base of the grass, his nose twitching with amusement. "Come down, little sister," he offered. "Come and tell me what you seek, out of your world and in mine."

She stooped and landed beside him, claws closing on grass stems as if they were a mouse. "An answer," she said, folding her wings with a careful flip to align the feathers properly, for a raptor's life depends on her feathers. "What is it that keeps me unworthy to become a pipebearer? Where have I failed?"

"I am not the one to ask," said Rabbit. His pink nose quivered as he tested the air, constantly, and his gray-brown coat blended perfectly with the dead grass of last year. "You know what my counsel is; silence and care, and always vigilance. I do not think that will help you much. But perhaps our cousin in the grasses there can answer you."

He pointed with his quivering pink nose at a spiderweb strung between three tall grass stems and the outstretched branch of a blackberry bush. Spider watched her from the center of her web, swaying with the breeze; a large black and tan orb-spider, nearly the size of her kestrel-head. Rabbit accepted her word of thanks and hopped away. In a moment he had vanished among the grasses.

She repeated her question to Spider, who thought it over for a moment or two, as the breeze swayed her web and flies buzzed tantalizingly near. "You must know that I am going to counsel patience," she said, "for that is my way. All things come to my web, eventually, and break their necks therein."

Kestrel bobbed her head, though she did not feel particularly patient. "That is true," she replied. "But it is more than lack of patience—I must be unready, somehow. There is something I have not done properly."

"If you feel that strongly, then you are unready," Spider replied, agreeing with her. "I see that you do have great patience—except, perhaps, with your Grandfather. But he is a capricious Little Old Man, and difficult, and his tricks do not make you laugh as they did when you were a child. I think perhaps I cannot see *what* it is that makes you unready. Why not ask one with sharper eyes than mine?"

She wondered for a moment if there was a hidden message in that little speech about her Grandfather, but if there was, she couldn't see it. Spider pointed to the blue sky above with one of her forelegs, and Kestrel's sharp eyes spotted the tiny dot that could only be Prairie Falcon soaring high in a thermal. Her feathers slicked down to her body in reflex, for the prairie falcon of the plains of the outer world would quite happily make a meal of a kestrel.

For that matter, if she let fear overcome her, Prairie Falcon of the *inner* world would happily make a meal of Kestrel.

But that was a lesson she had learned long ago, and the tiny atavistic fears of the form she wore were things she had overcome many times. She thanked Spider, who turned her interest back to a dewdrop threatening her web, and launched herself into the air.

She returned to the steam-laden sauna with no answers, only a load of defeat, and the surety that she was not only unready, she was unworthy. Not good enough.

And she still didn't know why.

Kestrel became Good Eagle Woman; Good Eagle Woman assumed the mask of Jennifer. She opened her eyes and stood carefully, feeling for the switch that turned the heater-box off, then finding the door latch and pushing it open, releasing the steam into the air-conditioned cool of the hall. There were old bathrobes hanging beside the sauna; she wrapped herself in one and headed for the shower.

As the hot water sheeted down her body, she tried to let it clear her spirit of depression. It didn't succeed, not entirely.

She should have been ready by now; she should have been good enough. She had mastered skills just as difficult in a shorter time frame—to save money, she'd gotten her four-year degree in three years, while continuing to study the shamanic traditions. *Not good enough;* that hung in her chest, a weight on her soul and heart, pulling her to the ground when she wanted to fly. It was time—it was more than time. She had spent years in this apprenticeship; she *should* have been ready by now. She should have been good enough.

How long had she been doing this, anyway?

Since I was just a kid, she thought, trying to remember the very first time her grandfather had singled her out for teaching. Then it came to her—

"You see Rabbit?" Granpa asked her, coming up behind her on the white-painted back porch, so quietly he had made no sound. But she had known he was there. She always knew where he was; he was a Presence to the heart, like a little sun, a glow, always shining with energy and cheer.

She had been sitting on the porch for a while, just watching the birds at the feeder, when the little rabbit had crept cautiously up to help himself to some of the stale bread her mother put out for the crows and grackles. He couldn't have been more than two months old; no longer dependent on his mother, but scarcely half the size of a grown rabbit. He never stopped watching all around while he nibbled; never stopped swiveling his ears in every direction, alert for danger. His fur looked very soft, softer than her cat's, and her fingers itched to stroke him. But she knew that if she moved, he would be off in a moment.

She nodded, not speaking. Granpa wouldn't frighten the rabbit no matter what he did or said, she knew that, but she also knew she would. It was just a fact, like the green grass. Granpa could walk right up to a wild deer and touch it. She wouldn't be able to get within a mile of one.

"No, not just this rabbit—" Granpa persisted, *"Rabbit."*

She had not puzzled at the statement, as virtually any adult and most children would have. She heard what he meant, not what he said, and looked deeper—

That was when the half-grown cottontail became Rabbit, grew to adult-human size and more, sat up, and looked at her.

"Hello, little sister," he said politely. "Thank your mother for her bread, but ask her if she would put some of the kitchen greens out here for us as well, would you? Carrot-ends taste just fine to us, and bug-chewed cabbage leaves, or rusty lettuce. Crow might like a taste of carrot now and again, too."

Wide-eyed, she had nodded, noting how modest he was, how quiet; how he had made his thanks before making his request. It came to her then, right into her mind, how hard life was for him—how everything was his enemy. He not only had to flee his ancient foes of Hawk and Coyote, Rattlesnake and Fire, but the new ones brought by humans, Dog and Cat. And humans hunted him too—she'd eaten rabbit often, herself.

But he survived by being quiet, by skill at hiding and running, and by being very, very fruitful. He sired many offspring, so that one out of every ten might live to sire or give birth.

And he did well by being something of an opportunist. Now that the land had been covered with houses with neat backyards, there were alleys full of weeds to eat and hide in, and sometimes the kitchen rubbish to eat as well. There were spaces between fences and under houses or garages to make into warrens. Dogs and cats could be dodged by escaping into another yard, or under a porch. And of the hawks and falcons, only kestrels hunted among the houses at all regularly. Rabbit had adapted to the world created by the Heavy Eyebrows, and now prospered where creatures that had not adapted were not prospering.

Just like us, she thought with astonishment. *Just like Mommy and Daddy and Granpa—*

Because they lived in a house in the suburbs of Claremore, because Daddy didn't get tribal oil money, he had a job as a welder, and that was the same for Mommy and Granpa, too. There was nothing to show that they were Osage and Cherokee except their name. They lived just like their neighbors, went to church every Sunday at First Presbyterian, and Mommy even had bridge club on Thursday afternoon—except, like Rabbit, they had a secret life of stories, traditions, and dances and special ceremonies that none of their neighbors knew about. They had their hiding places in between the "fences" and under the "porches" of the white ways, where they did their Osage and Cherokee things—

Granpa had laughed, and Rabbit dwindled and became a half-grown cottontail, who had fled like a wind-blown leaf into the dark shadows under the honeysuckle.

That was when he had taken her by the hand, led her in to Daddy, who was finishing his breakfast, and said, "This one."

That was definitely it, the moment she had begun training at Grandfather's hands. There hadn't been many children her age in their neighborhood and there weren't any of them she really cared to hang around with; Grandfather had taken pains to make the training into games, and she hardly missed not having playmates. At some point, though, it had turned serious, no longer a game but a responsibility.

She rinsed her hair with a torrent of hot water, wryly congratulating herself on putting in the biggest hot-water tank available. A small luxury, like the sauna. An advantage of being an adult with your own home—though when it came to responsibility, she had been an adult for years before she had moved out of her parents' home. Maybe they were both a little environmentally excessive, but she was frugal with her energy use in general, and she confronted her conscience with the stacks of recycling bins in the kitchen; she recycled everything, and food leavings went either to the neighbor's compost heap or to feed the birds, squirrels, rabbits, and freeloading cats.

There was no question when *that* turning point of adult responsibility in her lessons had happened; it had been at one of the powwows in the Tulsa area, and she had been thirteen.

Until tonight, the powwow had been a lot of fun. Dad had won the Traditional Fancy-dancer Contest, but although she had been urged to compete by several of her friends, Good Eagle had remained in the stands during the ladies' contests, held there by a growing feeling of tension. For now—there was something in the air, and not just the hint of the thunderstorm that usually put in an appearance every year during this particular powwow.

The ponderous heat of August, nearly one hundred to-day, had baked the area in and around the grandstands as thoroughly as if they were inside a giant oven. The grass lay parched and burned to soft brown, limp strands of fiber, with only a hint of green near the roots; the earth still radiated heat, cracked and baked flint-hard. That was one reason why the adult contests were always held at night—to prevent the participants from passing out with sunstroke.

And although rain threatened, it had not fallen, and the arena lights made a haze of the dust raised by hundreds of dancing feet. Tonight there wasn't even a breeze to clear it away.

Something else weighed heavily tonight besides the heat; Grandfather felt it too, for he was unusually quiet. She kept looking around at the stands, wondering who or what it could be—then beyond the stands, up into the sky, where heat-lightning flickered orange behind the trees. Grandfather's hand took hers, and she started as a kind of electric charge passed between them.

It jolted her out of herself—but not into the other worlds. She was still in her own world, standing beside her body as Grandfather stood beside his. To any onlooker, they were only an old man and his small granddaughter, enraptured by the dancers.

"Someone is trying to make trouble, Kestrel," Grandfather said. "Two someones, I think. One of them is white— he wants to cause a fight and blame it on the Peoples. But the other is Osage, he wants the fight too, but he wants it to get power over some of the young hotheads. That is what we feel. We must deal with both these young men."

"But Grandfather, how are we to stop this fight—like this?" she asked, puzzled. "Shouldn't the policemen take care of it?"

An innocent question; at thirteen, she had still trusted the police. She had still trusted in white man's justice. Grandfather had not disabused her of that—because he was wise enough to know that sometimes the wrongs were not entirely one-sided. Perhaps that was why she had gone into law in the first place. . . .

"I will deal with the white boys; I am more used to this way of things than you are," he told her. "But I need a young warrior to deal with the other—" His eyes sparkled as he looked at her, and she knew that she was the one he meant. Excitement had made her shiver; this was an adult task. And Grandfather made it clear that she was to deal with this young man without supervision.

She saw then that he had his own medicine-costume on; it looked much like his dancing-gear, except that he carried his implements openly, not hidden in their pouches.

"He is taking peyote," Grandfather continued, a faint note of disgust in his voice. "He has taken it already, thinking it will help him dance better, to raise the power he needs to control and impress his friends. He has not even done it properly; he has not followed either the West Moon or East Moon Church ways; he has simply made up some nonsense of his own. He will be able to see you. You must go and stop him."

It never entered her head to tell him no. Grandfather was right; this was important. There had been trouble at this site before, and there were people who came to the powwows purely to harass the participants. The only way to get permission to use public land like Mohawk Park was to make the event open to the public; that meant open to troublemakers, too. Liquor was a problem, for people often brought strong alcohol with them; heat and hot tempers did not help in the least.

"He is down among the dancers, there," Grandfather said, and slid down under the grandstand, into a shadow. What came out of the shadow was not a human but a rangy old coyote, who gave her a hanging-tongue coyote grin and was gone.

If her responsibility was down among the dancers milling around the entrance to the arena for the next competition, that gave her an advantage. She only needed to go down there and walk among them in spirit. There was no reason for a woman to be in their company, and her target would be the only one who would notice her, since she would not be wearing her body.

No sooner decided than done; she dropped down under the grandstand and drifted through the crowd there to the place where the dancers had gathered. Then she walked among them, staring each one in the face.

They ignored her, intent on their preparations, unable to see her, except perhaps as a ghostly shadow.

All but one.

He glared at her, and looked ready to speak. She saw the peculiarly fixed stare of a Peyote-taker, and knew that he was the one her Grandfather had meant.

She gave him no opportunity to speak. Instead, she seized him by the wrist, and as he started in surprise and tried to resist, she stepped off into the other worlds, taking his spirit with her.

As she pulled his spirit from his body, she sensed his body collapsing; not too surprising, for Grandfather claimed that the Peyote-takers who did not follow the proper Ways relied on the drug rather than discipline to walk among the worlds, and as a consequence had no control over their bodies when they left them. He did not approve of Peyote at all, really, but he would not condemn others for using it if they were properly prepared, as this man was not. She had transformed herself as she stepped over the threshold; now she was no longer a little girl in a buckskin dress but a tall young man, modeled after her brother, in full warrior's gear. She sensed that this young man would not listen to anyone except someone he deemed stronger than himself.

He pulled out of her grip; she let him. He stood looking about, at the open prairie, full moon overhead, with no sign of humans in any direction he cared to stare. Slowly, his eyes widened, as he realized where he must be.

"You meant to cause a fight," she said flatly, knowing what he had intended without needing to ask him. "You just wanted to get on television, so you could look important to your friends. You tell them that you're a big civil-rights activist, but all you want is to look like a big shot. You've been telling them that you're a Medicine Person, a shaman, but you aren't a shaman; you're just a phony, a faker, and everything you do is just tricks and drugs."

If her accusations surprised him with their accuracy, he wasn't going to admit it. He simply crossed his arms over his chest, and she sensed he was going to try to bluff his way out of this.

"While you're pretending to have Medicine Powers, all you've done is have a couple of sweatlodges and taken a lot of peyote," she continued sternly. "You didn't even do the sweatlodges right, and you might just as well have gone to a health club instead."

He needs to learn a lesson, she thought. *That is what Grandfather wants me to do—see that he gets it. He cares more for himself and what he can make people do than whether or not it is good for them—*

That was when she realized who should deliver the lesson, and what it should be. As he regained his courage and turned a frowning face to try to bully her, she stepped back a pace, and transformed again.

This time, she wore the semblance of the She-Wolf, and she raised her nose to the moon to summon the Pack.

Howls answered her from all sides, and before the young man could blink, he found himself surrounded by the Wolves of the Pack, both the great gray timber wolves and their smaller cousins of the prairie, and even one or two of the rangy red wolves that were long gone from her world. They all stared at him with great yellow eyes, fur tipped with silver from the moon above.

"You called the Pack, sister," said the Pack Leader, gravely.

She bowed her head to him; as a female, she need not bare her throat in submission to a male. "I did, brother," she replied. "This is one who leads his pack into danger for the sake of his own ambition and prestige, and does not care what will befall them so long as his power is increased."

"So," said the Leader, turning his golden gaze on the young man, who shrank away. "You think perhaps I should challenge his right to lead, then?"

Again she bowed her head. "As you wish, Pack Leader," she replied humbly. "I am but a young female; I only know this one needs discipline."

The Leader grinned toothily. "Then discipline he shall have."

In a moment, there was a young Wolf where the young man had stood; another moment passed while he trembled with shock and surprise; then the Lead Wolf was on him, treating him as he would any young fool who dared to challenge him for the right to lead the Pack.

There would be no killing—oh no. But before this one was sent back to his body by the contemptuous fling of a pair of lupine jaws, he would be certain he was about to be killed, not once but a hundred times over. Likely, he would not again dare to reach for Medicine Powers he was not entitled to, with the help of peyote. Not after this experience.

Satisfied that the Lead Wolf had the situation well in hand, she stepped back across the threshold and into her own body, just in time to see the competition begin. Paramedics were taking the young man who had collapsed to the first-aid tent; they were probably assuming heatstroke. He would wake up soon—and with no more thoughts of causing trouble tonight, at least.

Grandfather's hand tightened around hers, and she looked up into his wrinkled, smiling face. "Well done," he whispered.

That was all. He never told her what *he* had done, but later her father told them a story he'd gotten from one of the Tulsa County Sheriffs, about a dog that had spooked the normally steady horse ridden by one of the mounted officers. The rangy dog—reportedly a German shepherd—had driven the horse right down a trail away from the powwow and into a gathering of young white boys who were carrying bats and chains, were drunk, and were obviously out to start a fight. The officer had rounded them up with the help of his suddenly cooperative horse, and had seen they were escorted out of the park—and had arrested the most aggressive for public intoxication. "Damndest thing they'd ever seen," her father had said, with a curious glance at Grandfather. "Those crowd-control ponies just don't spook. And to head in the right direction like that—"

Grandfather hadn't said anything, and neither had Jennifer. But from that moment, the games ended, and the serious work began.

From then on, she'd applied herself with the same determination that she'd given to her studies. There hadn't been much room in her life for anything else, particularly not once she started her sideline of "finding." The first time it had been by accident; she'd been working on a case that had taken her up to Indiana, tracing the movements of a child-support dodger. She'd found herself in a tiny town with four hours to kill, and had in desperation followed a sign that pointed the way to a "county museum."

"Museum" wasn't exactly what she would have called it. It looked more like the leavings of the attics for miles around for the past several generations. There was an attempt at outlining the county history in the first room, but after that, it had been dusty glass case after case full of mostly unlabeled flotsam. Without a doubt, some of it was genuine and valuable; the Civil War artifacts, for instance—

But right beside war diaries that screamed for proper preservation were stuffed squirrels, stuffed birds, stuffed fish . . .

. . . a mummified mermaid . . . a shrunken head . . . someone's collection of jelly jars. . . .

And the relics.

She nearly doubled over with nausea; she couldn't even bear to touch the case. Scalps, medicine bags, articles of clothing, weapons, and three or four dozen skulls, all of them crying out to her of death. Bloody, horrible death. Kestrel had come very near to starting a mourning keen until the Jennifer persona took over.

She staggered to the front of the museum and managed to ask about that particular case. The attendant, a girl who was obviously trying to do her best, first described the terrible problem she was having, trying to preserve the things worth preserving with no money. She carried on at length about the importance of the papers and belongings of the settlers.

Gradually it dawned on Jennifer that this girl never said a word about the Indians; so far as she was concerned, the history of the area began and ended with the white settlers.

When she finally got the girl to tell her about the case of bones and artifacts, the girl shrugged dismissively. "Mound builders of some kind," she said. "Abram Vanderzandt found them when he arrived looking for a place to homestead, and they were all dead. Probably some other tribe killed them, and he could have taken credit and turned in the scalps for bounty, but he was an honest man and he just collected a few souvenirs."

The girl continued, apparently blithely unaware—or uncaring—that Jennifer was Native American, that she had dismissed the taking of "souvenirs" from the victims of the massacre as casually as if they had been nothing more important than the stuffed squirrels.

For a moment, Jennifer was outraged—until the girl continued. And it became clear that she attached sanctity to *no one*'s dead, and would have happily looted every graveyard in the county if she thought she could get any kind of information from the graves.

And it was her attitude that only those who had left *written* accounts of themselves—the white settlers—were worthy of attention that gave Jennifer an idea.

"Well, the reason I asked about that particular case," she

said, interrupting a plaint of how the Civil War relics were falling to pieces, "is that I collect Indian relics. I don't suppose you'd be able to sell me those, would you?"

The girl gaped at her, then stammered something about "county property." Jennifer nodded, and said, "So who's in charge of county property? The Assessor? Or the County Commissioner?"

It took several phone calls before it was established that the County Commissioner *did* have the authority to sell property deeded to the museum. Jennifer was not going to let this opportunity slip through her fingers, and the volunteer was not about to lose a chance at some funding for *her* pet project. So when Jennifer urged, "Let's go ask him," the girl led the march straight to the tiny office on the fourth floor.

She had the feeling that she could have bought half the museum if she'd wanted; the Commissioner was overjoyed to sell something the girl assured him was "worthless." He was probably very tired of her pleas for money; now she had some, and maybe she'd leave him alone for a while.

Jennifer was fairly certain that the sale was only quasilegal at best, and she hadn't cared. It was doubtful that anyone would pursue her.

It had taken every ounce of determination to take the box of relics, smile, and thank them.

The place where the settler in question had discovered the massacre was now in the middle of a state park. That made things easier.

Whatever the tribe's rites had been, no one knew them now. Jennifer could only inter them near where they had died, trying to recreate a rite as best she could from her own intuition and Medicine knowledge, as well as from things she had learned about the Peoples who had once lived in the area, gleaned hastily from the county library. She found a place she thought would be undisturbed, one of the lesser, less interesting mounds near what had been the village, and spent most of the day digging into the side. At sunset, she had laid them to rest as best she could.

Then she covered her tracks, and went back to the job she was being paid to do.

But that had given her an idea. There were hundreds, if not thousands, of artifacts in profane hands, all over the country. Not just museums, but in the hands of people like private collectors, and in the hands of the descendants of Indian agents. Some agents had been good, well-intentioned, if woefully Judeo-Christian–centered people, but some had been thieves who took anything they could get their hands on, and others had felt the only way to "pacify" the Indians was to destroy their culture. Most of those artifacts didn't matter; much—but some—

For some, it would be as if collectors had robbed the tomb of Abraham Lincoln for the sake of the bones, or stolen the relics of Catholic saints out of their shrines. As if some museum knowingly bought the Black Stone after it was stolen from the shrine at Mecca. The remains of Ancestors deserved a proper interment—and medicine objects deserved to go back to the hands that cherished them. That was when she had decided that *she* would do something about the situation; tracking these objects down and returning them to the appropriate hands. There were plenty of people at work on the major museums, using publicity and lawyers to regain lost artifacts and remains; she would concentrate on getting the things back in the hands of private individuals. Grandfather had approved, and that was all she had needed.

It took time, but she had time—and what else was she doing with her life, anyway? Certainly there were no men in it. She might as well do something useful with her free time.

Now I'm getting depressed—no, I'm depressing myself on purpose, she decided. *This is ridiculous. What I need right now is a good night's sleep.*

She turned off the water and wrapped her dripping hair

in a towel, bundling herself back up in a robe. A big glass of orange juice, then bed.

The living room was dark, the house locked up; Grandfather had gone off to bed himself already. She shook her head at the time; she hadn't realized it was that late.

But as she slipped in between the cool cotton sheets, she felt a familiar tingling that told her that her Seeking hadn't ended in the sweatlodge. She barely had time to settle herself before she found herself out in the Worlds again.

But this was no World she knew; the place was grim and frightening, calling up a feeling of disturbance inside her that made her feel a little sick.

Beneath a gray overcast sky, a dead, chemical-laden wind stirred the branches of withered trees planted in little sterile circles of hard-baked earth. Except for those tiny circles of dead ground, the rest was concrete as far as the eye could see. She turned, slowly, and saw nothing else; nothing but leafless trees and lifeless earth—a parking lot for the damned.

Then, beneath one of the trees, she saw, with an internal shock, the desiccated corpse of a bird.

Hesitantly, with her stomach churning, she approached it. In a moment she saw that it had been a bald eagle; it lay sprawled ungracefully on the bare gray concrete, lying in a way that suggested it had dropped dead—perhaps from poison—rather than being shot or knocked out of the sky. The harsh breeze stirred its feathers as she stared down at it.

Something about the eagle jarred a memory—hadn't there been something about that mall-project on the Arkansas River near the eagles' nesting site?

She looked up, suddenly, and realized what this World symbolized.

I've been concentrating so much of my attention internally that I've been ignoring my connections to my own World and what's going on around me. Maybe that's what's been holding me back. . . .

As if she had somehow satisfied something—or someone—with that thought, she found herself moving out of that World and back into her own. She started to relax—

Then something dark, shapeless, and completely evil loomed up, interposing itself between her and the way back.

It looked at her for a moment, while she tried to shrink into something so small she could evade its gaze. The ploy didn't work; it reached for her, with eager, greedy interest.

Fear overcame her. She turned and fled.

CHAPTER TWO

"I DUNNO," LARRY Bushyhead said, staring meditatively at the raw red earth of the site of the new Riverside Mall. About half the site had been rough-cleared of brush, a quarter of the whole site leveled out flat and even, so the yuppies wouldn't have to park their cars on an incline. The scrub oak and cottonwood, weeds and tallgrass might not look like anything worth saving to a town-dweller, used to manicured lawns and landscaped shrubbery, but Larry was a hunter. They saw weeds; he saw habitat for rabbit, quail, squirrel and meadowlark, and hunting territory for hawks and even bald eagles. Habitat going under the bulldozer blade. His baloney sandwich dangled from his fingers, momentarily forgotten. "I dunno, Johnny. I took the job, a guy's gotta work, but I'm still not sure I like this." Larry leaned against his bulldozer, which served as an impromptu perch for half a dozen of his fellow workers.

"I know what you mean." Rich Blackfox, one of the other dozer operators, nodded agreement as he swirled the

Coke around in the bottom of his can. "It's not just another damn yuppie mall going up, it's this site. The elders of most of the tribes around here didn't like it—Sutton didn't like it either."

"Sutton who?" asked someone else on the other side of the dozer, a white guy none of the three knew very well, in the usual hot-weather "uniform" of sweat-soaked T-shirt and work jeans. His hard hat had "Cliff" stenciled on it. "Who's Sutton? What's not to like about a mall?" He lit up a cigarette. "My wife can't wait for this one to go up, so she can go run up the charge cards."

"Sutton Avian Research Center, over to Bartlesville," Rich told him. "You know, the eagle people, the ones that run the tours up by the dam in February."

"Oh, yeah!" The man brightened, and he grinned. "Yeah, I went up there this spring, watchin' the birds fish, saw that little gal from Sutton with the tame one. Boy, she's got guts, I wouldn't let anything with a beak like that anywhere *near* my face!" He took another drag on his cigarette, then discarded it. "So what is it they don't like?"

Rich stared upriver, squinting against the sunlight. The Arkansas was at a low point after three weeks without rain. In fact, it looked as if you could walk across it, with sandbars rising out of the water all across the basin. "Sutton says we're too close to the places those eagles are nesting. They say we're gonna drive 'em away, and there just aren't enough good places for 'em to go, especially where people won't take pot-shots at 'em. My tribal elders say the same thing."

"Huh!" The other man followed Rich's stare, as if he expected to see one of the birds right then and there. "How many of them are there?"

"Eight pairs, at last count," Larry put in. "That's the most nests in fifty years." He sighed. "Here they got a pretty good chance—someplace else, they got odds of ending up in some scumbag's trunk."

Even Cliff nodded at that; eagle-poaching had made the headlines again; a poacher had been caught during a routine traffic-stop, with his trunk full of dead birds. There hadn't been a man or woman on the crew that hadn't been outraged by the discovery.

Larry shrugged. "But Fish and Game says they'll stay, says they're used to us now, and we won't scare them off. I dunno." He looked around the site again. "If you ask me, whoever decided to plant a mall here is dumber than dirt. What happens the next time we get one of those 'hundred-year storms' and the Army Corps of Engineers has to open the floodgates upriver?"

"We get bigtime flood sales down here," laughed the other man. "Seems like we've been getting those 'hundred-year storms' of yours about every three or six months lately!"

Larry nodded. "You got it. Dumb as dirt, man."

The placid Arkansas River, with sandbars rising out of the yellow-brown water like the backs of a pod of beached dolphins, and lower than it had been all year, hardly looked like a candidate for flooding. But before the Army Corps of Engineers had put in their flood-control program, parts of Tulsa had suffered more than one disaster. And it could happen again; if there was too much rain, floodgates would have to be opened, and the Arkansas could turn into the raging devil some old stories painted it. When it did—not "if", but when—this mall could well be underwater.

So why put it here? That was what Larry didn't understand. There had to be a dozen sites that were better candidates, especially given the proximity of this one to the eagles. That particular fight had cost the developers plenty in extra studies and court costs.

He'd had a bad feeling about this place ever since he'd set foot on it—but he knew better than to say anything about *that*. He got enough ribbing from the guys on the crew about being a superstitious Indian, just because he had a medicine wheel his daughter had made him dangling from the rearview mirror in place of the fuzzy dice from his street-rodder days. He didn't need to give them any more ammo.

Still, there was something creepy about this place—and the boss. Rod Calligan didn't fit the profile, somehow. Larry had seen a lot of developers in his time; some were slimy scum, some were just guys, but Rod was a different breed of cat, all right. Or maybe snake. The man was cold, he had a way of looking at you that made you think he was totaling up your entire net worth right there on the spot. But he was smart, real smart; he could gauge the amount of time a crew would have to spend clearing a particular site right down to the hour, and he had a penalty clause built into the contract that kicked in unless the cause for delay was weather that *he* said was too bad to work in. Basically, he had to come down to the site, agree that the weather was too rough, and let them go home—then he would go up to the site office and make a note on the contract, extending the due date.

He sure seemed too sharp to have made the mistake of putting a mall on a floodplain.

Larry glanced at his watch and finished his sandwich in a couple of bites. Lunch was about over, and you never knew when Calligan and his Beemer were likely to show up. Bad feeling or no bad feeling, there was more ground to clear before quitting time.

He shooed the rest of the guys off his dozer and started the engine, wondering where he ought to take her when this job was over. The powerful engine roared to life, drowning any other sounds, and filling the air with diesel fumes. The seat vibrated and rocked as he sent the dozer over the little hillocks they hadn't smoothed down yet. There were rumors that Rogers College was thinking of putting up another building—but weighed against rumors of a job around town was the certainty of work on the turnpike up around Miami way. . . .

He swung the dozer around to the place he'd quit, engaged the blade, and put her in motion. It sure was hot out here; he was more or less used to it, but he figured he must go through a couple of gallons of water a day. It kind of made him mad to be plowing up trees just so a bunch of yuppies from Tulsa had more places to spend their money.

Suddenly, the uneasy feeling he'd had built to a crescendo; there was something *wrong* with the way the earth felt under the blade—

He braked, and killed the motor—and looked down.

And froze, for the treads had stopped a mere inch away from a skull.

A human skull.

It must have been at least ninety-five out in the sun, but Larry still felt cold, chilled right down to his gut, which was in knots. He'd backed the dozer off, you bet, and damn fast when he'd turned up those bones. For one horrible moment, he'd been certain he'd uncovered some kind of dumping place for the victims of a serial killer or something, like the guy in Ok' City. The other guys had come at his yell of surprise and—yes, fear. They clustered around the dozer, and the place where the blade had stopped. There were more bones there, more skulls.

Only a closer look showed that the bones were old, really old, and what was more, there were broken pots and things mixed in with them. It was Keith Pryor, another Osage, who said out loud what had been trying to break out of Larry's own muddy thoughts.

"It's a burial ground," Keith said flatly. "We've been digging up sacred ground."

That was when Larry realized that he had *known*, from the moment he'd seen them, what those artifacts were. They were Osage. He'd been digging up the graves of his own ancestors. Old tales flitted through his mind; there were terrible things that happened to those who desecrated graves.

"Oh, man," he said, unhappily, wondering if old man Talldeer could be talked into an emergency ceremony. Not that he *believed* the Little People were going to take revenge for this, and it wasn't as if he'd done it deliberately, but—

—but he didn't care. He was Osage, and the Osage honored their ancestors. He needed someone like Shaman Talldeer to let the ancestors and the Little People know that he meant no disrespect, no sacrilege. And then, to kill the trail from this desecrated site back to him.

One part of his mind was wondering how the hell you purified a dozer, while the rest of him stood back and watched the ruckus spread. About half the crew was Indian—or "Native American," as some of the activists liked to say—Osage, Creek, and Cherokee blood, mostly. Whatever, they were all Indian enough to be mad as hops about being asked to plow up a burial ground.

The foreman was as white as you got, though, except for his red neck, and he was ready to fire the lot of them.

Rich was right in the center of it, nose-to-nose with the foreman, giving him hell. "Look, you *can't* make us doze that lot over!" he yelled, his foghorn voice carrying over everyone's, even the foreman's. "That'd be like asking Tagliono there to plow up the Vatican—or at least, the graveyard at St. Joseph's!"

That shut them up—at least for a minute. And Larry felt some of the chill leaving him as he saw that with that single sentence, Rich had managed to get some of the white guys over on their side. Because the graveyard at St. Joseph's church had been under threat for a while, back in the early eighties and the boomtown days of high-priced oil; and Tagliono and some of the other guys on the crew had been picketing the Skelly Building for wanting to dig up their grandparents and transplant them so they could put up an office complex. Transplant them to a city cemetery, not a Catholic one; a cemetery without the blessings that old-fashioned people thought absolutely necessary for their rest to be in holy soil. *Way to go, Rich!* he congratulated, silently, as the dynamics shifted and some of the white guys, Tagliono in particular, took the couple of steps necessary to put them on the other side of the invisible line separating the foreman and the whites from the Indians. And when Tagliono came over, so, eventually, did everyone but the company suck-ups.

The foreman knew when he was outgunned. With a muttered curse, he stalked over to his truck and picked up his cellular phone.

Larry drifted over to the rest. "What's next?" he asked no one in particular.

"Five to two he's callin' Calligan," Tagliono said, and spat off to one side.

Larry nodded. "I figured," he said. "Question is, what's Calligan gonna do about it?"

Silence for a moment; traffic noise from the highway nearby warred with the piercing wails of killdeers overhead. Then one of the dump truck operators spoke up.

"I was on a project that hit somethin' like this," he offered. "Feds made 'em close down."

"Permanently?" Tagliono asked. The man shook his head.

"Naw. Just long enough for some college guys to get in there and dig the stuff up, like on TV." He scratched his head, meditatively. "But that was like, some old fort or something. I dunno what they'd do about somethin' like this."

Neither did anyone else, it appeared. The foreman was deep in conversation on his phone, and the rest of them were at something of a loss. Not for the first time, Larry regretted that he hadn't popped for the cost of one of those phones.

He'd have liked to put in a couple of calls—to the Osage Principal Chief for one, and to old man Talldeer for another. But he didn't dare leave the site, because right now, from the dirty looks he was getting, it looked like the foreman would be willing to use any excuse to fire him.

The foreman shoved the phone back into his car and stalked back, the look on his face boding no good for anyone who got in his way.

"The boss says that he wants us to dig the stuff up and trash it—burn it or throw it in the river or bury it or something," he said shortly. "Otherwise the Feds are gonna get in here, drag in the college people, and start holding things up while they screw around."

That was when Larry decided that no amount of money was worth violating a burial site. He got on his dozer, with a silent apology to those buried there, and backed up. Carefully. Doing his best not to disturb things any more than he already had.

The dozer was a cranky old bitch, and he used his long familiarity with her to kill her and flood her carburetor. She coughed and died; he made some elaborate "attempts" to restart her, then held up his hands.

"Sorry," he said, face carefully blank. "I guess she needs some work."

The foreman's face turned tomato-red, but there wasn't anything he could do if the dozer had stalled, no matter what the cause. The way he was glaring at Larry boded no good for the future, but he had no choice but to order a second piece of equipment forward.

He chose one of the dozers leased directly to the construction company. Unfortunately for discipline, he chose the machine normally driven by Bobby Whitehorse. Bobby was young—but Bobby lived at home with his parents. He was single. His car was paid for.

In short, Bobby could afford to get fired.

"No effin' way, man," Bobby said, putting the machine in

idle, and sitting back on the seat, arms folded over his chest. "I'm not diggin' up *nobody*'s ancestors."

Larry got down off his dozer, for now that the center of conflict had switched from himself to Bobby, he thought he just might be able to sneak away and call someone, though he wasn't quite sure just who to call. If they'd uncovered a nesting site for Least Terns, it would have been Fish and Game, but who would you call to get a staying order on a gravesite?

Maybe if he just called the cops, and pretended he didn't know these were ancient bones . . . by the time they figured it out, there'd be media here, lots of publicity, and the right people would know about it. And he'd have a chance to get in touch with the tribal elders.

The nearest phone was the cellular in the foreman's truck. Not a good idea. Next nearest was the one in the office-trailer on the side of the site. Maybe not such a good idea either. There was a Quik-Trip down Riverside—

Larry moved a little farther away as the foreman climbed up on the machine, getting right into Bobby's face and screaming at him. Bobby was screaming right back. No one seemed to notice that Larry was defecting.

Then he heard something; a high-pitched whistle, exactly like one of those sonic garage-door openers or motion-detectors that people "weren't supposed to be able to hear," but he heard all the time.

He didn't even get a chance to wonder what it was.

Because at that moment, the dozer exploded.

The machine rose three feet into the air on a pillar of flame and smoke, then came apart, sending shrapnel everywhere. Larry's instincts were still those of a combat vet; he hit the ground and covered his head and neck.

Things rained down out of the air onto him, dirt and debris, pieces the size of a handball and smaller. He kept his head covered while they slammed into his back, shuddering under the impact, feeling the sting of cuts—something came down on his head, knocking him out for a second. It was the pain of his smashed fingers that brought him around.

He looked up. It looked like something out of a war movie.

The dozer had broken in two and both halves were on fire; his machine was on her side. There were bloody bodies everywhere, some moving, some not. Of Bobby and the foreman, there was no sign.

Larry had been the farthest from the dozer when it went up; he was the least injured. He shoved off from the ground and sprinted for the foreman's truck, ignoring his throbbing head and useless right hand. It only took one finger to push 9-1-1, even on a cellular phone.

Rod Calligan took pains to seem perfectly cooperative to the detective; he'd gone over every inch of ground with them, and had answered every question civilly. Many men would not have gone that far.

The total was four dead—two of them, the ones who had actually been on the bulldozer, were hardly more than assorted body parts—and a dozen injured. He rubbed his temple anxiously, trying to figure out if these would be workman's comp cases or not—if the police proved sabotage, did that let him off the hook?

On the other hand, if he fought the cases, the local media might pick up the story. Bleeding-heart liberals. They could make him look very bad. Better not.

"Mr. Calligan?" the detective said, as if he had asked Rod a question.

"What?" Rod said automatically. "I'm sorry, I was kind of preoccupied. What did you say?"

"I asked you if you thought there was any reason why someone would try to sabotage your operation here." The detective's face was bland, but Rod had seen the Forensics and Explosives people swarming over the wreck of the bulldozer, and he was fairly certain he had also seen them carrying something off.

The Tulsa Police Department, for all their internal troubles and the incompetence of some of their patrol officers, was no half-baked and slipshod operation when it came to forensics. They had the use of some very sophisticated lab facilities. Rod had no intention of underestimating them.

"My foreman called some time before the explosion," he said, carefully. "It was on his cellular phone, so I'm sure you can find out exactly when that was. He said that the crew had uncovered some kind of Indian remains, bones or something, and that the Indians on the crew were rather upset about it and refused to go back to work."

"But that was only a few minutes before the explosion," the detective replied, dubiously. "There wouldn't have been any time for anyone to get a bomb in place."

"Perhaps not," Rod replied, watching the detective's expression very carefully, "but this isn't the first time I've had trouble with Indians on my crew here. They—" he paused, and selected his words very carefully. "They have what I would call a 'flexible' idea about time and work-schedules, and I am a very precise man. I don't tolerate unnecessary overtime or goofing off on the job."

The detective's lips tightened, just a little, and he squinted in the hot sun. It occurred to Rod that the polyester suit he wore must have been like wearing a sauna, but Rod wasn't much more comfortable in the linen blazer he used as summerwear. Rod wasn't about to take it off, though, despite the sweat that trickled down his back, tickling him. He wasn't going to sacrifice an iota of his edge in dealing with the police. Police respected a man in a suit; he'd learned that lesson quite completely over the years. They would treat a man in a suit a hundred times better than a man in blue jeans, and they were significantly more likely to listen to him than a man in shirtsleeves.

"Why would a troublemaker, Indian or not, go and blow

up his own people?" the detective asked, finally.

"Why do terrorists do anything?" Rod countered. "I've never seen a fanatic who wasn't willing to sacrifice a few of his own to get the enemy. What's more, if you take out a few people, it tends to make others take you seriously when you make a threat in the future."

Slowly, the detective nodded. "Sounds like you've studied the situation."

Rod let a tiny hint of a smile creep onto his face. "You know what they say; know your enemy. These days, a developer never knows who is going to decide he's oppressing them. Animal-rights nuts, ecology freaks, special-interest groups—we'd already had some problems before we started clearing this land. Troubles with the eco-freaks and the Indians, over the eagles and what have you. Maybe this is just an extension of that kind of thing."

The detective didn't look as if he was convinced. "I can't see where a bunch of back-to-nature nuts is much of a threat—and I can't imagine why they'd plant a bomb in a bulldozer."

There; he'd let it slip. They *had* found the remains of the bomb. Rod schooled his face not to let his satisfaction show.

"You should ask loggers about that," he replied, allowing himself to look and act a little heated. "Ask them about the tree-freaks driving railroad spikes into trees they're about to cut. You know what happens when a logging-grade chain saw hits one of those spikes?"

Evidently the detective had handled a chain saw or two in his lifetime; he winced. "But a bomb?" he persisted.

"I wouldn't actually put my money on ecology nuts," Rod said with a sigh. "I don't know what it is, but those Indians have it in for me. I think maybe this was their way of saying I'd better watch my step." He let his smile turn bitter. "Funny thing about people who claim they want equal rights—they *don't,* not really. What they want is superior treatment, not equal. And they squawk if they don't get it. Sometimes they do more than squawk."

" 'All pigs are equal, but some pigs are more equal than others,' " the detective quoted, in a kind of mutter. He made a few more notes in his book, and flipped the cover closed. "All right, Mr. Calligan, I think that will be all for now. Thank you for being so cooperative."

"Thank you," Rod Calligan replied automatically. "Keep me posted on what you find out, will you?"

"Sure thing," the detective replied. He wouldn't, Calligan knew that, as he knew they both had to go through the motions.

But as the detective headed for his sedan, and Calligan for the cool interior of his air-conditioned BMW, he was still a most contented man. The seed had been sown. Now to nurture it, and make it grow.

Jennifer tucked the phone between her shoulder and cheek, and waited for Ron Sinor's secretary to see if he was "in" for her. Meanwhile, with one hand she grabbed the stacked sheets of paper off the printer, and with the other, she reached for a tamperproof Tyvek envelope.

"I'm putting you through to his office now," the secretary said, and there was a click, and a short ring, picked up almost immediately.

"Miss Talldeer, glad to hear from you—" Ron said, cautiously.

"You should be even gladder when I tell you that the background checks you asked me to run took less time than I estimated," she replied, evening the edges of the pile of papers and slipping them neatly into the Tyvek envelope. "They're done; do you want me to send them by regular mail, or would you rather I called a messenger service or dropped them over myself?"

"How 'eyes only' are they?" Ron asked cautiously.

"Depends on how you feel about alcoholics," she said.

"Personally, I wouldn't want one writing my software. Sometimes I suspect that was what was wrong with the last release of my word-processing package."

Ron chuckled; he could afford to, since his company wrote oil-field analysis software, not word-processing programs. "Overnight mail, and make it registered, too," he replied decisively. "That way only Judy and I will see it."

"Done and done." Jennifer slipped the tamperproof envelope into a bigger Priority Mail bag, and grabbed a ball-point pen to fill out the adhesive waybill. One advantage of having an office a half block from a local post office. "The bill's in there, too."

"Good. Thank you, for being so quick." Sinor sounded genuinely pleased. "A couple of those people looked really good on their resumes, and I didn't want someone else to hire them out from under me—or find out that they were only good on paper."

Let's hope one of the ones he wanted isn't the guy who drinks his breakfast, she thought, but didn't say. "Thank the modern computer environment," she said instead. "If I'd had to type this the old way, you'd still be waiting for it."

He laughed, and they said their good-byes. Jennifer put the envelope in a stack of mail to go to the post office by three.

Her watch read 2:15; that gave her just enough time to call Claremore and the old homestead while she sorted receipts. Claremore was a good forty minutes away from Tulsa; if there was anything someone needed she could bring it out when she and Grandfather came over for Saturday dinner.

The phone only rang twice. "Yo!" said a familiar young male voice.

"Yo yourself, creep," she replied cheerfully to her youngest brother. "When did you get back from the lake?"

" 'Bout fifteen minutes ago," Robert Talldeer said, and paused to gulp something. "Didn't take as long as we thought it would. Never recharged the A/C on an RV before, those things don't take more than a pound. So what's up in the life of Nancy Drew?"

"Same song, different verse, little brother," she said, with a yawn. "Grandfather is fine, although I'm afraid one of the neighbor kids addicted him to Tetris. At least it's better than soap operas, but I suspect he's beating the kids out of their allowance money. Thought I'd catch up on family gossip before I went to the Post Awful."

"I could get to like recharging air-conditioners," Robert said, and paused, before adding scornfully, *"Not!"*

"Then be glad you've got a job to pay for college, Wayne," she told him, making neat little stacks of receipts. "You'll make a better engineer than a heating and A/C specialist. How's Dad's ostrich-fence project coming?"

Robert laughed, although she wasn't sure why. She sorted out a couple more gas tabs. Then he explained. "Twice as many of the eggs hatched out as the guy thought would. He had to get a guy in from Tulsa to build more shelters, and Dad's gonna have to weld twice as many fence lines."

Jennifer shook her head, and laid a McDonald's receipt on the rest of the business meals. *At least no one can claim I'm trying to deduct booze and steak. Running a flat per-hour rate may be a pain when it comes to accounting, but it's what got me a lot of clients pretty quickly. Glad Mom thought of it.* This ostrich thing was surely one of the wilder get-rich schemes she'd ever run across. "He hasn't talked Dad into—"

"Investing? Not a chance. Pop thinks the whole ostrich boom is gonna bust in a couple of years. Every chick this guy raises is going out to a new breeder. Once you run out of people who want to be breeders—how many feathers, hides, and five-pound eggs can you sell? Those things die at the drop of a hat, and they eat like a mule. Or maybe a goat; they'll eat anything that'll fit down their throats, whether or not it's really edible. By the time you get one big enough to be worth something, you've lost six more."

Jennifer was relieved; it looked like everyone had seen the fallacy in this ostrich thing, at least in her family. She'd been half afraid her father would get talked into investing. She'd seen this breeder on the news, and he was very persuasive. He was making a lot of money—quite enough to pay her father for his work up front, all at once.

She had been concerned because it looked good on paper—now. Like the guy in Claremore who'd tried to sell concrete dome houses—the idea looked good in theory, and they were certainly tornadoproof, but the reaction of most people in Oklahoma had been "Maggie, that's weird," and the poor guy had lost his shirt. She should have known better than to worry; the Talldeer were sensible people, and not easy to talk into something.

Well, most of us are, anyway. Present company excepted. She dropped a bill for dry cleaning down on the stack of "miscellaneous," and noted on it "removal of client's blood from silk blouse." Not that it had been anything serious, like a murder. Marianne's husband had beaten her up, that was all, and she had gotten the blood all over her blouse taking the woman to the emergency room. But it should shock the hell out of any auditors. She loved writing little notes like that. If the IRS ever decided to double-check her, they'd certainly have an interesting time.

Well, it was a good thing her father hadn't gotten wrapped up in the ostrich scheme. Besides, according to everything she'd heard, the damn things were not only stupid, they were vicious. "Like six-foot turkeys with an attitude," one of her clients had said. There were already enough things with "attitudes" in their lives; the Talldeer family didn't need to cope with giant birds too.

"Mom has a hot prospect for that white elephant—the earth-sheltered place in Mannford," Robert continued. "An artist; told her to show him everything weird, so long as it had land, a view, and privacy."

"Sounds good, but is an artist likely to go for that?" she asked dubiously. "You think he's ready for a one-lane gravel road with a twenty percent grade?"

"He picked Mom up to go look at it in a Bronco with a lot of mud on it," Robert said. "I'd say so. He was wearing snake-boots, too. I think he knows what he's going to go see."

That sounded promising; maybe all artists weren't crazy. She'd seen the place; it had an impressive view and with the addition of a windmill for electricity it could be completely self-sufficient. Maybe that wouldn't be such a bad thing for an artist.

Mortgage. Twenty percent, office space. She'd thought about the place too; wonderful view, and for someone with *her* interests, it would make the perfect place to detox from the modern world. With ten acres, she could have had a dozen real sweatlodges out in the woods and no one would ever know.

But it was no place for someone who had to make a living in the city. At least an hour away in good weather, and during the January and February ice storms, you wouldn't be able to get out without a Land Rover and chains.

"Listen," Robert said, "Mom left a note in case you called and she wasn't home. Can you pick up some of those good glass crow-beads and the porcupine quills at Lyon's downtown? Dad's adding to his dance gear again."

"Who's going to mess with the quilling?" she asked, aghast. Porcupine-quill embroidery was not quite a lost art, but it was one even their ancestors had gladly abandoned in favor of using glass beads. "Not Mom—"

"Nope. He is. Says he'll just have to put on a dress and do it himself." That was the perennial joke; when her father wanted something particularly difficult done for his costume, and her mother swore she didn't have the time or inclination, her father then said he'd have to "put on a dress to do women's work."

"He isn't really going to do it this time, is he?" she asked, giggling. "Remember the time he got as far as Mom's closet?"

"Naw. Auntie Red Bird is holding a quill-embroidery class and she said she'd do his costume stuff as the demonstration. So he's saved again." Robert snickered. "One of these days Mom is going to call his bluff, and I'm gonna be there with a camcorder."

"Do that, and I get the popcorn concession," she replied. "So what does he want for this piece of Osage haute monde?"

Robert read the list and she made careful notes on the back of a plea for money from a televangelist. She always saved her junk mail to use for notepaper, especially the stuff from televangelists. She figured that it ought to serve some use before she recycled it.

"Okay, young buck, is there anything more I need to know?" The last of the receipts went into the "it might be deductible but I'm not going to take it" pile—the one she intended to present to the IRS with all the rest if that audit ever came. The way she had it figured, they'd probably end up owing her money.

For the entertainment value alone.

"Not a thing. Don't talk to strange men, sis."

"I'm talking to the strangest one I know right now," she countered. "I'll pick the stuff up some time tomorrow, okay?"

"That'll be great. Watch your back."

"I will," she said, and only after she'd hung up did she wonder why Robert, the least disturbed about her job of any of the family, had chosen to say that.

CHAPTER THREE

IT WASN'T EXACTLY an appointment, but Jennifer wanted to catch both of the Ambersons home. According to her research, Ralph Amberson usually arrived home at about 4:30; his wife Gail, who had a part-time job with an advertising firm, got home just before her children did. If she didn't catch them before dinner, she might not be able to get them to answer the door. The neighbors said that Ralph was something of a martinet, and insisted that the phone be unplugged and the doorbell ignored at dinnertime. And after dinner—well, the neighbors said that only business would pry Ralph out of his home office.

It was Gail who most interested Jennifer, for Gail's maiden name had been Gentry.

That was not an unusual name, but it was of particular interest to Jennifer. It had been an Abraham Gentry who had served as one of the government agents on the Lakotah reservation from 1892 to 1904. During that time period, any number of interesting things happened between the Lakotahs in question and the agents who were supposed to be protecting their interests, no few of them reprehensible by anyone's standards, but the one that concerned Jennifer was the disappearance—after "confiscation"—of several sacred Lakotah religious items. The policy at the time was to "civilize"—which meant Christianize—every Native American on the continent. Native ceremonies were often outlawed altogether, on the flimsiest of excuses; children were taken from their parents' custody and sent away to boarding schools where they were forbidden to speak their own languages or to worship in their own ways. Freedom of speech and religion were not an option for anyone who accepted the "beneficent guidance" of the United States government.

So much for "land of the free."

Jennifer grimaced, partially at her own bitterness, partially at those long-dead officials. Exactly what these particular objects had been, she did not know. The inventory was sketchy at best, and did not describe much that a shaman-in-training would recognize as a specific relic.

The objects disappeared about the time that Abraham Gentry took his generous government pension (and whatever else he'd managed to scam out of his post) and retired to Oklahoma. None of the other leads Jennifer had followed had produced any information. But Abraham's private papers, available at the Osage County museum, indicated that *he* was the one who had taken them into "custody," and there was no indication that he had ever given them over to anyone else, either privately or publicly. Abraham had a penchant for taking souvenirs; that was obvious from the inventory of his personal possessions made for his will. Some of those souvenirs of his posts on various reservations were in the museum, but most were not.

Now came genealogical research. Abraham had one child, a boy, Thomas Robert. That boy had inherited all of Abraham's possessions, gave some to the museum, sold the family farm, and moved to Tulsa one step ahead of the Dust

Bowl. Thomas Robert had married and had a single male child, who had married and had a single female child. That girl was Gail Gentry, now Gail Amberson, and according to Jennifer's research, she had recently inherited a number of things from her recently deceased grandfather.

Among those things, Jennifer had deduced, were the Lakotah relics. "Memorabilia from Abraham Gentry's estate," was how the will had read.

If they were in the Amberson residence—and Jennifer would know the moment she came anywhere near the house if they were in the Amberson's possession—she hoped she would be able to persuade the couple to let her have them. Granted, they had a certain value as artifacts, but their value to the Lakotah went far beyond that. These would probably not even rate very highly as artworks; at that point in their history, the Lakotah were not spending a great deal of energy on making things of power "pretty"; instead, they were purposeful and often unornamented, the better to focus their intent.

Unless someone knew their history, they would not be valued according to their true worth. With luck and the will of *Wah-K'on-Tah*, no one would know that history. She would send the relics to the Lakotah elders if she could get her hands on them. If she couldn't—

Well, she had the paper trail leading to this house, this family. That was enough to get a restraining order, and to start a lawsuit. Legally, the situation was the same as if Gail Gentry had inherited a stolen painting. Before the Ambersons could sell any of relics, they would have to admit they had them—and at that point, there would be lawyers ready to take them to court over their right to possession. It would be a long and drawn-out court battle, and even if the Ambersons won it, they would lose far more than they could ever realize in the sale of the relics simply defending their "right" to have them at all. Only a major museum could afford to fight a legal battle like that. Most of the people

Jennifer had turned in capitulated when it became obvious that a court case would involve far more than they wanted to commit. Often when the first suit was filed, they capitulated—especially if the Lakotah could offer them some token payment in return for the relics. Usually they did not offer the payment first, even though that would seem to be the easiest route. Experience had shown that offering payment generally led to a bidding war, and legitimized the claim of the possessor. It was better to file the suit first, to establish exactly what the situation was.

She hoped, as she steered her battered little Subaru Brat through the winding streets and past the manicured lawns of yet another middle-class suburb, that this would be one of the "easy ones." A couple of cases had ended nastily; in one instance of "dog in the manger," the person who had the relics had destroyed them rather than give them up. She still felt rotten about that one, even though it had been out of her hands by then.

Still, from a shamanic point of view, sometimes it was better for those items to be destroyed rather than be in profane hands. Artifacts of any kind of power could generate some pretty bad medicine just by being in the hands of the "enemy"; the Little Old Ones had known that, making the protection of their shrines for the Sacred Hawk, the *Wah-hopeh*, of paramount importance during warfare. Certainly many of the ancestors of other nations would have agreed with that assessment; that was what the Seminoles had said when they told her the artifacts had been lost to them permanently.

She parked the Brat a block away from the Ambersons' address, and the moment she stepped out of the truck's air-conditioned cab and into the hot evening air, she felt as if she had been hit with a double blow—one to the body, and one to the spirit. The hot, muggy air slugged her even though the sun was halfway to the horizon. And the blow to her spirit was just as formidable. She knew, with no room for doubt, that not only were the objects in question in the Ambersons' possession, but that she *had* to obtain them, by whatever means it took. For this particular set of relics, she might consider almost anything to get hold of them.

From a block away, even though their power had not been renewed for nearly a century, it struck her hard enough to stagger her. Whatever it was that Abraham Gentry had taken as his private memorabilia of the Lakotah was strong enough for her to feel its influence with a strength she had not expected. She closed her eyes against the sense of terrible pressure, as if there was a tremendous thunderstorm just over the horizon. She couldn't remember a time when she had ever felt something from this far away, except when the objects in question were in the custody of practicing shamans.

She steadied herself against the pressure, and walked as briskly as the heat allowed toward the Amberson residence. In a moment or two, the sense of pressure eased, as if something out there recognized her and her intent, and had acted accordingly. Perhaps something like that *had* happened; shamanistic regalia tended to develop a spirit of its own.

She walked along the curb, watching for traffic, although there was very little of it in this sheltered cul-de-sac. Ralph's (relatively) low-priced BMW was in the driveway; through the still-open garage door, Jennifer caught sight of the rear of Gail's minivan.

Good. That means they're both home. This was not the first time she had been here, but she appraised it with the eye of the daughter of a successful real-estate agent, with a view to assessing the mental state of those within it. The house was just like every other house in this neighborhood; which rather annoyed her, truth be told. A house should have character; these had none. Clearly built in the late seventies or early eighties, it was a split-level, with the requisite stone-and-cedar exterior, recessed front door, attached garage, six-foot cedar privacy fence. The backyard was probably short-shorn grass with a tiny bordering of garden and a few hanging plants on the patio; the manicured front lawn, with two evergreens and two maple trees, was just like the neighbor's. Every house here had an energy-wasting cathedral ceiling in the living room to give it an air of spaciousness—yet the attic would be all but useless and the three bedrooms barely big enough for a bed and a little furniture. Jennifer appraised it with a knowing eye. At the time it had been built, during the oil boom, it probably had sold for between $120,000 and $150,000. Now—if the Ambersons could find a buyer with so many companies laying off middle-management or moving their personnel elsewhere—it might sell for as little as half that. There was no sign on the front lawn, but that did not mean they had not tried to sell in the near past. The depreciation of their dreamhome would have come as a dreadful surprise.

If they have any brains, they'll get the place reassessed and have the property taxes refigured on that basis, she thought to herself. It was advice her mother had given many a potential client trying desperately to unload a house that he could no longer afford. At least lowering the property taxes a little gave a feeling of illusory relief.

The neighborhood itself was too new to have any of the character of her own neighborhood. The houses were clearly built by the same company, to one of three plans. They were crowded quite closely together by the standards of the older neighborhoods, with barely five feet to the property line. The backyards would be half the size of hers, and the trees—except in the few cases where the homeowners had planted fast-growing cottonwoods or other softwoods—had not attained enough growth to really shade the houses. The sun beat down without mercy here, and with fully half the front yard of each house taken up by its driveway, the heat was terrific. If she hadn't been so used to it by now, she'd have felt as limp as a wilted leaf of lettuce.

There weren't even any children playing out here today; the heat was too much even for them. Although it was possible, given this area, that the children were at some carefully structured after-school activity, where nothing as frivolous as playing ever occurred.

There were no sidewalks in this subdivision; when these houses were built, it was presumed that everyone would drive everywhere, and that the kids would play only in their own or their friends' backyards, out of sight, sequestered, like little animals in their exercise wheels. Jennifer often thought of those builders whenever she saw a subdivision like this one. No one in Tulsa in the seventies and eighties had ever given thought to oil shortages, or pollution high enough on windless summer days to be dangerous. No one in Tulsa—then—could even conceive of a day when some-one might want to—or need to—*walk* somewhere. Every-one had a car then; everyone. The absence of road salt extended the lives of cars so much that back in the fifties and even the sixties it had been a common practice to simply drive an unwanted old car into a field somewhere and aban-don it, even if it still worked. Life had been generous to those living high on the profits of scarce oil; if you *wanted* to work back then, you had a job. Guaranteed. And with a job came the requisite car, the only way to get to that job.

Nor could those long-ago Tulsans imagine that anyone who lived in a subdivision like this one would be caught dead on mass transportation; the old street-car system was gone, the bus system totally inadequate for a city half the size of Tulsa, and it wouldn't come within a half mile of a neighborhood like this one. Jennifer had occasionally tailed people using the bus; every time it was a nightmare. Every few years there was some talk of a monorail, a BART-type train that would link the downtown with its industrial cen-ters and outlying apartment complexes and malls. It came up whenever the mayor didn't have anything else to talk about. But now that the days of high employment and major oil and beef money were over, the Tulsa monorail was about as likely as a Tulsa space shuttle.

Access to the house was from the driveway, which had so slight a degree of slope that it barely qualified. Jennifer got into the scanty shade provided by the overhang on the tiny square of cement that called itself a "front porch," and rang the doorbell. In front of her was a fake wrought-iron storm-door, with double-pane glass on the other side of the metal. It looked protective, and the Ambersons probably thought it was. Jennifer could have jimmied it open in about thirty seconds.

She was hoping for Gail Amberson, but instead, she found herself confronted by the suspicious face of her husband Ralph when he opened the inner wooden door. It was not a good omen. He was still wearing his tie, although he had removed his suitcoat, and even in the supposedly relaxed atmosphere of his own house, he was as stiff as a catalog model. His brown hair was cut in the clonal Businessman's Style, his brown eyes were as expressionless as mud, and his nondescript face matched any one of a thousand other men. His suitpants were gray, his shoes shiny black, his tie a solid blue-gray. It was held in place with a plain gold pin. Jennifer wished she could look that anonymous; camouflage like his might have saved her a time or two.

"Whatever you're selling, we don't want any," he said stiffly, completely ignoring the fact that she wasn't carrying anything other than a very slim briefcase. And ignoring the fact that she was not wearing either a door-to-door sales permit or a solicitor's badge. "And I give through United Way at the office."

He started to close the door in her face; she stopped him with a single sentence and by flashing the badge-holder containing her P.I. badge and license. It looked impressive enough; not quite coplike, but enough to intimidate a little.

"If you're Mr. Ralph Amberson," she said quickly and

clearly, "my client is very interested in some property you have." She did not say "may" have, although she probably should have, ethically speaking. It had been her experience in the past that those who genuinely did not know what she was talking about showed it immediately, and those who *had* the relics showed that as well. Besides, she knew the Ambersons had the stuff; there was no point in *not* showing this card, and throwing Ralph off-balance by letting him know she knew it.

The word "client" caught his attention, and he opened the door again. There was a touch of cautious greed about him, and a hint of unease. Now there was only the storm-door between them, but that was still a psychological barrier she could have done without.

"What property?" he asked. "What client is this? Who are you, anyway?" Good questions, all of them, and perfectly reasonable. She could not take offense at the words.

But the way he had said them made her tense her jaw and count to ten. His implication was that not only did he not believe her, but he felt the only reason someone like Jennifer Talldeer should be in *his* neighborhood would be as a maid.

She took a deep breath; he radiated hostility, and she had the feeling that she wasn't going to get very far with him. He had her pegged for a minority, and she was already a woman. Two strikes against her on the empowerment scale. Someone as low-status as she was could safely be brushed off. Still, she had to try. "I'm Jennifer Talldeer, and I'm a private investigator representing the Lakotah Sioux," she said briskly, trying to put as much authority into her voice and the somewhat exaggerated relationship with her "clients" as she could. "My clients have traced a number of Lakotah artifacts to your possession, sir—or rather, to your wife's possession. These articles were illegally obtained by her great-grandfather from tribal hands. They would like them returned to tribal hands."

With someone friendly she might have added other

things; that there would be no reprisals and no adverse publicity, that the Lakotah would consider anyone who returned these objects voluntarily a friend. Not with this man; he was The Enemy, and he had made himself into The Enemy from the moment she knocked on his door.

So she would act as if she had more authority than she really did, and give him only the barest of the facts. There. That was it. Now he would either admit he had the things and hand them over, or—

Well, that was about as likely as pigs flying. He looked more than ready to give her a fight. He must have had someone tell him that the artifacts his wife had inherited were worth a lot of money to a collector.

She saw Gail Amberson peeking over her husband's shoulder, and pitched her voice so that the woman would be sure to hear what she was saying, even through the double-pane glass of the stormdoor. She could not see Gail well enough to read her expression, but her husband's was a mixture of guilt and anger, just a flash of it. The same kind of expression she saw on the faces of people who had bought "hot" merchandise.

Then it changed, turning first calculating, then complacent. *I've handled your type before, bimbo,* she all but read. *You're just a woman and a stupid Indian. You can't prove I have the stuff; you can't prove anything. I hold all the cards here, and you don't even have a bluff hand.*

But he kept tight control over his manner; his voice held a world of haughty disdain that she knew she was meant to hear. "I'm afraid you have the wrong information, miss," he said, clearly and precisely. "I haven't the slightest idea of what you're talking about."

He was using his height, race, and male authority to try to intimidate her, but sometimes an equal show of authority would make someone like Ralph back down. It was worth a try. "I'm talking about some Lakotah artifacts your wife, Mrs. Gail Amberson, just inherited from her grandfather,

Thomas Robert Gentry," Jennifer persisted, taking slow, deep breaths of the stifling air, and fully aware that this man was *not* going to allow her inside his house where he stood in air-conditioned comfort. "Those artifacts were obtained illegally, and—"

"And even if I knew what you were talking about, you have no way of proving that," Ralph interrupted. Then he smirked—which she was also meant to see. She found herself pitying any woman who worked for him; sometimes intimidation was worse than harassment, for it left the victim feeling utterly worthless. His tone hardened. "Now I suggest that you take yourself back to whatever reservation you came from. You're trespassing on my property, and I'm fully within my rights to call the police if you don't leave."

And with that, he shut the door in her face, and only the air pressure between the inner door and the storm door prevented him from slamming it.

She counted rapidly to ten in Osage, then in Cherokee for good measure. "Fine, jerkface," she muttered to the closed door. "Then we'll see you in court. Hope you enjoy spending money on lawyers."

Then she turned on her heel and marched back down his driveway, carefully avoiding stepping on his precious grass so as to escape any "destruction of private property" charges. She was fully aware that he was watching her and probably *would* call the police if she didn't leave. Not that they'd come; she wasn't wearing her gun, he had no reason to say that she had threatened him in any way. She was totally within her rights so far, and in the eyes of the law she was no more than a minor nuisance. The Tulsa P.D. was too shorthanded to send anyone out on a nuisance call. But he *might* correctly remember her name, and it would be a royal pain to have her name on the police log for something like this the next time her license came up for renewal. Some people on the licensing board weren't happy with a Native P.I.; some others were incensed at a woman doing a "man's job." Her only defense was her spotless record. Well, mostly spotless, and she had never been *caught*. . . .

She *would* see him in court; as soon as she got back to the office, she would be calling one of the local tribal lawyers she worked with, and he would file a restraining order on Ralph, preventing him from selling *anything* until a licensed appraiser had a chance to look at it. And right now, she was going to ask him to word it in such a way that Ralph would be violating the law if his wife took something to a garage sale. The lawyer would also see to it that the appropriate legitimate buyers of artifacts were notified that Ralph Amberson was trying to dispose of the artifacts that were illegally obtained. Then he'd consult with the Lakotah elders, and so would she; after she told the Lakotah shaman what she had sensed, the upshot would probably be a lawsuit.

Of course, Ralph *could* dispose of the artifacts on the black market, but Jennifer wasn't terribly worried about that. Someone like Ralph, with all the appropriate yuppified attributes, had never done anything more illegal than cheating on his taxes or pilfering from the office. The odds were high that he wouldn't have the kinds of contacts he needed to get rid of the relics, and it would take him time to find them. By then, the number of buyers would have decreased to a handful, and although the relics had power, they probably were not of a rarity sufficient to interest the few buyers who would be willing to purchase something they could never display. Something from one of the famous chiefs, perhaps—or something of tremendous artistic value or a one-of-a-kind item—but not what was in Amberson's hands. Nothing she sensed led her to believe that the Lakotah items were of that nature. While Jennifer had heard rumors of another sort of buyer—the kind more interested in the power of artifacts rather than their rarity—she had never encountered one of those, and she figured it was unlikely that she would this time.

If we were talking about the Holy Grail, the Shroud of

Turin, Sitting Bull's coup-stick, or Little-Eagle-Who-Gets-What-He-Wants' fetish-shield, maybe. But not this time. I think these things were made in secret, and charged with power to protect their people from what was to come, then confiscated before they were used.

Then she noticed something else. The objects were moving.

Damn him. He's jumping the gun and getting them out of the house!

She wanted to turn around and go right back, but she had better sense than that. A confrontation would only cost her. Her anger made her walk faster than she had before. She was halfway down the block, lost in her own plans, when she snapped to attention, alerted by the sound of someone running after her, someone wearing sneakers or other soft-soled shoes. Definitely chasing her; there was no doubt in Jennifer's mind.

She stopped and turned, ready to defend herself if she needed to—and Gail Amberson, wearing a high-fashion jogging suit, matched pink-and-white Spandex shorts, shirt and sweatbands, nearly collided with her.

"Excuse—" Jennifer gasped. Gail backed up a little, worry lines creasing her lovely, well-scrubbed face, and shoved a dusty cardboard box, brittle with age, at her.

"Here," the woman said, glancing back over her shoulder furtively. Her ash-blond hair, cut in a shag style, flared a little with the nervous movement. "This is what you want. Take it, please!"

Jennifer accepted the box reflexively, and the moment it touched her hands, she felt something very akin to an electrical shock. Whatever she was about to say was driven right out of her head. The sensation unnerved her enough that she lost the sense of what she had been thinking; lost even her previous anger.

"But—" she stammered awkwardly, "I don't—"

She glanced instinctively down at the package in her

hands. The paper felt like dried leaves, and smelled of mildew. Now she saw that the box itself was wrapped in yellowed newspapers; the date on one page was May 15, 1902. It looked as if no one had touched this parcel for the past ninety years.

"Ralph is having an appraiser in to look over everything grandfather left me," Gail interrupted, babbling her explanation, her brown eyes narrowed against the sun glaring down in both of them. "But he doesn't have any idea of what is in all those boxes or even how many boxes there are—he's so neat; he hates dust and dirt and you couldn't get him to handle the stuff himself for any amount of money. I had to unpack the crate myself." She laughed nervously, and looked back over her shoulder again. "He's so afraid of germs—but some friend of his told him what Indian things are going for these days and that just started him up. He's sure what we've got is worth a lot of money, and the minute that appraiser tells him anything he'll be sure it's worth twice or three times what the appraiser says. His brother's a lawyer; suing him wouldn't do anything to get what you want; anybody who's ever sued him has gotten tied up in countersuits until they gave up."

"But—" Jennifer said again, still mentally dazzled by the throb of Power coming from the box in her hands. "Won't he know you gave me something?"

Gail shook her head violently. "No, no, I promise! Right now, though, he doesn't have any idea this box exists. And it's what you want, I know it is," Gail continued, on a rising note of strain. "Whatever is *in* there has been giving me nightmares since the crate arrived."

Her eyes widened with something very like fear as she glanced down at the box and away again. "You have to take it—just take it and go—"

Jennifer cradled the box protectively against her chest, and the fear left Gail's eyes. "Thanks—" Jennifer managed.

"Don't thank me." Gail Amberson shuddered, and now

her eyes looked more haunted than frightened. Jennifer wondered what kind of dreams the box had given her. "I may never be able to watch another Western for the rest of my life."

And with that, she wiped her hands convulsively on the legs of her running shorts, as if to rid them of something unpleasant, and jogged off down the street.

Jennifer stared after her, watching until Gail turned a corner and vanished into the heart of the subdivision. *She must have used running as an excuse to leave the house.* One part of Jennifer's mind admired the woman for her quick thinking, while the rest of her vibrated on the very edge of trance just from being in contact with what was inside that innocuous cardboard container. And Gail Amberson had been absolutely correct—this *was* what she had come after, and there was nothing more back in that expensive paean to suburban living that she was even remotely interested in. Nothing. There was not even a whisper of Power in the Amberson house now, and Ralph could have whatever pots and beadwork, "tomahawks" and rifles that were left, with her blessing.

And What Was In The Box was now purring with content that it was back in something approximating appropriate hands. There was no doubt in her mind that It knew who and what she was, just as she knew what at least one of the relics in The Box was. And a good thing it was happy with her, too. The Lakotah and the Osage were near-enough "relatives"—and Jennifer had more than enough of the proper training—that the artifacts in there were evidently content to "rest" until they were back in tribal custody. Jennifer wasn't surprised that Gail Amberson had been having nightmares. Anyone with any degree of sensitivity would have, especially with That working at him.

A derisive caw made her look up. There was a raven watching her from atop a streetlight, an old one by the dusty feathers, the wear on his beak, and the way he was tilted a little to one side, as if one of his legs was weaker than the other. When the bird saw that she had seen him, he cawed again, but did not seem inclined to move. Not that she figured he would, all things considered.

Well if I stand around out here, there's always a chance that dear hubby Amberson is going to spot me with a box in my hands and want to know where I got it. And while a rap of "robbery" would be easy enough to beat, since she hadn't gone anywhere inside the Amberson house, she didn't think it was polite to get Gail Amberson in trouble with her spouse after she had gone out of her way to smuggle The Box out to Jennifer Talldeer.

She ignored the heat and sprinted to the Brat. She hadn't bothered to lock the doors, not here, and not since she really hadn't thought she'd be away from the truck for that long. She carefully and reverently placed The Box on the floorboards, started the engine, and drove away as quickly as the speed limit allowed, and didn't even take the time to reach over to turn on the air conditioning until she was six blocks away.

And although The Box was content now, that did not mean it was any less powerful. It still throbbed, pulsating through Jennifer as if she were seated in a drum circle, and it certainly was not comfortable cargo to have aboard.

It's like sitting next to an unexploded bomb, she thought, as The Box decided to make its contents known to her in a flash of insight as clear and distinct as a Polaroid. The vision of the Lakotah shamans creating their instruments of Power, colorful and as vivid as the real world, interposed itself between her eyes and the road for an instant, and it was a good thing that she was half prepared for something like that to happen, or she might have run into a ditch.

It's FedEx for you, my friend, she told The Box. *I am not having you in my presence for one minute longer than I can help. You just might take a notion to recall the days when the Osage and your people were something less than brothers. . . .*

Fortunately, there was a Federal Express pickup booth not that far from the Ambersons' subdivision.

With the dry, cool air from the air-conditioning vents blowing onto her face and drying the sweat, and now that she was well out of Ralph Amberson's reach, she felt a little calmer. The Box still throbbed at her, but its contents seemed to understand what she intended to do about them, and unless she was terribly mistaken they might even be closing themselves back in. *It would be a real good idea to go quiescent while FedEx has you,* she thought at The Box silently. *The less you rouse people, the more likely you are to make it home safe.*

Thank goodness she had her address book with her; she would be able to ship this thing directly into the hands of one of her Lakotah contacts without even having to call Grandfather to read the address off the Rolodex in the office.

The girl minding the FedEx desk didn't show any particular interest as she packed The Box by nesting it in progressively larger containers, then secured the final box with strapping tape. She did sit up and take notice when Jennifer insured the contents for the maximum allowed amount.

"You haven't got jewelry in there, have you?" she asked suspiciously. "That insurance doesn't cover jewelry."

"Archeological artifacts," Jennifer said shortly; the girl pursed her lips and looked through her book, but evidently couldn't find any exclusions for "archeological artifacts." Which was precisely why Jennifer had chosen than particular description of the contents; this wasn't the first time a shipment had gone out from her under that heading.

An "archeological artifact" wasn't something that would tempt theft, either—although by insuring the package for that much, she had red-flagged it so far as would-be thieves were concerned. The company would be keeping its electronic eyes on this little parcel.

She didn't breathe easily until the girl took The Box into the back to join the rest of the packages leaving tonight. By ten tomorrow morning, Jay Spotted Eagle would have a little—surprise. And at that point it was his worry, not hers.

She left the chill of the FedEx office for the humid heat of late afternoon. She didn't even look up as a mocking caw from the roof of the office behind her greeted her exit. She knew what was there.

The Raven called three or four times before giving up and flapping down to land on the roof of her Brat for a moment. He cocked his head to one side and stared at her with one bright black eye. She stared right back at him, refusing to drop her gaze, challenging him.

Finally, she took another step toward the Brat, her keys out, still watching the bird. The Raven opened his sharp black beak and made a series of noises that sounded like barks, then took off. He shoved off the top of the truck and flapped his wings clumsily in the heavy, still air with that typical corvine rowing motion, dropping down to within a foot of the ground before finally getting up enough speed to fly to the wires behind the parking lot.

She unlocked the Brat, got in, and headed straight for home. It had been a long day. . . .

Grandfather was waiting in the living room, sitting cross-legged on the couch across from the television set, with the Nintendo joystick in his strong, age-wrinkled hands. He hit the "pause" button as soon as she entered the room and dropped her purse on the floor beside her favorite chair. He grinned, showing a strong set of white teeth, and looked up at her.

He was a tall man, like her father and brothers, and still held himself straight as a man decades his junior. Sometimes he reminded her of Jacques Cousteau; he had that same tough resiliency, like a weathered blackjack oak—and although age had weathered him, it had not twisted him. He wore his iron-gray hair long, in a single tight braid, though forty or fifty years ago he had sported a crewcut like everyone else in his neighborhood. He had been an aircraft mechanic, first with the Army Air Corps, then the Air Force, then at the small-aircraft side of the Tulsa Airport. No one who knew the family casually would have guessed then that he was Osage. No one who knew the family intimately would have ever thought otherwise, but there had been few who knew the Talldeer intimately, and they were all to be trusted with the secret that could have instigated discrimination.

Now he wore his heritage openly, much to the delight of the neighbors' children and grandchildren. He told them stories, taught them simple things, got involved in their ecology projects, all things their parents had no time to do. Things that their grandparents, who might be half a continent away, could not do. Half the neighborhood called him "Grandfather." And he tricked the children as well, teaching them with his tricks that the world was not a universally friendly place for a child, teaching them in ways that would not hurt them to be careful even with people they knew.

That was not "traditional" teaching although it grew out of Osage tradition; it was teaching adapted to the modern world. The neighborhood kids learned Osage legends—but the lessons were to respect and protect nature. They learned how to defend themselves against the adults who would hurt or even kill them. They learned that Native Americans, far from being ignorant savages, had knowledge and information and a wisdom no different from their schoolteachers.

Grandfather often pointed out the success of the sparrow hawk as an example—the sparrow hawk, who like the rabbit had moved out of the meadows and into the suburbs. That was not the original way of the Osage, who had been more apt to construct deeper and more complicated layers of ritual around the core of their traditions when those traditions failed them. Grandfather—and, she suspected, his father before him and his own grandfather—had changed that. They had begun to change, to move as quietly into the world of the Heavy Eyebrows as they once had through their beloved forests; to hide themselves under the camouflage of jeans and workshirts, of square wooden houses and neat yards. With that change, they had changed the Medicine, until it began to work well again, as it had worked when it was concerned with hunting and fishing, stealing horses and averting danger, winning brides and conquering enemies. Adapting the Medicine had worked with other tribes—but the Heavy Eyebrows were different, so different that an adaptation would not work. It had to be change, much as the Little Old Men disliked change.

That had been what Grandfather had said, at any rate, when she had asked him.

"Well?" he said, looking up at her, his bright black eyes shining with some secret amusement. She didn't pretend not to know what he was talking about.

"You know very well I got it, Grandfather," she sighed. "There's no point in pretending you don't know. I might have believed that a raven cawing at me from the wires was just coincidence, but not one that landed on the roof of my truck and stared me in the face, then laughed at me."

Grandfather shook his head, mockingly. "Damn," he replied. "I must be slipping. I shouldn't have tipped my hand that way."

"So why were you following me?" she asked, kicking off her shoes, and reveling in the feeling of soft, well-varnished and blessedly cool wood under her bare soles. She walked around the living room, picking up the little bits of popcorn and empty cups that told her he'd had the kids inside today, probably during the afternoon. He seldom let them into the house in the morning, teaching them instead the Osage games his father had taught him, and running the fat of too much television watching off them. But even he agreed that when the temperature climbed above ninety, there was no point in courting heatstroke. These were kids raised in air conditioning, born to parents with health insurance, not tough little Osage brats who never saw a doctor and ran around mostly naked in the Oklahoma heat. Toughening took time and required the parents' cooperation and participation—perhaps when the children were older, he might teach them the way of the Warrior, if not Warrior's Medicine. Grandfather agreed; the seed was planted and he took the long view of any of the gentle *Tzi-Sho* gens. Let the seed sprout and mature in its own time; these children would at the very least be a little less credulous, a little less inclined to let others run things for them, a little less prone to give up and go with the system, a little more likely to fight for themselves and their world. And of course, they would not be content to accept the stereotype of the "lazy, drunken, ignorant Indian." For him, that was quite enough.

"Why were you so afraid of what you recovered?" Grandfather countered—and before she could dodge out of his way, those strong brown fingers had slipped off the joystick and she yelped as he pinched her rear. "And when are you going to start being nice to me?" he continued, with a meaningful leer. "A pretty girl like you should know an old man like me needs—"

Oh, so he's in that *mood. Should have guessed that a strong dose of Respectable Elder was going to bring out the Old Reprobate as soon as I got home.*

"An old man like you needs a good whack upside the head!" she countered, skittering past him before those fingers could pinch the other cheek. "Don't you know you're supposed to be senile by now? You're supposed to be drooling and in diapers so I can keep you in your bed and you wouldn't be able to get into any more trouble!"

He chuckled, and shook his head at her.

She finished her cleanup, and dropped the popcorn bits in

the paper bag she kept for bird scraps. The grackles would love the popcorn. "How's the garden doing? How many kids did you bilk out of their allowances today?"

"Their hand-eye coordination is improving," he told her serenely, "they're starting to tie me. When they start to beat me, I'll start them on target shooting. I made five bows that should be cured up and ready about now."

She straightened abruptly. "So *that's* why you wanted me to get you that Nintendo!"

"Is it?" His eyes practically disappeared in a nest of wrinkles as he smiled. "The garden is doing well. The corn will be ready to pick in a day or two."

She gave up, and collapsed into her chair.

He restarted his game, and only then said casually, "Oh, I almost forgot. Someone from Romulus Insurance called."

She sat straight up in her chair and stared at him. He continued, as calmly as if he hadn't "almost forgotten" a potential client—and an important one.

"The man said they want you to investigate some trouble at a construction site. I think he mentioned a mall."

Make that a real client. And an insurance agency! Insurance agency cases often meant lots of time, and time was money. She launched herself out of the chair and sprinted down the hall to her office.

There was the pad beside the phone, with what was presumably the Romulus phone number noted on it, in Grandfather's handwriting. And a name, Mark Sleighbow, presumably the man who'd called.

If they found someone else—if I've lost this one—

She wasn't sure what she'd do. Maybe it was time to get a phone service. Grandfather occasionally "forgot"— accidentally on purpose—when he thought that a job "wasn't right for her."

I'd prefer to make that determination for myself. Particularly when the mortgage payment is due. And right now, with that background-check job over, she needed another piece of steady work. Anything for an insurance company was bound to be steady. . . .

She dialed the number quickly, and waited while the phone rang, glancing at the clock on her desk and hoping Mark Sleighbow hadn't gone home for the day. *It wasn't quite five—where is this area code, anyway?* If it was just in this time zone, or even west—

Someone picked up.

"Mr. Sleighbow?" she asked, trying to sound businesslike and brisk. "This is Jennifer Talldeer, returning your call."

Mooncrow concentrated his outer awareness on the video game—the only one he ever played, something involving small odd-shaped blocks dropping down from the top of the screen—and pondered the many problems his beloved granddaughter was coping with. He watched her constantly, and he was well aware how she must be feeling right now. After all, he had gone through his own version of her particular balancing act.

That must be exactly what she felt like; as if she were a tightrope dancer. When one was very young, the balancing between life among the Heavy Eyebrows and life as a shaman was not particularly difficult. There simply were not many points of intersection, and no real points of conflict that could not be resolved by appeal to a parent to intercede with authority outside the family. But as one became older, the responsibilities became greater, and the number of conflicts increased. And there was no one to intervene on an adult's behalf.

No one could remain forever in the Spirit World, not even in the long-ago days. The Little Old Men had also hunted and taken the war trail, raided and planted, until they grew too old. Then they remained behind to guard the village when younger men went on the hunt. But they did not sit always in the Lodge of Mystery, speaking to the spirits; they had their outer lives as well as their inner ones. But in these days, it was much more difficult to balance the secular life with the sacred—perhaps more so even for Kestrel than it had been for him. He had been a man with a simple job, one which began at seven in the morning and ended at three in the afternoon. It did not follow him home, disturb him in the sweatlodge, ring his phone at odd hours.

He understood her better than she knew. She must pay for this house; she must earn the money for food and clothing. She was the hunter, and the quarry was far more capricious than any buffalo. And yet she must also be the shaman-in-training. The clock must drive her—and yet, she must learn to let things come at their own time, to ignore the clock and the calendar and the demands they made on her concentration.

When he had been her age, he had not had this particular crisis; he had been far too busy dodging the bullets of Japanese fighters as they strafed the runways of the strange Pacific islands he had been stationed on. He had been concerned with his own survival, the survival of his fellow Indians, the survival of his fellow Americans. He had been a Warrior, and the only Medicine he had needed to practice had been Warrior's Medicine, for the hawk had fallen with his head to the west, and as in the old days, it had been from the west that The Enemy had come, for all that they called themselves men of the Rising Sun. His Medicine pouches had been tucked into little corners of the Corsairs he had serviced—and he had been proud when *his* planes and pilots returned, beating the odds.

No, his crisis had come later, when he was a man of peace again, and he had a home, a wife, and a small son to provide for. That was when he had felt the pressing of the Heavy Eyebrows' world of the clock, against the Medicine world of the seasons. He had often felt as if he were juggling knives.

She must feel as if she, too, were juggling knives, and the nature of her job meant she might also be tossed a red-hot poker at any time. But she was a Warrior. He had known all along that she would be a Warrior. The path of the Warrior-Shaman was that much harder, the balances more complicated. Her blood was of the peacemakers; her path of the fighters. The dance she danced was no traditional one, but an intricate weaving of steps that would leave a Fancy Dancer exhausted, akin to the skill needed for Hoop Dancing.

He half closed his eyes and his thumbs danced upon the control buttons, and the little blocks fell and fell, falling into place. Not always neatly, but he kept ahead of them. That was the object, after all—to keep moving, keep ahead of the falling blocks.

Kestrel had another sort of problem, for she had always been a very earnest and responsible child. One of the Heavy Eyebrows words for what she was, he suspected, was "over-achiever." She always wished to do everything perfectly, quickly, greeting each new conquest with the need to do more. This was partly his fault, he thought; he should not have permitted her to take on any of the internal paths of the Heavy Eyebrows. He had allowed her to become contaminated in her thinking—

Now, that was not right. He had not taught her to put that part of her that dealt with the Heavy Eyebrows world into a box. That was what *he* had done, ultimately—and when that part of him was in the box, he did not allow it to touch his inner self. In the past two years or so, he had noted a tendency in her to wish to *control* things, to direct them, rather than simply permitting them to happen and then dealing with the results. Those knives she was juggling would in fact juggle themselves—if only she would learn to trust in them, in the Spirit World, and in herself.

That was the reason why he continued to tease her about sex. The Little Old Men of the past had sequestered their virgins until a husband chose them or the husband's family chose her for him—or until she found a man to her liking and an uncle to broker the match. That was one of the customs that made no sense in these days, for there was no way to learn the world while being sequestered. And besides, as a shaman, it made no sense for her to be a sequestered virgin, for how could she understand the powerful medicines that sex created between man and woman if she knew nothing of them herself? Not that Kestrel was a virgin—he was perfectly well aware what she had been up to, and while she might have thought it was her mother who had put the condoms in her underwear drawer when she was sixteen—

Still, in some ways he might just as well have sequestered her away. For the past two years, at least, she had been living like a Heavy Eyebrows nun. No men, not even a suggestion of a man—no, nor a woman either. That was unfortunate; one needed to take care these days, but abstinence was doing nothing for her.

It seemed to him that she needed some sort of outlet for the tension inside her, and that sex would be a perfectly good release. It would certainly help her to balance herself; it would be the best of Good Medicine, with the right man. She needed to find herself another youngster, and rediscover one of the simple things. She would discover by giving up control of herself to a sensation how many of her problems could be dealt with by giving up an attempt at control and letting them happen.

This thing, this obsession of hers with earning the pipe—receiving a sacred pipe would signal the next level of her achievement as a shaman, would, in fact, mean that she was no longer his "apprentice," but his equal. The trouble was that she was so certain that it was *time* for that to happen, as if things in the Spirit World were punched in on some kind of celestial time clock. It was the control thing that was holding her back, and she could not see it. Nor could he tell her; she must see it for herself. He was trying to lead her in that direction by being suggestive, a dirty old man, using the shock to send her to find a more appropriate partner, and so to see what it was she needed to see.

Yet for all his hinting and suggestions, she was so intent on *time*, on control, on Outer World responsibilities that she could not seem to see past his joking with her to his serious intentions.

Or else she didn't want to admit that she could actually need or learn from something as "simple" as sex.

He sighed. He could only continue to do as he had been doing, and hope that sooner or later he would find another path, or she would find one. Until that happened, Kestrel was certainly a bitch to be around.

"I'm glad you called, Miss Talldeer." The tinny voice did not *sound* terribly glad, but that could have been either Corporate Manner or simply the bad speaker in her phone. "You caught me just before I left for the day."

"I was out on a case," she said simply, hoping that it was either of those two. "I called as soon as I got your message. There was something about an investigation of trouble at a construction site? I hope you haven't found someone else."

She pulled pad and pencil to take notes within easy reach. Both lay in a patch of late sunlight on the warm worn wood of her desk. She hoped that the answer to her question would be "no."

"No, we haven't," Sleighbow said, and she stifled a sigh of relief. "There aren't many people with your particular qualifications; certainly not in the Tulsa area."

Qualifications? That was an odd thing to say. And something she'd better check out before she took this job.

"I'm not certain what you mean," she replied cautiously. "There are certainly plenty of competent private investigators in this area; I'm sure there are many you've worked with before. Has one of my former clients referred you to me?"

"Not exactly—" he temporized.

It took a good ten minutes of verbal song-and-dance before she finally got Sleighbow to cough up his reason for calling *her*, and no one else. Yes, she had come highly recommended by former clients—which was pleasant to hear, but not enlightening. Yes, her record was quite good. Yes, he was pleased that she had a good relationship—or at least, she didn't have a *bad* relationship—with the local police. None of those were the reason why he had called her, nor the reason why Romulus did not particularly want to use one of their usual firms. And he wouldn't tell her exactly what the job was; he kept asking her questions. She was usually pretty good about figuring out which "interview" questions were loaded, but this guy was slick; she'd have to have a voice-stress analyzer to get anything useful out of some of the things he asked her.

"Does this have anything to do with the fact that I'm female?" she hazarded, a little impatient with the man. "Or that I'm a—ah—minority? If this is a bow toward tokenism, I'll take your job only if I'm really suited to doing it. Otherwise I would be very happy to recommend someone else who can handle it better and you'll have made your federally mandated attempt." She'd taken a "token" job a few times in the past; they had always turned out to be unmitigated disasters. Now, even if she needed the money, she always turned them down. There was a "PITA" factor— "Pain In The Ass"—that only very generous pay could compensate for.

"It has everything to do with the fact that you are Native American, Miss Talldeer," Sleighbow replied, relief quite obvious in his voice. "And no, there is no one who is better qualified, and it has nothing to do with federal mandates."

"All right," she said, feeling that this time he was coming straight with her. "If you've got time, I've got time. Why don't you start at the beginning, and I'll sit and listen."

CHAPTER FOUR

"Are you familiar with the Riverside Mall project, Miss Talldeer?" Sleighbow asked. His tone didn't tell her much, but her instincts told her to be careful. "Rod Calligan is the developer there."

"Vaguely," she replied with caution. Not a good idea to tell him she had been among the protesters when the area had first been proposed for development. He might take a dim view of that. Not that it mattered much anymore, really. She and everyone but a few diehards had finally given up on stopping the project when it became painfully clear that the developer had everyone, from the Feds on down, firmly in his back pocket. There was no other way to explain why so many issues she and the others had raised had been so neatly "taken care of." But there had been no way to prove corruption, so she had dropped out, as had most of the others.

"There'd been some trouble with Native American protesters back when the site was first selected," Sleighbow continued, his tone completely noncommittal. "When Calligan came to us, he presented us with a package that indicated that every objection had been taken care of. Frankly, we thought his presentation was a good one, and when the developer made a point of hiring as many Native Americans as he could, far beyond the point of government—ah—recommendations, our specialists assured us that there would be no further problems from that angle. That was why we agreed to insure him. Romulus does not specialize in high-risk insurance." The last was said with a certain emphasis, and agreed with everything she had heard about his company.

She noticed two things; he said "Native Americans" with no sign of self-consciousness or irony, and he had avoided the taboo word "quotas." Interesting. She thought she detected a little more relaxation in his voice as well. She relaxed a little further, and let her instincts talk to her for a moment. Her feeling after a few seconds was that since he had decided to come straight with her, he was being quite open and honest.

"I take it there seems to be a problem at the site, then?" she asked. It seemed an obvious question, and she wondered how big the problem was. And why the insurance company was now involved. Had there been some property damaged?

He sighed. "I take it that you haven't seen the news tonight."

She felt her eyebrows rising. "No, actually, I haven't."

"Ah." He paused a moment. "Then let me lead you up to this carefully, so that you get everything in order. According to Rod Calligan—and mind you, he only came to us with these allegations *after* the incident today—he's been threatened and harassed by Native Americans. Phone calls, threatening letters, nuisance sabotage at the site, that sort of thing. No real property damage, or threats that came to anything. He did not report any of this to the police. He says he didn't want to alarm his family or trigger anything worse by starting a police investigation. He had a number of Native Americans quit; he hinted that the threats might have been coming from them."

"Oh?" she replied noncommittally. "Interesting." He was taking his own sweet time to get to the "incident," but she had the feeling that everything he was telling her now was important. She had learned enough from Grandfather's teaching-stories not to rush him past information she might need.

"We thought the same." His tone was full of irony, and she sensed that he found these stories just a little too pat. "Still, that doesn't change what happened today. If there really were threats, it went beyond them to action."

"And this is what was on the news?" she asked.

"And will probably make CNN," he confirmed. "It's ugly, Miss Talldeer, and I've got some small experience in sabotage. There's no way to soften this—someone blew up a bulldozer, and killed four people, including the foreman. There are a half dozen more workers in the hospital or who were treated and released." He paused for a moment to let that sink in.

It came as a shock, still. That was the kind of thing you expected to hear about in Greece, or the Mideast, or even New York. Not in your own backyard. "My god—" she said, finally. "What happened?"

"Preliminary investigation indicates that there was an explosive device planted somewhere on the bulldozer, one that was triggered by an electronic detonator." He took a deep breath, but it did not cover the anger in his voice. He was outraged by this, personally. As well he should be. "It was probably something like a garage-door opener."

The analytical part of her mind was the first to recover. "Not easy to trace." She made notes rapidly as things occurred to her. First and foremost, this was a job for the police, not a private investigator.

"True, given that there are several hundred thousand of

them in the Tulsa area alone. But that is not what we want you to look into. The police can handle the criminal investigation." Sleighbow was firm on that, and she appreciated it. She was *not* a Magnum, P.I. She'd never handled anything worse than a spouse-beater before this, and she really didn't want to start butting in on police territory now. "That's their job, and we are willing to let them do it," he continued. "It'll be murder charges before this is over, and an insurance company does not need to handle a potato as hot as that. What Romulus wants you to do is to look into who or what is behind this. *Is* it a conspiracy, and if it is, did the developer try to defraud us by concealing it? Or was this simply an isolated act of a single disgruntled employee? That's what we want to know. Was there fraud going on; was the developer deliberately misleading us?"

"I can live with that," she told him, much relieved. "More, that's something I *can* do." It would not be the first fraud case she had handled, although it was certainly the biggest, and potentially the nastiest. "Now, why me? Because I'm Native American and you figure the crew and the protesters will talk to me where they won't talk to the police?"

To her surprise, Sleighbow chuckled. "That, and because you are by all accounts a very attractive and small woman. Construction workers are less likely to think you're a threat."

She answered his chuckle with one of her own. "You're figuring out all my secrets. But you're putting me between a rock and a hard place, you know. If I find out there was a conspiracy—"

"That's all we need to know. We *don't* need to know if the conspiracy actually performed the sabotage. I want you to understand that from the beginning."

"In other words," she said dryly, "no Nancy Drew."

"Right." He sounded relieved that she understood. "All we need to know is that there really were threats previous to the explosion, that there was a reason to think that the risk was greater than we had been informed, and that because of that, this developer went into the contract with the intent to defraud us." Sleighbow's sincerity came through even over the bad speaker on the phone. "If you uncover anything else, you know what you have to do. I would turn anything suspicious over to the police, and I think you will too, but I'm not going to dictate to *your* conscience. And Romulus will not be double-checking on you. In the words of Rhett Butler, 'Frankly, Scarlett—' "

"Uh huh." She couldn't fault him or the company, really. Criminality was *not* their business, and he was evidently quite conscious of the fact that he was hiring her to find information that might prove to be harmful to her people. This was the best compromise he could offer.

Yeah, I know what I have to do—turn the evidence or even the suspicions over to the police. This is murder; my duty lies with those who were killed, even as an Osage shaman—or at least the kind of shaman Grandfather has taught me to be. But that doesn't make doing that duty any easier.

Still, how many times had Grandfather made it clear that the time for purely tribal loyalties was gone? That her "tribe" was humanity? Besides, there were plenty of P.I.s in Tulsa who would be very happy to find him the proof of conspiracy he wanted—even if it wasn't there. They'd at least be getting a fair shake with her in charge.

And there were those pesky bills to pay—

"Well, Mr. Sleighbow, I guess you've just hired yourself a P.I.," she said slowly. "I'd rather it was me than someone with a prejudicial axe to grind."

"So would we, Miss Talldeer." Yes, that was relief in his voice too. "This way no one can be accused of not giving the Native Americans under suspicion the benefit of the doubt. Send your invoices to me, directly—"

He dictated an address, which she noted down; while this seemed to be a perfectly legitimate job, she would be taking no chances. She'd be checking both the job and Sleighbow, tonight and tomorrow before she actually did anything at all on the case. There had been cases of people pretending to an authority they did not have; there had been hoaxes perpetrated on P.I.s too.

They both made polite if hurried good-byes, and she hung up the phone. But she did not return to the living room; instead, she remained at the desk, thinking hard, absently doodling on her notepad. Dust danced in the golden light coming in through the miniblinds at her office window, and there was a pair of blue jays pigging out at the feeder just outside.

She had to think this thing through, very carefully. She had to be absolutely sure of her own feelings and motivations before she found herself tangled in something she was not prepared to handle, emotionally and mentally.

If there was a conspiracy—if it was activists—

Her own people. Possibly a cause she had been involved in herself. One she was emotionally supporting—

I still have to turn them in. This was murder, terrorism. I can't play cute little semantics games and call them "freedom fighters."

Yes, that was it. There was a line that had to be drawn. What was the old saying? "The freedom to swing your fist ends at my nose." The freedom to be passionate about a cause ended when people could be hurt because of that passion.

People who murder innocent people in the name of a cause are still terrorists, no matter how noble that cause is. She had drawn that line for herself; now she must stick to it.

I hate terrorists. I hate them and everything they are. They're cowards who won't face the enemy honorably. They're like the cowards who used to scalp women and claim they had taken warriors' scalps—like the ones who attacked villages when the men were on the buffalo hunts.

That was another line of demarcation; the line between

"warrior" and "terrorist." A warrior was one who fought an enemy who knew he was the enemy—who fought other warriors, openly. There had been times in Osage warfare when coups were not even counted by taking a warrior's scalp, but by merely touching him and getting away again. That was the purest form of warfare. . . .

But there had been times when the enemy did not abide by the rules, when he too became a terrorist. There was a site not that far from her home in Claremore where that had happened, where a band of mixed Heavy Eyebrows scum, renegade Cherokee, and rejects from other tribes had overrun an Osage village, killing, torturing, and raping the women, old men, and children left behind. Claremore Mound, it was called now. She could never come near the site without feeling rage overcome her, a rage triggered by all that helpless blood spilled—by the powerful grief and fear and pain left behind by the victims.

Anyone who sets bombs in bulldozers is no warrior, and he deserves to die like a poisoned dog, without honor, without a way for Wah-Ko'n-Tah *to recognize him, so that his spirit joins the* mi-ah-luschka *and he wanders forever—*

She felt that old rage building in her and stifled it.

You can't just condemn an entire race for things people who weren't even their ancestors did. That was why she had broken with the more ardent activists back in college. *You can't shove everyone into the same pile just because of their bloodlines.* She wanted her rights, and the rights for all of the Native Peoples, just as much as any of them did—they'd all been cheated and lied to for too long, deprived of homes, of religion, of heritage—

Even her family, who had only kept their ways at the cost of hiding them, who had not until her father's generation been able to be Osage openly.

But she could not take those rights like a thief and an assassin; not at the cost of murder. Not at the cost of the lives of people who had nothing to do with the problem.

Because you couldn't put all Heavy Eyebrows into the same category, any more than you could every Indian, or even (and this could get her in a world of trouble from some of her own people, or those of other nations, who had their own little sets of prejudices) every member of a nation or tribe. Pawnees weren't Osage, who weren't Cherokee, who weren't Apache, who weren't Algonquin, who weren't Mohawk—

There were people of every type in every nation; no one was Noble and Honorable just because he (or she) was Native American. There were people from nations traditionally her "enemies" that she would trust to cover her in a life-or-death situation, and people of her own nation she wouldn't trust as far as she could throw them. You couldn't even pigeonhole people by their professions, for not every Indian made a living on the reservation weaving blankets and making jewelry. There were Mohawks who couldn't stand heights, Navaho physicists, and Algonquin computer programmers.

There were people like Gail, who had tried in her way to right the wrong that had been done by her ancestors, and people like her husband, whose ancestors had never *seen* an Indian, who had been quite prepared to continue that wrong.

So just because someone's grandfather did something awful to my grandfather, that doesn't make him responsible, unless he decides to continue the wrong. Yeah, better me in charge here than someone else. Seems to me that occasionally it was one of the duties of the shaman to play judge and executioner—or at least cop—

"You still didn't tell me why you were afraid of the box."

Grandfather's voice behind her made her jump; she hadn't heard him come up behind her, and she hadn't heard the door to her office open, either.

She pushed off from the desk, turning her chair to face him. He stood there with his "teaching" face on, which meant that he wasn't going to leave until she said *out loud* what it was that had so troubled her.

"Because there was a sacred pipe in there, that's why." She frowned at him, angry at being forced to admit her own weakness and her own deficiencies. "Not just any pipe, either, but a powerful one, created by and for a Lakotah shaman's use. Dammit, Grandfather, you know I'm not a pipebearer! You *know* why, too; you know I'm not strong enough, I'm not *good enough* to handle it safely if it had remembered that the Lakotah and the Osage weren't exactly best buddies, and decided I was a threat!" She stared him straight in the eyes, all her bitterness there for him to see for himself. "You've told me that often enough, and you know you have."

But Grandfather did not seem in the least disturbed, not by her half-accusations, nor by her bitterness. "I've told you that you'll be ready only when you stop thinking you should be ready. You should listen to what I say, not what you think you hear."

And with that, he calmly turned and went back into the living room. Back to his Nintendo, no doubt.

She counted to ten, slowly, in English, Osage, and Cherokee. Useful, to have three languages to do it in. Four, if you counted her rudimentary Spanish—so for good measure, she did it in Spanish, too.

Well, now that he'd gotten that out of the way, he'd probably leave her alone about it. Sometimes she wondered just what he thought he was doing when he asked her things like that. . . .

No, he knows what he's doing. I just don't understand it. She sighed, and picked up the little table-fetish one of her clients had sent her as a gift. Bear, and she wasn't Bear clan—and Zuni, and she wasn't Zuni—but the thought had been kindly and the gift had meaning because of that. She cradled it in her hand, a lovely cool piece of soapstone, comforting to hold because of its gentle curves.

She had been the only one in the family to have Medicine Power; she would be the only one he had time to train before he died. Was he feeling frustrated too, having to work with a flawed tool?

After all, he'd been teaching her so many things that she was not, by tradition, "permitted" to know. The Medicine of all the other gentes, for instance; and men's Medicine as well as woman's—and Warrior's Medicine.

Well, he's always been pretty contrary—what do the Lakotah call it? Heyoka, I think. Part of that comes with the territory, I suppose, and part of it comes with being a changer and not just a traditionalist. Still. You put what you have in the only pot you have, I guess, even if the pot is flawed. And you hope the flaw isn't going to be a fatal one.

Oh yes, part of the shamanic training was to be able to put yourself in the place of another, to see if you could understand what *he* must be going through. And she could understand it—

But why couldn't he understand her? Why couldn't he just tell her what it was that was holding her back?

Kestrel still hadn't heard him, although she had listened to him. She had paid no heed to what he had said; she had only heard what she expected to hear.

Mooncrow reminded himself not to grind his teeth; it made his jaw ache afterwards. That girl; that incredibly stubborn girl! For all of his years and patience, there were times—

There would have been times with any pupil, but it was all the more frustrating with his granddaughter. She had not been the only choice to be his successor in the family—no, there had been others, including a cousin or two. But after he had seen her with Rabbit, and had seen how fearlessly and effortlessly she had dealt with the Spirit World, there had not been anyone else in the running. She was, in fact, the best apprentice he had seen in all of his life, and she had no idea just how good she really was. Things it had taken him until late in adulthood to master she had achieved in her early twenties. But he would not tell her that; it would not help her to know that, and might harm her. It would certainly reinforce her certainty that she was "ready" to be a pipebearer, and that would do her no good at all.

It might also harm her to know just how strong she was, for that might either frighten her or make her try even harder for control. She would command more Power than he ever had, once she loosened up a little, and got over this current fixation of hers with how she must be the one who held the reins and guided everything.

As he contemplated his own frustration in dealing with Kestrel, he closed his eyes and told himself to relax. He remembered a car-enthusiast friend of his seething with a similar frustration during a televised race. When Mooncrow had asked why, the friend had explained how the power of the particular car he favored had been deliberately lessened by restrictive devices placed on it by "rules". Now Mooncrow understood that frustration, watching Kestrel flounder. All that potential—and until she stopped making up the rules that restricted her power, the potential would never be fully freed.

No matter how he tried to tell her this, she simply did not understand, because she would not understand. To understand what he was trying to tell her would mean that she must give up some of her control, and put herself in the hands of *Wah-K'on-Tah* and all the mysteries. She wanted things, concrete things—"if *a,* then *b* and *c*"—not times and places where there were no rules, or where she would have to find the new ones.

And he could only relieve his frustration by stacking little electronic blocks. . . .

* * *

Jennifer had succumbed to the cable temptation some time ago, mostly for the news, but also to give Grandfather a little more choice in what he watched. Interestingly, what he watched was, in order, CNN, Discovery, and MTV. Sleigh-bow had been right; it was a relatively slow news day, and the explosion not only made the local news, it made the networks as well as CNN. In fact, the national coverage was better than the local, probably because the big guys were a bit less squeamish about gore than the three local stations.

Not that she blamed the local folk. The pictures, even "sanitized" for general viewing, were pretty ugly, and the local news people knew that there would be friends and relatives watching tonight. The local anchors hadn't gotten around to listing the victims yet; CNN had. And one thing hit her immediately when she heard the names—most of the victims had been Indians, presumably the ones who hadn't quit. Not whites.

That made her sit back in her chair and stare at the screen, ignoring the flash-flood story from Arizona that followed. *Most of the victims were our people.* Would an activist, even a fanatic, have planted an explosive, then triggered it, under conditions where most of the victims were his own people? You killed the enemy, not your own warriors. You killed "The Man," not the presumed victims of his oppression.

It didn't make sense. It didn't even make sense if you figured in the possibility that he might have counted anyone working for this developer as a traitor. He would *know* how other Indians would feel about deaths in their own ranks. Especially very insular types who still harbored prejudices against any Indian from another nation. She'd heard enough stories about treacherous Blackfeet and—from her own folk—traitorous Cherokees to know that. An incident like this would not foster solidarity, it would create divisions.

No. No, this was not adding up. This made no sense whatsoever.

Time to call home again. Dad's got the best grapevine in the county; maybe he's heard something. If he hasn't, and I ask him to keep his ear to the ground, he might.

She dialed the familiar number without even looking at the buttons, and waited. It was picked up on the first ring this time.

"Talldeer residence, Sarah Talldeer speaking. Can I help you?"

Jennifer grinned to herself, and replied in Cherokee, "Beloved Mother, you are going to get yourself stolen by a marauding Japanese seller-of-goods if you continue to answer the telephone that way. We shall have to go on the war trail in order to steal you back, and you know the Japanese have no good horses to take! How shall we get your worth in raiding with no horses to carry off?"

"Jennie darling, you are going to confuse the hell out of the nice FBI man tapping the phone if you keep speaking foreign languages," her mother countered, this time in English. She laughed, and so did Jennie.

That was a family joke, although at one point there probably had been a tap on the phone, either because of Jennifer's activism or because of her current occupation. There might be again. Oddly enough, no one in the family really cared. Sarah Talldeer's attitude was that since no one in her family had anything to hide, there was no reason to worry. Jennifer, although she would have been outraged when she had been in college, was now fairly philosophical about it. And both her brothers and her father took a kind of puckish pleasure in the idea that some poor fool might be listening in.

Sarah thought the whole idea of a phone tap was rather stupid. If someone really *wanted* to listen to long conversations with her real estate clients, or the trials and tribulations of the adolescent and college-age Talldeers, they were welcome, so far as she was concerned. And heaven help them if they weren't also fluent in Osage and Cherokee; the family used all three languages, as they had all their lives, to make certain that their children were fluent in the tongues of their heritage.

"By now they probably have translators," Jennifer told her. Then, in Osage, she made an indecent suggestion about what could be done with the late FBI founder's body—just in case someone *was* listening.

"If your Grandfather taught you that one, I don't think I want that translated, honey," Sarah replied serenely. "It has to be something obscene. Poor Mr. Hoover, he must be spinning in his grave like a high-speed lathe. Your brother told me you'd called; has something come up?"

"Sort of." She licked her lips. She might as well come straight to the point. "Have you—ah—seen the news yet? Any news?"

Although Sarah was not strictly a Medicine Woman, Grandfather had hinted that at least part of Kestrel's ability might have come from her mother's side of the family. Kestrel didn't doubt that at all, for Sarah had an uncanny ability to cut straight to the subject someone wanted to discuss, whether or not it had even been mentioned.

That ability did not fail her this time. "You mean the explosion? The one where the bulldozer blew up and all those poor men were killed?" Her voice sharpened with anxiety. "Isn't that a police thing? How did you get involved?"

"Obliquely. Don't worry, I'm not going to get underfoot with the cops, I don't think." Quickly, she explained as much as she could without betraying client confidentiality, then continued. "Basically, I need to know if Dad's heard anything that might apply—you know, young hotheads shooting their mouths off just before they shoot themselves in the foot—or if the Principal Chief has."

"Hang on a moment, I've got my real estate books and

mortgage calculation sheets spread out all over the table, and I want to write all this down so I get it right." She listened to the background sound of paper shuffling for a moment, as her mother restacked her work and reached for something she could take notes in. "All right, would you take it from the top for me?"

Jennifer repeated it all, carefully. Sarah had been a secretary and kept her shorthand up; a skill she had taught Jennifer. It had come in useful in college, and both of them still used it, although Jennifer had augmented her notetaking with a microcassette recorder.

"Dear, this developer—can you tell me his name? I might get something, if I nose around a little." Sarah's offer came as something of a surprise, and Jennifer found herself staring at the wall with her eyebrows lifted. She hadn't considered her *mother* as a possible information source, but Sarah was right—if it had anything to do with land, real estate agents heard about it, and they talked. She could have hit herself for not thinking of it, too. Normally she was a bit better at thinking of the obvious.

"Mother, that would be fabulous," she said honestly. "And yes, I can tell you, since it's pretty well public knowledge. They'll probably say something about it on the ten o'clock news; they might even have an interview with him. It's a fellow named Rod Calligan. And I would love to hear every juicy little rumor you have on him."

"I can tell you right now that he hasn't made any friends in this business," Sarah said immediately. "If you asked someone in Tulsa, they would probably talk your ear off, but even out in Claremore we know about him. He's cutthroat, and they say he's cut-rate. Anything he builds never meets more than the absolute minimum standards and whenever he can he builds outside municipal boundaries so he doesn't have to meet city codes."

"Interesting." That wasn't illegal—but it was cheesy by some standards. And someone who built things that way might be tempted into something just as cheesy.

Or maybe not. He might not think he was doing anything cheesy—he might think he was simply being a good businessman. He might not even consider shading the truth to get cheaper insurance to be fraud. She'd have to have more information, and she said as much to her mother.

"Well, I can get it for you, honey," Sarah said cheerfully. "I think Marge had some dealings with him, and you know how Marge loves to talk."

"Only too well; she cornered me at your last company picnic," Jennifer groaned. "I thought my ear was going to fall off."

"Jen—I hope you know I worry about you, but I wouldn't ask you to stop what you're doing." Sarah sounded hesitant, but Jennifer knew why. They'd had this little talk before.

"I know, Mom. You can't help worrying; I'm your kid. You'd worry about any of the guys, too." Jennifer couldn't help smiling. "You also know how good a shot I am, and that I'm pretty good at martial arts. And I don't think that being a shaman hurts."

"I know all that. I also know that people have a breaking point—and that if you push them too hard, sometimes they get ugly." Sarah did not sound like a nagging mother; she sounded like a concerned one. Not worried, but cautious. "I don't like what I've heard about this Calligan man. He sounds like he's used to getting his own way, and if you cross him—"

She did not complete the sentence, but Jennifer did it for her. "If I cross him, he is very likely to react badly. So I'll do my best not to cross him." She hoped the slight smile she wore now crept into her voice. "If I can manage it, I won't be more than another reporter; I'll try not to let him know what my job really is. If I have to talk to him, I'll try to make him think I'm just a dumb Indian babe." Now her tone turned ironic. "Sometimes a prejudice can work for you."

"That's my smart daughter," Sarah chuckled. "I'll give this to your father as soon as he comes in; if you call back tomorrow, he'll probably have a little something for you, if there's anything at all to know."

"Thanks, Mom," Jennifer said. "Now what's all this about quill embroidery?"

They talked of ordinary things for a while longer, then Jennifer hung up when she heard the "call waiting" click on her mother's side of the line. Besides, she still had some more work to do before she gave up for the night.

She had two lines, one for the phone and one for her computer. She wasn't the only P.I. in Tulsa using a computer, but she thought she might be one of the few to use it to its full potential. There were a lot of databases available to people who knew how to get into them, all of them quite legal to access, so long as you knew how.

A little cross-checking proved that Sleighbow's number was indeed one of the Romulus internal numbers. A little more cross-checking showed that Romulus, like many other companies, had voice mail. And since Sleighbow had said he was going home—

She reached for her phone and dialed his number again. After the fourth ring, there was a pickup. She listened as the voice-mail service told her she had, indeed, reached Sleighbow's number and told her how to leave a voice-mail message. She hung up without leaving anything.

But she had learned that Sleighbow worked for who he said he worked for. Now to find out if he had the authority to hire her.

She looked through the database for the number of the live internal operator, and dialed that. After a moment, a real person answered.

"Do you have the number for the accounting department?" she asked.

The operator was perfectly happy to give it to her, and then, somewhat to her surprise, added, "Since it's month-end, there are probably a lot of people still down there. Would you like me to put you through now?"

"Yes, please!" Jennifer replied, trying not to sound as surprised as she felt. If she could confirm Sleighbow's authority to hire her, she could be on this case tonight.

A few more hours to chalk up to the Romulus account wouldn't hurt.

The phone rang through, and someone picked it up. Jennifer explained who she was, and why she was calling, and the young man at the other end replied, "I'm just a programmer, man, but hold on a sec, I'll get the supervisor."

This was going better than she had any reason to expect.

Five minutes later, she hung up the phone, still blinking in pleased surprise. Not only had she confirmed that she had been hired by someone with the authority to do so, but the supervisor of accounting had laughed, and told her he'd seen the account with her name on it opened just before quitting time.

She pinched herself, just to make certain this wasn't some kind of dream.

Then again—

She sobered, suddenly. There were usually reasons for things going this well, early in a case. It meant that the case itself was going to be a bitch.

Well, if it's going to be that bad, I'd better get on it tomorrow early, while my luck is still running. She closed down computer and modem, picked up her purse, and headed back out. *And meanwhile, I'd better make a good grocery run, because I bet I won't have time for one once this heats up.*

As she passed him in the living room, Grandfather looked up, and gave her one of his Patented Inscrutable Expressions.

Now what in the hell was that all about? she wondered. *With him, it could be anything from toilet paper on my shoe to the fact that I'm about to walk into a trap and he doesn't feel like telling me about it.*

As she closed the front door behind her and headed for the truck, the shrill *klee-klee-klee* of a bird screamed out above her head. She looked up.

There was her Spirit Animal, a kestrel, sitting on the phone line above her head. The little falcon, a female by her markings, stared down at Jennifer and screamed again.

"That's easy for *you* to say," Jennifer retorted, inserting her key into the lock. "You don't have to live with him!"

CHAPTER FIVE

ROD CALLIGAN HAD not expected so many reporters to show up; he would have thought by now, after a day had passed, that the explosion was old news. He managed to send the last of the reporters packing, turned away to his car, and straightened his tie, just in case there was a camera still operating somewhere around. This was a hell of a way to spend a hot afternoon, standing out in the direct sunlight, courting a sunstroke. One of the advantages of being the boss was setting your own hours, and he liked to take his afternoons off. It was well past the time he'd usually have been home, and he was damned tired of nosy reporters demanding answers to questions they had no right to ask. What did his wife have to do with this, anyway? He was angry, but he hoped he had not showed anything other than contempt for the "reporter" in question. This had not been in the plan, and he had not been prepared to face all those inquisitors.

Still, he thought he'd handled it all pretty well. He'd

managed to field their questions cautiously and carefully, and he thought he might have succeeded in planting the idea that the explosion had been the fault of terrorists. He hadn't actually come out and said that terrorists did it, but he'd talked about the vandalism and sabotage at laboratories that used animals, and the spiking of trees in logging areas. He'd even managed to work in the supposed trouble with Indians in almost the same sentence, so without actually coming out and accusing anyone, he figured plenty of people would put two and two together for themselves. With luck, one or two of them would be reporters; there was a right-wing regional rag that would probably report things that way. There were plenty of people around here who thought Indians were trash; they'd be only too happy to believe anything bad about them. The neo-Nazis and skinheads would probably start rumors for him.

The jerk at Romulus had sure been a pain, though. His regular man had been away from his desk when he'd called in the bombing, and that Sleighbow was a suspicious bastard. He had as many questions as the reporters. *"Why didn't you say anything about these threats before?" "And when, exactly, did you start getting phone calls?" "Did you save the letters?" "Why didn't you report this to the police?"*

He thought he'd gotten through that all right, but he'd better make sure. Before he headed home, maybe he'd better check up on the state of things at Romulus. It didn't do to have loose cannon rolling around on the deck. He got into his car, started it and the A/C, and dialed the contact number on his cellular phone, savoring the cool sterility of the air-conditioned breeze coming from the vents.

This time his man was in.

Calligan let out a sigh of relief, although if John hadn't been there, this time he could simply have hung up. There had been a certain amount of urgency about getting the explosion reported to Romulus; now he could afford to take things the way he had planned them. He explained what had happened, quickly. "I got assigned to a guy named Sleigh-bow, a real company man. He gave me some trouble. What's he doing about this?"

"Call me from your office," the man said. "I'll have to check his desk. I saw him leave, so that shouldn't be a problem. Just let it ring until I pick up." There was a click, and Calligan hung up quickly. No use paying for minutes of cellular for nothing but an open line.

Calligan stared out the windshield at the remains of the bulldozer, a little smile on his face, then drove the short distance to the site office, a portable trailer. He had an auxiliary office and phone in there. He'd be alone; the secretary was long gone, since he'd sent everyone at this site home early. There would be no problems with being over-heard. He wouldn't have that security at home.

The window in his office looked out over the same area of course, though from a different angle. There were still police swarming all over the remains of the dozer, but it looked to him as if they had gotten everything they were going to. After all, they'd had all night and all this morning to glean clues. And there were a couple of cars and trucks parked off on the shoulder, their occupants peering out the windows at all the activity. *Bunch of ghouls,* he thought with contempt. They were no better than the bloodsucking reporters, who wanted to know "how extensive the injuries were."

He allowed his smile to become a grin now that there was no one to see it. The explosion had worked perfectly, all according to plan. The dynamite came from the company stores, a shed most of the construction workers had access to. The detonator came from there, too. And the garage-door opener came from K-Mart. There was nothing to trace back to him that couldn't lead back to anyone on the crew as well.

His hand went to his inside jacket pocket, and he took out a palm-sized bundle of what seemed to be soft, mahogany-brown leather. It was wrapped around other things, bones, feathers, who knew what; old, brittle, and dark with age. He put it on the blotter and fondled it as he picked up the phone with his other hand. He left it alone just long enough to dial the number of his contact, and then went back to caressing it.

His good-luck piece, he thought. And grinned again.

It had been a real piece of good luck, finding this thing, although it was not the sort of object he would normally have touched, much less picked up and taken with him. After acquiring it, he'd visited one of the Indian museums to try and identify it. He thought it might be a fetish bundle; it looked like the ones in the museum. Whatever it was, finding it had given him the key to making this whole scheme work.

He still remembered, clear as day, when he'd found it.

He had come across it right after the flood on Mingo Creek—the one his Mingo development had caused. Not that he'd ever told anyone. He hadn't really expected any problems, at least, not that soon. Just because he'd paid off the team doing the environmental-impact statement to ignore that little drainage problem that Sunnyvale was going to produce—

Of course, they hadn't dared admit that, or they'd have been in just as much trouble as he would. So everybody had kept their mouths shut, and the worst thing that had happened was that a bridge had gotten washed out along with some creek bank, and the Army Corps had extended their flood-control project on Mingo to go a bit above Owasso. No big deal. Too bad that bridge was gone—there wasn't enough money in the county budget to cover replacing it, so the hicks in the sticks would just have to do without it. It didn't make a lot of difference to him.

They'd said that a big chunk of land had gotten washed out, that Mingo had temporarily changed its course, and the Army Corps had to put in a fair amount of work to get it to go back to its bed. Well, that was baloney. Rivers and streams changed their beds all the time in Oklahoma. They couldn't point the finger at him, or at anybody. It just happened.

But he'd had to take a stroll down there himself, when it had happened, just to make sure that there was nothing that could point to him and his development as the cause. That was when he'd found his good-luck charm.

The little fetish bundle was simply lying on the ground beside the now-shrunken stream, in the middle of a flat patch of sand, as if it was waiting for him. God only knew where it came from; it was as clean as it was now. He picked it up.

And he still didn't know why. But ever since that moment, things had been going all his way.

Even then, the Riverside Mall project was sinking like a lead boat. There were no stores signed up, and no prospect of any. It was a combination of the abysmal economy and the fact that there was no one who was fool enough to sign up for a site that was inevitably going to flood some time in the next twenty years. Tulsa summers were getting wetter, not drier; "hundred-year floods" were happening every couple of years.

He had a choice at that point; close the project down and take a loss, or keep going and chance a bigger one. But the rest of the investors in the project would demand their money back, and that would be a disaster.

Until he picked up the bundle—and "John Smith" at Romulus Insurance gave him that fateful little call. His name wasn't Smith, of course, but that was how Rod was told to refer to him from the time of that conversation.

It started badly, with "John Smith" telling him he'd been checking into the Riverside Mall project for Romulus, and that it didn't look good. That he didn't see how Romulus could possibly insure a project that was going to go under at any moment.

Rod tried to bluff; John Smith wasn't having any.

But then the conversation took an abrupt U-turn. Smith suggested that he might "forget" some of the things he'd uncovered in his report, for a price. But that wasn't all Smith had in mind.

"You're a good businessman, Mr. Calligan," Smith had said. "Let me make you a proposition."

John suggested that there might possibly be a way to close down the project and still turn a profit—if he could find a way to get some kind of extremists or terrorists to close the project down for him because of sabotage.

He was holding the bundle at the time, and that was when the entire plan sprang into his mind, as if it had been placed there. He and Smith had most of the details worked out between them before he'd hung up.

First, he would go to a remote Indian burial ground on private land, a place he knew existed because he had camped and hunted there as a young boy. The place was supposed to be haunted, and none of his friends would stay there overnight or take any of the artifacts that occasionally surfaced in the area. Now he was glad he knew it existed, because it was going to be the key to his plan. He would dig up some of those graves, take the bones and artifacts, and seed his own site with them.

He would wait until his men uncovered the planted "graves"—and being superstitious Indians, they would, of course, raise a fuss. Probably they would even refuse to continue working there; certainly they would refuse to work until he brought in some kind of witch doctor. He would order them to continue digging and to burn what they found—and if they were not already refusing to work, that would ensure that they walked off the job. Then he would arrange a "terrorist bombing" that he could blame on the Indian activists.

While he was setting all this up, he would be siphoning development money into a fund at Romulus; probably some kind of investment fund that he and John Smith had access to. He would invoice things he had not purchased and put the cash into the fund. He could blame the Indians for stealing the supplies, too. Once the first bombing took place, he would have a scapegoat. Indian activists.

He could then stage several more "accidents," giving credence to the idea that Indian activists had turned to terrorism. Then he would complete the plan with a final bombing that would destroy the office, his office computers, and all the records, covering his embezzlement.

At that point, he could even declare bankruptcy; it was about time to get out of the development game in Oklahoma anyway. The gravy train had run out a long time ago, and the economy of this region was not likely to get better until the year 2000. He wasn't prepared to wait around, working on piddly shit, until that happened. He could try something else. Ostrich farming, maybe; there would be good money in it for a while.

Whether or not he declared bankruptcy was secondary anyway. He'd also be able to collect insurance money from Romulus. So, he would have his secret nest egg, shared with John Smith, and his insurance payment.

Well, right now he'd worry about Phase One: making sure all the blame for the bombings and other sabotage fell on the damn Indians. With any luck, he could make himself look really good—make a big point about how he'd gone out of his way to get them jobs, and carry on about ingratitude and superstition. He'd have to wait until the press came out and *asked* him if the rumors of Indian terrorists were true, but the way he figured it, that should happen some time later in the week. Certainly it would happen as soon as the second bomb went off.

The phone rang on. Periodically, Rod would hang up and hit the redial button, just to end the monotony. Smith picked up his phone, finally. And as always, Calligan activated the tape recorder. He had all kinds of recordings and paper trails, just in case. It always paid to have "insurance". . . .

"Calligan. I got to the records. We have a problem."

Rod frowned; he'd gotten to know the subtle cues in Smith's voice over the past few weeks, and Smith was nervous.

"So what's the problem?" he asked cautiously.

"Sleighbow hired a Private Investigator to make sure you didn't know there was real trouble *before* the bombing," Smith said. "He's looking for conspiracy to commit fraud—that's not just civil, that's criminal."

Rod didn't see the problem. "What's the big deal?" he asked. "There's nothing to find. There wasn't any conspiracy, remember? We made it all up."

"Yeah, and that's the problem—that there isn't anything. You don't have any way to substantiate this terrorism shit." Smith definitely was nervous. "If there isn't *anything* there, the P.I. just might look deeper, and find some of our tracks. Or else clue the cops in."

"No problem." Rod had dealt with small-timers a lot; he knew how to handle them. "We just wait until he doesn't find anything, slip him some change under the table to quit right there and—"

"The big deal is the P.I. he hired," Smith interrupted. "For starters, this one isn't on the take. She's as clean as they come. It's a woman, a local, and she's likely to know what to look for. And she's Indian, so you can bet she's going to be looking for things that will clear her people. I've got a file on her right here—Romulus hasn't ever done work with her before, but one of the companies we bought out not too long ago did. According to this, she not only refused a payoff, she had herself wired by a security firm, and reported the bribe with the tape as evidence. She got some Olympia people fired over that one. She's straight, and she could be trouble."

But the moment Smith revealed his opposition's sex, Rod

knew he had the situation sewed up. Indian and female—uneducated, unthinking, relying on instincts; no way was this chick going to give him a hard time. "No woman is going to be trouble," Rod said arrogantly. "I haven't seen a bitch yet I haven't been able to outclass and outthink. But I need more information—I need to know where I can get some leverage on her. See what you can dig up for me, and see if you can have someone at your end throw her a red herring. Get somebody to tell her there really was trouble with Indians before the explosion."

Smith snorted; he was clearly not that confident. But then, he didn't know Rod, did he? "All right—" he said reluctantly, "but it's your funeral if you screw up."

Then he hung up, abruptly, leaving Rod with a dial tone. Rod dropped the receiver into its cradle, frowning, and killed his recording. This was stupid; Smith was spooking over nothing. One insignificant female P.I., Indian or not, wasn't going to ruin the plan. All he needed was a little more information, a way to get a handle on her, and that would be it. Was Smith a weak link in this? He might be, and Rod needed to think about a way to protect himself from his ally.

Finally he got up and tucked his fetish-bundle back into his jacket pocket. It was time to be heading home, before another stupid reporter decided to track him down. He was not ready to deal with them yet. He needed to think out everything he was going to say and do before he confronted another reporter. He needed to control them; he could not let them take the situation out of his hands again.

He locked up the office and at last took refuge in his car. Only when he was speeding down the Broken Arrow Expressway heading for home did he feel secure. He would plan every day from now on, prepared to confront reporters, prepared to get control and keep control of every situation.

But as for the P.I.—Smith was overreacting. He was far more worried about the reporters uncovering something, because of some slip of his own tongue. No, there was no female in the world that was a match for him. He'd plow this bitch under like he plowed under brush. She'd be just another weed in his path. . . .

But still, the conversation left a bad taste in his mouth, one that lasted through the rest of the evening.

Jennifer pulled the Brat up to the edge of the cyclone fence surrounding the construction site. She parked there, and waited until the police were gone, even though she had no intention of getting onto the property.

Yet.

There were a half dozen other cars here, full of people watching the police, avidly. They were good camouflage for her. Finally Calligan left the site office and drove off in his ridiculously expensive sedan. Then the last of the cops packed up and left, and when they drove off, so did the sensation-hungry observers, leaving her alone.

The place was deserted now, yards of yellow POLICE LINE—DO NOT CROSS tape all around the area of the explosion, flapping in the breeze. It looked like any other construction site she'd ever seen; yards of plowed-up and leveled dirt, heavy equipment scattered around—the river in the background, low now—heat rising in waves from the open areas.

But there was something really wrong here. Something that had nothing to do with the yellow police tape, and the spilled blood that cried out to her for justice. Something that lay deeper than that, buried under the raw earth.

She had checked on all the permits, and they were clear. Calligan had not stepped one inch outside the law. She had spoken to other contractors, and no one was willing to say anything against him.

Nevertheless, there was something wrong here, something permits did not cover.

It was more than just the plowing up of land she had last seen alive and covered with native grasses and cotton-woods—although that disturbed her on a deep level, the level that saw waste and pillage and wanted to strike out at the author of that wastage.

There were several things obviously wrong, beginning with the sort of thing anyone could see.

First was simply the area itself. She hadn't quite remembered what the site had looked like before she got here, for it had been too long since the last protest—now she was struck by the complete inappropriateness of the land for *anything*, much less a mall. There were no really major arteries coming anywhere near here, so traffic was going to be a bitch. But most of all, this was floodplain. Granted, the Army Corps had been doing a lot since the floods following the monster in 1984 on Memorial Day, but when it came right down to it, they were playing a game of catch-up. There was a lot more rainfall around here than there had ever been before, but that was not all. There were more recreational lakes and water-retention projects than ever before, and that meant that there would be a little more water in the local ecosystem with every passing year.

That meant more danger of flooding. The Army Corps only fixed something after the floods, not before. And if *they* had to order a water release further upstream, there would be nothing that would save this place from the rising waters.

I sure wouldn't want to buy anything built here—not unless it was on a barge or came with a flotation collar.

And it was a lot closer to the eagle-nesting area than she remembered, too. True, eagles were even nesting on golf courses in Florida, but Florida golf courses supported a lively little ecosystem of their own, what with bunnies in the rough and fish in the water hazards. There was food on the golf courses; what would the eagles eat here? Big Macs?

Maybe I gave in too quickly. Maybe I should have used some of my out-of-state connections to put some pressure on

*the county boys. I know they had to be on the take—maybe
I should have done a little legwork and found a way to
prove it.*

She had watched Rod Calligan handle the reporters, dive
into his office, then drive away in his yuppiemobile, all
without bothering to make contact. She hadn't left him
alone just because he'd looked like he was in a hurry, either.
There had been something really off-kilter about him, something that just plain didn't fit his public face.

It was as if he'd been wearing chrome-yellow socks and
purple Nikes with that Armani suit of his, although it was
something that did not show on the surface. Something that
didn't match that yuppier-than-thou exterior. . . .

Abruptly, she realized what it was. *Bad Medicine.* It had
been all over him, an aura perhaps only she could have
detected.

She'd done a little checking with Karen Miles, a reporter
friend of hers for Channel Three, who had interviewed him
for the early news yesterday. Mr. Calligan had not made a
good impression on Karen—"offensive," "arrogant," and
"chauvinistic" were the kindest things that Karen had to
say about him. That had been another reason to put off
confronting him face-to-face; Jennifer had not felt up to
dealing with a pain in the behind just yet. She might not
have to meet with him at all; the job required investigating
him, and it might be better if he didn't know she existed.

For a moment, she toyed with the idea that he might
simply be putting her back up because his attitudes were so
ingrained that they tainted everything around him. But she
had to deal with offensive white males all the time; her
obvious racial heritage and sex often counted against her in
Oklahoma. In fact, there had been a time or two when
patience and doing a damn fine job had turned a couple of
those guys into allies.

No, this was all Bad Medicine, the real thing. The feeling
of hate, of a grudge or even a curse. It was as if Rod

Calligan had been tagged by something; something unseen, something malevolent. And it *wasn't* just because he had desecrated a burial ground, although that was part of it. That would bear looking into, as well. But the Bad Medicine that raised her hackles right now was something bigger, and it involved his cooperation. What was even odder, she hadn't noticed it until he'd come out of that office, as if something he had done in there had activated it.

She filed that away for future thought. And for a possible discussion with Grandfather. How could a whiter-than-white guy get involved with malevolent Medicine?

Well, she wasn't going to get any more answers standing around here—and if she lingered much longer, there might be a cop along to find out if she was just a morbid-accident groupie, a chick who was stupidly curious, or someone who might know something. The truism that criminals always returned to the scene was just that, and if she didn't want to become a suspect herself, she had better get out of here. Time to get moving with that list she got from Calligan's personnel girl. The best time to catch people was when they were home for supper.

Supper. Would there be time to get something? Well, maybe she'd better just grab an apple and some cheese from the fridge.

There was a derisive caw from above her head. She looked up.

Above her on the telephone pole was a huge raven, one with a worn beak and who listed a little to one side.

Still watching me, hmm?

She suppressed an urge to stick her tongue out at it.

Instead, she looked directly up at it and said, "Don't you *dare* order a pizza while I'm gone! You know it's bad for your heart!"

The raven cawed again, this time a series of short croaks that sounded like someone laughing, and it flew off, wings pumping hard to get any kind of lift out of the hot, heavy air.

She looked around guiltily to see if there was anyone who might have heard her talking to a bird.

Yeah, and who might call the folks down at the Home to find out if they'd had any escapees.

But there was no one in sight, and with a sigh of relief she started the truck and drove off.

Interviews. Not her favorite part of the job, although as a shaman she had a better-than-average chance at knowing when someone was lying to her. Home first, though, and grab something to hold until she could get a real meal; lunch had been an apple and some yogurt. Someone else might have called—or her father might have gotten back with some information that would help when she talked to the construction guys who quit. Every little bit of leverage was useful on a case like this one, where no one was going to want to talk to anyone else.

Sometimes it was useful to be going the opposite direction of everyone else. Rush hour around here began at three, when the plants and factories let out. She made pretty good time getting back home—while the sides of the streets heading out into the suburbs were still congested, the sides going into town were pretty empty. She pulled up into the driveway, dashed into the house, and poked her head into the living room, feeling a bit more cheerful than when she had left.

"Anybody call?" she asked Mooncrow, who was up to some obscene level on Tetris.

"One call," he said, never taking his eyes off the screen. "I left the number on the pad in the kitchen. The man would only say that he was calling about Native Americans."

Would that be Sleighbow, calling to see if she'd gotten started on the case? Surely not. Surely he would not be that impatient. In her experience, insurance people didn't understand the meaning of the word "fast."

She tucked herself into the tiny kitchen, barely big enough for one. Older houses usually had enormous kitchens, but this house must have been built for a woman who hated to cook, because you couldn't open the oven and refrigerator doors at the same time.

The number on the pad had an area code that seemed familiar, but the number wasn't Sleighbow's. It occurred to her that it might be FedEx about the package she'd just sent, or even one of the Lakotah calling to see if she'd made any progress.

No, wait, it's not an 800 number, so it must be the Lakotah. I did tell them I was going to know by today whether or not the relics were where I thought they were. Maybe my contact wasn't home, and whoever got the box doesn't know what it is.

She dialed the number, then dug into the fridge for an apple and string cheese while it rang. She was short on time, short on energy, and short on fuel.

"This is Jennifer Talldeer. I sent the box already," she said, checking her watch, as soon as someone picked up on the other end. *Make this fast and get on the road,* she thought absently; she needed to bolt this and get out of here. She felt a growing irritability, maybe even a little lightheadedness; the apple was wearing thin. "You should have gotten it before ten this morning."

Silence for a moment, then the person on the other end said, "What box?"

"The relics you—I mean, the Lakotah elders—wanted me to track down," she replied, rattling on quickly, and thinking she must be talking to a younger relative who was not privy to what the elders had been doing. "Just tell Charlie Wapiti I got them and I sent them this afternoon."

"I—uh, Miss Talldeer, I did call you, but it wasn't about Lakotah relics," the man on the other end of the line said. "I'm Franklin Morse, I'm with Morse Construction in Kansas, and I was told by a Mr. Sleighbow you might want to talk to me about Rod Calligan."

"Oh, good grief!" she exclaimed, exasperated with herself and blushing. "Mr. Morse, I am sorry—I have more than one case going at a time, and I just assumed you were calling about one I just wrapped up. Yes, I would like to ask you about Rod Calligan, if there's anything at all you can tell me. But I don't have a lot of time."

"Shoot, that's all right, it *is* your nickel," Morse replied. "Just what are you looking for?"

"Information about the way he operates," she said with caution. "I'm a private investigator, and I'm looking into an accident on one of his sites." That was ambiguous enough; nothing that Calligan could take exception to if he got word she was asking around about him.

"Huh." Morse was silent for a moment. "I go head-to-head with Calligan on a lot of bids, and I do have to tell you, miss, that he's a sharp one. Never makes a bad move, businesswise. Even when it looks like he's making a mistake, it always turns out he made the right move."

Interesting. Especially in light of all the real-estate failures lately. "What about his crews. Do you have any idea how he gets along with his employees?"

Silence for a moment. "Rides his boys pretty hard, makes sure every minute on the clock is a minute of work. I can meet and match his bids, though, and I can guarantee I don't have the kind of labor problems he does."

"Labor problems?" she asked, trying to prompt him without sounding like she was doing so.

"Who've you been talking to?" Morse countered. "I could tell you better if I knew."

A shrewd man; she had the notion that he wanted to know if anything *he* said could get him into trouble.

"Some of his employees," she said absently, trying to get down the apple without sounding like she was eating. "I may talk to some other people who aren't working for him right now."

"Well, miss, like I said, he's kinda hard. There's some folks that just don't like him being that tight on the clock, and they kinda got a problem with that. Are you working with that fella name of Sleighbow that called me?"

She decided she might as well loosen up a little. If Sleighbow had sent this man to her, it was probably safe to be a little less obtuse. "Yes, actually," she replied.

"Well, I got some of Calligan's people here, they're Indians—they don't think too highly of the man. They said he's got an attitude about things they feel pretty strong about." He sounded as if he was feeling her out. "Pardon my asking, miss, but are you Indian?"

"Yes," she said, figuring it wouldn't do any harm. "Why?"

Silence again. "I talked to them, trying to figure out why they left. They said it was because they figure he's disrespectful of the earth, and if you was Indian too, I reckoned you'd know what they meant." The man sounded puzzled. "I don't get it, but they feel pretty strong. They say he's disrespectful of the ancestors too; the way they carry on sometimes, you'd think he was out there every day bulldozin' down churches or something."

"Well, I think I can understand how they feel," she replied, trying to think of a way to give this apparently well-meaning fellow some insight. "Imagine how you'd feel if some punks got into the graveyard where your grandparents are buried and wrote graffiti all over the gravemarkers."

"I guess I'd get pretty hot about it," Morse admitted. "I guess they are too, then."

"Could be." She checked her watch again. "Mr. Morse, thank you. If you have anything more specific to tell me, call me collect, all right?"

"That'll be fine," he said cheerfully. "Glad I could help. G'night, Miss Talldeer."

"Thank you, Mr. Morse." She hung up; unfortunately,

the man hadn't told her anything she hadn't already heard from Sleighbow. Getting steamed about something and doing anything about it were two different things. And this still sounded more like a terrorist action than something concocted by a disgruntled employee. People who hated your guts came after you personally with a gun; they didn't blow up a bulldozer and take out only fellow employees.

Well. It had been a long day, and it was likely to get a lot longer. She'd better get on the road again.

The phone rang just as the Calligans were halfway through dinner. Toni Calligan started, her hazel eyes going wide, and pushed away from the table to grab it before it disturbed her husband. But Rod waved her back to her seat, before she could get up.

"I'm expecting a call," he said. "Go ahead and eat; this won't take long."

He left his dinner on the table, knowing that if it *did* take longer than he thought it would, Toni would automatically take his half-finished plate off to the kitchen to rewarm it. He had her well trained.

He picked up the phone on the extension in his office just as it got to the fourth ring. "Calligan," he said, shortly. If this was a siding salesman—

"Smith," said the voice on the other end. "You wanted more information, I got it for you."

Rod took down notes as Smith rattled off a short biography of this "Jennifer Talldeer" who had been assigned to him. Mother, father, brothers, grandfather living with her— there didn't seem to be a lot of leverage there, except for strong-arm tactics, and it wasn't at that level yet.

Then he got to the interesting tidbit. "Seems like she takes on some no-pay cases on her own time," Smith said. "She goes after Indian bones and artifacts and sends them back to the tribes they came from. She just shipped off a box of stuff like that within the week, in fact. If she's doing this for nothing, I'd say she's pretty motivated about it."

"Oh, really?" Rod Calligan's hand moved of itself to his good-luck charm in his pants pocket, but his eyes moved to the boxes of loot from that Indian graveyard, artifacts that had looked like they might be worth something, and which he hadn't used to salt the construction site.

He smiled.

"What do you mean by that?" Smith demanded testily.

Rod's smile widened. "Only," he replied softly, "that I think I can promise I know how to pull her strings."

CHAPTER SIX

THIS HAD BEEN her first full day on the case. By now, sunset was only a memory, and Jennifer was just grateful she knew the entire Tulsa metroplex like her own backyard. Otherwise it would have been impossible to find all these addresses. Some of these little suburban areas had streets that wound around through them with no plan that *she* could make out. This was one of them, and it took her fifteen minutes to find the right "Ridley," for there was a "Ridley Street," a "Ridley Way," a "Ridley Court," and a "Ridley Place," all within blocks of one another. She pulled the Brat up in front of the third house on her list, only to find it dark, with no signs of vehicles anywhere. Not in the garage, nor the driveway, nor the street outside.

What is this, bingo night? It's too early in the year for softball league, and too late for bowling. This was ridiculous; there hadn't been a single soul home so far who was on her list of Calligan's ex-employees. It was beginning to feel like an episode of "The Twilight Zone."

Well, no point in sticking around here. There was some traffic on the road, but not much. She waited until the car behind her had pulled around her parking place, then got back on the street again. Surely someone was going to be home!

The fourth name on her list was a guy who lived out in Sand Springs, not Tulsa. With any luck, whatever it was that had pulled everyone out of their houses here in town would not be something that someone in Sand Springs would want to drive all the way into Tulsa for. At the end of a long workday, a twenty-minute drive could seem much too long.

Unless it's a Garth Brooks concert or something. Nothing too much to go through for a Garth Brooks concert.

That was a facetious thought of course. If there had been anything that big in town, she'd have known about it weeks ago.

The drive out to the Springs was uneventful; sunset brought cooler temperatures, and she was able to roll the windows down instead of using the A/C. Heat lightning flickered in the clouds overhead, illuminating them for a brief moment in a flash of orange. The color always made her think of orange sherbet, a childhood hangover from nights spent sitting out on the porch, watching the lightning and the lightning bugs, and sharing a bowl with one of the cats.

Her next target lived a little out of town on a county road, and as she neared the house, she knew that this man, at least, was not off somewhere. His driveway was full of cars and trucks, and his yard held the overflow. The little white frame house was lit up inside and out, and it was clear that the owner expected all this company.

As she pulled into the driveway and parked her car behind the last one in the line (a red pickup), she had a sinking feeling that now she knew where everyone on her list was. Someone had gotten wind of trouble, and this was how they were dealing with it.

Too bad her father hadn't heard about this; it would have been nice to have had some warning.

Looks like I've walked right into a meeting, she thought grimly. *And I don't think it's the Kiwanis or the Tulsa Pow Wow Club.*

She turned off her car lights, and as she did so, she noticed the curtains at one of the lighted windows move.

I'd say I've just been spotted. Man—I wish I'd had some warning about this, though I guess if some of my buddies got blown up and people were looking for scapegoats, I'd get together with everyone else too. So I've got what, two dozen hostile people waiting in there? The prospect was not one she enjoyed. Still—on the bright side, it would save having to run them all down. And she could get all her rejections over with at once.

Aw guys, it would be so nice if you'd cooperate. It would look so much better on the report if you'd just play nice. . . . She squared her shoulders, put on her best professional manner, and opened the truck door.

As she came up the walkway and into the light from the porch lamps, she saw the curtains at the window move again, and a shadow move toward the door.

Here comes the welcoming committee.

Just as she reached the porch, someone opened the door and walked out to intercept her.

For a moment, a shock of recognition froze her.

He leaned up against the doorframe and crossed his arms, a sardonic expression—not quite a sneer—on his face.

She unfroze, took two more steps, and stopped, one foot on the low wooden porch. "Hello, David," she said, evenly. "I hope it's nice to see you again."

"Wish I could say the same. It depends on whose side you're on." Impossible to pretend she didn't know David Spotted Horse; not when he was the first guy she'd ever slept with, the guy her folks had thought for sure she was going to marry.

And the last guy she'd ever been at all serious about, as far as that went.

"I'm not on anyone's side, David," she replied, keeping her voice even, and not betraying what she was really feeling. "You ought to know that, if you pretend to know anything about me."

Her stomach was one tight knot; her heart fluttering. Rival feelings warred for possession of her body. *It figures that he'd be here. A possible incident building, involving Native Americans, and right in his own stomping grounds? They must still be scrubbing the marks off the driveway where he peeled out of there.* "There" being North Dakota, and "they" being the activist group he'd joined in college, right before he'd dropped out. And right before they'd had that screaming fight that ended in a breakup.

She still couldn't figure out why he'd bailed out of college. When he dropped out, he was scuttling a promising career in law, and the Powers knew the Native American movement needed lawyers. But he said it was a waste of time. She stayed to graduate. His decision to bail had been only one of the reasons why they'd broken up. . . .

He was posed right under one of the porch lights, and she couldn't help but make mental comparisons with the guy she used to know. The guy she used to know wouldn't have *posed* like that, making a macho body-language statement, clearly blocking her way. The old David would have stood a little to one side, to give her a chance to push past him. So he was used to blocking the way, to forcing a confrontation, whether or not the other party was prepared for one.

The years had improved him, that was for sure. Gone was the conservative haircut; his hair was almost as long as hers, now, parted in the middle and tied back with a thong decorated with a beaded redtail feather. She had no doubt he'd earned it; had no doubt that he'd probably earned eagle by now, and just chose not to wear it every day. He'd put on muscle; the open collar of his blue workshirt showed the strong throat, encircled by a hair-pipe collar, and it was pretty obvious from the straining seams across his shoulders and chest that he'd been exercising more than rhetoric since he'd been gone. She guessed he was actually wearing a size smaller jeans than he had in college, at least in the waist; the silver and leather concha belt buckled over his hips was new, and with that and the soft blue jeans, he looked good enough to be in the movies. The chiseled face and dark, farseeing eyes could still make her heart beat a little faster, if she ignored the sullen and challenging expression there.

That expression helped her get herself back under some semblance of control. *Yeah, he's a babe-fest all right. But the years haven't improved his manners any.* She grinned, but only mentally. *Or his command of body language. Inscrutable warrior, my ass! He might as well be writing his intentions on a blackboard.*

He was taking the offensive and aggressive path right from the start, and her efforts at keeping nonconfrontational weren't working. He'd already made up his mind about her, and she didn't think he was going to listen to anything she said. Still, she had to try.

"If you're not on our side, Jennifer, you're on The Enemy's side," he replied angrily, and giving "enemy" the emphasis that put a capital "E" on the word. "That's the way it is, and you'd better get that through your head right now. You may think you aren't on anyone's side, but you were hired by The Enemy, and you're The Enemy's shill, whether you know it or not."

Right. I thought that kind of thinking went out in the six-ties! She kept her expression calm, although she was any-thing but. "First of all, David, it's none of your business who hired me. But that hardly matters, since secondly, you can't possibly *know* who hired me or what they want me to find out, because that kind of information hasn't made it out on the street yet, and believe me, I'd know if it had. And thirdly, you're right out of line, because you haven't the faintest idea of what you're talking about." She tried not to sound anything other than logical and cool, but nothing she said or did was going to penetrate that thick (and ridiculously attractive) head.

He sneered. He actually sneered. She hadn't thought anyone used that particular expression outside of bad movies and worse TV shows. "I know more than enough," he replied. "I know how you were when I dumped you, that you figured you could get along with The Man. I know that's shorthand for selling out. You're still letting *wasichu* tell you what to do, what to say, what to think. You haven't changed, Jennifer."

You dumped me? Yeah, fer sure, and I'm a blond. She didn't know whether to laugh at him or herself. *Oh David, like you aren't a tool of The Man whether or not you admit it. The Man manipulates you just by being for something— even if it was good for you, you'd be against it. And don't think that smart people aren't able to figure that out after talking with you for two minutes.* But she didn't say anything; she just sighed after a long moment. "Look, I have a job to do, and it happens to be *for* our people. Are you going to get out of the way?"

"There's nothing in there for you, Jennifer," he said, not moving. "There's no one in there who wants to talk to you."

Since he obviously hadn't *asked* anyone in the meeting if they were willing to talk to her, that patent untruth made her lose her patience. "I'd like to hear that for myself, thank you! And I'd like to get a chance to talk to someone who just might know something that could help all of us, instead of a fool who acts like a white man and makes assumptions without waiting to hear the facts."

She could have slapped herself for calling him a fool, but it was too late to take it back.

He didn't move. He just stood there with that scowl on his

face, in what had to be an unconscious reflection of a James
Dean poster. "That's what this meeting is all about," he said
abruptly. "We're making up our minds about what we're
going to do about this situation. There are at least some
people here who have the sense to talk to experts instead of
waiting to get trapped by smart cops."

"We?" she raised her eyebrow, which so far was the only
change she'd made in her expression. At least she could take
comfort in the fact that she had more control over her body
language than he had over his. "I hadn't noticed you driving
any bulldozers lately. Or have you suddenly turned into a
construction worker in the past week?"

He ignored the remark. "I'm here to advise these people,
before they get into something too deep to pull out of. We're
going to vote on whether we should talk to anybody at
all—whether we should take everything straight into the
courts as a minorities harassment case. That way we get
protection and bypass all the bullshit."

A harassment case? She was incredulous. There was blood
spilled out on that site; some of his people and hers were
dead. How could he possibly be thinking of something so—
petty? How dare he reduce this situation to trivialities?

That was when her temper went the way of her patience.
This was not a law-class exercise, this was the real world—
and there were real people who were really dead.

"Dammit, David," she snarled, "there's more than just a
harassment case going on when you've got a body count!
You jerkoff, there's *dead people* involved here, kids whose
daddies aren't coming home, and somebody's responsible
for their deaths! That's *murder* in my book, and not some
two-bit legal sideshow!"

She dug into her pocket and came up with a handful of
business cards. She shoved the cards at him, feeling her
blood pressure rise with every second. "When you and the
boys get tired of playing Indians and cavalry, give me a
call," she said sarcastically. "Maybe *then* we can start get-

ting things settled, and maybe together we can find out who's responsible."

He didn't take the cards; they dropped to the ground at his feet.

She turned on her heel and walked off, so angry she could hardly see. She stalked stiff-kneed and stiff-spined all the way back to the truck, threw herself inside, started it up, and backed out with a spinning of tires and spitting of gravel. This time she left tire marks on the road.

But at the crossroads, her temper cooled; she pulled over and beat her hands on the steering wheel. She wanted to beat her head on it—but that would leave bruises, and a bruised forehead would be hard to explain to the folks.

Oh, I just ran into David Spotted Horse, and I started beating my head against a wall. . . .

Then again, they'd probably accept that.

"Good job, Talldeer," she muttered under her breath. "Really good job. Congratulations. You really made your point, didn't you. Damn, damn, damn—"

Why did *he* have to be there? Why couldn't it have been some other macho asshole from the Rights Movement? She could have handled a stranger. She wouldn't have lost her temper. She'd handled every flavor and color of macho jerk there was, including those of her own people who had accused her, openly or veiled, of selling out to the White Man. Of being an Apple—red on the outside, white on the inside. She'd done it successfully, too. If it had just been a stranger—

But it wasn't a stranger. It was *him.* All the old memories, all the old attraction—all the old baggage. If he wasn't such a jerk—

The hormones gave her another thrill along her nerve endings. *They* didn't care if he was a macho idiot. All they knew was that he had been cute and now he was a hunk-arama, right in the same style and league as some of the gorgeous guys who'd been making beautiful scenery in *Last of the Mohicans* and *Dances With Wolves*. Yeah, it was all still there.

"If he wasn't such a jerk, you'd be in bed with him in a New York minute," she said aloud, scolding herself. "Jennifer, you are such a pushover!"

Jennifer, you are such a dope. The minute David shows up, you've got helium heels.

She put her head down in her hands, and tried to think around the hormones and the anger. *I was yelling loud enough to be heard in the next county. I'm sure they heard me inside. If I'm lucky, someone in there will pick up one of those cards, or make David give him one. If I'm really lucky, it'll be someone with the sense Wah-K'on-Tah gave a gnat, and he'll call me. If I'm not lucky, I'm going to have to try and talk one of these guys into hearing me out before he pitches me out on my butt.*

Well, there was one man who would not be at that meeting. At least one of the men who'd been injured was still in the hospital and not so drugged up that he couldn't talk. Larry Bushyhead had had something fall on him when the dozer exploded; from the tally at the hospital the injuries were cracked ribs and broken fingers, but not much else. If she left now, she could make it before visiting hours were over.

He wasn't an ex-employee, either; he was a witness to everything that had happened before the explosion. He could have some valuable information about the guys who'd quit, and about what had happened that day.

And at least *he* wouldn't be someone who made her hormones prance around like performing dogs.

The hospital corridor was empty; most of the patients on this floor were drugged into happy—or at least pain-free—oblivion. They'd turned the corridor lights down for the benefit of those who wanted to sleep.

I really hate hospitals, she thought absently. The places always smelled like disinfectant and dead flowers, and they were always too cold. No wonder the nurses wore sweaters on duty. She listened to her own footsteps and the mingled sounds of a dozen TV and radio stations as she walked the empty corridor to a room halfway along its length.

"Hi," she said cautiously, poking her head around the doorframe. Larry was in a double, but there wasn't anyone in the other bed, and the nurse on duty said that his wife was out looking for some dinner. It was the usual hospital semi-private; Larry was in the bed nearest the window and the bathroom; Hillcrest had their bathrooms on the outside wall rather than the inside. The curtains were closed, and the TV was off, with only the light over his bed still burning. This was a good time to talk to him.

Heck, it was a great time to talk to him; if he felt like talking to her, he wouldn't be inhibited by the presence of a roommate or his wife.

"Hi," he said, looking up from the paper he was trying to read; from the way he'd been squinting at it, he wasn't having much luck with it. "What can I do for you?"

He looked interested, at least, and not like she was imposing on him. She took another step that put her in the doorway. Now that she was closer, there was no doubt of his Osage blood. Tall, rangy, with dark brown hair and mild eyes that were probably deceptive, he looked enough like her father to be a cousin. He'd gotten someone to bring him real pajamas, which was just as well, because she figured that, tall as he was, the hospital gown was just long enough to save him from technical exposure.

"I'm Jennifer Talldeer, and the insurance company that covers Rod Calligan hired me to ask some questions," she said, carefully. "I promise I'm not from Workman's Comp, and nothing you tell me will have any effect on your hospitalization. Do you feel like answering them? If you don't, I'll be happy to leave you in peace, but if you do, it might clear up a lot of things."

"I feel like just about anything other than watching a rerun or trying to read this paper," he said, giving her a wan but friendly grin. "They gave me a little stuff for the pain, and it makes fine print damn hard to read. Just don't make me laugh or ask me to shake hands, okay?" As he put the paper down, she saw that three of the fingers on his right hand were splinted and bandaged.

So, I got lucky, Davidwise. Either he doesn't like being bossed around by anyone, whether or not they're an activist, or they just haven't gotten to him yet.

Encouraged, she entered his room and took a seat beside the bed. "I'd like to start with some questions about some of the guys who quit," she said. "Was there bad blood between them and their boss?"

Bushyhead thought about her question for a moment, then shook his head. "Not really. A couple of them got better offers from the State, a couple got long-term offers from a road crew, and a couple of them just couldn't stomach plowing up good animal habitat for a stupid mall and went off to see if anyone else had a job opening. But I didn't ever hear any of them badmouthing him; they all got other work, and I hang out with most of them, off and on."

"So there were no threats against the company that you know of?" she asked.

"Threats?" His surprise was genuine. "Hell no, not that I ever heard of. Definitely not from the guys that quit."

"What about outsiders?" she asked. "You know there were a lot of protests over the choice of site."

He nodded. "I signed the petition. But once the county signed off, there was never anything seriously said or done. No threats, and that's for sure, or I'd have heard about that, too."

She gave him a skeptical look, and he grinned. "I sweet-talk the secretary; get her lunch sometimes so she'll let me know when something's up. She gets the mail first; if there were threats, I'd have known—these days, you can't be too careful. I worked on a site that got bomb threats once, and once was enough for me. The wildlife people kept trying to post injunctions, but they never went through, and that is *all* I ever heard of. You know, what with some of the crazies that are out there, there's a couple of us that'd think twice about working a site with somebody making threats around."

He could be bluffing—he could simply be ignorant of what was going on. But she didn't think so. He had no reason to lie, and every reason to tell the truth.

Besides, all of her instincts were telling her he was divulging everything he knew.

She decided to try a different angle. "Do you think you can remember exactly what happened just before all hell broke loose?" It had occurred to her that he might have noticed something that would tell her what kind of hand had been behind this.

"Yeah, I think so." He nodded. "I went over this for the cops, though—"

"I'm not likely to get access to that," she pointed out. "Was there anyone hanging around the site that you noticed?"

"No, and we kind of watch for that," he told her. "We've had some problems with people pilfering stuff. In fact, the guys told me this afternoon that the dynamite inventory doesn't match the stores—"

Bet that's where the explosives came from. "Did anything odd happen that day?" she persisted.

"Uh—I didn't tell the cops this, but, yeah." He was frowning, and she asked why.

"Well, something really bad happened right before the explosion, only it wasn't the kind of thing the cops would consider bad." He hesitated a moment, then gave her a sharp look. "Can I ask you a question first? About your family?"

"Sure," she said, wondering what had caused the look, but getting the feeling in her bones that he was about to tell her something very important. "I don't see why not."

"Is your grandfather the Talldeer that's the Medicine Man?" Despite being fogged by drugs, he was watching her very closely—and the question startled her a little, and increased the feeling of urgency.

"Well, yes, actually." She wondered where he'd heard of her grandfather, and if she should say anything else, but he said it for her.

"So you're the Medicine Woman, the kid he's been teaching—" He sighed and looked relieved. "Okay, you'll understand, then. You know, if this had happened the day *before* the dozer suicided, I'd have been sure somebody had planted a bomb because of it—but it couldn't have been more than a few minutes before—"

He was rambling, possibly nerves, possibly the drugs, probably both. But in the ramblings, there were important clues. Suddenly, this wasn't just an insurance job. She suddenly felt like a hunter who has just heard the warning caw of a crow. She stiffened. "So what *did* happen?" she prompted.

"We—we dug up bones." He swallowed. "Old bones, pots, you know what I mean?"

"You're saying you found a burial ground. I mean, one of *our* grounds," she said, trying to control the feeling of danger that made her skin crawl. There it was. Out in the open. "Not just some old graveyard from around the Land Rush days."

"Yeah, at least that's what we all think." He shook his head. "It really spooked us, even the white guys. The stuff looked like it might be real old. And you know what digging up sacred ground means. . . ."

He was getting more and more agitated the more he

thought about it. "Yes," she told him. "I *do*. Can I help?"

He brightened at that. "Yeah, if you get a chance, would you ask your grandfather to come do a cleansing on me? Not that I'm superstitious but—"

"But you've already had enough trouble; no problem," she replied, mentally hitting a "reset" button and looking at the situation in a whole new light. Now it definitely was no longer just an insurance job. She had a real soul-stake in finding out what had happened, and too bad if the cops didn't like her poking around. "So you—ah—disturbed relics. Then what happened?"

"We backed off pretty quick, you bet—and we told the foreman we weren't gonna dig there. He got hot; called the boss on the cellular. The boss said we by god *were* gonna dig, and what was more, we were gonna burn the stuff we found or throw it in the river and not say anything about it." He gritted his teeth, and it didn't take a shaman to sense his anger. "He said if we told anybody, there'd be people from the college and everything coming in and stopping work."

She grimaced. "And you were mad—"

"I wasn't the only one!" he said. "We started arguing, and we even got the white guys on our side. I was just about to see if I couldn't sneak off and like, call the college or something, just to delay things, when—" He shrugged.

She sat silent for a moment. "So, what do you think happened to cause that?" she asked cautiously.

"Well—I thought it was just faulty equipment, but the guys said it was sabotage. My brains say somebody probably planted a bomb in the dozer, and god only knows why." He shook his head. "Nut cases, who can tell, with them? But my gut—"

She noticed he was sweating, and she knew why.

"—you know, I am really *glad* you're the Medicine Woman and all," he said, and he sounded genuinely grateful. "Anybody else would laugh at me for this, but—my gut says it happened because the Little People are after his ass, and they kind of got us because we were involved. You know how they are."

She did, indeed, know how They were. *Mi-ah-luschka* had a mixed reputation. Vindictive, vicious at times. "You didn't hear any—owls—did you?" she asked. "Just before the explosion?" The *mi-ah-luschka*, the Little People, often took the form of owls. . . .

"Not that I'd noticed, but I wasn't noticing a lot except the fight between the foreman and the other dozer driver." He sighed. "That's why I'd really appreciate it if your grandfather could get on over here, you know?"

"Oh, I know," she assured him. "Uh—wait a minute, let me check on something—"

She dug into her purse, vaguely remembering that trip to Lyon's and the one to Peace Of Mind earlier this afternoon. Some things she always had with her, of course, but others she didn't necessarily take with her all the time. She'd picked up some herbs for herself and Grandfather, as well as the goodies for her father. Had she taken the packages out of her purse yet?

No!

"Would you accept a Medicine Woman instead of a Medicine Man?" she asked him carefully. "I won't be offended if you'd rather it was Grandfather."

"You mean, you've got stuff with you?" Bushyhead looked ready to kiss her, and a little light-headed with relief. "I don't mind telling you, with the full moon coming up, I've been kind of nervous about sleeping."

A cleansing was one of the easiest ceremonies to perform. There was just one precaution she was going to have to take. She took a quick glance into the hallway, made certain that the nurse was still deep in her paperwork, and closed the door. Then she climbed up on a chair, and stuffed facial tissue into all the openings of the smoke detector.

* * *

Ten minutes later, the ventilator in the bathroom was clearing out the last of the tobacco-redbud-and-cedar smoke, and the nurse was none the wiser. Larry Bushyhead looked *much* happier, and Jennifer was back in her chair, her implements neatly stowed back in her purse. Just as if she hadn't been chanting and wafting smoke around with a redtail feather a few minutes ago.

"If it makes any difference, I didn't feel as if They had tagged you," she told him. "But if I were in your shoes, I'd have wanted someone to do the same. I—I don't suppose you got any kind of a look at what was dug up, did you? Enough to really, honestly, recognize whose ancestors you were messing with?"

He hesitated, frowning. "I'm not an expert," he said, after a long moment. "And you know how much swapping around there was between the nations, even a long time before the white guys took over."

"A guess," she urged.

"Well—it wasn't Cherokee, or Seminole, and it wasn't Cado. If I was guessing—I'd guess it was our people. Osage. That's what I thought at the time." He licked his lips, as if they'd gone dry. "But that's just a guess. Could'a' been Sac and Fox. Could'a'been Creek, or Potawatami."

"Do you have any idea what happened to those relics?" she asked. "Because no one has mentioned them—and you'd think with cops crawling all over the site, somebody would have."

"I got two guesses," he told her. "The stuff we first dug up was either blown to bits or buried again. And the stuff that didn't get blown to bits, Calligan probably snuck in and got rid of. If he hasn't yet, I'm betting he will. All he needs to do is bring in a bunch of white guys who don't give a shit, as soon as the cops clear out."

She nodded, thoughtfully, and looked at her watch. "Oh

hell, visiting hours for us nonfamily types are up—'' And right on cue, the nurse showed up at the door, to remind her of that fact.

She stood up, swinging her purse over her shoulder, and gave him her best smile. "Thanks, Larry—you were a really big help."

He grinned. "So were you, Jennifer."

She made her way out of the hospital and down to the parking lot, only half aware of her surroundings. A burial ground—well, that certainly explained the "trouble" Sleighbow had mentioned, and why she had the feeling that there had been *something* there. The problem was, there wasn't supposed to be one there.

That may not mean anything. We haven't charted all the old burial sites yet, not by a long shot. The Arkansas wandered around a lot before the flood-control and irrigation programs settled it in one bed with all the dredging and dams. But—right on the riverbank is an awfully odd place to put a burial site. Especially an old one. And there should have been cairns, not underground burials; the Old Ones hated underground burials. Shoot, they wouldn't even build the cairns until months after the wind and weather had their way with the dearly departed.

The ancestors had tried not to put burial grounds anywhere near the Arkansas or any other river for just that reason—there was no telling when it would change its course and wash out the site.

Still, if it's really old, like when the Osage got forced down here from the north, and they didn't know the Arkansas tended to wander—and if it got buried by some accident or other—

Without actually seeing any of the artifacts, she had no way of telling how old it was, and if that was a possibility.

With a start, she realized that she had reached her truck; she opened the door and got in, reflexively locking her door again. But she didn't move; she was still thinking things through.

Really old grounds that had been "lost" were being rediscovered all the time in the course of development. Some were even uncovered by digging deeper under a building that had just been demolished—that was how they'd found that bat statue in Mexico not long ago. Since there hadn't been anything built on that site before, maybe it wasn't surprising that no one knew anything about it—

But that felt wrong, somehow. It matched the few facts as she knew them, but not the feel of the place.

It felt as if there had been some very powerful, very old relics there—but the feeling was—transitory, I guess. As if they hadn't been there long.

But *that* wasn't consistent with the idea of it being a burial ground.

One thing it did explain, though, was the definite scent of Bad Medicine about Rod Calligan. If he'd violated sacred ground and then destroyed bones and relics, he had definitely incurred the anger of the Little People.

But an Osage burial site—there—it just didn't add up.

Maybe if someone ripped the stuff off from another site and cached it there?

But who, and why would they have chosen that place to leave the loot? And why didn't they come back for it?

Could there be more caches around the site? Again, if she found anything, she would know right away if it was a cache or a grave—and that would at least put one question to rest.

Maybe I'd better go run a quick check on the construction area again. And maybe I'd better go check some of the old burial grounds too, the ones out in the boonies.

One thing was for sure; that feeling she got with just her brief glance at Rod Calligan meant that the Little People were after his hide—and given how vindictive they could be, the hides of everyone else connected with him.

She shivered at the thought. That was not a position that she would want even her worst enemy to be in.

CHAPTER SEVEN

IT WAS A good thing that the traffic was light, because she had most of her attention on the possibilities of the *mi-ah-luschka* being involved in all of this. The prospect was not one she would have guessed when she took this job.

Mi-ah-luschka. The Little People—different from the other kind of "Little People," the Little Mysteries that stole breath and made people sick—were not something she wanted to get involved with, particularly not if they were very old and very powerful Little People. And if this burial ground was old enough that her people had even forgotten it existed—

Jeez, I can't even talk about this to anyone but Grandfather without them thinking I've been drinking too much Irish whiskey. Little People. I don't even know what other nations call them; I'd sound like a refugee from a St. Patrick's Day parade.

"Little People" was a poor translation of *mi-ah-luschka,* when all was said and done. They were spirits; some of them were the spirits of those who had not been recognized by *Wah-K'on-Tah*, who had died without paint, or been buried in such a way that Wah-K'on-Tah could not see them—or worst of all, had perished in a way that kept their spirits earthbound. *Executed, murdered, died in cowardice, buried without the proper rites, without paint . . . not happy spirits.*

She had seen them. Once. On Claremore Mound. Grandfather had sent her there specifically to see them; it was part of the trials of becoming a shaman, to recognize spirits on sight, to face down spirits and learn to deal with them. That time, they had been mannerly; but then she was a woman, and it was mostly men who had trouble with the *mi-ah-luschka* of Claremore Mound, who had perished quite horribly at the hands of a band of renegade scum. Even though they had met her gravely, and had not even played any relatively harmless tricks on her, she had sensed the power and the possible menace in them; and had been glad to accept the token that would tell Grandfather she had passed this trial so that she could get back to safer territory.

According to Grandfather, there were other kinds of *mi-ah-luschka* too, that had never been human, but she had never seen any of *that* kind. Sometimes *mi-ah-luschka* were only lonely—sometimes they were just interested in making trouble, of a harmless kind.

But only sometimes.

Real Jekyll-and-Hyde types. She knew far too many stories about the Little People for her own comfort; especially the ones that ended up with someone dead or driven mad.

But were there ever any stories with—oh—modern "weapons"? Like blowing up bulldozers? First time I've ever heard of them planting dynamite on something. . . .

Well, what if they were active around the site, but not responsible directly for the explosion? Or what if they were working through someone, using a person or persons who already had a grudge against Calligan? Pushing that person over the edge enough to make him commit murder?

It could happen. . . .

The one thing she had on her side was that it was very difficult for them to work in the daytime, and the time they worked best was during the full moon. That would give her some margin of safety to go check the site out a little more closely.

She pulled up at a traffic light, and began tapping her fingers on the steering wheel in a drum pattern. The Little People would be handicapped if they were operating against someone who not only was not Osage, but wasn't even a Native American. Still, if this particular lot *was* very old, and very powerful, they might be able to work right through that nonbeliever resistance. And every time they succeeded in pulling something off, it would make the next strike easier.

And potentially a lot more deadly.

If this line of reasoning was true, well—it meant that the explosion was not the end, but was only the beginning. There would be more incidents, unless she could pacify them. More things for which mortal humans might be blamed.

Now she was very glad she'd smudged Larry Bushyhead down. If the *mi-ah-luschka* were on the trail of his boss, they might be inclined to take out Believer targets first. If they had picked up the magical "scent" of Calligan when the first dozer unearthed the relics, they would not let go of the trail. His workers, his wife, his family, they would all be fair game. They would have *his* scent as well, and as arbitrary as they were sometimes, the Little People might just start sniping at random.

Honking behind her jarred her out of her reverie; the light had changed, and she was still sitting there like a dope. Flushing furiously, she tapped the accelerator and moved into the intersection.

Shoot, the Little People could be causing all kinds of "accidents" that I don't even know about! Things like—making a

*driver see a green light when it's actually red. Or, Wah-K'on-
Tah give me patience, sending David here to get those poor
guys into more trouble by thinking he's getting them out of it!*

That would be like the *mi-ah-luschka* too, she thought
sourly. Get everyone entangled in a big mess. What would
be worse; going to jail for something you didn't do—or
getting flattened at an intersection? And which would those
construction workers pick?

*Me, I'd prefer to get flattened. The idea of a prison cell
gives me the creeps.*

She turned down her own street, several blocks earlier
than she usually did. The stop signs were all facing her
direction along here, and if she was going to go all fog-
brained, better to go along here than on the busier street.

Small brick-and-frame houses lined both sides of the
street, set back under trees that dated back to the thirties.
The street looked very safe and suburban without the sterility of the modern subdivisions. Little porch lights gleamed
warmly down on curved sidewalks and small porches with
a chair or porch swing waiting. No kids out tonight; just as
well, given her inattentiveness right now.

*If I want to see if there's Little People out there on that
site—damn it all, I'm going to have to go out there at night.
I don't want to see, but I have to find out. I might as well go
tonight or tomorrow, before the full moon. If they catch me
while they are not at full power, I can probably convince them
I'm on their side.*

But she had no intentions of prowling around a place
where the Little People had any chance of appearing without some special preparations. *Momma didn't raise any stupid children, oh no.* Besides, what was the use of being the
student of a Medicine Man if you couldn't ask his advice?

The driveway loomed up much faster than she had expected it to, and she overshot. She backed up slowly, making *certain* there weren't any kids playing in the street before
doing so, and pulled the truck in as neatly as she could.

The unmistakable scent of pizza greeted her nose as soon as she opened the door.

"Don't try to hide it; I already smelled it!" she shouted, closing the door behind her and walking into the living room. As she had expected, Grandfather sat in front of the television watching CNN, a Domino's box in front of him, and a half-eaten slice of pepperoni still in his hand. He looked up at her with his beady black eyes, and grinned without a trace of guilt.

"You know very well that my cholesterol count was fine, the last time we had it checked," he said. "And besides, I was hungry, and you weren't here to fix me anything."

"As if you aren't a better cook than I am," she retorted, then threw up her hands in defeat. "All right. I give up. I just hope you saved me some of that."

He smiled again, affectionately. "I knew you'd be hungry too; the past two days you haven't had a single proper meal. You work too much and eat too little." He picked up the first box to reveal a second, and opened it up, tilting it to show her another intact pizza. "Mushrooms and black olives, your favorite. All for you. And I made apple cobbler, for later. You're never going to find a husband if you look like a stick."

She helped herself to napkins and a fat slice; he was right, she was starving, and right now she would have eaten the cardboard if there'd been cheese on it. "What are you, Jewish now?" she jibed, and mimicked a thick New York accent. "Eat, eat, eat, you're too thin, how you gonna get a husband, you so thin—"

"So? Maybe they've got the right idea about some things." He chuckled, and put another couple of slices on a paper plate for her. "There's French Vanilla ice cream to go with that cobbler."

Jennifer suppressed a groan; she was never going to be able to resist that combination. She had been even hungrier than she had thought; she inhaled the first slice and looked longingly at the rest before licking her fingers clean and opening the mail.

It was a Good Mail Day; two checks. One from a divorce case, and one from a client whose steakhouse was being pilfered. That would take care of a couple of bills, while she worked this thing. . . .

This thing.

She picked up her second piece of pizza and cleared her throat, and Grandfather looked up quickly.

"The insurance case," she began.

"You smudged someone," he replied, before she could find the right words. "I smelled it on your clothes when you came in. So it isn't just an insurance thing anymore, right? Now it's a Medicine Thing, too."

She sighed with relief. He had gone completely serious on her, every inch the shaman. "Right. Exactly. Let me give it to you as I got it, so you can see the path I was following—"

He kept quiet as she related the entire story from the beginning, only pursing his lips from time to time without interrupting her.

"So." He sat quietly, thinking for a moment. "I have to admit that I have *never* heard of that particular place being a burial site before. Of course, I don't know everything, and there have been plenty of things lost to us besides the locations of burial grounds. Still. I think you're right; I think that this business with the relics is very bad, and I would not be in the least surprised to find that the *mi-ah-luschka* have been aroused."

"Oh, *hell*. I was afraid you'd say that." She finished her meal and wiped her fingers clean, before settling back in the chair. "I wish I knew what else to make of this. Half the facts I have make Calligan look like a bad guy, and the other half make him look like some bozo who was just doing something stupid and incredibly selfish. Stupidity on one person's part shouldn't be punished by blowing up other people; selfishness is generally its own punishment, sooner or later. On the whole, if Calligan did plow up a burial ground and order the relics destroyed, I think a hefty fine from some kind of government agency and a bad mark on his record would do everyone a lot more good than setting the Little People on him. And where the devil did that *bomb* come from? The Little People never went around planting bombs before that I ever heard of!"

Grandfather shook his head. "I don't know what to make of that, either. If you are thinking that you need to get deeply involved in this because of the blood spilled, though—well, you are right. It is your duty, and not only to your own people. Murder must be balanced." He tilted his head to one side, and continued, very gently this time, "I am afraid that you made some very serious mistakes in the way you handled young David, though, little bird. You may have made an enemy out of him; you certainly shamed him before the other young men. He was never very good at dealing with blows to his pride before, and I doubt that he has improved with the passage of time. The young men he has taken as his mentors have the towering pride of most young hotheads, and it bruises easily."

"I didn't make him my enemy," she said, rather sourly. "He did that all by himself. He'd already made up his mind before I ever got there, and he never was one to let facts get in the way of a good opinion."

"True." Mooncrow nodded. "I suspect that you are going to have to go to this construction site yourself, either tonight or tomorrow night, to see if the *mi-ah-luschka* really are out there. I would suggest tomorrow night, very, very strongly. You will need a ceremony to prepare and protect you, and it will take more time than we really have tonight. I think that tonight you should simply cleanse yourself. You have had many stresses today, and you are not thinking clearly."

He had been very serious right up until that moment, but suddenly the impish twinkle in his eye warned her that he was about to zing her.

"You know, I *could* show you the Osage Blanket Ritual."
He leered. "It would help you, the way you are right now."

"Thank you, O Wise One, O Wisest of the Little Old
Men," she said with heavy irony. "Just like a man. Suggesting
that the cure for all my problems is a good medicinal
fuck."

In a way she had hoped to shock him a little with the
vulgarity; she was doomed to disappointment. He chuckled,
and continued to chuckle as she made her way back to her
room.

Just as she reached it, the phone rang. She reached for it
automatically, before Mooncrow's warning "It's David"
could stop her in time to let the machine get it.

"Talldeer," she said, in as neutral a voice as she could.
She didn't bother to wonder how Grandfather had known
who it was; that was why he was the shaman and she was
the apprentice.

"Home already?" David said, in a voice dripping with
sarcasm. "Or couldn't you find anyone who'd fink for you?"

"Grow the hell up, David," she replied wearily, and hung
up before he could launch into a tirade or a threat.

She sat down heavily on the side of her bed, and took the
phone off the hook for a moment while she thought. He was
not going to leave her alone. Maybe he *had* to keep coming
at her until she conceded defeat; maybe it was more than
just pride. Maybe he'd do anything just to renew the contact;
maybe the hormones were getting to him as badly as
they were her—

"And maybe monkeys will fly out of my butt," she muttered.

Still, she knew that he was not going to give up tonight;
she'd rattled his cage, and he was going to have to try to
reassert his masculine superiority. He was either going to
keep calling until he'd delivered his threats, or he was going
to come over in person to deliver them. Probably on the

front lawn at the top of his lungs if she wouldn't let him in the house.

All right, you jerk, I'll force your hand. If you're going to play games, you're going to do it on my turf.

She replaced the phone in its cradle, then dialed one of her clients quickly. This was a child-support case, and while she didn't strictly *have* to call Angela with the information she'd gotten two days ago, since she'd already turned it over to the state's attorney and to Angela's own legal-eagle, it would make Angela feel better to hear it from the source.

Besides, Angela was a regular one-woman talk show. She was good for tying up the line for at least forty-five minutes:

"Hello, Angela?" she said as her client came on, after being pulled away from "The Golden Girls" by her daughter. "Listen, this is just a follow-up, but I thought I should let you know what I dug up on Harry so you can go bug your attorney and the state about this, okay? . . . Yeah, I sent the copies to them yesterday, so tomorrow or the next day at the latest they should have all the files—"

Just as she had figured, Angela was only too pleased to have someone to talk to; there were at least six "call waiting" beeps as someone—*David*—tried to ring through. She ignored them gleefully.

Finally, when there hadn't been any more beeps for at least ten minutes, she exited the conversation gracefully, reminding Angela that they both had to work in the morning, and hung up.

She glanced over at the clock on the nightstand; it was 10:18. She watched the minute-hand move. At 10:22, the doorbell rang.

She got up, but only went as far as the living room. Grandfather gave her an inquiring look, and went to answer the door at her nod. They both knew who it was; David was being *David* so hard that the walls might just as well have not been there. So—first get him off-balance, by having Grandfather meet him. The bunch of activists he was working with at least had *respect for the elders* drummed into them three times a day by their leaders. Seeing Grandfather here would probably set him back a peg or two. He wouldn't want to be rude around Mooncrow, and he wouldn't know why Mooncrow was living with her, when he was obviously able-bodied enough to be on his own.

She hadn't told David anything about her medicine-training; she'd been very reluctant to talk about it for a long time—and then, when he might have been interested or at least impressed, it had been too late to tell him.

Mooncrow led David into the living room, playing the herald, with every iota of his dignity and power wrapped around him like an invisible blanket. From the odd look on David's face, she knew that their first trick had worked. He *had* been startled to find Grandfather here. He had been even more impressed by Mooncrow's aura of authority; his posture and the way he moved told Jennifer that Grandfather had asserted himself without saying a single word.

"David Spotted Horse is here to see you, Jennifer," Mooncrow said formally, then moved around behind her, leaving David standing on his own at the entrance to the hallway. As Mooncrow faced away from David, he gave her a slight wink; she took her cue from that, and used her own Power to augment her presence, just as he was doing. Then Grandfather was behind her, deferring to her, which should have told David that he was walking on dangerous ground.

But he seemed oblivious to the nuances; or else he had made up his mind and was resisting anything that might change it. He took another pose, scowling, trying to intimidate her.

On my own ground? I don't think so.

"I think you said everything you needed to, earlier this evening, David," she said calmly, before he could start in on whatever speech he'd memorized. "Unless, of course, you are here to apologize for misjudging me."

That triggered an explosion of temper. The scowl turned

into a glare, and the warrior lost his cool. "Apologize? For *what*? Look, woman—I came here to give you one warning—"

She pulled her head up, and stopped him with a look. Behind her, she sensed her Grandfather doing the same— but this was *her* show, most of the Power was coming from her. What Mooncrow was doing was only enough to show solidarity.

And later, when David thought all this over, that might shake him up some, too.

Enough to make him really *think? Not likely. But I'll have given him his chance.*

"First of all," she said into the heavy silence, "I am not the enemy. I do not know what is going on over there. *That's what I was hired to find out.* I am neither judge, nor jury; I am impartial investigator. If the men working for Calligan are innocent, they have nothing to lose, and everything to gain, by talking to me. I am trained in investigation—you aren't and neither are they. I may see or hear something with their help that will allow us to find whoever *did* cause that explosion. What's more, you seem to be operating under some assumption that I'm working for the police or some other investigative organization. I'm not. The insurance company that hired me *doesn't care* if those men are innocent or guilty; all they want to know is if Rod Calligan concealed evidence that his company had been threatened before any of this happened."

That obviously took David aback. "They don't care? They—I get it, if Calligan was concealing threats, it would invalidate his claim, right?"

Jennifer had to give him credit; David could pick up on things quickly if he chose to. "Exactly. But there are plenty of people in Tulsa who would like to get an easy conviction. And if those workers are innocent, *I* might be able to convince some of the cops who are on the case that Calligan's men had nothing to do with it."

David's face hardened at that. "If?"

She let her own face assume the mask of the warrior. "Just what I said. If. Because·if they're not innocent, they'd better truck their asses out of town as fast as they can, because sooner or later either I'll find out what happened or the cops will—and if it's me, I'll turn them in. I won't lie to you, David; I'll turn in anyone else who uses terrorist tactics and death to make a point."

His eyes narrowed, and his teeth clenched as his temper rose again. "That makes you a traitor, in my book—"

She cut him off, this time using the Power to choke the words in his throat. His mouth worked, without anything coming out. He was, however, so angry that he hardly seemed to notice.

Her own temper had reached the snapping point. "Just who the hell am I being a traitor *to*, David Spotted Horse?" she snarled. She couldn't help but think, perhaps with some conceit, that her temper was the trained warhorse—and his the wild mustang. "Why don't you go take a quick trip over to the morgue before you start on me? So far there are four people *dead*. Go look at what's left of the damn bodies, if you have so much courage! *I* did! A fair share of those dead bodies are *our* people, and red or white, their blood demands retribution!"

He continued to fight her control of him. She released her hold on his words before he really did choke. He spluttered for a few minutes before coming out with something coherent.

"Your problem is that you've forgotten that you're Indian—"

She choked him down again, reined in her temper to a walk, and gave him a Mooncrow Look from half-lidded eyes. "Oh, no. I haven't forgotten. But *your* problem, David Spotted Horse, is that you have forgotten the words of the greatest spiritual leaders of all our nations. You have forgotten that we are all *human*. You are Cherokee first, then

Indian, *then* human." She finally let her temper show, just a little. It was enough to make him back up an involuntary step. "When you get your goddamn priorities straight, and figure out that it should be the other way around, you can talk to me. Until then"—she gathered her power, and sensed Mooncrow following her lead—*"get out of my house."*

She pointed, and Grandfather mirrored her, both of them using their power to send David away. David tried to fight them; his muscles tensed, and his face writhed as he tried to stand where he was and continue the argument. But it was no use, not against the combined force of Jennifer's anger and Mooncrow's sheer ability. He found himself walking out of the door, down the steps, and to his car at the edge of their property.

As a final touch, Grandfather made the door slam shut behind him.

She stayed where she was, listening for the sounds of his car starting up and pulling away. When they finally came, she let her temper and her power go, taking deep breaths to help her release her anger, letting it all run away into the ground.

Then she yelped in outrage, as Mooncrow pinched her rear. She pivoted, to see him several steps away, too far away to have touched her—

—*physically, the old goat*—

—with his arms folded, grinning like a coyote. "About that Blanket Ritual," he prompted, puckishly.

"When I can take *you* on a genuine Osage Snipe Hunt," she snorted; then he laughed, and she headed back to her room to finish cooling off.

For the next hour or so she sat quietly in the middle of her room, relaxing every muscle and nerve, trying to get rid of that incredible buildup of tension. There was more there than she had guessed. Was David making her *that* angry? Or was it something deeper than that?

And along with the anger, she was having to deal with a very sexual electricity, a force that had sprung up between them even while she was facing him down as if he were an enemy. Which might just be the reason why Grandfather had made that jab.

Odd. When I was really small, Grandfather was very open about everything. Never avoided any subject. Then when I hit puberty and I was feeling touchy and shaky about anything sexual, he kept things very low-key, and very clinical, and never brought it up unless I did. He never said anything about David or Saul or even Ridge, and I thought for sure he'd have a few choice comments about Ridge! But now, especially lately, it's like living with a New York street crew! He's flinging innuendoes at me all the time! Why? Is it because I can handle it now? Or is he trying to tell me something?

Like maybe I could use a good, therapeutic—

She shook her head, and bit her lip. *No, it can't be that simple.*

Mooncrow had not said or done anything "simple" for the past four or five years. Whatever he was trying to tell her, it must be something else entirely.

She shook her head, loosening her neck muscles. *Maybe he's trying to tell me I should become a nun,* she thought wryly. *Shoot, I might as well, for all the action I've had lately. The safest sex there is—none.*

Now she was feeling sorry for herself. Any more, and she'd start playing Morrissey records.

Sauna, then shower. Just sauna, simple steaming out of nerves and anger, no sweatlodge stuff. Then I'll see if I can't get some direction in dreams.

The sauna made her relax in spite of her tension, and the shower, turned to "massage" setting, pounded out every muscle in her neck, shoulders, and back. She concentrated on making everything that was bothering her wash out with the water and run down the drain, in one of the oldest cleansing rituals there was. Her people had always been ones for cleansing by water, both spiritually and physically; that was one reason why they always tried to camp beside running water. Even in the dead of winter, Osages would bathe.

Breaking the ice to take a bath. Glad I'm not living back then. I'd never survive a winter.

The missionaries had been appalled. They had been certain that so much bathing was immoral.

She came out of the steamy bathroom to find that Mooncrow had anticipated her needs, and had left a hot cup of—well, "tea" wasn't exactly the right word for what was on her bureau. It was black, so dark it looked like strong coffee; redolent with two or three dozen different herbs and plants, it was without a doubt exactly what she would need for a minor vision-quest among her dreams.

She lifted the cup in an ironic salute to the electronic beeping in the living room, and downed it in as few swallows as she could manage.

As expected, it was absolutely vile. With no honey in it to cover the taste. Grandfather had never believed in disguising bitterness, either in Medicine or in truth.

Which is why we are so much alike. And probably why we get on each others' nerves.

Lights out, she did not exactly fall asleep, but the kind of trance she achieved was much deeper than the kind she had in the sweatlodge. This time, instead of looking for an answer within herself, she took form as an owl rather than a kestrel. She needed the senses of a night-flyer; she was going to be looking at a world only a little removed from the "real." In this shape, she soared into a sky that was an analog of the real sky over Oklahoma. The buildings of Tulsa loomed beneath her, and she kited on the thermals rising from hot asphalt.

Where should I look next? That was the question she needed answered. She framed her problems carefully in her mind. First, where should she go for clues? Not the site—she already knew she would have to make a careful examination there. But where *else* should she look? Somewhere out there was evidence—and it might not be in obvious places.

Brothers, sisters, show me the places that are not obvious. I have a shattered jar, and only a few of the pieces. Show me the places where some of the pieces might be.

Although in the real world it was still night, dawn-red crept into the eastern sky. Without thinking, she shifted from owl to kestrel, for now she was completely in the Spirit World, and now she did not need the special night-vision of an owl. She widened the circle of her hunt. Below her the landscape blurred and shifted. Her prayer had been heard.

Movement below her caught her eye, a pair of redtail hawks crying out over a despoiled nest.

In this world, there were always deeper meanings to things that seemed obvious. There was a deeper meaning to this than a hawk pair who had lost their nest to some interfering human.

And the redtail was, above all other birds, the sacred bird to the Osage. It was the redtail whose skin went into the sacred *Wah-hopeh* shrine, the redtail whose tail feathers were as red as the sun at dawn and sunset, and the redtail who told the Osage when it was to be war, or peace.

So—she folded her wings, and dropped lower.

The hawks faded; the nest became a shrine. One of the sacred *Wah-Hopeh* shrines of woven grass that housed the hawk that guided her people. The shrine had been broken into and the pieces scattered.

She kited closer. The broken shrine became landscape; roads and hills that she recognized; a house and several barns. A place up near Rose; a burial ground that was on private property.

A place she recognized, with a feeling of *personal* violation. *Her* ancestors were buried here; most of the Osage in the area knew about this place, though no one was likely to talk about it to an outsider.

She wasn't certain whether to curse or be perversely pleased. This probably meant that the relics that had been bulldozed up had *not* been buried there originally. Which meant that this might be a case of two crimes and two criminals; one grave-robber, and one terrorist.

Or—

Another thought; what if the grave-robber had cached his stolen relics and had blown up the dozer to *prevent* them from being uncovered? The idea had enough merit that even if it wasn't true, she might be able to get the cops to take an interest in it and take some of the heat off the construction workers and the local activists, at least for a while.

She beat her wings rapidly to take her up into the sky again, and resumed her quest. She might get more answers. She might not. But in either case, now she had another place to start looking. And she had until morning to keep asking.

Brothers, sisters, where should I look next?

Chapter Eight

Toni Calligan kept glancing apprehensively at the closed door of Rod's office every time she went past it, going between the kitchen, the utility room, and the kids' rooms. And not only glancing at it, but hurrying past it as quickly as she could without actually running. It gave her the creepiest feeling, as if there was something lurking behind the door, listening to her, waiting for her to turn her back on it.

It's the boxes, she thought, burdened with an armload of clothing from the hamper in Jill's room, wishing that Rod had never brought the things in the house. *It's whatever's in those boxes. I keep having bad dreams about them. I feel like I'm in a grade B horror movie, and Rod is the evil scientist who's brought his work home with him. Ever since he dragged those boxes home. I keep getting the feeling that there is something in his office that is watching me, laughing at me, waiting for me to walk in there so it can get me.*

This was not rational, and she knew it. There was probably nothing in those boxes but old papers. If she told Rod

how she felt, he'd laugh at her in that way that made her feel about ten years old.

She began sorting laundry with one ear listening for Rod. *Or if he's had a bad day, he'll have a fit and chew me out until I feel as if I was six years old and mentally retarded to boot.* It would depend on how he felt.

Well, everything depended on how Rod felt. Rod was the center of this little household universe, and everything revolved around him. That was why Toni didn't have a job, although she had been a good executive secretary, and had enjoyed the work. Rod had been so masterful; *he* had taken her out for dates, never accepting "no" for an answer, he had proposed and made all the wedding plans, he had insisted she quit her job immediately. And for a while she had enjoyed feeling dependent, leaving all the decisions to him. Now, she simply endured it, because that was the way it was, and Rod was a good provider. He always bought the best for her and the kids. He never raised a hand to any of them. Independence was a small price to pay for that kind of security. And if he was kind of finicky about things—if he was kind of demanding—well, he had earned it, hadn't he? Look at all the good things he provided for them. . . .

So what if every moment of her waking hours was spent literally serving him? If she had to be available for whatever Rod might need, whether it be secretarial services, dinner, or whatever else he might require? Her "job," Rod had explained very carefully, many times, until Toni could recite the entire lecture by heart, was *him.* Even the kids were secondary, since they were only extensions of him.

"This is a cutthroat business. I have to be like a surgeon; I have to know that an instrument is there waiting for me when I put out my hand for it. You have to be the nurse that hands me the instruments. Things have to be perfect at home, so I can keep my mind on my work, or the work won't get done. It's your job, your full-time job, to keep them perfect."

How could she argue with that? He worked hard, and it

was a cutthroat business. All kinds of things could be problems for him, things she hadn't even dreamed of. *"You married the business when you married me."* She must be sure that neither she nor the kids were anything other than a credit to him. That they didn't ever embarrass him. That people would look at him and envy him, because in the construction business an impression was everything, and the impression she and the kids made could gain or lose him a job. He had to know that if he brought a client home unexpectedly, the house would be spotless, the yard picked up and trimmed, the dinner ready and waiting, the kids well behaved and quiet. *Always.* There was no room for weakness, no vacations, no time-outs. If the kids were sick, they must be out of the way where they wouldn't interfere with business. If she was sick, she must not show it.

Not that he had ever brought home a client unexpectedly. There was usually so much fuss over a client's appearance that anyone would think he (never she) were visiting royalty.

And his office must be twice as perfect as the house itself. Everything must be squeaky clean, dusted and polished, every paper filed, every note attached to every file. He must be able to put his hands on anything he needed at any time.

So why had he brought home those four filthy cardboard boxes—and why was he keeping them in his office? No client was going to be impressed with *them* in there, smelling all musty, stained with oil and dirt, and looking as if he had pulled them out of some farmer's chicken coop.

Not that she wanted to get near them, even to clean. Ever since he'd brought the things home, she'd cleaned around them; she'd even been afraid to let the vacuum touch them. She hated to open the office door, but left it open during the day because she hated the feeling that something was hiding behind the door even more.

And now the kids had started getting bad dreams, too. Not so much Rod Junior, but the youngest two, Ryan and

Jill, in particular, had been waking up in the middle of the night for the past three nights running. They couldn't even describe their dreams, but if they had been anything like hers, there wasn't much to describe—just dark shapes looming up out of the dark to grab, and a feeling of absolute terror and despair. But they did keep mentioning "the boxes," and she knew *she* hadn't said anything about the boxes in the office, so there had to be some other explanation for why the three of them felt so uneasy around the things.

Maybe it's just that they're so much like me, she thought, trying to keep her mind on sorting the laundry properly. One time she'd gotten a single red sock mixed up with the whites, and had spent the rest of the day with a bowl of color remover, bleaching out each article carefully, so that nothing was damaged. *Maybe they're just picking it all up from me.* It was true enough that there was no doubt whose kids the two youngest were; they looked so much like Toni that it was uncanny. *Maybe they're just good at reading my body language, and I'm jumpy, so they're getting jumpy.*

Certainly Rod Junior, who looked as much like his dad as Ryan and Jill looked like Toni, hadn't had any nightmares lately. Maybe it *was* all her imagination. Maybe she *was* letting her nerves run away with her.

It was easier to believe that than to believe there was some kind of malevolent force penned up in those boxes in Rod's office.

I can't say anything; it all sounds so stupid. And the one thing that Rod absolutely would not forgive was any hint of what he called "nerves." He wouldn't even say the words "nervous breakdown." He didn't believe in any such thing—like the old British generals who had men shot in World War I for showing fear. If she ever gave him a reason to think that she was suffering from "nerves"—

Well, she didn't know what he'd do. Certainly there would be no visits to psychiatrists, or helpful prescriptions of drugs. He hated and despised psychiatrists, and loathed the very idea of medicating what should be taken care of by will-power alone. At least, that was what he told her.

She had one ear cocked for her morning signals, and heard the bathroom door open and shut again. She dropped the T-shirt she'd picked up and hurried back into the kitchen—

—past the door—

Then, with a sigh of relief, she reached the safe haven of the kitchen itself. Quickly, she broke eggs into a pan, started the toaster, heated precooked bacon in the microwave. As Rod settled into his chair, paper in one hand, she put a cup of coffee into his free hand and slid the plate of bacon, eggs, and toast onto the table in front of him. He'd eaten exactly the same breakfast every morning for the past twelve years. Two fried eggs, four strips of bacon, two pieces of buttered toast, one cup of black coffee. He had not noticed when she had substituted the precooked bacon for his freshly cooked bacon, so that saved her one step, at least.

He read the paper steadily, eating and drinking with one hand, oblivious to her. Or—seemingly oblivious. If she had done something wrong, had made scrambled eggs instead of fried, or burned the toast, he would have delivered a lecture on her job, her duty, that was as bad as a beating, while she stood there flushing with shame.

Rod didn't cut himself or anyone else any slack, as he always pointed out at the end of the lecture.

The three kids slid quietly into their chairs while Rod ate and read. Ryan got his Wheaties, Jill her Frosted Flakes, and Rod Junior his breakfast identical in every way to his father's except for the coffee. All three kids got orange juice and milk, by Rod's orders.

But this morning, Ryan and Jill seemed fidgety. All three ate in silence until Rod finally put down the paper, but the two youngest were obviously waiting for the few seconds when Rod would give them his attention before he went off to work.

Suddenly, it occurred to her what they might want to ask him about. *Oh no—they aren't going to ask him about the boxes in the office, are they? I should have warned them—*

But it was too late now.

"Uh—Dad?" Ryan said hesitantly. "Dad, is there something in your office? Something bad?"

For a moment, Toni would have sworn that Rod was startled. But the next minute, she thought she must have been seeing things. He wore the same bored, impatient look he always wore when he had to deal with Ryan or Jill. "No," he said shortly. "There is nothing in my office, bad or otherwise. What makes you say something that stupid?"

Ryan winced, but continued bravely on. "It's just that— Jill and me—"

"Jill and I," Toni corrected, automatically. Ryan gave her an "Oh, Mom!" look, but corrected himself.

"Jill and I, we've been getting nightmares. About something in your office, something awful—"

She suppressed a wince, knowing what was going to happen. When the kids said or did something out-of-line, it always came back to her. And as expected, Rod rounded on Toni, frowning. "What the hell have you been telling these kids?" he asked, accusingly.

She shook her head, helplessly, and spread her hands placatingly. "Nothing," she protested weakly. "Nothing at all! I don't—"

"Then you've been letting them watch too damn many horror movies on cable," he interrupted irritably. "Stephen King, Dracula, aliens; Christ Almighty, no wonder the kids are having nightmares! Every time I turn on the TV, there's a bucket of blood spilling across the screen. Don't you ever check to see what they're watching? What kind of a mother are you, anyway?"

It was no use to protest that the kids only watched what

he approved, that he himself was the one who selected the programs. He'd simply accuse her of letting them watch things behind his back, and she had no way to prove that she wasn't doing anything of the kind.

"That's *it*," he said, slamming his hand down on the tabletop, making them all jump. "No more cable TV unless I'm here to supervise what you're watching."

Jill opened her mouth to protest, but fortunately Toni managed to silence her with a look. Poor Jill; no more afterschool Nickelodeon.

"What are we allowed—" Ryan began timidly.

Rod hit his head with the heel of his hand. "Do I have to tell you kids everything? You can go outside and play, dammit! You kids spend too much time in front of that thing, anyway. You can play Nintendo if it's bad. You can even watch a movie from your special cabinet." His voice became heavy with irony. "You *might* even actually read a book *for fun*. I know that may sound impossible, but people *do* read for fun. But no matter what, no more cable TV unless I'm here to supervise!"

Toni carefully refrained from pointing out that there were horror books, too. And it was hardly fair to take that tone with Ryan, who, if not a bookworm, was certainly a good reader. She just bowed her head submissively, and murmured something conciliatory.

Rod Junior kept right on with his breakfast, ignoring the whole thing. Rod finally turned to him after a moment and asked, "And what about you, son? Any stupid nightmares?"

Rod looked up, first at her, then at his younger siblings, and shook his head. "Nightmares are for babies," he said contemptuously, polishing off the last of his eggs.

Rod gave her a *there, you see!* kind of triumphant glance, as if that had proved something. Presumably that she should have somehow trained the younger kids out of nightmares by now, weaned them away from bad dreams as if she were toilet-training them.

All it proves is that Rod is his father's child.

And that Rod Junior knew how to say the things that his father wanted to hear. Young Rod was Rod's unconcealed favorite. He succeeded at the things Rod Senior thought were important; he had learned how to parrot every opinion his father had, whether he understood it or not. But most of all, it proved that he hadn't a gram of imagination.

Of course he doesn't have nightmares. He doesn't have enough imagination to produce them. But she could hardly say that to Rod, who spoiled the boy something awful. Or even if she did—imagination wasn't the kind of thing that Rod valued. "Guts," "smarts," "brains," "gumption,"—all those mattered. Not sensitivity or imagination.

She wondered what that little "I don't believe in nightmares" remark was going to earn Rod Junior this time. Every time he came up with some comment that showed how much like his father he was, he generally got a reward by the end of the day. Probably the CD player he'd been wanting. Not that the other two had any real use for a CD player, but Rod Junior's room was stuffed full of the toys and treats his father brought him every time he said something his father considered clever. Or, in other words, proved himself to be a copy of Rod. It happened at least once a week, and it wasn't fair to the other two.

She sighed, though strictly internally. *But life isn't fair. They're just learning that a little early. I think it's time to change the subject before he starts in on Ryan and Jill.*

"Rod, I hate to bother you"—she always began her requests with that phrase—"but the dryer is getting unreliable. I'd really like to call a repairman to come and look at—"

"Is it still running?" he asked, folding his paper neatly. Next he would get up, put on his suit jacket and tuck the paper in the inside pocket, then head for the office.

She made a little grimace of doubt. "Well, yes, it is, but—"

"Is it making any noises?" he continued, standing up, his own face reflecting his impatience.

Again she hesitated. "Well, no, but—last night, I thought I smelled—"

"You didn't smell anything," he said, interrupting impatiently. "You imagined it. I was right here last night, and I didn't smell anything. If I didn't smell anything, then neither did you. Or if you did, it was probably just some lint overheating. Clean the lint-catcher once in a while. I'll look at it later."

"Yes, Rod," she sighed, as he shrugged on his coat and headed out the door. A moment later, he pulled his car out of the garage, down the driveway, and was gone. She began picking up the breakfast dishes and setting them into the dishwasher. School had only been out for about a week, but already the kids had established their summer routines. Jill wandered back down the hall to her room; Rod Junior went out to ride his bike. Ryan stayed with her to help. She smiled at him, and hugged him comfortingly. He still looked disturbed and unhappy, and not just from his father's unkind words.

But her mind was on other things now. *It's a good thing I turned off the dryer last night when I thought I smelled something burning, and remembered to unplug it first thing this morning,* she thought, closing the dishwasher and starting it. *With an electric dryer, you can't always be sure it's off unless you unplug it. I guess I'll just have to dry clothes on the line outside until he gets around to looking at it. I wish he'd let me call a repairman. . . .*

Actually, she wished he'd let her buy a new dryer. One with some of those special settings for delicate things like Rod's silk shirts, and a door rack for the kids' sneakers. There was always enough money for new suits, but never anything for a new dryer. Probably because *he* didn't have anything to do with the dryer—

"Mommy!"

She jumped, as if shocked. The shriek was Jill's and it was full of terror. *"Mommy! Fire!"*

Her heart bounded into her throat; she came out of her trance of shock, dropped the butter-dish she'd been holding, and ran for the utility room. But Ryan streaked past her and into the hall, something large and red in his hands.

The fire extinguisher from the kitchen, under the sink—he'd been closest to it—

The smoke alarm went off, shrilling in her ears, galvanizing her with fear, as Jill broke into a wail of her own.

"Mom-EEEEEEEEEEEE!"

Her mind was stuck on *hold*, but her hands and body acted without any direction from her gibbering mind. As she reached the utility room and grabbed the extinguisher beside the door, Ryan was already emptying his own extinguisher on the blaze eating into the wallboard behind the dryer. Jill wailed in terror, plastered against the back wall of the utility room, clutching her stuffed bunny.

That's right, the bunny was still in the dryer. My God, she could have been electrocuted!

Toni joined her son, playing the chemicals from the extinguisher on the blaze, amazed that her hands and his were so steady. Doubly amazed that he had such enormous presence of mind for a ten-year-old. If he had just been a little taller, he could have reached over the dryer as she was doing and sprayed down behind it; from the looks of things, he'd actually tried, then given up, keeping his spray on the areas he *could* reach. But he had given her the extra few seconds she needed, confining the fire to the area in back of the dryer, keeping it from spreading any further until she could really put it out.

The last of the flames died. The plug, still in the wall socket, spat a spark; she dropped her now empty extinguisher, wrapped a rubber glove around the cord, and yanked, pulling it free of the wall.

Then she fell to her knees, gathered both her precious

babies in her arms, and the three of them laughed and cried
in fear and relief.

Then she called the fire department, told them what had
happened, and had them send a truck over to make certain
that the fire hadn't somehow gotten in between the walls. It
made for quite a bit of excitement in the normally quiet
neighborhood; Rod Junior came streaking in on his bike
after the truck, and was nearly beside himself when he realized it was coming to *his* house. The first thing he wanted to
know was if his room was all right. And predictably, by the
time the truck left, Rod Junior had usurped Ryan's place in
the tale of how the fire had been extinguished, at least where
his peers were concerned.

It was only after the firemen had checked and found the
house safe, only after they had made certain that it was the
dryer plug and not the outlet that had shorted out, and only
after she had called and left a message with Rod's service
about the "accident," that she had time to think. And remember.

She had pulled the plug out of the wall this morning, just
before she started sorting laundry. Rod never went into the
utility room, and the kids couldn't possibly have reached it
to plug it back in.

She had pulled the plug out of the wall. She had made
absolutely certain to do so, in case one of the kids might go
swimming at the neighbor's and throw a wet bathing suit
into the dryer before she got a chance to stop them.

So who had plugged it back in?

Jennifer loved driving in the early morning at this time of
the year. Mornings in June were just warm enough to be
comfortable, and not so hot that you needed the air condi-
tioner. In July—in July you would; the temperature often
didn't drop below eighty, and sometimes stayed in the nine-
ties until two or three in the morning.

But in June—the air was full of flower scent and bird song. Scissor-tailed flycatchers were performing wild aerobatic maneuvers in pursuit of bugs, and mockingbirds informed the rest of the universe that *they* knew every bird's song there was. Cows grazed placidly, knee-deep in ridiculously green grass, with adorable calves frisking alongside.

In June, the entire state looked like a travel brochure, or scenes from *Green Grow the Lilacs*. Not from the musical *Oklahoma!* that came from the play, though; the musical had been filmed by people who knew nothing about Oklahoma, and had perpetuated the myth of Oklahoma, Land of Flat and Treeless.

Where did they think all the wood came from to build all those wooden farmhouses, anyway? Hollywood. I'm surprised they didn't film Lawrence of Arabia *in the middle of the Serengeti Plain.*

It was going to be such a nice day that she had packed a lunch; half a dozen apples and some cheese.

Not only was this part of Oklahoma anything *but* flat and treeless, once Jennifer got outside the city limits of Tulsa, the landscape looked a lot more like Brown County in Indiana than anything in *Oklahoma!,* the movie. Long, rolling hills; high, sandstone ridges topped with blackjack oaks; redtail hawks soaring above the highway, looking for roadkill. . . . She tuned her radio to something she could sing along with, and resolutely enjoyed the drive, because she was probably not going to enjoy the march across country to get to the burial ground.

The farther north of Tulsa she got, the more rugged the country became, and the fewer the inhabited farmhouses. A lot of farmers had given up in the last ten or twenty years; had sold out to bigger ranchers, or just let the land go to the bank. This kind of land was no good for anything but cattle, really; full of stones, hard to clear, hard to plow, and utterly unforgiving in the years without much rain. Selfishly, she was pleased. The cattle could graze under the blackjacks without disturbing the general balance of nature too much; the land was going back to the kind of territory her people had known and roamed. There seemed to be more redtails this spring than ever before; she saw them perched every mile or so, on top of telephone poles, or in the tops of snags, the old, dead blackjacks that simply hadn't fallen down yet.

This was not "farmland" as people in the north or east, or even south, were used to thinking of farming land. Even during the Dust Bowl, this part of Oklahoma had not been affected much, because it had not been cleared much. This was almost all grazing land, wild and hilly, overgrown with poison ivy, sumac, tangles of wild blackberry vines, and wild plum thickets with thorns as long as a thumb. The blackjack oak reigned supreme here; a tree that was as tough and hard to kill as the Osage that used to call this land their home. Blackjacks seldom grew tall enough to attract lightning, except on the sandstone ridges; their thick, rutted bark resisted penetration, and the tannin in their leaves and bark discouraged insects. Their allies were the woodpeckers, red-bellied and downy, who probed their bark for boring insects persistent enough to stomach a bellyful of bitter tannin. In return, they sheltered birds of all kinds all through the winter, with leaves that turned brown but didn't fall until they were pushed off in the spring by new growth, and branches that bent down toward the ground in a prickly snarled tangle that left protected, predator-free spaces around the trunks.

It was hard to penetrate country like this, on foot. Jennifer wished she knew someone out here with a horse—unfortunately, the owner of the property didn't have one. If groves of blackjacks didn't block your way, in the open spaces between the groves, huge thickets of wild plum made it impossible to pass, and where they didn't grow, vines of honeysuckle waited to trip you, and wild blackberry bushes were perfectly prepared to act like tangles of barbed wire. It looked lovely from the car, but Jennifer was not looking forward to forcing her way in to where the burial ground lay. In all probability, if it *had* been raided, the farmer on whose land it lay would not know. Out here, people often didn't bother checking over rough parts of their wooded pasturage on foot, unless there was an animal missing. And even then—well, ranchers and farmers weren't dumb; they quickly adopted every technological aid they could afford and get their hands on, and these days there were plenty of folks who checked over their herds from treetop level, in ultralight aircraft. You could even do some limited herding with an ultralight, she'd been told. The cattle didn't much like their noisy two-stroke engines, and would often move away from a circling farmer.

I'll ask at the house, she thought with resignation, as she approached the tiny village of Rose (population less than one hundred), *but he'll probably just tell me I'd better check for myself.*

Tom Ware was home, and getting ready to clean out his henhouse and spray for mites when she pulled into his driveway. And he said exactly what she thought he'd say.

"Shoot, haven't been anywhere near that section since deer season," he replied, his eyes crinkling up with worry. He pushed his hat back with his thumb, and squinted in the direction of the burial ground, grimacing. "I didn't put any cows out there this year; figured I'd let the ground rest for a year. Shoot, the Ancestors aren't gonna like it if someone's been gettin' in there."

Ware was Osage, although his family had long since adopted Christianity. But even though he didn't follow the Old Ways, he respected them, and respected Jennifer and Mooncrow. Part of the reason he'd bought the ridge when it came up for sale years ago was to protect the old burial ground. While Jennifer shrugged, and made an answering grimace, he seemed to be making up his mind about something. "Look," he said, finally, "it's not easy gettin' back in there. I just broke a ridin' mule last fall for deer huntin'.

You want to saddle her up and use her, I reckon she could use the exercise."

Well, that was going to make her job a hundred times easier!

"Thanks, Tom, I would really appreciate that," she said gratefully. "Just tell me where the tack is, I'm not so green I can't round her up and saddle her myself."

Tom's eyes crinkled up again, but this time with amusement. "I dunno about that, Miz Talldeer," he said, clearly holding in chuckles at the idea of her bringing in his mule. "She hasn't been under saddle much since fall."

She went ahead and laughed. "But I'm my grandfather's granddaughter," she pointed out. "I'll save you some work if I can, and if she won't behave, I promise at least that I won't spook her and send her into the next county."

Still looking amused and dubious, Tom Ware showed her where he kept the saddle, blanket, and bridle, then went on with his planned work. Jennifer took only the bridle with her when she went out into the field where the mule stood, ears up, under a tree, watching her from the middle of a cluster of very pregnant nanny goats.

Jennifer looked fixedly at the mule's tail—it being bad manners to stare any animal directly in the eyes—and relaxed, putting her mind in that peculiar state where she saw not only the mule, but Mule.

Sister, she thought, when Mule flicked her ears in acknowledgement of Kestrel's presence. *Sister, will you help me? I need this younger sister's strong back and thick skin to get to the Sacred Ground.*

Mule considered this for a moment. *Will there be an apple?* she asked, finally, on behalf of Tom's real-world mule; practical, like all mules.

Two apples, Jennifer promised, upping the ante. Mule's jaw worked at the thought.

Yes, Mule replied, after time to think about the effort involved in terms of reward. That was, after all, how mules operated, and why they had such a reputation for stubbornness.

As Mule walked forward out of the herd of goats, she dwindled, and became Tom Ware's old riding mule, responding to Jennifer's whistling and coaxing. She bent her head to take the bridle, and even accepted the bit with good graces. As Jennifer led her to the shed that held the rest of the tack, Tom Ware came out of the chicken coop, and his eyes widened.

"Well, I'll be!" he said, with admiration. "You *are* the Old Man's granddaughter! Never could see a critter that could resist him!"

"I just promised her apples," Jennifer replied, laughing. "Good thing I brought some with me!"

The mule remained well mannered, mindful of the promised apples, and didn't even blow herself up to keep the girth loose—an all-too-common trick mules and horses alike liked to play on inexperienced riders. Within ten minutes, Jennifer was in the saddle, guiding the mule in the general direction of the ridge but letting her pick her own way. Mules were better at avoiding tangles than any human, and had more experience threading their way through dense undergrowth.

Ask anyone who's tried to catch one that didn't want to be caught. It was just a good thing that since time immemorial, Mule never could resist a bribe.

She had more than enough to worry about at the moment, because there was one particular section of this burial land that only she and Grandfather knew about. There was only one, very ancient, cairn there—and even someone who knew about this site would probably not know about this particular grave.

Her vision had not been specific last night; it had only indicated that resting places had been looted, and not *whose.* She was hoping against hope that this one had not been found.

It was a very special cairn, covering a very special person. *Moh-shon-ah-ke-ta.* Watches-Over-The-Land. Her ancestor, from the days when Heavy Eyebrows first came up the river. The shaman who had a vision of things to come that was not believed. Or, if you used Kestrel's interpretation, the shaman who had seen so far forward in time that no one believed what he had seen, simply because their visions had not been of a future so distant and so wide.

Watches-Over-The-Land had seen something of what was to come, and what was currently happening far to the east; the encroachment of the Heavy Eyebrows and Long Knives, driving other Peoples before them. The loss of territory. The plagues of smallpox and typhoid. Further loss of territory. The end of the great buffalo herds on which the Osage way of life depended. And worst of all—that the old medicine ways would no longer protect the Children of the Middle Waters.

At first, he himself had not believed these things. At that time, the Heavy Eyebrows came as admiring postulants, seeking furs and protection from the tall Osage warriors. There were no other Peoples who could stand against them when they met in warbands of two or more gentes, and they roamed a territory that stretched from what became Illinois right down to the Texas border, and from Arkansas to almost Colorado. How could people who regularly defeated the Sac and Fox (whom they called the "Hard-To-Kill-People"), warriors who drove the Cado right down into Texas, ever be defeated? But the visions came, again and again, and more terrible in detail each time.

He determined to do two things. First, that he would learn *all* the medicine ways of the Osage in order to save as much as he could, and second, that his children and theirs would learn to hide among the Heavy Eyebrows as easily as he hid among the trees. So he sent out his son, *Wa-tse-ta,* to the Heavy Eyebrows traders, to learn of them the one trade that all Heavy Eyebrows needed, so that they would not scorn to bring money and work to a "redskin."

So *Wa-tse-ta* became both *Moh-se-num-pa,* Iron Necklace, and Tom Deer, blacksmith. He let his roach grow out, and hid his features under a bluff-paint of soot. And he learned two trades, that of the smith, and that of the shaman. As quickly as Watches-Over-The-Land learned the medicines of a clan and gente, so quickly did Tom Deer, his son, until as many of the medicines as could be learned were learned; both had become Medicine Chiefs, and Watches-Over-The-Land left his land and people for the Other Country.

Tom Deer taught his sons both trades; his son James Deer saw the warning signs that his grandfather had spoken of, and took his family out into the world of the Heavy Eyebrows for a time. When they returned, the whites thought that he was one of them; he settled on the reservation as an outsider, and only the Osage themselves knew that he was not. When the time came to register, he did not, nor did any of his descendants, all of whom were "Sunday Christians" and practiced their Osage ways in secret.

As a result, they lost their share of the oil money that finally came in, belated payment for all of the land that had been stolen, the Brothers and Sisters slaughtered for hides, and poor compensation for an entire way of life lost. That was not in James's time, but Kestrel doubted he would have cared. The money was not enough, not nearly enough; apologies at least would have been in order, and were still not forthcoming from the government that had robbed so many of so much.

Last night, Mooncrow had imparted another bit of tradition to his granddaughter. It seemed that James Deer had also begun another project mandated by Watches-Over-The-Land; he was the one who had begun *changing* the medicine ways he had learned, until once again, they began to work. That was not the traditional path of the Osage; the Osage way was not to change, but to add to a medicine path, like a spider adding to a web, making it ever more complex. But Watches-Over-The-Land had seen that this would not serve, and had charged his family with finding new ways, borrowing from other Peoples, but keeping the Osage ways as the center. James was the first, Mooncrow the latest, to follow that mandate. Instead of spinning a tighter and tighter web, the Talldeer spiders had descended from the web, becoming hunting spiders, and yet remaining, in all important ways, still spiders; still Osage.

If other Medicine People had received the same visions as Watches-Over-The-Land, they had not acted on those visions. At least, not so far as Kestrel knew.

Of course I can't claim to know everything, even if Grandfather would like me to believe that he does! There could be plenty more people like me in other Nations, and like me, they are next thing to invisible. . . .

That was moot; the important part was that Watches-Over-The-Land had been one of the most powerful medicine men of his time; perhaps of *any* time. Certainly right up there with *Wo-vo-ka*, also called Crazy Horse, or any of the other great Medicine Chiefs. He, however, had chosen Rabbit's way; to hide and be silent, in order to preserve things for future generations.

Many of his medicine objects had been laid to rest with him. If his resting place had been looted. . . .

The mule picked her way delicately through a mess of blackberry vines that would have snared Jennifer and kept her tangled up for fifteen or twenty minutes. She glanced at her watch, and was surprised at how little time had passed.

Next time we have to come up here, if Tom's mule isn't available, I'll find a way to borrow horses or mules from someone else. This beats thrashing through the brush all to heck!

As the mule rounded a stand of blackjacks, the ridge Jennifer wanted loomed right up in front of them, mostly tallgrass-covered slope. Persimmons grew at the foot, young blackjack saplings dotted the slope, and the older trees crowned the ridge. The slope itself faced west; that was what made it perfect for a "burial ground," especially an old one. The Osage of the past exposed their dead to the sky and *Wah-K'on-Tah* for at least a season, to give the spirits time to rise. Afterwards, what was left was placed under a cairn of rocks. That was one reason why this ridge was covered with a rubble of small stones. Over time, a lot of soil had settled here, some of it blown in from the rest of the state during the Dust Bowl, burying the remains of the cairns and what they protected. Nature, and not man, had given these graves a covering of earth.

The burial site looked no different from any other brush-covered ridge out here, and if she hadn't known what it was, she would never have been able to pick it out.

Normally. She halted the mule and squinted up at the ridge, shading her eyes with her hand.

The damage was obvious as soon as she was able to pick out what was shadow and what was disturbed ground. *Oh, hell.*

She nudged her mount forward and up the slope to the site of the looting, then pulled the mule up, ground-tied her, and dismounted. It was no better at second viewing. The shallow graves piled high with crude cairns of rocks were lying open. There were a few signs that the looter or looters had been in a hurry still lying about in the form of odd beads, broken pottery, crumbling baskets. Everything portable had been taken, down to the bones.

The bones. Theft of possessions would not have riled the Little People. Theft of *remains*, however . . .

Some five or six graves had been looted; from the grass sprouting in the turned earth, and the amount washed back into the holes, it looked as if it had happened right around April.

Damn, damn, damn.

This was more than Kestrel could handle easily; she

wanted to start a mourning keen right here and now. But a mourning keen would not help, not now. So she put on her Jennifer mask and persona, invoked her experience as a P.I., and began collecting what little evidence there was. She had two cameras with her; a Polaroid and a 35-mm. Clinically, dispassionately, she began to fire off Polaroids, then took a full roll of 35-mm film for later development.

Meanwhile, she went mentally through all the possibilities for some sort of official investigation. *I could call in the cops, but this is the county, and they're overworked. The only way they'll catch whoever did this is if they come back, or start boasting. Even if they caught whoever did this, what could they do? If we were* lucky, *the perps would get the standard slap-on-the-wrist for graveyard desecration. Lucky, because this isn't a registered, official county graveyard, which might mean that the law wouldn't even allow us that much. What is* the law about graveyards on private land? I *don't even know that; it's never come up before.*

She hung both cameras over the saddle horn by their neck straps once she had all the evidence there was to get. Then, biting her lip a little in apprehension, she went farther up the ridge, to the very top. Right where the sun lingered the longest, and the view was the best.

Right where the remains of a cairn were the most obvious to someone who knew what to look for. And where a hastily-dug hole in the ground was equally obvious, once you got past the bushes that screened the place from below.

Oh, shit.

Watches-Over-The-Land's resting place was as empty as the other six graves.

The strictly physical was easy to take care of, so long as she kept her Jennifer persona in place. There was absolutely no point in trying to sort out whose bits belonged to whom, and really, even for the medicine it didn't much matter. The spirits of those left here had long since gone into the West, and what had happened here would not materially affect that.

Unless, of course, the person who had taken the bones had been some kind of magician or medicine person himself. *Then* he could use the relics to draw those spirits back, against their will . . . imprisoning them in this world, making *mi-ah-luschka* out of them.

Which might very well be why the feeling of dark anger lay over this hillside, dimming the sunlight.

She picked the deepest of the holes, gathered everything that was scattered, and carefully laid it all on the bottom, covering it over with loose dirt and rocks. She hadn't brought a shovel, so she used her hands.

When she finished and straightened, she already knew it wasn't enough. The air vibrated with the rage of the Little People, exactly as if she stood in the middle of a swarm of angry bees.

The menace was there, not for *her*, but for whoever had done this. And there was a sense of frustration and bafflement, too, as if the *mi-ah-luschka* had somehow been prevented from tracking this person, or that he was protected in some way from their vengeance. . . .

Which argued even more for it being some kind of medicine practitioner.

Well, there was one thing she *could* do. Provided that none of the Ancestors *had* been drawn back, that is. She could invoke the fire of *Wah-K'on-Tah*, and burn away all connection between those spirits and their remains.

This was not something her own Ancestors would have known how to do; it was another of the innovations of the Deer/Talldeer family. An innovation made necessary by the number of Heavy Eyebrows stealing from gravesites, not only for museums and collectors, but for darker purposes.

Or even purposes they didn't *realize* were dark. How many turn-of-the-century Spiritualists had unwittingly called back spirits to be their "Indian Guides" to the Afterlife, using stolen bones? Probably quite a few, judging by the old papers of the Spiritualist Society. . . .

There was sage on the hillside, and sweetgrass; redbud along the creek bed, the blue mud for paint. Everything she needed was here. Maybe this was all that was needed for the Little People to settle down.

Maybe.

The sunlight seemed thinner on the hillside; she hadn't even worked up a sweat reburying the remains. And although she *did* get hot and sweaty collecting her redbud and sweetgrass, when she returned to the site it was like walking into a shadow.

Not a good sign.

She started her fire and her little smudge of smoke, painted her face with the charred end of a redbud twig, then stood tall and straight in the eyes of Grandfather Sun. She closed her eyes and raised her face, the warmth of the sunlight full against her cheeks, steadied her breathing until she reached a still, calm center and filled herself with Power.

Let it begin.

The creek was safe enough to wash in, although she would not have tried drinking it. She splashed cold water all over her face and arms, flushing off the paint, scrubbing away the dirt she'd accumulated.

She glanced back over her shoulder at the hillside, glad enough to be down off the site. The anger up there had diminished a bit, but it was still a potent force, and she would *not* want to go up there after dark. And although she had a certain level of calm—after all, she had at least done *something*—there was also a corresponding level of frustration. Some force was working against both the Little People and her own attempts to discover just *who* was responsible here. Something was clouding the trail. Yes, this site had been robbed. Yes, it was possible that the relics had been taken from here and cached at Calligan's development site. But the trail had been broken and muddied past all retracing, and there was no way of knowing for *certain* unless she could actually get her hands on an artifact from the development.

It was just as possible that whoever had robbed this site had no connection with Calligan at all—even though the vision quest she had undertaken had seemed to imply a connection. Medicine worked the way it wanted to, sometimes, and that vision quest *could* simply have been telling her, "*that* job is not important—*here* is something you should be doing something about."

There were seldom any black-and-white answers in Medicine, at least as Mooncrow taught it.

It took a while to get the dirt out from under her fingernails, but if there was one thing she hated—and one thing that gave people a really bad impression—it was dirty fingernails. By the time she finished, she was starving.

So she took just long enough to share her lunch with the mule, while she tried to think of something she had left undone, or anything *else* she could do. Finally she shook her head, and swung herself back up into the mule's saddle.

It was going to be an uneasy ride home.

CHAPTER NINE

JENNIFER DROVE BACK to Tulsa with the radio off, her thoughts full of thunder, thirsting for revenge, and in no mood to appreciate the lovely weather.

She had put as much back into the vandalized graves as she had been able to find, and at least the bones could no longer be used for Bad Medicine, but most of the resident spirits—and more importantly, the Little People—had not been in any mood to settle. The feeling of the place was as bad as anything she had ever felt on Claremore Mound, and it was as plain to her as the blackjacks on the ridge that the *mi-ah-luschka* were out for blood, and nothing less would satisfy them. She didn't blame them, and in fact she would normally be more than pleased to let them have their way.

The trouble was, that wouldn't get back the medicine objects that had been taken from Watches-Over-The-Land's grave—and if someone who knew how to use them got hold of them—

Or worse yet, if someone who *didn't* know how but was

open and vulnerable got hold of them—

Some poor fool trying to "get in touch with his roots"—or at least, the one-tenth of his roots that were some kind of Native American—oh, the *mi-ah-luschka* would have a wonderful time with someone like that. True, he'd be a bonehead to buy artifacts from someone who wasn't a reputable dealer, but being a bonehead didn't necessarily warrant the kind of trouble the *mi-ah-luschka* would visit on him.

They might even succeed in killing him.

And meanwhile—meanwhile there was the very real possibility that the things looted from Tom Ware's ranch were the same ones plowed up by Rod Calligan's men. And if that was the case, the Little People would be after every man on that crew like flies on a deer carcass. *They* certainly didn't deserve retribution! The *mi-ah-luschka* might even be indirectly responsible for the dozer explosion; that meant they'd already killed. Blood fed them; there would be more killings. And the Little People were definitely of the "kill them all and let *Wah-K'on-Tah* sort them out" philosophy.

She rubbed the back of her neck and stared at the road ahead, trying to think in practical terms. First, she needed to have *someone* alerted to the desecration, so if the relics came on the legitimate market they could be confiscated. *Let me think. Nobody on either side of my family is registered with the B.I.A., so there's no way I can lodge a formal complaint, either with the B.I.A. or with the Principal Chief.*

Here was where the flip side of not being registered came up. There were ways in which Jennifer was handicapped in dealing with government authorities. Registration was a touchy point with a lot of Native Americans, and definitely with the Bureau of Indian Affairs. It was a touchy point with the B.I.A. precisely because of the whole reason the B.I.A. had been created in the first place; to *control* Native Americans. The Bureau had theoretical control over tribal lands, tribal moneys, over the stipends that whites thought were "welfare" and were really nothing more or less than the pittances the United States Government *owed* Indians for the lands that had been taken away from them, stipends paid out over so long a period of time that even some Indians didn't really know what they were for.

We take away your hunting grounds, we take away your lands, we take your children and your traditions, and in return, we will give you the food and shelter you need. That was how the treaties read, when you cut out the bullshit and fancy language. How the Bureau had carried them out was something else entirely.

Jennifer was already angry; the inevitable recollections of what the Bureau had done to every Native Nation only made her angrier. She gripped the steering wheel as if it had become a weapon.

All right, better just let the anger run its course, and not let it fester. She let the associated memories of long-ago wrongs play through.

More often than not, the Bureau read the treaties as an excuse to kidnap Indian children from their parents and lock them up in "boarding schools" where they were forbidden to speak their own language, practice their own customs, or worship anything but the White Christian God The Father Almighty.

And people wonder why so many of us became alcoholics.

The last treaties had been written with the understanding that the Indian was a vanishing creature, to follow after the buffalo, and the Great White Father would simply look after him in his decline and move in to take the little that had been left when he was gone. And in the case of some Nations, that was precisely what had happened. . . .

O for a time machine, and a gunpowder and rifle factory. . . .

And registration was a touchy subject now with many Native Americans because it was easy for someone to *claim* to be a nonregistered Indian, and attempt to cash in on the stipends, and the Native Arts Movement. Or even to claim Medicine Power and set up as a New Age Shaman, crystals and all. There was a life and a spirit to Indian art that was hard to find elsewhere, and an ability to tune into nature that many people wanted.

Just proving how hard we are to kill, either in body or in spirit.

As a result, there was money to be made, in everything from jewelry to fine-arts oil paintings. There were quite a few artists Jennifer knew who resented white people muscling in on that market. And a whole lot more folk who resented the New Age movement hauling their crystal vibrations into traditions that white folks had tried to destroy not that long ago. Rightfully . . . in many ways.

But not being registered was going to make reporting the desecration a good bit more roundabout than Jennifer liked.

Well, that's the way it has to be.

Having brought the anger around to the end of its course, she was able to let it go. What was past, was past. It was time to take care of the present.

There was a slightly more direct route to authority . . . through her father and mother. He was good friends with the Principal Chief on the Osage side.

And Mom used to go to school with Cherokee Principal Chief Wilma Mankiller before Wilma and her folks went off to California. But I'd rather deal with this from the Osage side. It's our burial site, and besides, Wilma has more than enough on her plate as it is.

She briefly considered bringing in Mooncrow; he packed a lot of clout when he cared to use it—mostly he didn't.

She knew why; he was saving that "clout" for a real emergency. This wasn't; not yet, anyway. Burial sites were looted all the time. There was no proof that this one had been looted with malice and intent.

She pulled onto the interstate behind a long-haul trucker,

and settled in to let him set the pace. *Clout is only good so many times; Grandfather is right. It's attacking, rather than persuading. We'd better save it for when we need it.*

Given that—

On impulse, she took the Claremore turnoff. With luck, Dad would be home for lunch.

It felt kind of odd to be back here, sitting across from her father at the kitchen table, B.L.T. in both hands, windows wide open to the light breeze. The house had been built in the days when a lot of things went on in the kitchen; most of the social life of the family, in fact. The kitchen was one of the largest rooms in the house, big enough that one corner of it had been set up as her mother's office, with a phone, a fax machine, and a computer, and there was still plenty of room left over.

The kitchen table stood under one of the windows, and it was nearly as old as the house, big enough to seat eight comfortably; a real farmhouse table. Right now she and her father were the only ones occupying it. Every time she came home, she got hit with nostalgia, of eating peanut-butter-and-jelly sandwiches with her brothers, of family holidays all around the big table, some of which did not correspond with things like Thanksgiving, Christmas, and Easter. . . .

"You ought to eat that instead of staring at it," her father said, after a few minutes of staring off into nowhere on her part. "Your grandfather says you don't eat enough to keep a bird alive."

She started, and grinned ruefully. "Grandfather doesn't see me hitting the fast-food stands, either," she admitted. "Man does not live by yogurt alone. There are also Frisco burgers, Rex chicken, and fry-bread and honey."

Dad laughed, and she obliged him by starting in on her own sandwich. Mom had redecorated the kitchen, with new miniblinds on the windows, and refinished the old kitchen table and the cabinets, taking them down to the natural wood. So while it held a boatload of memories, at least it didn't *look* the way it had when she was a kid.

She'd told Dad everything she knew—which wasn't much—concentrating on the desecration and looting of the burial ground, and trying to keep speculation to a minimum. She showed him the Polaroids, and left the 35-mm film to give to the Principal Chief. He in his turn had told her he'd asked around, and no one, *no one*, had heard anything about threats being made or even hinted at against Rod Calligan, either by hotheads or activists, before the explosion.

That had been the reason for staring off into space, while Mom's favorite mockingbird sang wildly from the tree in the backyard; thinking over what he had told her. It did not jive with the information Calligan had given the media, or the situation the insurance company had suspected. If no one had been threatening him, *why* had he told the media and the insurance company that they had been?

Unless he was deliberately constructing a scapegoat. But in that case, who had planted the bomb? And above all, why? Suddenly she had come to a dead end she hadn't expected, and a whole pile of loose ends that didn't match up with anything else.

She chewed thoughtfully; Dad made a darned good sandwich—the bacon was from a half-hog they bought every year, and the tomatoes were fresh from the garden. She had given her father half the Polaroids as well as the film; he had promised to give both to the Principal Chief, who would tell a little white lie and claim to have taken them himself. So at least Officialdom would be notified and if this was simply a coincidence—

—*not likely*—

—the looting would be registered and the legitimate market tightened up.

She noticed that her father was watching her with a little

frown line between his eyebrows, although he was usually as hard to read as his arc-welder. When he continued to stare at her that way, she finally put the sandwich down and returned the stare. He was not easy in his mind, and although she suspected she knew the reason, she decided to get it over with.

"All right, Dad," she said. "You're worried about something. Cough it up."

He cleared his throat self-consciously. "I always worry about you, Jen," he temporized. She noticed that more of his hair had gone gray at the temples, and that there were a few new wrinkles at the corners of his eyes. "You know that. You picked a tough profession, tough even for a guy and a white—you being a woman and not, well—it's tougher."

That wasn't it, and she knew it, but it was a place to start. "I'm paying the bills," she pointed out. "And you know darn well I can take care of myself. Between marksmanship and martial arts, I'm not too bad—and overtrained for chasing philandering hubbies and deadbeat daddies!"

She chuckled, and he finally joined her. "I know," he admitted. "I know the only reason you didn't qualify for state trooper was because of your height."

"And whose fault is that?" she asked, archly, deciding to try and inject a little more humor into the conversation. "You're the one who wasted all those good Osage height-genes on my brothers! And left *me* the runt of the litter! I call that unfair!" She made a face when he laughed, and went back to the original subject. "Look, Dad, as a P.I. I can get things done that need to be done. Sometimes I can actually do more than the cops can. There's no one watching over my shoulder to make sure I have probable cause, telling me I can't bodyguard someone because her nutcase boyfriend hasn't already *done* something. And right now— well, I can do a *lot* for our people. My hands aren't tied, there's no one telling me I have to find a quick set of suspects, because CNN is watching and the mayor is embarrassed." She rubbed the side of her nose. "In fact, if I drop some hints to the cops, they're likelier to start watching *their* step, because they know me, they know I'm honest, and they know *I'm* watching."

He reached up and scratched his temple, making a slight grimace. "I know all that," he said uncertainly, "but honey, this job is different. Now, I know I told you that there wasn't anything going on with the young bucks *before* the explosion—but—well, there is now."

She sat straight up, sandwich forgotten. Outside, a blue jay called alarm.

"What?" she demanded. "Tell me!"

He sighed, and looked pained, but this time she could tell the frown was not for her. "I've been checking around some more, especially after I heard that David was in town and getting himself into this—well, I heard some things. For one thing, I heard Rod Calligan has been pointing a finger right at the Indians on his crews. 'Course, in some ways I can't blame him, since David seems to be so set on making himself a target." He shook his head. "But if you'd figured that Calligan and the cops would really like to pin this one on our people, well, you're right. I heard they've been getting pretty heavy-handed with some of the guys involved, and that they aren't looking real hard for any other suspects."

She put the sandwich down, all appetite gone. It was one thing to speculate; it was another to hear your worst mundane fears confirmed. "Have you heard anything else?"

"Yeah." The worry line came back. "I heard that David and his buddies were likely to play rough with anybody that gets in their way. Like—"

He left the sentence unfinished, but she finished it for him. "Like me," she snarled. "And I'll break his skull for him. Dad, if you have a way to hear *from* him, messages can go the other way. You let that bunch of overgrown adolescents know that there's a lot more going on here than he thinks—

and that's *not* from Jennifer Talldeer, P.I., it's from Kestrel-Hunts-Alone, Mooncrow's designated apprentice. I think at least some of his friends will get the message and back off a little. I hope. If they don't—I am *not* going to place myself between them and a bunch of angry *mi-ah-luschka*. And that's *my* word on the subject." She sniffed disdainfully, as her father winced at the mention of the Little People. "That won't stop David, of course. He's probably gotten so damn sophisticated that he doesn't believe in anything anymore."

Her father was quiet for a long moment. "Well—that was the other—the *real* reason I was worried. I may not have the Medicine, but I've seen it at work. This is old and powerful stuff you're messing with. You weren't making any inferences, but I can read between the lines. Somehow, this looting and the explosion are related. Watches-Over-The-Land was an unusually gifted man. The medicine stirred up against someone who stole his bones is going to be pretty severe. I don't *want* you standing between the Little People and anybody."

"I knew the job was dangerous when I took it, Dad," she replied flippantly, but then sobered, and smiled at him reassuringly. "Remember, I have Mooncrow. He's a horny old coot, but when things get serious—well, he's as good as they get. If we can't handle this together, no one can."

Finally her father's expression of concern faded. "I guess you're right, and I really can't make any good assessment—it'd be like you trying to figure out a weld. You know what you're doing, honey. And you know what you need to do. So does the old man, as far as that goes, though sometimes I wonder how you put up with him living with you."

She shrugged, secretly pleased that her father had given her the ultimate accolade of an *adult*—"you know what you're doing." "Maybe I'm more than a little contrary myself," she admitted. "After all, it's man's medicine that I'm learning—"

Her father sighed. "Now you know I wouldn't be a good

parent and a good Osage if I didn't worry about that, too."

She tilted her head to one side, giving her reply a lot of thought. This was the first time he had actually come out and *said* that, and it deserved a decent reply. "I can understand that. But please, remember that *he* is the Teacher; I was the one he chose, it wasn't the other way around. Not using this power—" she shook her head, "—no, I couldn't let it just lie there, it would be—it would be denying a responsibility. As if I had all the ability of a great artist and refused to draw. No, that's not right either." She considered for a moment more. "It's a demand on me, in my heart. It's more than that, because it's not just something for me, it's something for my family, my clan, my gente, my nation— it's more as if I got elected president and refused to serve. I kind of got elected to this, so it really would be the wrong thing *not* to do what's right with the power. . . ."

She let her voice trail off; he looked into her eyes, and finally nodded. "I think I understand. You know, the old man told me once that the only time I really touch the Power is when I'm dancing—and I know what you mean about it being a demand on your heart. When I'm dancing, even in competitions, I feel like I'm *doing* something, something important, even if I don't understand what that is. I wouldn't give up dancing, even if they quit having competitions, even if only women danced, even if it were illegal the way it was in his father's day."

She held his eyes and smiled, feeling a wonderful warmth and relaxation come over her. Oh, he would still *worry*, because he was a parent, it came with the territory. But now he understood.

"Thank you," she said softly. "That means a lot." Then she cleared her throat, and took a more normal tone. "Look Dad, if you can, just pass on what I told you, all right? It might at least keep some of those poor construction workers out of the line of fire. And see if the law will move its fat ass about the vandalism." She sighed. "Not that I have much hope—but since there's a county election coming up in September, maybe the sheriff's department will feel some pressure, especially if it comes from the Principal Chief. Osage oil stipends are still a major source of county income up there."

He nodded. "I'll try," he replied. "You've got a good point about the stipends. I sure wish David Spotted Horse would be a little more—more—"

"Sensible?" she supplied, doing her best not to sound *too* snide or catty. "Reasonable? Thoughtful? I'm afraid those are pretty foreign concepts to Mister Spotted Horse. I learned that the hard way. *His* way is to overreact to everything, and his overreaction is one of the reasons we broke up."

She got a sudden suspicion from the way her father's eyes narrowed that he was about to bring in personal matters.

She wasn't mistaken.

"You know," he said carefully—and a little hopefully, "your mother and I always kind of hoped you'd get a little more serious about David."

She dashed his hopes by groaning. "Puh-lease! He was *way* too busy being the Big Man in the Movement." After a moment of consideration, she decided to let him in on a little personal secret that had finally stopped hurting. "I never told you what it was that finally precipitated my breaking up with him. He quoted Huey Long at me."

"Huey Long?" Dad replied, puzzled. "Wasn't he a Black Panther or something? What was the quote? How could that break you two up?"

"You'll know *how* when I tell you." She cleared her throat. "I was trying to point out why bailing out of college was a bad idea, especially for someone who claimed he wanted to do some good for our people. I even pointed out how much good *I* could do, being both in criminal investigation and in the Movement. He said, word for word, 'the only place for a woman in the Movement is on her back.' "

Her father stared at her for a moment, and his face spasmed. "I don't imagine you put up with that—" he choked, trying not to laugh.

She shrugged. "For his pains, I egged him into trying to shove me around, then I put *him* on *his*—to let him get an idea of how it felt."

That was too much for her father; he broke up laughing, and she grinned, feeling just a little smug now that the confrontation was old, old news. It had hurt at the time. What had hurt even more was that she had known, then and now, that it was *meant* to; David had an uncanny ability to pick the most hurtful words possible and use them.

"Well, he thought the reason I was taking tai chi was just to keep the fat off my hips and make me a good dancer. Boy, did *he* get a surprise!"

Her father chuckled. "I'll bet he did. And I'd be the last person to tell you he didn't have it coming, after a crack like that."

She shook her head. "Needless to say, when I told him as much, he called me a flint-hearted bitch—among other things—I called him a male chauvinist pig—among a *lot* of other things—and we called it quits."

Her father picked up a napkin and wiped his eyes. "That's *my* daughter. If you hadn't, and I'd found out about it, I'd have disowned you myself."

She picked up her sandwich again, and stared at it, before taking a pensive bite. "You know, Dad," she said after swallowing it, "it isn't easy being a flint-hearted bitch. It takes a lot of work."

To her surprise, he reached across the table and patted her free hand. "You mean," he said, quietly but firmly, "that it isn't easy being a warrior. *That* is what you are, and only a foolish young man with no experience and unable to get past his own ego would fail to see it."

She looked up at him in complete shock.

He nodded, and gave her a smile warm and bright with

approval. "Just promise me this. Watch your back very closely. Not because you need to, but to please your old man, who probably worries too much about the girl he remembers as a baby in his arms."

She blinked, and agreed.

"Good," he said with satisfaction. "That is all I have any right to ask you. Now—can I force some strawberry cobbler on you?" He arched his eyebrows at the refrigerator. "There's fresh homemade ice cream to go with it," he continued temptingly.

All she could do was laugh, and agree.

She was thinking about the conversation as she made notes in her office after she got back. It had been a very enlightening and surprising little talk, on a lot of levels—

"Sometimes it would be easier not to be such a rebel," Grandfather said from behind her, making her jump. "Easier on you, as well as your parents. But sometimes it is something that you must be."

She swiveled her chair around. There he was, standing in the door to her office, looking inscrutable. "Are you eavesdropping on my brain again?" she asked, shaking a fist at his ear. "Dirty old men shouldn't eavesdrop on ladies' thoughts!"

He ducked, and chuckled at her, waggling an admonitory finger at her. "No respect," he chided. "You kids have no respect for the elderly and wise—"

It was hard to stay even annoyed with him for more than a minute when he was in this mood. "If you were either, I might," she retorted. "You're an oversexed sixteen-year-old contrary, an Osage *heyoka* and there *isn't* any such thing, and you're just *disguised* as a wise old medicine man! You've got my real Grandfather tied up in a closet somewhere. You're Coyote, that's what you are, and not Mooncrow at all!"

His eyes crinkled up as he grinned. "Could be, could be," he replied. "But I was just reading the thoughtful look on your face when you came in, and put it together with the pan of your mother's famous cobbler in the fridge. That meant you stopped to see my son, and since you brought the cobbler home, he must have let you know he's worried because you're so different, but since you aren't annoyed, he told you he knows you can take care of yourself. Hmm?"

She shook her head. "I am *never* going to be able to do that. You sound just like Sherlock Holmes, and I feel as stupid as Watson," she sighed, then hooked a chair with her toe and kicked it over to him. "Sit, Mooncrow, my Teacher. I am troubled, and in need of counsel. We have a lot of problems that should fit together and don't. I need your help, Little Old Man."

He took the chair, losing his smile. When she called him *that*—which was a title of high honor among their people— he knew the situation was more than simply serious. And he knew that she would not ask him for help unless she really was out of her depth.

She told him what she had told her father, but with more details, particularly the Medicine details. Although he was wearing his very best stoneface, as befit a Little Old Man, she thought that he became alarmed when she told him about Watches-Over-The-Land's looted grave.

He began to ask her some specific questions about what graves in particular had been looted where, and she had to confess that she had been so upset that she couldn't remember precise details.

"That's why I took these," she said, pulling out the Polaroids, and handing them to him. "Each set is from a specific grave; see, I put a number on a note right in the middle of each one, so you can tell which was which. I put everything back that I could, but with the bones gone, I got the feeling that my ceremonies were about as effective as blowing smoke into the wind. I did at least break the spiritual connection to the bones, but the *mi-ah-luschka* are looking for blood payment."

He leafed through them, carefully, his face gone stony and cold. Finally, when he came to the last set, he took a quick intake of breath. That was all, but it was enough to tell her that he was as upset as she had ever seen him.

He closed his eyes for a moment, simply holding the photographs in his hands. When he finally opened his eyes again, though, he did not look the way she had expected.

He was angry, but that wasn't all. He was *disturbed*, and perhaps a little frightened. Something had happened that he had not expected.

"You are correct in remembering that this was Watches-Over-The-Land's resting place," he said, after a long silence. "As I have told you, he was a Medicine Chief, and a very great one."

He paused, and she waited. He would tell her what he knew, but he was clearly thinking this through as he spoke.

"There is something wrong—besides this vandalism," he said after that long pause. "I am looking at these pictures, and there is more malice in the last looting than in the rest. There are *no* bits of pottery or beads left there; absolutely everything was taken. Further, no one but you, or I, or some other immediate ancestor, should have been able to find that grave. *Not* simply because it is—was—hard to find. Because they should *not* have been able to see it. Because it was protected."

She nodded, slowly, and then with vigor. *Of course! That was what the back of my mind was trying to tell me! Of course the place would be protected—how could it not have been, with a son who was a Medicine Chief himself seeing to the cairn? And with every descendant since watching over the site?*

Magics like that were only supposed to grow stronger with time, not weaker. And now she knew what Mooncrow had been up to, each time they had visited the place. He had been reinforcing those protections.

So what had gone wrong?

"So something has gone wrong," he said, echoing her thoughts. "Something has gone very wrong with all of the protections that we tried to keep in place." He pondered again for a moment. "So, here is something new to add to your equation. A new story for you, and it is one of ill omen; one I would have told you when I taught you the rituals to protect our Ancestor. There was a—a thing—that Watches-Over-The-Land defeated. This was later, after his visions, or he would not have been strong enough to defeat it. It was something evil, and he defeated the evil man that created it as well, killed him, and buried him with all his evil things. Watches-Over-The-Land told his son that he had seen another set of visions, visions that showed that if he did not defeat this man and his evil object, the Osage would go the way of the Hard-To-Kill-People, and disappear; and lose *all* that they had to the Long Knives, like the Thing-On-Its-Head-People did."

The Osage disappearing, like the Sac and Fox, where I don't think there's a single pure-blooded member of the tribes left. And losing literally everything, like the Cherokee, who were driven out of the lands in the South, had homes and farms and businesses stolen from them by government order. . . .

"He said this evil man meant to get power by helping the Long Knives, and that he would have done terrible things to the land itself." Grandfather shook his head, and his eyes were very troubled. "That is why Watches-Over-The-Land had to try to defeat him and his *thing*. It was like a *Wah-hopeh*, the sacred hawk-bundle, but it wasn't. It was like an evil *Wah-hopeh*, meant to destroy everything that was sacred, to contaminate everything that was good. That evil man *would* know where Watches-Over-The-Land was resting. He would see through all the protections, for he is very powerful. And he would take great pleasure in seeing the sacred things stolen, the bones taken. . . ."

Mooncrow's voice trailed off, and he narrowed his eyes,

his attention no longer really on her. Abruptly, he stood up.

"I must think on this," he said, and left without another word, leaving her to stare at the chair he had sat in.

This does not give me a warm and fuzzy feeling of confidence, she thought, unhappily. She particularly was not fond of the way that Grandfather had spoken of this "evil man" as if he were still alive. Or, at least, able to act.

Of course, if he was that powerful, he would be able to act. He would not leave this earth; he would not be at all interested in going into the West. If he left the earth, he would be weighed by Wah-K'on-Tah, who would not be very pleased with his actions. So it would be in his best interest to stick around and see if he could break the bindings that my ancestor placed on him, then find someone to act through.

If? From the look of things, he *had.* And some of the pieces of the puzzle were beginning to fit together to form a very nasty pattern.

In the past, the evil one had worked against the Osage and with the whites, even if the whites had not been aware of it. And in the present—

In the present, there had been relics plowed up, a terrible explosion in which mostly Indians had been killed, *for* which Indians were being blamed, by whites. Some Indians were being stirred up against *her,* the ancestor of the evil one's great enemy.

The two patterns matched.

Too well. Far, far too well.

CHAPTER TEN

DAVID SPOTTED HORSE stifled a yawn, wishing he hadn't stopped smoking. A cigarette would at least have given him something to do with his hands.

The gathering in the back room of somebody's cousin's smoke shop was not going the way he'd planned. He wanted to warn the guys from Calligan's construction site not to talk to Jennie, no matter what they heard on the grapevine. He hadn't called this meeting to hear about superstitious crap, but that was what he was getting, especially from the Osage.

He couldn't believe they were wasting a single moment of time on this. He leaned back against a stack of heavy cardboard cartons, and crossed his arms over his chest, trying to at least keep his face straight. *First Jennie and her cute little stagetricks, making the door slam on me, and now this. And if I don't at least listen to them, they won't listen to me.*

The guys on Calligan's construction project had all gone back to work the day before yesterday—against his advice—when Calligan had promised to cordon off the particular corner of the property that seemed to be "sacred ground" now that the cops were done playing at evidence-gathering. He'd been dead set against them going back, on the grounds that they were playing right into Calligan's hands, but some guy named Rick had said stubbornly that if they *didn't* go back to work, it would pretty well prove that Calligan was right about one of them being in cahoots with terrorists. "The best way we can prove we're innocent is to *act* like we're innocent," he had said, over and over, until the rest agreed with him.

But now, from all the stories being told here, as soon as they went back, everything started to go bad again. Not just heat from Calligan, either, although the bastard was there every minute of every damned day, supervising everything himself. Probably making certain nobody slacked off, although the guys said he told them he was watching for more sabotage. No, it seemed like every time somebody turned around, there was one accident after another.

Weird stuff, too; stuff that couldn't have been like the dozer explosion. Holes opened up right in the path of equipment, big ones, and equipment would fall in and have to get hauled out, wasting time. A load of steel pipe broke its straps and came down right on one guy, who was lucky to get off with a broken leg. Every piece of heavy machinery was out of commission by the end of today, with gaskets blown, fuel lines leaking, hydraulics shot, piston arms broken. Something had gotten into the dynamite shed and chewed on every single stick, letting in damp—which made them likely to be unstable and useless. The only thing stupid enough to chew on dynamite was a possum, but there weren't any holes under the shed or in the roof big enough to let a possum get inside. And it was a good thing that the guy going after the dynamite had looked it over good, or the bad sticks could have killed someone.

He hadn't heard such a litany of woes since Hurricane Andrew.

And of course, every single one of those accidents was "proof" that the Little People were angry, that there was a curse on the project.

How can people who are so smart be so gullible? he asked himself for the thousandth time. *These guys aren't stupid; it takes a lot of brains to horse one of those rigs around. I should look on the bright side. When they stop jawing, I can probably talk them into staying off the job now. But how can guys who laugh at people who're afraid of black cats turn around and believe in the Little People?*

He used to believe in all that nonsense—well, maybe not Little People, since that was an Osage thing and not Cherokee, but in spirits, and totemic animals, vision-quests, and all the rest of it. Medicine. Stuff that got all the New Age, Dances-With-Credit-Cards crowd so misty-eyed.

Newage. Rhymes with sewage, and the same watered-down crap. He suppressed a smile at his own cleverness.

He had more sense than that now; it was just one more way for people to delude themselves. Look what had happened to *Wovoka* and the Ghost Dance Movement! More of the People had been shot down because they believed that those stupid white shirts would keep them bullet-proof. . . .

Peyote, and too much imagination. That's all right if you're making a painting, or writing a poem, but we're trying to keep some People out of jail, here.

Oh, he went to various rituals; even Peyote ceremonies, although he wouldn't go so far as chewing the stuff himself. Partially because he didn't like giving up control to anything, he liked knowing he was always completely in control of his mind and all his senses. But he went because his mentors pointed out it was important to go—"politically correct," as it were. It would look bad if he didn't participate, as if his spirit wasn't in helping his People.

And he did believe that there was something Sacred out there, that there were special places that had a special power for the Peoples. Hell, even white people had places like that, places where powerful things happened, like Lourdes, Mecca and Jerusalem. It only made sense that there were places like that for everyone. And the earth itself was sacred, if only because it was the only place to live that humans had, and when they didn't treat it like it was sacred, they messed it up.

And there's something out there that's for us, all the Peoples, something that doesn't fit the white idea of God the Caucasian Father. That only makes sense too. The Judeo-Christians don't have a lock on truth any more than anyone else does.

But he just couldn't handle all this superstitious stuff. He believed in the power of Lawyers, not Little People; of Media Pressure and not Medicine. You could smoke a sacred pipe till you choked; it wasn't gonna do you a damn bit of good against a bunch of U.S. marshals with guns.

I'd rather have a restraining order on my side than all the eagles in the country overhead when I'm facing the Feds.

He sighed, and continued to listen to the latest story. The way he had it pegged, the mystics were deluding themselves . . . confusing the symbols of power with the real thing.

But if it makes them get their act together to save their tribal identity and maybe do something so that the whites are forced to get their act together, well, fine.

And despite Jennie's accusations, he had a larger goal in mind, too. The way he saw it, the Native Movement should be taking a larger role in ecological matters. Since so many of the eco-freaks were looking to the Indians for spiritual guidance, the Peoples had damned well ought to give it to them. *We have to do something to save the world from poison. If it takes talking to crystals, it's all right with me, as long as they start cleaning up the air and water too.*

We all have to live here. The whites aren't going away, and that's reality. So the best we can do is get as much back as we can, and shame them into cleaning up the rest. . . .

At least Jennie has that part right.

He frowned a little, and caught himself. He took a quick look to see if the latest speaker had seen the faint grimace, but the guy was so wrapped up in his own story that David could probably have stuck his tongue out without the man noticing. The smell of tobacco back here was overpowering. Made him *really* sorry he'd given up smoking. But damned if he was going to let a stick of dried weeds rule his life.

But that made him think of Jennie again, since she'd been on him all the time to quit, and that just reminded him of that last confrontation. He was really glad none of the guys here had known anything about *that.* How the hell had she managed to get him to leave when he hadn't wanted to? The door trick, that was easy to figure out, but not the rest. He'd still had plenty to say to her—but somehow he hadn't been able to get the words out of his mouth, and he'd found himself walking right out the door on top of that!

That crazy old man, her grandfather, was with her, too. Shit, he used to be able to do some weird things, back when we were kids. . . .

Hell, now I'm starting it! That stuff the old man did, it wasn't anything more than sleight of hand and the suggestibility of kids!

What was the old man doing living with her, anyway? That only complicated matters. Especially since a lot of the guys here held the old man in pretty high esteem.

"We've got to talk to old man Talldeer, that's what," the guy holding the floor was saying, and to David's dismay, there was a murmur of approval, even from some of the guys who weren't Osage. It was obvious from that it wasn't just *some* of the guys, but all of these guys had respect for the old man. Hell, that was all he needed!

"Maybe we oughta talk to Jennie Talldeer too," said another. "Larry did; he said she's got the right stuff. Last time I asked the Old Man for a blessing, he had Jennie do my work for me, and she's good. Old man Talldeer's training her right."

Another murmur of agreement—

"She showed up at the first meeting," said someone else, giving David an oblique glance. "Spotted Horse wouldn't let her in. He said she was there for Calligan, but what if she was trying to give us some Medicine help? What if the old man sent her?"

Oh shit. Now how was he going to convince them *not* to go to her when she had the old man in her corner?

So far none of them had gotten wind of the message she'd sent to him by way of the Osage Principal Chief; if they did, there'd be no keeping them away from her or her grandfather. And he wasn't sure if what she'd sent him was a trick, or if she really believed it herself—

But the message had been, couched in no uncertain terms, that there was Bad Medicine involved in this Calligan mess, and that he'd better butt out or get involved in some constructive manner.

How can she believe that stuff? She went to college!

How had she forced him out of her house when he didn't want to leave? And how come ever since then, any time he dialed her number, no matter *what* phone it was from, he always got the "your call did not go through" message? She hadn't changed her number, and it happened even when he went through the operator. The operator had been just as confused, and had muttered something about a short in the line.

On the whole, for the last day or so, things had not been happening according to David's idea of a logical and predictable universe. In a perverse sense, he would have liked to blame it all on Jennie, but he doubted that she had gone out and dug holes in Calligan's land for equipment to fall into. Short of ascribing supernatural powers to *her.* . . .

Dammit. And what the hell do they mean by "old man

Talldeer's training her right?" Now that he thought about it, hadn't her message said something about being her grandfather's apprentice? Shit, maybe she *did* believe all that crap!

The entire bunch was looking at him now, waiting for him to say something.

He almost grimaced, and covered it in time. No matter what he said, he lost in some way. If he told them *not* to talk to Jennie or the old man, he'd lose them completely. They had that shaky, panicked kind of look about them. Then they'd go do whatever Jennie told them to do.

"Well," he said slowly, keeping his expression just a shade on the dubious side, "you can talk to the Talldeer girl if you want, if you're really going to insist on it, but if you do, don't be surprised if everything you tell her shows up as evidence on Calligan's side when he takes you all to court. You know she's a private eye, and none of us know who hired her, but I'd bet on Calligan before I'd bet on anyone else. And anything she hears, if it has any bearing on the explosion, she *has* to tell the cops."

I wouldn't, but she will. Little People, my ass.

"What's she gonna tell him?" the man asked, scornfully. "That we think the jerk's got a curse on him? She already *knows* that, and so does he! We told him to his face, more than once! And last time I looked, curses weren't admissible in court!"

Ah hell, I have lost them. Bitch.

They turned their backs on him and began deciding who was going to approach the Talldeers, and whether they were going to go straight for the old man or work through the girl first. He finally got up and left; it was obvious that he'd lost this round.

Time for round two. He pushed through the stockroom door and passed through the front of the smoke shop, empty except for the cousin at the counter. The cousin kind of grunted good night; he returned the courtesy, and walked out into the earlier dusk. His car was off to one side of the tiny parking lot, under a cottonwood.

He hadn't meant to start clandestine operations this soon, but it looked as though he wasn't going to have any choice. Whether or not Jennie was working with Calligan was moot. If she was—well, he was about to show these guys how stupid they were being. If she wasn't—

Then at least he'd have collected some other evidence. People always left paper trails; they couldn't help it. There would be something in that office he would be able to use, if only by leaking it to the press.

He had the document camera, the rubber gloves, and the lock-pick set all hidden in the side panel of the front door of his Jeep. Tonight would be a good night to go raid the office at the site. The cops had all gone away, and with the workers back on the job, Calligan had no reason to be nervous. And no one with any sense broke into a site office; there was never anything worthwhile there. Not even pawnshops took electric typewriters anymore. That, and oversized calculators and beat-up old office furniture was all anyone ever kept at a site office.

And, of course, records. . . .

Not that I've ever been caught, he thought, not bothering to hide a smirk, since he was halfway to his car and there wasn't anyone to see it. *Damn, I'm good. . . . We'll just see if there's something in those records at the site that leads back to Jennie—or anything else that can be used against Calligan himself.*

Kestrel-Hunts-Alone was on the hunt—armed to the teeth, metaphorically and spiritually speaking—crouched at the edge of the fence surrounding Calligan's construction site. It was very dark out here with no moon and only the light of the stars and very distant streetlights, but she wasn't depending entirely on her night vision. She had already spent some time here before sundown, memorizing the positions

of bits of cover, planning the route she would take to get to
the ground that had held the relics.

Both she and Mooncrow had decided that it was time to
do a little more investigation; after dark, during the Little
People's most active hours, this time. Mooncrow had ar-
mored her to the best of his ability, and she had layered on
her own protections and "assurances" on top of his. At best,
the Little People would recognize her as an ally against the
real enemy. At worst, she had enough defenses that she
would not need to fear their anger.

She hoped.

There was only one way to be sure, however, and that was
to test it all under fire, in the field.

No one had plowed anything else up since the explosion,
but that was because Calligan had put off digging any further into the disputed corner until after the forensics and
university people got done checking the area out. Calligan
was pretending to cooperate; at least, she thought it was
pretense, despite his claim that he had contacted people at
O.U. to come check out the disputed area. Of course, he
could have assumed that the explosion had powdered every
relic left. He could be assuming—probably correctly—that
O.U. was too short on money to send anyone to do a real
archeological investigation. Or he could have come in on his
own and removed everything—it would have been a little
harder with the cops here, but it could have happened.

One thing was certain; if she could rely on her own Medicine senses, this place was *not* a real burial site. She had
sought visions here both while in her car and crouched at
the edge of the fence as near to that corner as she could get.
There simply weren't any of the appropriate signs, or the
proper "feel" to the place. There *had* been a faint echo that
something had been kept there, briefly—and there seemed
to be a bright point, as if there was still some kind of relic
out there, but it was all in one place, not spread out as it
would be if this really were a burial ground. But there was

nothing more, and she was not going to go into a full Medicine trance in a place where she was so physically vulnerable. So—that probably meant that what had already been dug up was a cache of some kind, as she had guessed. And she needed to find out now if there were any more caches out here, or if that point of power meant only a relic or two still intact after all the turmoil. Even one object would tell her if what had been dug up had actually come from the Osage cairns.

The only way she could do that was now, at night, when there would be no one around to interfere—or try to blow *her* away for uncovering their stash.

She slipped under the wire fence—ridiculously easy to do, since it wasn't anchored very firmly, and it was obviously there just to define the area of construction and not to form any kind of protection.

Didn't Larry tell me that there'd been some missing supplies? I'm not surprised, if this is the level of their security. An amateur could break in here.

She froze for a moment, scanning the area, then scuttled silently to another patch of cover, a stack of something with a tarp over it.

Working her way carefully across the site, moving from shadow to shadow, occupied all of her attention. She did not bother to "watch" for Little People; if they wanted her, they would be able to ambush her without any difficulty. They were spirits, after all, and it was rather difficult to keep a spirit from materializing in front of you if it wanted to!

She had gotten halfway to the "forbidden" corner, when she realized that she was not alone.

And whoever was out here was at least as good at being "invisible" as she was, or she would have noticed him? her? long before this. In fact, the only reason she *had* spotted the other invader was because he had run in front of a light-colored piece of equipment just as she looked at it.

Oh shit!

It occurred to her then, as she cowered in the shadow of a huge bulldozer and watched for some sign that *she* had been spotted, that she just might have run into the original looter. If there was an "original looter." The signs sure pointed to one. And if so—he would also be the most likely candidate for saboteur, trying to wreck the equipment before it dug up his cache.

Just what I needed for my birthday. The guy who wired a dozer with dynamite and killed four people. Not likely he's going to play nice and surrender if I catch him. Not likely he's going to congratulate me on my expertise if he catches me!

Assuming this person was human at all. That was not a good assumption, really. The Little People could take on all the attributes of a flesh-and-blood human when they chose, and there were other spirits that could do the same.

This might not be a looter, a saboteur. This might be something much worse.

She was afraid to move, lest she be spotted, and afraid not to move. She certainly couldn't stay here forever! She strained her eyes against the darkness, but she couldn't make out much more than a darker shadow against a pile of sand or gravel. If she hadn't seen him move there, she wouldn't have known he was in that blotch of darkness. She'd never have guessed that the shadow was alive if she hadn't seen it in action.

Then it moved again; so quickly that her heart jumped up into her throat. It was spooky; maybe a couple of pieces of gravel fell, but otherwise the lurker was silent. It was heading over in the direction of the roped-off corner.

So, does that mean it's the looter, another would-be scavenger, one of the Little People, or somebody else altogether?

She followed, heart pounding, palms sweating, and wishing she had a night-scope.

Then it occurred to her that she *did* have a kind of night-scope, after all. The only problem was that it was hard to move if she went into the kind of mental state where she could See things, see the purely physical, and See Medicine things. If this other lurker *was* something other than human, he would really betray himself at that point. But she would be severely handicapped—

That's why you're a Medicine Woman, stupid. "Hard" doesn't mean "impossible." Just try not to move too fast when you're double-sighted, or you'll trip over something.

She froze for a moment, putting herself in the right frame of reference.

She knew she'd matched it, when instead of only the shadow of a human lurking over by the dirt dug up by the now-wrecked dozer, she saw not only the stranger, but a stag, standing beside him.

Interesting. So her unknown had a medicine-animal self. At least that meant he wasn't one of the Little People; they didn't have medicine-animals, spirit-totems, since they *were* spirits. And it meant he was indeed a "he"—it was a stag, after all, and not a doe—and that he probably wasn't white. Although she had met white people who had medicine-creatures, there weren't many of them in the Tulsa area. He didn't fit the profile of someone who would be grave-robbing, either; a medicine-animal would have left him, if he'd done something as appalling as that. No one she knew had a stag for a medicine-animal. . . .

But he didn't seem aware of his medicine-animal; at least, he paid no attention to it, staring instead very fixedly at something lying just inside the roped-off area.

That was really odd; how could he not *know* he had a spirit-guardian? And for one to appear, to try to force him to become aware of it, he had to be in some kind of danger. . . .

The stag was very agitated, frantic; surely he had to feel *something*! Even if he was only marginally in touch with his spiritual self, he had to feel it! The stag kept alternating between threatening gestures with its horns toward the man's right, and pawing at the earth, threatening something *there*, where the man was looking.

She concentrated a little more, and narrowed her focus. *Whatever this is, it's very small—and I think it's in that area where I spotted something earlier.*

Finally, something clicked, and she saw it, or rather, saw the medicine-self that was the echo of its physical self.

It was a single artifact, a small one. A medicine-pouch, hardly bigger than the palm of her hand. She had missed seeing exactly what it was the first time because she had been "looking" for a mass of relics, not a single piece.

A real, physical light flashed on, startlingly bright in all the darkness. The other person had a penlight and was shining it on the object, and she cursed him mentally for a fool, showing *any* kind of light out here at night! Anybody driving by would see it; anybody keeping watch for saboteurs or troublemakers would see it! How could he be so *stupid*?

That's the same kind of dumb trick David would pull—

Whoever the idiot was, he didn't act as if he'd expected to find the pouch there, and she wondered how he had spotted it in the first place. Maybe he was marginally sensitive—

Maybe pigs sing arias. He probably saw something reflective.

He *was* studying it, carefully. Although it was too much to hope for that he'd leave it there. . . .

Dammit. That alone would have told me if it was from one of the looted graves. But I won't know that unless I can get my hands on it, and get the "feel" of it, to see if it matches the "feel" of any of the gravesites.

The stag feinted toward the right again, and this time movement there, movement in the spirit world, made her focus her attention in that direction.

Oh hell. Oh no—

Little People. Lots of them. In human form, in the dress of her people from the time of the first French traders, but

with faces too wild and too hungry to ever pass for human.
Waiting and watching, avidly, their eyes glowing with a
feral, anticipatory light that made her shiver. They crouched
in a group, making her think of a waiting pack of coyotes,
or a mob of crows. Waiting for dinner to kill itself. Watching some supremely stupid young creature, who was just a
heartbeat away from doing something fatal.

Fatal?

She turned her newly sharpened spirit-sight back toward
the medicine-pouch, following the gaze of the Little People.
Yes, that was what they were watching; it looked as if they
had been *waiting* for this man to find it—

Fatal? She strained her abilities to the limit, and prayed
a little for good measure—and *knew*, suddenly and completely, what it was that was "fatal" about the pouch.

It was the bait to a very mundane trap—it was wired to
a bomb!

She didn't stop to think; she just acted. She flung herself
across the intervening space, hurled herself at him, tackled
him and rolled him sideways, just as he started to reach out
to pick it up.

Together they rolled right into the crowd of Little People,
who flowed about them in confused eddies, momentarily
deflected from their purpose.

She felt their anger, hot on her skin; their rage, at being
cheated of their rightful victim. And she looked up to see
them surrounding both her and the stranger.

David had intended to head straight for the portable office
on the site, but something made him take a little detour
instead. A feeling that there was something out in the "forbidden" area that he really should know about.

He hadn't been certain about the hunch, but it was too
strong to be denied. But he'd stopped, right by a pile of dirt,
feeling a little stupid at following a "hunch," and played his

penlight over the area—

A flash of pale blue caught the light, and he aimed the circle of illumination there, expecting to see nothing more than half an old plastic cup.

Instead, the light shone on the deep reds and blues of really old beadwork, surrounded by the remains of quill-work, all set into what had to be a truly ancient medicine-pouch.

He stared at it, transfixed, unable to look away. He forgot what he had come for in the first place. After a few moments, the fascination turned to something else.

Desire. He *had* to have this thing. It was meant for him. It had called him to take it, called to him out of the darkness. He *must* take it—

He reached out for it, slowly, with his free hand—

And something hit him from the side, knocking all the breath right out of him, sending him sprawling.

He had not been ready; he had not even been close to ready. He hit his head on the hard ground as he toppled over, and that partially stunned him. On top of that, his attacker had knocked the breath out of his lungs with the blow, something that hadn't happened since the last time he'd been "sucker-punched" in grade school. He and his assailant rolled over and over in the dirt, finally coming to a halt a few feet away from where he'd been hiding.

He tried to suck in air, flailing around for balance, or to put up a pretense of defense. All he could manage was a vague idea that his attacker must have been one of Calligan's hired stooges, a rent-a-cop or something. But he was too busy trying to force a breath into his lungs, which burned with pain, and felt as if they'd collapsed. His attacker ignored him, and scrambled to his feet.

Finally, after a terrible muscle spasm, his chest unclenched, and he sucked in a long and painful breath in something close to a sob; a breath that hurt so much that his eyes watered. He looked up, through tearing eyes, to see who had hit him—

Jennie? What the hell?

She stood over him, her face set in a tight, fierce mask, a she-wolf defending her cub. *That* was when he looked at what *she* was looking at.

And nearly stopped breathing all over again.

His mind babbled that he wasn't seeing this—he couldn't be seeing this—that it was all a hallucination.

No. Oh no—I'm going crazy. I'm seeing delusions. I'm still knocked out—

But shaking his head didn't make them go away. And despite all his rational thinking, college learning, and disbelief, they were still there.

The Osage Little People.

He *knew* what they were; old man Talldeer had spun a tale or two for him and the rest of the neighborhood kids, back when he and Jennie were both in grade school. And any Indian kid in Claremore knew about Claremore Mound, the Little People there, the things that would happen to males who were stupid enough to climb it; boys used to dare each other to go up on it, and none of them ever would.

Yeah, he knew what the Little People were supposed to look like. And they *had* to be spirits; for one thing, they were transparent, and for another, no Osage had dressed the way they were dressed for the last hundred years or so. Wearing only gypsum-rubbed deerskin leggings, with roaches of deer-tail hair and turkey-gobbler beard attached to the long roaches of their own hair, which had been shaved in the style that the whites called a "mohawk," they surrounded him and Jennie, their eyes gleaming with mingled rage and hunger.

Their eyes glowed.

And one other thing told him that they were Little People, and not ordinary spirits.

No feathers. No face paint. Each of them should have been wearing an eagle feather in his roach; either a soft, under-tail covert if he was of the *Tzi-sho* or a full tail-feather if he was *Hunkah.* The Little People wore neither, nor were they painted. If they had once been human, they had died in such a way that they had no honor, and must go through a strange afterlife stuck here on earth and not in the Summer Country, existing without paint or eagle feathers. . . .

Just as old man Talldeer had whispered to them, on those long-ago October nights.

"They are hungry for blood. They search for prey—"

If they had once been human, they could have been killed by his people, in the raids that left no one in an entire village—every man dead, every woman and child made a slave. To die a slave—to die in a sneak attack and rot where you fell, without paint or ceremony—that would leave your spirit wandering.

At any other time than the night of the dark of the moon, you might be able to talk them into sparing you. They might even content themselves with simply pulling a trick on you. But during the dark of the moon, they became pretty single-minded killing machines.

David did not need to scan the sky; he knew it was the dark of the moon. He'd planned on that, when he'd decided to make his little raid tonight.

The Little People were ignoring Jennie for the most part, staring avidly down at *him.* Whatever was going on, she seemed to have some kind of protection from them. He didn't.

I'm dead, he thought, his mouth going dry with a terror so profound it couldn't even be called *fear.*

Then Jennie pulled something out of the inside of her jacket; a beaded feather—no, two feathers, eagle-tail and eagle-covert bound together with beadwork, like a peyote-fan, but different in a way that felt important. She held it before her like a shield—

He blinked to clear his eyes of the strange triple vision that suddenly came over him, but the vision remained. There was Jennie, legs braced slightly apart, the Jennie he knew, in blue jeans and a beat-up jacket decorated with Osage ribbon-work embroidery and ribbon-weaving—

And Jennie, in full Osage regalia, but with some additions; a kind of shell necklace he *knew* was only supposed to be worn by men, a beaded *Tzi-sho* eagle feather braided into the hair on one side of her head, and a beaded *Hunkah* feather on the other, a modified warrior's roach, and some other things that she didn't wear to the powwows—

And over all that, a bird. A kestrel.

And the second and third images were a *lot* stronger than the "real" one.

The Little People slowly raised their eyes, and stared instead at Jennie, and David began to hope that maybe he wasn't going to die after all.

One of the Little People straightened up from his crouch. He stood much taller than Jennie; he must have been at least six feet in height, and towered over her, but she didn't seem the least intimidated.

He said something in what David recognized as Osage; he didn't know much of the language, but it was Siouan in derivation, and he knew Lakotah. He understood just enough to get the basics.

You have interfered with our hunt. This is our rightful prey.

She shook her head, and replied in the same tongue.

David didn't understand *any* of what she said, and it was a fairly long speech. The rest of the Little People straightened and surrounded her, looking down at her, ignoring him.

Oh, please don't make them mad, Jennie. I don't think kung fu, or whatever it is you know, works on them.

Finally she finished with something he vaguely understood. *Sorry about this, but he's with me. He's a little stupid, please forgive him.*

He didn't know whether to kiss or kick her. Maybe he'd better not do either. They might not like it.

The leader looked down at her, taking her measure; looked down at David, and there was no mistaking the contempt in his eyes. Finally he raised his chin in agreement, though it was obvious that he did so grudgingly. The glitter in his eyes spoke volumes. Here was a man, saved by a woman who was more warrior than *he* was, at least in the estimation of the Little People.

David felt his ears reddening.

The leader folded his arms across his chest, and slowly faded from view; the rest of the Little People followed him a heartbeat later. And the strange triple vision of Jennie faded as well, leaving only the Jennie he knew.

David finally remembered to breathe.

He thought that Jennie would say something, probably scathing, but she ignored him. Instead, she tucked her feathers back into her coat and returned to the place where he'd been crouching, and dropped down to sit on her heels and stare at the medicine-pouch he'd found. . . .

Which was no longer so desirable. In fact, he didn't want it at all anymore; his earlier lust for it made him a little nauseous.

She stayed there for an awfully long time as he slowly picked himself up out of the dirt and assessed the damages. Not bad, really. A couple of bruised ribs, some other bumps and bruises and scrapes. *She* didn't seem the least interested in him anymore, and he was torn between being fawningly grateful and really pissed off. If there was a death worse than fate—well, she'd just saved him from it.

If the Little People had gotten hold of me, they'd have killed me, and they'd have taken their time about it. Not only that, but I'd have had to join them. . . .

He shuddered, and his nausea increased. An eternity of hunger and frustration, never being able to leave the earth, never doing anything constructive . . . and he could just imagine the reaction Calligan and the press would have had to finding him cold-dead on Calligan's property.

Calligan would have had a field day, and David probably would have inadvertently taken a lot of innocent people down with him.

Not an hour ago, he'd scoffed at the Little People as being no more than superstitious drivel. Oh, he was a believer now.

Jennie continued to ignore him. He decided not to say anything. In a strange way, he was actually *afraid* of her. Where had she gotten that kind of power?

Maybe the stuff she had done the night he'd come over wasn't all stage-magic crap after all.

Maybe? Get real, Spotted Horse. She's got it, whatever it is. You should be glad she just shoved you out of her house, instead of a million other things she could have done to you for talking to her like that.

In his mind, she took on a kind of mythic status; a kind of Great Mother, like Spider Woman or Changing Woman. He wondered if he should just try to slip away before she noticed him again.

Then she spoke, and the sarcastic tone and completely ordinary words shredded his building mental image of her to rags.

"You blow your own mouth off often enough," she said quietly, "you happen to know anything about bombs?"

Bombs? He blinked, suppressed an automatic and equally sarcastic reply, and walked over to join her.

She had his penlight in her hand; evidently he'd dropped it when she hit him. She had it focused on the medicine-pouch, and she had moved some of the dirt from around it. Now he saw the trip wires leading to it—and now he knew why the Little People had been waiting for him. They hadn't been planning on killing him themselves; they were going to let him blow himself to pieces.

"Happens I do," he said, carefully. "At least, I do know

about things that are this primitive. We had to learn how to look for bombs in our cars, and booby traps people would set up in barricades."

She glanced at him sideways, but didn't comment. She didn't have to; it was all there in her glance. He took a deep breath to calm himself; he'd earned that particular doubtful glance.

"Honest," he said, with complete truthfulness. "Jennie, I can swear to you that I have never set a bomb in my life, and I only took apart bombs that whites set on Native property. Okay?"

She nodded. "Okay. So, how about if I hold the light and you deal with this one?"

He was still wearing his rubber gloves; she couldn't possibly have missed that, but she didn't say anything about it. The bomb was ridiculously simple to take apart, leaving them with a potentially dangerous device, and a "device" that was probably equally dangerous, in another direction entirely.

"Now what?" he asked.

"Now we take this sucker back to my car to store as evidence," she said. "You carry it; you've got the gloves, and if there are any latent prints I don't want them messed up. I'd let you take it, but since you're a known activist, if anyone got probable cause to search you and your property—"

"Yeah." She was right, dammit. "Why not just leave it here for the cops to find?"

She tucked the medicine-pouch inside her jacket and dusted her hands off before answering him. "Because I'm afraid it won't be here in the morning," she finally said. "I'm afraid it's going to mysteriously disappear. It *was* meant for me. You just happened to fall over it."

He didn't quite snort at what he would have considered an outrageous statement a few hours ago. He simply amended it. "You, or anyone else who might have recognized it for what it was. There are supposed to be some O.U. people here, sooner or later. It would really look bad to blow one of them up."

She held one hand over the lump in her jacket where the medicine-pouch was, and nodded, slowly. "That's true, and I can't explain it, but I know it was meant for me. And I would probably have done just what you started to do if you hadn't gotten there first and sprung the trap. I wasn't looking for a trap like that."

He thought about the sudden avarice that had overcome him at the sight of the pouch, and his mouth went dry again. This was getting to be a lot more than he had bargained for.

She continued, gesturing for him to pick up the remains of the bomb. "I didn't even see the bomb until after I spotted you, and I—ah—let's just say I used medicine to find out who and what you were."

He let out his breath in a sigh, and shook his head. "If I say I'm confused—it's been a strange night." He gathered up the explosives and the rest of the component parts and followed her. Presumably she'd parked her truck somewhere nearby.

Strange night, hell. I've been figuring she was just pushing buttons, and here she is talking about and using Medicine like it was part of her. Maybe it is. . . .

"Yeah." That was all she said, but it sounded, if not conciliatory, at least a little less hostile.

Apologize, Spotted Horse. Get it over with.

He gritted his teeth, then unclenched his jaw, and calmed himself enough that the words wouldn't sound forced or false. "Jennie, I'm sorry. I've said a lot of stuff that was out of line. I think maybe we *are* on the same side. Maybe we ought to start at least talking a little more."

She made a little skeptical sound, but she didn't tell him to go jump a cactus. Finally, as they reached a looming shape that turned out to be her little Brat, she answered.

"Put that stuff on the floorboards and follow me home," she said, sounding more tired than brusque. "We need to talk."

CHAPTER ELEVEN

JENNIFER FINALLY SENT David back to his motel at about three in the morning, after she realized she had begun to repeat herself. Her eyes felt swollen, and they had begun to burn with fatigue—although Grandfather was still wide awake and perfectly prepared to sit in on the discussion if it carried on till dawn.

At least they were friends again—or as much friends as she, wary and watching, would permit. Grandfather had helped with that.

So had the fact that David had apologized.

David hinted he wouldn't mind staying; she ignored the hints. He gave her a mournful look as she opened the door for him—in the normal fashion this time. She blithely waved good-bye and shut the door as soon as he was on the sidewalk.

She rested her back against the door for a moment, then locked it, and walked back through the house to her bedroom, turning off lights as she went. Grandfather was already in his room; as she passed his door, light shone from the crack underneath it. Just as well; she wasn't up to any more deep discussions at the moment.

At least she and David had achieved a truce, if not precisely a reconciliation. And at this point, she wasn't certain she wanted a reconciliation, with all the emotional baggage that came with one. She wasn't even certain she wanted a relationship that *didn't* involve a reconciliation! It wasn't as if she didn't have her hands full.

Full in more ways than one. She still had the mundane investigation for the insurance company, a couple loose ends to wrap up for other clients, and her own private investigation of Calligan and the looting of the burial ground to deal with. The last thing she needed at the moment was David Spotted Horse on her doorstep.

Or in my bed.

Even if he had completely changed his ways, there were still certain demands to be met when one had a lover. . . .

She closed her bedroom door, and shook her head. "No," she said aloud. "I don't think so."

Not with what Grandfather had taken to his room to complicate an already complicated situation. David had turned the trap, bait and all, over to her with only minimal argument. The medicine-pouch was Osage, was from one of the plundered cairns, and there was no way to tell how it had gotten there, or even how long it had been there.

She had turned it over to Grandfather after determining where it had come from. Handling it was not her concern at the moment. There *was* another car in the back drive—it was Mooncrow's and he was a perfectly good driver. He could very easily take the pouch back and reinter it, if that was what was needed.

She shook her head, and went straight to bed, wondering if she would ever learn anything more than that.

Unfortunately, the bomb wasn't likely to tell her much of anything. The trigger had been a simple one, a trip wire. The explosives could be found at any construction site where blasting might be needed, including any of Calligan's. In the morning she would dust the bomb for prints, but even if she found them, unless the owner of said fingerprints had a criminal record, it wasn't likely she'd find a match. Her request for a match check would go into a long queue of other similar requests from private agents—which had a lower priority than the requests from law-enforcement agencies. So even if she found prints and the bombmaker did have a criminal record, she might never get an ID until after the case was solved or something forced her off of it.

Mooncrow couldn't make anything more of the pouch than she could, except to assure her that although Watches-Over-The-Land had made it, it had not belonged to him. In a way that was both reassuring and disappointing. It would have been good to recover at least one of her ancestor's looted possessions, but she wasn't certain she had whatever it took to handle something once belonging to a shaman as powerful as her forefather had been.

In the end, when she looked at the clock in her headboard and saw the time, she realized that all she was going to do now was think in circles. Almost four in the morning, and she knew very well she was completely exhausted. She stripped and climbed into bed; but once she turned off the lights, she stared up at the ceiling, unable to go to sleep.

Well, I can force myself, she thought. *I can make myself relax if I want to. But do I want to? Obviously there's still something bothering my subconscious. I suppose if I don't deal with it, it'll be showing up in my dreams. I sure as hell don't need that.*

It wasn't hard to figure out what that something was. *David Spotted Horse, that's what.* He'd come back like the proverbial tomcat.

Though tonight he'd probably lost one of his nine lives from fright alone. He'd had a good scare thrown into him by the Little People. . . .

But now that she thought about it, she wasn't entirely certain that he had been in real danger after she knocked him on his ass. A scare might have been all they intended after that moment. They were so unpredictable; they were perfectly capable of changing their minds within a few seconds.

They're almost as contrary as Mooncrow. Hard to tell what they intend from one moment to the next. Certainly the leader had been willing to listen to her, and although he had given in, it had been without much of a protest, much less a fight. Was that due to the effectiveness of her protections, to her own ability, or to the fact that they had decided not to bother with David anymore and accept that she was protecting him? There was no way to tell besides asking them, and no guarantee that they'd tell the truth if she did.

Oh, if David had managed to get himself killed, they'd have taken him, all right. He fit right into the category of "those condemned to roam the earth, out of the sight of *Wah-K'on-Tah*." There wouldn't have been enough *left* of him to paint if the bomb had gone off in his face; he'd have been lawful prey. Messing with stolen Osage relics, dying without paint, being buried without paint—she had the feeling they'd have had him even if he'd been white.

Granted, he was a Cherokee, and normally Osage of her forefather's time hadn't much use for the Thing-On-Its-Head People, but these were *mi-ah-luschka*, and they were a law unto themselves. It didn't take much to wind up swelling their ranks, if they decided to take you.

But after she had saved him from blowing himself to bloody bits, and had confronted them, they had truly seemed less angry than resigned. There hadn't even been any serious argument when she claimed David was already under her protection and implied that he was acting on her behalf.

They *did* make certain he saw every single one of them, though, and they took a great deal of glee in his obvious fear. It was probably the first time he had Seen something not of the physical world, but of the Medicine world, at least as an adult. It had obviously come as quite a shock. And she had to admit, she had taken just as much enjoyment in his fear as the Little People had.

Maybe they knew that; maybe that was why they hadn't given her much of a fight.

So now he was a believer—in the Little People, at least. And she *thought* he might have seen her two spirit-echoes as well, her Medicine Woman-self and her Kestrel-self. The way he kept giving her strange looks when he thought she wasn't watching was proof enough that he had seen something odd about her.

Grandfather had hinted obliquely at something of the kind, and David had gotten a queasy look. David hadn't wanted to believe. He was one of those for whom the old legends were wonderful, but hardly applicable to modern times.

Odd. *She* should have been the one with that attitude. She was the one living in the Heavy Eyebrows' world, making her living their way. She was the one who actually fit into that world, at least outwardly. He was the activist, the rebel, who wanted at least a partial return to the Old Ways.

But that wasn't the oddest thing she'd had to deal with lately. On the face of it, she was as contrary as Mooncrow. . . .

At least David's experiences had made him a lot more tractable when it came to persuading him that there was a lot more going on with this situation than what appeared on the surface.

After talking with him for four hours, she had to concede that he had changed some over the years. He wasn't as much of a chauvinistic brat as he had been. He wasn't as narrow-minded as she'd assumed, either. He still wasn't going to win the Nobel Peace Prize by any means, but he wasn't as bad as he had been; he could compromise; he could be flexible when he chose.

He might even be a useful ally in this mess. He could go places she couldn't, and Calligan's men were already talking to him. She could get information back to them. He could be *very* useful, really.

She grimaced into the darkness. *Face it, Jennie, you want more than an ally. You really didn't want to send him off to his motel tonight . . . not when there's a nice bed in here, quite big enough for two.*

Well, she had wanted to send him away, and at the same time, she hadn't. She had—because it gave her a lot of satisfaction to prove to him that not only was he not the hot stud he thought he was, but she could resist his blandishments with ridiculous ease. As good-looking as he was, he probably had no problem getting all the women he wanted. He wasn't used to being turned down, particularly not by a woman he thought was already "broke to his saddle." The brief look of incredulous shock as she closed the door had been worth it.

The trouble was, she had to admit to herself that it had been very difficult to resist him. It would have been nice to be able to say that she was going to sleep tonight without any desires more carnal than a yearning for a bowl of the chocolate-fudge-brownie ice cream in the freezer—but not even a bowl of ice cream was going to make her forget the way the lamplight gleamed on his hair, or the broad shoulders under that black turtleneck, or the warmth in his eyes when he looked at her. Ice cream was no substitute for what she really craved.

Nope. You're not a pushover, Talldeer, but you're really going to have to watch your step with him. It would have been all too easy to suggest he spend the night instead of driving back across town. And then it would have been even easier to suggest that he save his money and move in with her until—

Until what? He didn't have any particular place he called

"home," he'd made that very clear. His folks were uncomfortable with his kind of activism, and he was doing his best to keep them out of it by keeping clear of them. He had no regular job, and everything he owned fit in the trunk of his car. So why should he move out again once he'd moved in?

Oh no. That was too easy a trap to fall into. And it was a mistake she didn't intend to make. *If* David Spotted Horse moved back into her life, he'd better be prepared to take her as an equal.

And he'd better get a clean bill of health before he does it. I don't know where he's been—and I wouldn't even take Mooncrow's word on the subject of HIV without a test. So there.

And *she* would want to be certain that he understood all the rules as clearly as she did before anything got any further than "colleague."

Still. . . .

David—my equal? In Medicine matters, he isn't even in the running! she scolded herself. *He hasn't even got both feet on the path yet! Oh no, if I get involved with him again, he had better have it clear that in Medicine, if I say something, I'm the expert. And in P.I. work, too. Maybe he knows the legal system better than I do, but I have my own areas of expertise. He has got to understand that and accept it.*

And all the veiled compliments and broad shoulders in the world weren't going to change that.

Still. . . .

Finally her libido decided it wasn't going to win the argument with her brain and gave up, and she got to sleep.

Calligan had hoped to be called to the mall site by the police some time during the night. He was certain his trap would be sprung, and the explosion would wake up everyone within a mile of the river. When the alarm went off without an emergency call, he woke feeling vaguely disappointed.

He'd been so positive that the Talldeer girl would take the bait. He'd never been so certain of anything in his life.

Well, if not tonight, then maybe tomorrow, he told himself. *She can't stay away forever, and she can't resist an artifact. I left the thing right where anyone prowling would be certain to see it—and she would have been looking for exactly that kind of object. She just didn't show up, that's all. No big problem; she won't stay away forever. Probably she's making certain I don't have a night guard on the site. I'll get her when she finally does show.*

So even though his wife seemed a bit jumpy this morning, he ignored her nerves. She hadn't slept well for the past several nights, and he couldn't get her to take a pill. Maybe he ought to tell her to go to the doctor . . . except that her restlessness hadn't disturbed his sleep any.

No, no point in making her see a doctor. Doctor visits were expensive, especially for things as intangible as "nerves." It was probably just hormones anyway. Women were slaves to their bodies, and half the time he thought they enjoyed it that way. It gave them excuses to become hysterical.

He ignored the slight shaking of her hands and the dark circles under her eyes. If he ignored this nonsense, she'd probably drop it. No point in reinforcing bad behavior by giving her attention for it.

He timed his arrival at the site so that he got there a good fifteen minutes before any of the men would. That would give him enough time to dismantle the trap and hide it away before anyone got there and became curious. He'd thought about leaving it in place—but some fool was only too likely to spot the pouch and try to pick it up. Or worse than a fool, a kid, messing around where he shouldn't be.

No, it was better to get rid of it during the day. He could hide the whole setup easily enough, then put it back after everyone was gone. That wouldn't be hard; the men left the site at quitting time fast, the goldbrickers. Not a minute of unpaid overtime on *their* sheets.

But when he got to the roped-off area and looked down, he got a severe jolt.

The pouch was gone. So was the bomb. Not buried, as he thought in his first burst of incredulous thought, but completely gone.

The first thing he thought of was that some stupid critter had decided to mess with it. He looked for signs of animal tracks or other disturbances, certain that something must have carried the trap off somewhere. How an animal would have done that without being blown to bits, he had no idea—but mice carried bait off out of traps all the time without springing them, and maybe a possum or raccoon had found the pouch and carried the pouch and explosives off. Maybe a dog had gone after it. Maybe a cat thought it looked tasty.

Nothing. Only the signs of enough digging to free the tripwire and bomb, and footprints of common sneakers all around.

His next indignant thought was—*They stole it! The bastards stole it! I'm calling the—*

Calling who? The cops? And do what, report that an illegal booby trap baited with stolen artifacts had, in turn, been stolen? Oh, that would be just brilliant.

Now he was glad he'd set the thing up wearing gloves. If Talldeer had taken it—

Well of course she took the pouch; who else would have? But how in hell did she know it was wired? He was absolutely furious; his neck and face burned for a moment with rage. How had she known? And how dared she *take* his trap *and* bait?

Another thought occurred to him, then, as he stared at the place where the bomb had been. If she had found it, she must want to know who had set it. So far, he thought he had managed to keep his trail clean. The cops didn't consider him enough of a suspect to watch. But what about Talldeer?

Could she be watching now?

He got to his feet and dusted his hands off, then moved to another area of the roped-off section, trying to look as if he were checking the entire corner for artifacts that might have turned up as the soil settled or something. He even brushed at the surface a bit, as if he were looking for something. The coarse, sandy soil came apart as he touched it, breaking down into dust. He'd have a hell of a time getting the stuff off his pants.

At least she wouldn't be getting any prints off the pouch or the bomb. While he didn't exactly have a criminal record, he didn't want to take a chance on finding out his prints were on file somewhere. The government had files on everybody, and with all the computers around these days they were probably doing searches via computer. There was always a chance someone, somewhere, in some law-enforcement agency, had filed a set of his prints away. Hell, the local cops might even have them. They'd certainly taken a set of prints after they'd dusted the remains of the dozer after the explosion. Would she get access to that file? She might, if she had friends in the department.

After taking his time with his bogus examination, he rose to his feet, brushed as much of the dust off his pants as he could, and finally headed back to the site office as the first of the men arrived, lunchpails in hand. He nodded to them as they came in, just enough that they knew he recognized them, not enough to encourage familiarity.

He retired to his office and sat down at his desk; drumming his fingers restlessly on the blotter, he watched the men arrive, and listened to the phone ring in the secretary's room. She was certainly fielding a lot of calls this morning.

He was annoyed, to say the least. The Talldeer bitch was smarter than he had given her credit for. And what was she going to do with his little surprise? Obviously she was smart enough to disarm it and then take it away, presumably to check for prints. Was she smart enough to realize that it could be used as evidence without prints on it? He hoped not. . . .

Or did she take it because she thought some of her own people might have set it, and she didn't want to leave any more evidence of sabotage for the law to find?

Or did she take it just so that he couldn't reset it with more bait and a better hiding place? Like the mice taking the cheese and then running off with the trap so it couldn't be used again?

Hard to say. But whichever it was, he would have to work to see that she didn't suspect *him*. He had feelers out, and none of the information he was getting made him think that the cops thought of him as a likely suspect. He had to see to it that Talldeer eliminated him from her list, too.

The secretary tapped timidly on his door, jarring his concentration.

"Come in," he said, wondering what the problem could be this early in the day. And a little irritated with the secretary as well. Why did she have to slink around like a timid little chipmunk?

"Mr. Calligan, sir," she said, with an air of someone who was bearing bad news. "Almost half the men have called in sick. They all say they're having dizzy spells and their doctors told them not to operate heavy machinery while they're dizzy." She paused a moment, then added, worriedly, "they don't know when they'll be back; their doctors all want to run tests. This is definitely going to put off the completion deadline, sir."

"I understand that," he snapped, as if he were angry, glad to finally have *one* legitimate outlet for his irritation. "I'll deal with it. You put an ad in the paper, then contact the state employment service and see if you can get me some replacements. We need them now! If those goldbricks think they can coast and find their jobs waiting for them, they're going to get a big surprise. And they'd better not file for workman's comp, either!"

She wouldn't find any experienced men, of course. After all the "bad luck" that had been hitting this project, only a fool would risk himself or his machinery.

Of course, if she did come up with anyone, he'd find something wrong with most of them. He'd be conducting the interviews and making the hiring decisions himself.

But she didn't know that he would be rejecting everyone she found, of course. She winced away from his obvious anger, and retreated back to the safety of her own little cubicle hastily, leaving him alone behind his closed door.

She would have been very surprised to see that he was smiling a moment later.

So, the plan was working. The little "accidents" he had arranged continued to mount up. Although—he frowned—there were some things happening that he *hadn't* arranged. Things that had no business occurring, like those sinkholes opening up under equipment. It was almost as though there really was a curse at work.

No, that was stupid thinking. Shit happened. Sinkholes opened up all the time, and possums would eat almost anything. Especially if it was greasy. No big deal.

Now the workers were calling in sick, and some of them were staying off the job. He would have to put in some extra work to make certain the roster stayed empty, and at the same time put up a convincing show of trying to replace the men gone absent. It would take a lot of time, going through the motions in order to keep his tracks covered, but with any luck the time of year would work for him. This late in the building season, virtually every heavy-equipment operator was booked for the rest of the year. Those who couldn't make a living here had moved on to other climes. Surely he could find a way to disqualify everyone who applied—

He pulled the medicine-pouch out of his pocket and stroked it, then grinned as the perfect answer occurred to him. Easy enough—just get into the records at night and change the phone numbers of those who applied! Then when Shirley gave them their callback, she'd get wrong numbers, no-answers, or disconnected messages.

And if the workers attributed *that* to the curse as well, who cared? It would only reinforce what he wanted.

That would put the project into a delay—delays would continue to mount, until it was at least a year behind schedule. That shouldn't take long; with half the workers already gone, he had doubled the time it would take to complete this thing—if it even could be completed. If anyone from O.U. ever did get down here, that in itself might shut the project down while they sifted dirt in search of nonexistent artifacts.

Then, as things looked to be at their worst, he would set fire to the office one night. Within a month or two he would be able to declare bankruptcy. And with no records left to betray where the money had all gone, he would walk out of there completely clean. The Indians would get the blame for everything, from setting the fires and explosions to breaking the back of the company by walking out on the job. The local economy was in piss-poor shape; that wouldn't win them any friends in the media. Two birds with one stone—and no one would be likely to be sympathetic to complaints about curses and other superstitious bull when a multimillion-dollar project had just gone belly-up. People were far more likely to figure statements like that to be half-assed excuses than anything worth a moment of time and consideration.

And his good buddy at the insurance company would pocket his slice of the pie, and pass Calligan's share on to him.

A foolproof scheme. All he had to do was to stay cool, keep his brains about him, and get rid of the Talldeer woman. Permanent would be best, but it was a dangerous goal, now that his initial trap had been sprung. He didn't think she suspected him, but if he made any more blatant attempts at taking her out, the chances of her putting him on her list increased with every try. There was no telling what she'd told her boss by now. He had to make certain she took a fall, and that the blame fell on her own people. Then he could spread some rumors that it had been to silence her, that she had been on the verge of discovering an Indian gang out here; one selling peyote and other drugs to guys on the construction crews.

Yeah, that would work. He'd get her and the people she was trying to protect, all at once.

Now that was a sweet scenario . . . and it was one he could even put into motion now.

His hand went to the desk in front of him, and he stroked the old medicine-bundle while he thought things through. Maybe it was already time to plant some of those rumors.

He picked up the phone and dialed a particular regional talk-show host who was known for his flamboyant, near-yellow journalism and his willingness to say anything about anyone so long as it was bad. One also known for being something of a bigoted jerk, as well, who'd made his feelings known quite strongly on the subject of Indian activism and Indian-run high-stakes bingo and other gambling. He was no friend to the red man, and that would put him right where Calligan wanted him.

The rumors would be flying soon. They might even spur some legitimate news investigations. That would make things difficult for the Talldeer woman and whoever was egging his workers on. *Now we'll see who the smart one is. . . .*

"Hi, is this Bob Anger? This is Rod Calligan of Calligan Construction. I've got a story you might be interested in. . . ."

Now, at last, days too late so far as she was concerned, Jennifer was able to talk freely with Calligan's ex-workers. As important to her investigation as the ones who actually saw something when the dozer went up were the ones who had been involved in other "accidents." Not in the least because not all of those accidents had the flavor of the Little People about them.

Now that she had seen them, she honestly didn't think this band of *mi-ah-luschka* was capable of setting explosives or sabotaging hydraulics. For all that they were powerful spirits, as far as she knew, they were limited in what they could do to *what they understood*. And that was important to her investigation.

There wasn't a one of those she had seen who was even familiar with a muzzle-loader, much less a bulldozer. Most of them came from the time of Watches-Over-The-Land and before. They could understand that the heavy machinery was a threat, and cunningly dig pit traps for it to fall into, just as they had dug pit traps for wapiti and even the occasional bison when they had been among the living. They could *not* understand that pouring sand into hydraulic fluid reservoirs would ruin a vital part of the machinery. They saw that the men on the site guarded and valued the dynamite sticks in the shed—which were only sticks to them. They knew that possums would eat anything, particularly if one poured bear fat over it. They would not understand that those sticks could be made to release lightning and thunder.

Not that they were stupid, and she suspected if anyone ever was around them·long enough to teach them the ways of the modern world, they would be more of a menace than even she could dream. But they were facing something completely alien to the world in which they had lived and died, and faced with the alien, they could only improvise with what they themselves knew.

So the questions remained; who had raided the burial hill and cached the relics here? Who had sabotaged the dozer? Who was continuing to sabotage the site? And who had set the trap that had so nearly caught David?

Most of all—were all these acts done by the same hands?

She had to report back to Sleighbow at Romulus that if there had been any threats against Calligan or the site before the explosion, none of his men had ever heard about it. So in that much Calligan was clear.

She had no doubt that the man was a snake; the stories her mother conveyed from other realtors made that perfectly clear. If she looked long and hard enough, she would probably find *some* way in which he had deceived Romulus. She needed a reason to continue to stay on the case, one that would continue to supply a paycheck, and one that would let her pursue the answer to her questions.

It was time to call Sleighbow and establish that reason. David himself was in her office when she made that call, so that he could see and hear just where her loyalties were with his own eyes and ears.

She put it on speakerphone so he could hear both sides of the conversation.

"Mr. Sleighbow," she said as soon as she had identified herself and what he had asked her to investigate, "I have to be up front with you. There are more unanswered questions than answered ones with Calligan so far as I'm concerned, but the job you asked me to do is finished. I can't find any evidence of any threats to Calligan and his property prior to the explosion. Whatever else is going on, he did not deceive Romulus in that regard."

David looked blank. He obviously could not see where her statement was leading.

"Oh?" There was a long pause. "I find your phrasing interesting, Miss Talldeer. Do you have any reason to think Rod Calligan has attempted to deceive Romulus Insurance in any other way?"

She sighed, as David frowned, and she made an abrupt gesture to him to warn him to be silent. "Let me just say this much, Mr. Sleighbow. The information I have leads me to think that Mr. Calligan is less than ethical in his business practices. He is continuing to suffer accidents—some appear to be outright sabotage, and some simply *seem* to have no possible natural explanation. It may be that he has some business rival that he has annoyed, or some less-than-legal associates that he has angered, and he is attempting to cover their retribution up by claiming that it is all the work of Native American and ecology groups. I am not going to attempt to guess what kind of policy he took out with you, but I suspect that such a situation would not be covered, especially if he deliberately concealed illegal activities and associates."

"You are quite right, Miss Talldeer," Sleighbow replied, his voice even and betraying no emotion. "And those are interesting speculations."

"They're only speculations, sir," she said warningly, making a hushing motion at David, since he looked ready to jump in again. "I have not found any evidence to indicate anything of the sort. All I *have* found is that he is considered to be less than ethical by his peers, and that there do not appear to have been any terrorist-type threats prior to the explosion. Other than that, I can only say that while I have not actually met the man, the things I have uncovered would make me unlikely to use his services even if he were the only contractor in the three-state area. I certainly would not recommend him to anyone else. My personal feelings are that a man like that collects enemies, and a man like that may well have been involved with some kind of organized crime figure at some time. But that is strictly a personal feeling and I have no facts to justify it. And I will admit to a slight prejudice against him because he seems to be attempting to make Native Americans into scapegoats for what has been happening to him."

There was a moment of silence, punctuated by the ticking of someone using a keyboard. "I respect and appreciate your candor, Miss Talldeer," Sleighbow said at last. "And I also respect the 'hunches' of a private investigator with some experience. 'Hunches' seldom prove to be as mystical as most people think." The keyboard clicks returned. "I've noted your observations. If you have no objection, I would like to authorize you to continue to investigate. However, in light of the fact that there have been more 'accidents' and that you yourself said that you are not Nancy Drew, you may feel free to withdraw, and I will find another investigator to take up where you left off."

David was practically bursting out of his chair, but he kept quiet, at least. Jennifer pretended to give the matter a moment of thought, although her answer was a foregone conclusion. "I would like to continue, sir," she said. "I hate to leave something half done."

"Good." A few more clicks signaled a few more keystrokes. Jennifer was now certain that he was recording this interview and adding it to the records. "You're on indefinite retainer. I respect your honesty enough to be certain you will tell me when you feel your investigation has come to an end. Two suggestions, please. Don't hesitate to call me if you feel you are in over your head. I'll see to it that you are fairly compensated. And if you do uncover some kind of criminal activity, please report it not only to me but to your local police and the state's attorney general."

"Yes, sir," she promised, with some satisfaction. Sleighbow hung up then, and she took the phone off "speaker" mode.

David practically exploded. "What were you *doing*?" he shouted. "I thought you were—"

"Didn't I just, truthfully, manage to get the suspicion away from the Rights Movement?" she interrupted.

"Yes," he said, after a moment. "But what was all that crap about organized crime?"

"Complete truth, just not *all* the truth." She leaned back in her chair and regarded him through narrowed eyes. "Calligan is the kind of man who might be involved with criminals, even organized crime. I said I didn't have any evidence. Sleighbow just gave me carte blanche to go look for some.

So now I have a legitimate reason to continue poking around Calligan Construction. I could hardly mention that I'd seen the Little People while I was poking around Calligan's site illegally."

David subsided. "I guess not," he said, reluctantly. "But I don't see why you couldn't do what you want."

She shrugged. "I have to have a reason for staying on Calligan's back if the cops ask," she pointed out. "My own personal curiosity doesn't count, and since I'm Indian it *could* be taken as harassment, and that's illegal. I've got plenty of evidence that no protest group *threatened* Calligan—now I have to prove that there weren't threats from sources he wouldn't report. It's still work, David, and it's work I can do while I'm checking up on other things." She stared up at the ceiling for a moment. "You know," she said, half to herself, "I'd kind of like to find something to nail Calligan to the wall. If half of what I've heard about him is true, he's long overdue to be nailed. I suspect him of being behind Bob Anger's broadcast this morning."

David looked blank. "Who?"

She blinked, and focused on him again. "You mean you haven't—oh, that's right, you haven't lived here for a while. Local talk-show host, makes Rush Limbaugh look like a Franciscan monk. The only reason he hasn't been sued is because the people he insults are either too poor to sue, or he doesn't name names when they have the money for lawyers." She reached into her drawer for the padded envelope that had come by messenger from the office of the Principal Chief of the Cherokee Nation, pulled the cassette out of the envelope, and stuck it in her cassette deck. "This was the broadcast this morning."

She watched David's face as he listened, his expressions running the entire gamut from incredulous, to disgusted, to angry . . . trying to guess the moment when he would go ballistic.

She was a little off. Before he could explode, she snapped the recorder off.

"There's more where that came from," she offered. "About another forty-five minutes' worth. Where are you going?" she added, as he launched himself for the door.

"I'm going to do something about that—"

"Wilma Mankiller's office is already handling it," she said, cutting him off. The news that the Principal Chief of the Cherokees was already involved stopped him with his hand on the door. "They sent me a copy of the tape, since I passed the word that I'm on the case to her office. I told them when Sleighbow hired me, just on the off chance that anyone in Cherokee Nation had anything useful to tell me that I hadn't already heard on my own."

"Oh yeah?" he said, still poised to go out. "And just what are they doing about it? That bigoted jerkoff, I mean."

"Ignoring it," she replied blandly. "And him."

"What?" He stared.

"Think about it, David," she said impatiently. "This idiot is only looking for publicity. Anything any Indian says or does about this is just going to give him more of what he wants. A *few* of the media press went over to Wilma's office this morning for her comments. Fortunately, she had a good zinger waiting for them. She simply looked at them and said, 'I thought you guys were here for the real news,' and gave them press releases about the improvements to the Tribal Police system."

"She's got to be doing more than that!" David cried.

Jennifer shrugged. "Why?" she responded. "This guy is nothing, David. The only people who believe him are people we'd never touch anyway—people who not only don't have a clue, they couldn't buy one if you gave them a roll of quarters. We've got a real problem to deal with. Let Wilma handle Bob Anger. If he keeps it up, she'll find a way to get him put down. Probably," she added thoughtfully, "by convincing the 'Morning Zoo' DJs to turn both barrels on him.

What they did to Oral Roberts is nothing compared to what they can do to him."

David shook his head, but returned to his chair. Jennifer went back to her list, crossing off "Call Sleighbow."

"You know," she said after a moment, "this business with Bob Anger—"

David looked at her hopefully. "We should do something about him?"

She shook her head violently. "God, no! No, now that I think about it—it smells like a trap. As much of a trap as that medicine-pouch was. We were meant to lock horns with Anger—to give his accusations some legitimacy."

He frowned at her. "Yeah? What makes you say that?"

"The timing, mostly." She ignored his growing scorn and took out the cassette tape to stare at it, as if by doing so she could make it give up its secrets. "Someone is getting nervous. Someone knows that you and I are working together, now. That someone is the person who tipped Anger off." She glanced at him sharply. "And before you ask, no, it isn't 'just a hunch.' It's my own trained deduction combined with Medicine skills. I sense the hand of The Enemy here, and threat from the West, the country of war and death. Here—" She held up the cassette and shook it for emphasis. "I see a false war-trail here; The Enemy has gone elsewhere. If we follow the bluff, we will lose him."

David shrank back a little in his chair, acutely uncomfortable. "Well . . . if you say so. . . ."

"I do," she told him firmly.

He sighed, and although she could see that he was struggling against a sharp retort, he kept his mouth shut. "All right," he said after a moment. "What's the plan?"

"Oh, your favorite." She pulled out a list, and he groaned. "Legwork, legwork, legwork," she said sweetly, and handed him his half of the list.

* * *

Jennifer leaned over the table at Ken's Pizza and batted her eyelashes flirtatiously at the plainclothes officer across from her. He batted his eyes right back at her, then wiped his mouth with a napkin.

"So, Jen, what is it you want out of me this time?" he asked. "You never buy me lunch unless you want something."

"Moi?" she exclaimed in mock-horror. "Want something? Why, Wild Bill, I am *crushed*! How could you say something like that? Can't an honest citizen buy lunch for one of Tulsa's finest without *wanting* something?"

"Not when they're you, they can't." But "Wild Bill" Cody, a casual friend of Jennifer's who'd recently been promoted to the Detective Unit, didn't look or sound as if he was unhappy about the situation, so Jennifer decided to continue pursuing the intention that had led her to meet Cody at headquarters and invite him to lunch.

She pouted. "You eat my pizza, you drink my soda, then you make terrible accusations that I'm *bribing* you."

"Statements, not accusations," he retorted. "And the Three-Ninety-Five all-you-can-eat Lunch Buffet is below the five-dollar limit that constitutes a bribe, as you are well aware. So what do you want? I don't fix tickets and I don't give out confidential information."

"I *know* that," she said with annoyance. "All I want is office gossip. You used to be in Fraud. What's the word on Rod Calligan?"

"Current or history? Never mind, both, I know." He took a long pull on his cola, and the ice clicked against the plastic when he put it down. "History is, Fraud has him on the list of people who might go over the line some day. You know, people who have enough complaints against them that we figure it's worth watching them in case their companies get in trouble and they start looking for creative ways to finance things? But you *also* know that list—"

"Is real long." She nodded. "That's the way it is around

here. A lot of people skate on thin ice but never fall in. Any hint he's ever been involved in the illegal artifact business?"

Wild Bill shook his head vigorously. "Nothing but the usual contractor-type stuff. But that's where the current gossip comes in. There are a lot of people looking *really* closely at this explosion of his. Could be what he says it is. Profile from the FBI says it also fits with someone who's trying an insurance scam. So we're stalling. Other thing is, normally when there's real terrorists involved in a bombing, *someone* slips up. Leaves fingerprints, or something that can be traced back to them, or—more often than not— somebody *has* to boast about what he did. Whoever set this one is either real lucky or real slick, and terrorists don't fit that profile."

She nodded, wryly. "Uh-huh. They're too busy being passionate and idealistic to be slick. Gotcha. So?"

"So we're being *real* careful. And Calligan is being a real pain, because we haven't arrested anybody." Cody played with his glass. "He doesn't bug the department about it— but every time somebody comes around to ask him a couple more questions, he *always* brings it up, real resentful." The officer gave her a look from under his bushy eyebrows. "That's off the record. Anything else is confidential."

"No problem." She picked up the check, and fished a ten out of her purse to cover it, handed both bills to a passing waitress, and waved away change. Cody rose, and so did Jennifer.

"That's all you wanted?" He seemed mildly surprised.

"That's all," she said cheerfully. "Painless, wasn't it?"

"Wish my dentist was that painless." He grinned broadly. "Make sure you call me next time you need office gossip. I can always use a free lunch."

"And I can always use a friendly face. Don't get into any trouble, Cody," she said, as they parted at the door. "And don't forget what my grandfather always says."

"What's that?" he asked, pausing for just a moment.

"Don't believe everything you hear." She arched her eyebrows significantly. "At least when it comes from the mouths of guys you have on lists."

He "fired" a finger at her. "Gotcha, Jen. Be seein' you!"

She laughed. "Next time you need a free lunch!"

CHAPTER TWELVE

So, ANOTHER DAY like the past six. Same song, different verse. David glared at the neat little scrap of paper—torn off as precisely as if it had been cut—and shoved it into his pocket. *Legwork. Right.* Jennie was awfully fond of sending him off chasing things, and half the time he thought it was just to get him out of her hair.

He wasn't used to being ordered around by a woman, much less by one who used to be his girlfriend. It was kind of hard to take.

But Jennie just wasn't the same girl he knew back in college—she was so serious all the time. Businesslike, imper- sonal. Hardly ever smiled, for one thing, much less laughed. Except when she was trying to get his goat, being sarcastic, or trying to give him a hard time. She always had some kind of smart answer, too.

And she didn't fit his idea of a real woman anymore, not with that cool, emotionless attitude of hers. Like she'd been taking lessons from Mr. Spock or something. Not a hint that they had ever been close.

She dressed so damned aggressively, in jeans, leather jackets, boots—or really severely tailored suits—no make-up, no jewelry, nothing feminine. She was obviously used to doing everything herself; even when he offered to drive her somewhere, she declined. Too damned independent, that was what it was. She wouldn't give up control for anyone or anything.

He'd *tried* making suggestions about this case; mostly she didn't even give him an argument. Instead, she just ignored them, acted as if he hadn't even said anything.

That was bad enough; he was used to people listening to him, and asking for directions. He didn't like being ignored. But what was the most humiliating was that when he'd gone ahead and followed through with his own ideas himself, what he'd tried had usually backfired on him. Like two days ago, when he'd tried to tail Calligan's new foreman, the guy who'd moved up from assistant after the first foreman went up with the dozer. . . .

He'd figured the foreman probably knew something, and tailing him seemed like a good idea. After all, no one on the whole crew had a better opportunity to plant something like a bomb than the foreman or the foreman's assistant. The man had spotted him, and had tried to lose him. Stupidly, he'd tried to keep up. That was when the foreman picked up his cellular phone and called the cops.

Too late, he'd seen the man talking on the handset and looking back at him. That was when David figured out what had just happened and had tried to get away.

At that point, the foreman had turned the tables on him and had started tailing *him*, keeping up a running cellular report as he did so.

The end of that story was inevitable. The cops had pulled him over, and he'd spent the rest of the afternoon at the station while they checked all fifty states for any outstanding warrants on him, even parking tickets. They didn't find any, but when they came back now and again to check on him, their file folder with his name on it kept getting thicker and thicker. He figured that before the afternoon was over, he'd cost them a couple hundred bucks in fax charges.

They couldn't hold him forever without charging him with something, but they could keep him for twenty-four hours at least, and they didn't have to make his stay comfortable. And they had the right to question him every time a new addition to his file came in. He could have shut up and demanded an attorney, but he figured that would only make things worse. They knew he was an activist by now, and for all he knew, Oklahoma had a "stalker" law he could be charged under. Or they could try and hold him on suspicion in the Calligan sabotage.

So he chose the appearance of cooperation. His story, made up out of desperation, was that he was trying to see if the foreman was the source of the anti-Indian stories in some of the papers. He *knew* what Jennie would have done to him if he had dared to drag her name in. Finally they let him go with a warning that any more incidents would leave him open to harassment charges, and that Oklahoma did indeed have a "stalker" law he could be prosecuted under. But now he was "red-flagged," and he was pretty sure they had that full file on him just waiting for the moment he did something else stupid.

He hadn't told Jennie about the incident. He knew what she'd say, and he wasn't in the mood for "I told you so." He hadn't tried anything that might get him the attention of the Tulsa cops again.

Whenever he suggested she might act along the lines of working Medicine, she just gave him an opaque look. He hadn't dared follow his own suggestions along those lines; for one thing, he didn't even know where to begin, and for another, even if he did, after his one and only experience with the Little People, he wasn't too eager to have anything more to do with the Spirits.

This list she had given him now—it was all perfectly ordinary stuff. Finding out if any Osage artifacts had been offered to any of the local galleries, antique stores, or collectors in the last six months. Tracking down everyone who was licensed to handle explosives in this area. Finding out everyone in the area who could be considered an expert on Osage culture who *wasn't* Osage. Interviewing all the men on Calligan's construction crew to find out if they had seen any person or vehicle hanging around the site a great deal, either before or after the explosion.

It looked like make-work, or something to keep him occupied while Jennie did all the important things. He resented that, but he didn't dare make the accusation that she was sloughing him off.

Why?

Because she had scared him, *that* was why! He had to admit that as well, and he resented both the fact and having to admit it.

She waited patiently for him to say something. He sighed with disgust.

"Isn't this more along your line?" he asked, patronizingly. "You could do most of this on the phone—"

"I could if I had the time, which I don't," she replied, imitating his tone perfectly. "If I could afford a secretary, it would be his job. Since there are things to do that only *I* can get way with, like trading information with the cops, you're going to have to do the other stuff if you want to get anything accomplished. It's a fair distribution of effort. I have other cases to work on, David—I have to make a living. No P.I. of my small-time stature works full-time on anything. You have the time I don't to do this kind of thing."

He came very close to wincing when she mentioned the cops, and he hoped she didn't notice. Or had she somehow found out about that little run-in he'd had? Was she rubbing it in?

It would be just like her, he thought sourly. Every time he tried to get into the dominant position with her, she just put him right back down again—and he had no doubt that if she *had* learned about the humiliating episode, she was saving it for later use.

"One of the guys called me this morning," he said, after a moment. "He got his buddy Paul Fry to keep *him* posted on what's going down out at the site. Calligan is trying to replace all the guys calling in 'sick,' but it seems like everybody who shows up for an interview is either an alkie or a fake."

"A fake?" Jennie looked up from frantically scribbling something on a pad by the phone. "What do you mean by 'a fake'?"

He straightened a little, pleased to have some knowledge *she* didn't have. "According to Fry, all the ones that have gotten callbacks turn out to have given bad phone numbers. Either the numbers have been disconnected, don't exist, or no one on the other end ever heard of the guy who interviewed."

Jennie tapped her eraser on the desktop in a curious and rhythmic pattern for a moment. "Doesn't that strike you as odd?" she finally asked.

He made a noncommittal sound. "I don't know. I know Billy said it was another sign of the curse on Calligan."

Jennie tossed her head, so that her hair whipped over her shoulder, and snorted. "Right. I don't think so. Not unless that particular lot of *mi-ah-luschka* has learned how to work the phone system. It takes a lot of power to fake out the phone lines, and a lot more knowledge that I don't think they have."

She didn't add *and I should know,* but she might just as well have. Both the authoritative tone of her voice and the fact that she mentioned it could be done at all confirmed his hunch that she *had* somehow messed with the phone system when he had tried to call her to chew her out.

And a little cold chill ran up his spine for a moment or

two. A Medicine Woman powerful enough to mess with the phone system—what did that take, anyway? Was there anything she couldn't do? Or—

He caught himself up sharply. *Dammit! She did it to me again!*

"So what *do* you think is happening?" he asked.

"My best guess is that someone might just be sending ringers over to Calligan to keep him from filling those slots." She gave him a sharp look. "That 'someone' wouldn't be you, would it?"

He brought his head up indignantly. "Me? Why the hell would I do something like that?"

"To keep Calligan from filling those slots," she said, logically. "Those are jobs theoretically being taken away from Indians. It would be a good way to preserve them until our guys came off the sick list."

"Oh." Damn, he wished he *had* thought of that one! "No, it isn't me."

"Then maybe I ought to find out if there really is a plot, because I don't think the Little People are behind this one."

"Neither do I," he told her—and actually, that did agree with the feeling he'd gotten when Billy told him this morning. He was beginning to get a feel for which incidents were caused by the *mi-ah-luschka* and which by purely human hands.

Not that the "feeling" made him any more comfortable. He would really rather not have anything to do with Medicine at all, except admire the showmanship from afar. . . .

Are you a shaman, or are you a showman? one of his friends used to ask the people he suspected of fakery, or of catering to the supermarket psychic crowd. Up until last night he would have said that anyone who claimed to be the former was really the latter.

Until now. . . .

"How sure are you about this 'false trail' stuff?" he asked, unwilling to make the concession, but also unwilling to let her get away with putting on a show rather than giving him real facts.

She snorted, delicately. "Sure enough to bet my life on *not* following it," she said. "But if you want more—"

Before he had a chance to protest that no, he really *didn't* want any more, thank you, she had reached into a drawer in her desk, and had taken out a little bag of something. As she dusted it over her desk-blotter and the cassette that lay there, chanting under her breath, he recognized it as corn pollen.

The pollen just lay there for a moment, a frosting of yellow specks over the dark brown blotter—but then, as the hair on the back of his neck began to crawl, he saw very clearly that it was moving. It crept across the blotter as if each bit of pollen was a tiny insect, but an insect moving in a purposeful way.

It formed into symbols even *he* could read. And last time he had looked, there was no scientific power on earth that would make corn pollen crawl into readable patterns.

A ragged circle around the tape cassette, with an uneven slash across it. A rough arrow pointing away, to the west.

Nothing vague or requiring interpretation. If she was calling on Medicine Spirits for advice, she had made certain it was advice he could read as well as she. Once again, his skepticism had been shattered. He looked up from his frozen contemplation of the pollen on the blotter, to see her watching him sardonically.

"I hope that's enough for you," she said, without inflection. "I asked for something you could understand and see for yourself. Anything more than this, you'd better ask from Grandfather."

He swallowed, with a little difficulty.

"I—ah—think that will do," he replied. Suddenly the idea of legwork had a lot more appeal.

* * *

Over the next several days, he had a few more occasions to have his skepticism shattered. Mostly, though, she didn't do it on purpose—but there were plenty of times he saw things—half-seen people and animals—around the house, appearing and disappearing without warning. Once, he heard her talking and heard something else answering, but when he opened the door to her office, there was no one else there. It was unnerving, to say the least, and he kept feeling as if he were off-balance and that everything he had always thought was true had suddenly come into question.

Finally it all became unnerving enough that he couldn't take it anymore. Something was going to have to break, one way or another. Either he was going to have to leave Tulsa, give up on this problem, and go back to his friends in North Dakota, or—

Or else he was going to have to take a good look at himself and his world and rethink everything he had accepted as true.

He didn't make a conscious decision; the morning was clear and cool, the sky cloudless—and instead of driving to Jennie's office, he found himself taking the opposite direction. Before long, he found himself on a dirt road, halfway between Catoosa and Claremore, out in the middle of nowhere.

Without thinking about it, he slowed as he came to an area without planted fields or fences. It seemed the right place to stop, and he pulled over onto the narrow shoulder, then left the car where he parked it. A narrow drainage ditch lined with young cottonwood trees separated the open field from the road; he jumped across it, hiked into a quiet spot, and sat down on a rock in the sun, to think. There was a slight breeze, and birds called off in the distance, but otherwise he might have been completely alone, ringed in with tall, nodding grasses that towered above his head as he sat there, cutting off his sight of anything but their tips and the cloudless blue sky. This might be the tallgrass prairie of the days of the buffalo herds.

No distractions. It was a good place to do some thinking. Hard thinking, in fact.

He lost all track of time, as he stared at the sky and the grass tips, and thought over everything that had brought him here. *Everything*, right back to the very day he had left this area in the first place. And he came to some hard conclusions.

He didn't usually act like such an idiot. Oh, maybe he had back when he was still in school, but he'd had some sense knocked into him since then. There just seemed to be something about this entire situation that had been bringing out the worst in him. Maybe it was being back home. Maybe it was being around Jennie, bringing up old baggage and old habits of behavior. Maybe it was just Jennie herself that both irritated him and made him want to strut and bugle like a young buck in rut. A bad combination, for sure . . . especially given Jennie's opinions of young bucks strutting and acting like fools.

There was very little doubt in his mind that Jennie was getting a certain amount of enjoyment out of putting him down—but on the other hand, every time she did so, it was because he was trying to pretend he knew more than she did about either P.I. work or Medicine. When he had an opinion on law, politics, or the Movement, he honestly had to admit that she listened and acted on his advice. When he told her what Calligan's ex-employees had told him, she listened and paid attention to what he told her. In fact, any time he voiced a fact or an opinion in an arena where he *did* have some real knowledge, she listened and used it.

He *didn't* deserve the snide way she enjoyed putting him in his place—

—well, maybe he did, a little—

—but she only did it when he was making a fool of himself, when it came right down to it.

She'd changed, like he'd thought, but not in the way that

he'd thought; she'd grown up a lot since college, and she had sure learned a lot that you couldn't find in classrooms. And man, it was sure hard to tell that he'd done the same, with the way he'd been acting around her.

He sat in the sun for a long time, just letting it soak into him, trying to rearrange his thoughts when it came to Jennie, to put everything he *thought* he knew about her on the back burner and try to look at the past few days and weeks as if she were a total stranger.

Several observations immediately sprang to mind. She knew her job; really knew it. The cops respected her enough that they often cut her a fair amount of slack. She was making a living at a man's job, and at a job that a lot of men couldn't make a living doing.

Back when they'd broken up in college, he'd said some pretty unforgivable things. So maybe some of that enjoyment she was getting at putting him in *his* place was only payback.

And when it came to Medicine—she was the best he'd ever seen except for her Grandfather, and old man Talldeer was better than anyone he'd ever heard of, outside of stories he'd never believed. He'd watched both of them as they tried to find answers to the questions that baffled them; they went at their medicine-ceremonies with a competence and a calm that reminded him of an expert silversmith that he knew. Twice he'd actually been allowed to participate, in a small way. It had stopped making him shiver and had started fascinating him, even if it wasn't "his" tribal Medicine.

Maybe it was time to make a fresh start with her. He'd sure taken enough hits to his ego to soften it up for the job. . . .

Funny thing was, when he opened his eyes on the field of tallgrass, he felt kind of light. And more relaxed. Maybe that ego of his had been heavier than he had thought.

The feeling of lightness persisted all the way back to town, to the point that even though the rush-hour traffic was horrible, he wasn't upset by it. He simply sat calmly behind the wheel, and let the traffic move when it wanted to; he even let people cut him off without snarling at them.

He pulled up into the Talldeer driveway and saw that Jennie's little Brat was pulled up under the carport. He felt a momentary twinge, then—

Come on, you said you were going to do this, now don't back out on it. Go in, apologize, tell her you were being an idiot and why, apologize for being an idiot when you broke up, and ask her to start all over as friends.

He took a deep breath, took the keys out of the ignition, and went in.

From that moment on, life became—if not easier, certainly easier to take. Jennie had been surprised by his apology, but he had sensed an air of skepticism, as if she had been certain his change of attitude wouldn't last.

But these days he wasn't in the habit of treating other women the way he'd treated her since they'd first collided on that doorstep. It wasn't so much a change of attitude as it was reestablishing the appropriate attitude.

He understood her skepticism, and he was determined to break it down by proving himself. After two days, her skepticism had softened into something like a pleased surprise. After three days, he decided to try dropping the bomb on her.

He was sitting in her office while she phoned in the results of another one of her investigations to her client. Personnel checks, apparently—these days a lot of people wanted to know if a prospective employee was in the habit of suing his bosses or had an inordinate number of workman's comp claims. The news was good, the client was happy, and Jennie was in a good mood when she hung up and turned to him.

"Think you can spare me a couple hours?" he asked, before she could say anything.

She looked surprised, but nodded. Not warily this time, which was a nice change. "Sure—you've been putting in an awful lot of time on our mutual case for me. So, what do you need?"

He sat back in his chair. "I need—hell, this is *really* hard for me—" He felt himself actually blushing. "I sound like some retro hippie or something. But—I've been watching you and Grandfather, and I need—I'd like—I—"

He had planned the whole speech out, and now it deserted him along with his confidence. "Jennie—I mean, maybe I ought to call you by your Osage name for this, but you never told it to me—I want—can you—help me?" He looked up at her hopefully. "I'm Cherokee and you're not, and I know what some of my people did to yours, but you and Grandfather are the only Medicine People I know well enough to ask."

She blinked at him, and for a long moment, said nothing. Then she took a deep breath, and said, very carefully, "Are you asking me to help you find your spiritual identity?"

He nodded, grateful beyond words that she had articulated what he had not been able to.

"Oh my." She blinked again, then suddenly grinned. "You know, your ancestors must be rotating in their graves like high-speed lathes. Have I ever *told* you what my people called yours?"

He shook his head.

Her mouth twitched. "It translates as 'Thing-On-Its-Head-People,' because you weren't particularly valiant by the arrogant standards of *my* people, nor were you particularly outstanding in any other way, and the only way they could think to distinguish you from other nations was by the bandana the Cherokees wrapped around their heads."

She started giggling then, and after a moment, he saw the joke.

"Well, if my ancestors are twirling, *yours* are probably trying to beat a path back from the Summerlands to whup some sense into your head," he replied, with a weak laugh. "That is, if you're even considering it."

"Considering it?" She giggled again. "Good god, David, Grandfather actually predicted this two days ago, and I didn't believe him! How can I not do my best to help you when *he* said that he was going to oversee the whole shebang?"

"The whole shebang" began with a three-day fast, punctuated with sweatlodge ceremonies, which honestly *was* something he had expected. He wasn't completely ignorant of Medicine Ways after all.

Grandfather Talldeer—who he was now supposed to refer to as either "Mooncrow" or "Little Old Man"—insisted that he move into Jennie's spare room for the duration of the ceremony. But he was to bring nothing, not even clothing, other than what he had on his back.

The first day of his fast he didn't see Jennie at all; Mooncrow led him through a special bath, followed by a long stint in the sauna-cum-sweatlodge. The old man was a lot more pragmatic than David had expected, handling things very calmly, as if he did this sort of thing every day.

"In the old days," Mooncrow said, as he took a seat on the floor of the sauna, and poured a dipperful of water over the heated rocks, "we'd have a drummer and a singer in here, chanting to put your mind on the right path. But these days—well, my drummer's in Talequah running his gas station, and my singer's splitting his time between classes and asking 'do you want fries with that?' So we'll have to make do."

"Make do?" David asked, wondering what the old man had in mind.

Mooncrow grinned, and took a towel off a bright yellow sports-model cassette player. "Got to deal with modern ways, sometimes. This thing doesn't mind the heat, and doesn't have a job and a mortgage and kids to feed. Doesn't get tired, either."

David raised a skeptical eyebrow. If it had been his call, he would have thought this was *way* too much like buying a videotape of enlightenment . . . but if Mooncrow approved it. . . .

But the tape Mooncrow started was not some synthesizer and Pan-flute, white-bread version of a drum chant. This was the real thing, recorded in a drum-circle, not a studio; it went straight into his chest and vibrated his entire body. His heart throbbed in time with it; his whole body swayed in time to it, and as Mooncrow lit a bundle of sweetgrass for smoke, David did not find it at all difficult to fall into the meditative state the old man demanded of him.

Three days of sweats and ritual baths, of tales and instruction, and in the end, it came down to this; standing barefoot in the middle of a clearing on some friend of Mooncrow's private land, wearing nothing but a loincloth of the old style and a medicine-bag Jennie had made for him. Mooncrow had awakened him this morning long before dawn, put him in his old pickup truck, and had left him here before the sun rose. David was light-headed from fasting, but his mind was clear, as clear as the sky overhead, and the breeze that brushed his body.

He felt like an entirely new and different person—one with more patience, fewer prejudices, and the wisdom to know he wasn't perfect. If this was a religious revelation— well—he figured he could get to like his "new self" in a hurry.

This part of the vision-quest was another change from the old days, Mooncrow told him, with some regret. In the old days he would have gone straight out into the wilderness from his own village and would have stayed out where he would never see another human, traveling in whatever direction the omens sent him, until he met his spirit-animal.

"Of course," Mooncrow had added with a chuckle, both strong hands holding the steering wheel, "in the old days you would have done this long ago, when you were a boy, and you would not have been permitted in the company of men until you *had*."

But there was no wilderness near enough to Tulsa to permit such a vision-quest; no place at all in the continental United States where he would not, sooner or later, encounter some other human if he began wandering.

So he would remain where he had been left, and his spirit-totem must come to him.

Along with the light-headedness of fasting, there was the light-headedness of excitement. He had been three days in preparation for this, and he had imagined many times what his spirit-animal might be. The Horse of his family name— the Puma—the Bear—the Wolf—best of all, the Eagle—

Don't focus on what you want, *that's what Mooncrow said,* he reminded himself. *Don't focus on anything. Just wait, without expectations. Open yourself to the Earth. . . .*

He did not even notice that he had settled, cross-legged, as easy as a leaf drifting down from the trees. He simply found himself sitting instead of standing, dismissed that, and as Mooncrow and Jennie had taught him, became a part of this little corner of the Earth, as still and as accepting as the grass.

He was not even aware of the passing of time, except as a change in the shadows and the patterns of shade and sunlight.

So when the white-tail buck stepped into the clearing and walked straight to him, he was not even excited. It was a beautiful animal, and he was lost in admiration of it. Sun gleamed on the buck's rust-brown sides, making him shine like a living statue of molten copper. He was a ten-pointer, and his rack shone black and bronze, gleaming as if it had been polished. His huge, liquid brown eyes stared directly at

David; his black patent-leather nose twitched as he took in David's scent. He picked his way slowly and deliberately across the clearing, his ears pointed toward David, each hoof placed with such care that the dry leaves barely whispered as he passed.

At least, David was not excited, until the Deer dipped his nose to look into David's eyes, and said, "Well. And it certainly took *you* long enough to see me!"

Mooncrow sat on a rock beside him, sunlight shining on his crown of gray hair, and chuckled. "The Deer, hmm?"

David was a little chagrined at the identity of his spirit-animal; not disappointed, but chagrined. After all of Mooncrow's admonitions not to *expect* any particular animal, he still had fallen into the trap of hoping for something, well, a little more macho. If his spirit animal *had* to be one of the deer family—it would have been nice to have something like the wapiti, the great Elk, and not the white-tail buck. A little more like a power symbol and less like Bambi. . . .

"You don't sound surprised," David remarked, after a moment. He had to be gratified by one thing, at least. It couldn't be more than noon, by the sun. His spirit-totem had revealed itself to him in a very short time. He had heard stories of it taking anywhere from one day to a whole week, sometimes more.

The old man smiled, giving him a sideways look out of the corner of his eye. "I'm not surprised," he replied. "I already knew. Kestrel saw him."

The first thing, the very first thing, that came into his mind, was *why didn't they tell me!* It was inevitable; if they knew, it followed by logic that this whole spirit-quest could have been bypassed.

But he knew why. What was the point in telling him? This was not some kind of Monte Hall giveaway; this was a quest, *his* quest, of self-discovery. What would the point have been of *telling* him? If they had, it would have meant nothing.

But the second question that occurred to him was to wonder when Kestrel—Jennie—had seen his spirit-animal.

"She saw Deer trying to warn you the other night," the old man went on, blandly, as David started again. Was Mooncrow some kind of mind reader? "It was when you almost tripped that bomb, and he was trying to get you to leave it alone."

"Oh," was all he could say. Mooncrow favored him with another enigmatic smile.

"Deer is a very proud creature," the old man continued. "Sometimes—too proud. He lifts his antlers high and displays for the ladies at times when he should be watching for hunters. The scent of a female can make him forget all caution. And when he scents another male—*that* makes him forget everything else but locking horns!"

David flushed and hoped Mooncrow wouldn't notice, because much as he hated to admit it, Mooncrow's description of Deer certainly fit David. . . .

"But those are his vices," Mooncrow said with a shrug. "I am certain that you can think of his virtues for yourself. But among the Children of the Middle Waters, his chief virtues are cleverness, speed, strength, and agility. Perhaps among your people he has virtues beyond those."

David shrugged slightly; he really didn't know. But once again, he had to admit that Deer certainly fit him. He liked to think of himself as being clever and a quick thinker; and in school, he'd been in track and field.

"This does not mean that you are to stop learning, Spotted Horse," Mooncrow went on, serenely. "Your spirit-animal only shows you what you *are*, and will be your guide to the other spirit-creatures from which you must learn. *Every* creature has virtues and vices, and you must learn to acquire the virtues and conquer the weaknesses. Reject no spirit as being unable to teach. Even Spider can teach a powerful lesson, *All things come to my web and break their necks therein.* That is why one of our gentes is the gente of the Spider, and why our women in the old days had the Spider tattooed upon their hands. Or Crayfish! Crayfish gave us the four sacred colors of clay! There is nothing so weak and small that it cannot have power—and nothing so powerful that something weak and small cannot overcome it."

David nodded, earnestly, and suddenly felt as if he were being watched by hundreds of eyes. . . .

He looked around, covertly. He *was* being watched by hundreds of eyes! The clearing was full of animals, all listening to Mooncrow and nodding their heads in agreement—and watching David to see if he was paying attention.

Is this a hallucination, or—

"A hallucination is only an uncontrolled glimpse elsewhere, Spotted Horse," Mooncrow interrupted the thought. "Sometimes the 'elsewhere' is the spirit world, sometimes it is only the inside of your own head. You should be able to tell the difference, soon. Both can teach you something."

David's temper flared a little. "Are you a showman, or a shaman?" he snapped, without thinking.

But Mooncrow only laughed, throwing his head back and crinkling up his eyes. Then he turned a face full of innocence toward David, and said, "Yes."

Just that.

Now, so far, every person David had met who had ever claimed to be a Medicine Person would react to that question with varying degrees of anger. Either shamed anger that he had caught them out, or anger that he would even *consider* that they were not what they claimed to be. No one had ever answered him "yes" to both!

He couldn't help it; he sat and stared incredulously, as the animals rustled and stirred, and seemed to be laughing too.

"David, that is a silly question," Jennie chided, from

behind him. He turned his head, and there she was, although he had not seen or heard her approaching. Like her grandfather, she was dressed in jeans and a T-shirt, although both of them wore eagle feathers in their hair, just as he had seen in the triple vision. The hard tail-feather on the right side, the soft under-tail covert, dyed red, on the left. Now he knew what that meant; that they knew the medicines of both the *Hunkah* and the *Tzi-Sho*, and of all of the *gentes* of both divisions. They were Medicine People the like of which could not have existed in the old days. Small wonder the Osage on Calligan's crews respected them so much.

"Why's it silly?" he asked, a little belligerently.

She chuckled. "Because it's either/or, very simplistic. But the real situation isn't at all simple, for every *good* shaman has to be a showman as well; sometimes people simply won't believe a thing until you've wrapped it up in fancy paper and ribbon, and bestowed it with a fireworks display. And because in order to counterfeit something that is genuine, you have to at least understand the *appearance* of the genuine, every showman has at least a little shaman in him. For that matter, there is no reason why a showman can't teach you something valuable. It's perfectly possible to learn all the right lessons from the wrong source, if your heart is right."

"Or as I tell the kids who come to play Nintendo with me," Mooncrow said, his voice still full of warmth and amusement, "Luke Skywalker learned as much from Darth Vader as he did from Ben Kenobi and Yoda. He *even* learned a thing or two from that ne'er-do-well, Han Solo!"

David looked from Jennie to her grandfather and back again. Finally he shook his head. "You two have been reading too much Joseph Campbell."

"Or *you* have been reading too little," Mooncrow countered, standing and beckoning to him. "Come. Jennie has your clothing, and the car is ready. It is time to go."

And that, so it seemed, was that.

Except for the thoughts that ran through his head while they drove him home, fed him, and put him to bed. Thoughts that kept him silent, danced behind his closed eyes, and percolated through his dreams, a welter of Deer and Bear, space fighters and ancient warriors—

His dreams took a turn they never had before. He found himself wandering in a virgin wilderness, watching, listening, and then—

Then hiding, from a strange black beast that was neither human, bird nor animal, that walked upon two legs and left the land waste behind it. . . .

This time Smith had called Rod Calligan, rather than the other way around, calling him at home. Rod took the call in his home office, after making certain that Toni couldn't pick up one of the other phones without him knowing. And the question the man asked him rather surprised Rod.

Brusque, blunt. "Are you getting anywhere with the Talldeer chick? How close are you to getting rid of her?"

"I haven't actually seen her once," Rod said, carefully, not mentioning the trap the girl had sprung and then taken. "She hasn't been out to the site that I know of, and she hasn't personally questioned anyone who's still on the project. I think I've thrown her a couple of fastballs, and at least she hasn't been actively interfering. No one's called me from your company. Why?"

"Because I have an idea," Smith replied, cautiously. "I want to be certain she's out of the picture before we do anything about it. It's a way to capitalize a little further on that land of yours."

As Smith outlined his "idea," Calligan began to smile. Once the mall project was dead, Smith would come in with a phony holding company, and some cash; Rod would supply the rest. Smith's company would buy the land for next to nothing—land already cleared and waiting, ready for any purpose they cared to put it to. Rod would use his leverage with the county commissioners to get the area opened for a landfill. He would look like a good guy, making sure that the land was used for *something* that would produce some county tax revenue. And there would be plenty of clean dirt and rock going in there—with all the flood-control work going on, the dirt dredged up had to go somewhere, after all. Even the tree-huggers would be happy, if Smith's company promised to build a park on it once the landfill was full.

"That's what'll go on during the day," Smith said. "And I know, there's not much profit there. But after hours, we'll be doing something else—"

Because John Smith had a contact at a drilling company, and his contact had a lot of friends just like them. Wildcatters and independent oil drilling firms were having a hard time keeping their heads above water as it was—and all the piddly-shit regulations about disposing of the chemicals that came out of wells were driving a lot of them under.

"You know anything about drilling?" Smith asked.

"Not much," Calligan admitted. The fetish-bundle in his pocket seemed to draw his fingers to it. The soft leather felt comforting.

"Well, they have to force water, sometimes steam, down into slow wells to force the oil up," Smith told him, while he listened intently. "The water that comes up out of wells along with the oil is full of chemicals, from cyanide to polycarbonates, many of them very dangerous. The old way was to bury or dump the chemically-loaded water, but new regulations say the water has to be cleaned, the chemicals removed. The marginal drilling firms just can't afford the cost of running an 'environmentally correct' drilling operation. That's where we come in."

So by day the big trucks full of river sand and construction rock would come in, and leave piles of sand that would be bulldozed to cover up the barrels of chemicals John's "buddies" had left there at night. There'd be big money all around for everyone, and by the time anyone found out what was being dumped there, he and John Smith would be long gone. And no one would even be able to prove that they had even known about the illegal dumping in the first place. The chemical barrels would be unmarked. Everything would be in cash; no way to trace the payoffs, no way even to prove where the chemicals came from.

It was a beautiful scheme. It was no less beautiful, in that John had tentatively picked out another site, although he had done nothing about acquiring it yet.

"That one would have cost a lot more," Smith said. "It would have been a legal hazardous waste site, although it wouldn't have been rated for the welded barrels my people were going to bring in. The EPA would assume those fancy leakproof barrels, not welded steel."

When Rod asked him about the second site, he discovered he had another reason to buy into Smith's plan. The other site was very near Rod's subdivision—

That would not have been possible to keep under wraps for very long. Smith said candidly that the operation would be a short-lived one; six to eight months at the most, before someone found out and pulled the plug. It meant high profit, but high risk; people watchdogged those sites all the time, and sooner or later, someone would have started asking questions about the trucks coming in after normal operating hours.

Certainly word would have leaked out long before Rod was ready to sell his house and pull up stakes.

Word would leak out about the same time the cyanide did, he thought, amused at his own cleverness.

"It sounds good to me," he told Smith. "Tell you what, if the bitch gets out of hand, you think you can give me some help with her?"

"I didn't intend to, when it was just you and this bankruptcy scheme, but if we add in the dumping, that makes it worth my time," Smith replied, as Rod smiled. "Just say the word. I have—contacts."

The next day, it was business-as-usual, although Jennie didn't seem to be lobbying for him to move out of the spare room and back to his motel. In fact, Mooncrow suggested he go check out of the motel—"for a while, at least"—and stay with them, to further his education in Medicine. He didn't need a second invitation; it took him less than an hour to get everything moved into the guest room; Jennie didn't say anything, and she had to have noticed.

It was business-as-usual, except for an incredible lightness of spirit, despite the strange dreams of last night. He just couldn't get angry at anyone for anything. He ran a few more checks for Jennie after he'd stashed his stuff in the room, while she took care of some smaller cases, tracking down spouses who'd split and were not paying alimony.

And he watched, and listened, to her and Mooncrow. Maybe he was seeing things more clearly now, but—

—but under all the teasing, the things that seemed like sniping, there was a very deep and abiding *love* between Jennie and Mooncrow. It kind of surprised him, in a way; he hadn't known they could have a teacher/student relationship and still have that kind of emotional bond.

He noticed something else, as well. Mooncrow was worried about something—about Jennie—but was keeping very quiet about it. Was it because he respected Jennie's ability to take care of herself? Or was it simply to keep from appearing to be an interfering old man?

If it had been anyone else, David would have said it was the latter. But not with these two.

And Jennie was beating herself over the head about something, something that had nothing to do with any of her current investigations. What it was, he had no idea, but as he watched her all through that day and the next, there was at least *one* thing she was doing that he figured he might be able to cure.

It was a trap he'd fallen into himself often enough to be able to see the same fault in her.

She was being way too serious, all the time; it was one thing to make sure the work got done, but it was another to let the work take over your life. She probably hadn't taken any time out just to have *fun* in years! There was a little tension-crease between her eyebrows that he wanted badly to smooth away, and he wanted to do it because he was her friend, and not for any other reason.

Well, mostly not, anyway.

Finally, he just couldn't take it any more. He had to try *something*. Otherwise he could see her turning herself into a knot in no time flat.

It was about nine; she typed a few things into her computer with the decisive clicks he'd come to associate with her finishing for the night.

"There," she said, shoving the keyboard drawer back under the desktop. "That's as far as I'm going to get with this Calligan thing tonight—"

"Then let's go," he said, quickly, before she could say anything about a sauna, or early bed, or catching the news.

She blinked at him, as if she had forgotten completely that he was there. "Go?" she said, puzzled. "Go where? Why? What's open at this time of night?"

He grinned. "You like techno," he stated. He knew he was right; he'd seen the CDs on her shelf, and he'd heard her listening to the techno-industrial alternative-rock radio program from Rogers College—or at least she had, before the college administration in their infinite wisdom shut it down.

"So?" One eyebrow lifted.

"So trust me." Before she could object, he came around to the side of her desk and held out his hand. She took it, dubiously. He pulled her to her feet, and led her out the door. She got into the passenger's side of his car with an expression of puzzled patience. It changed to an expression of disbelief when he headed downtown, since most of the downtown area locked up by 5:30 at night.

Most of it.

He took her to a rave, at a "club" that hadn't been there a month ago, and might not be next month, in a building that had been everything from a factory to an art gallery.

They were probably the oldest people there; it was hard to tell. The lighting was not particularly conducive to taking a good look at peoples' faces. Interesting thing about techno; the heavy beat was not all *that* dissimilar to drumsong. He hadn't done any fancy-dancing in a long time, but when the beat caught him up and he found himself gyrating as if he were wearing his old costume, he simply let his body do what it wanted to. Jennie clapped her hands and grinned like a maniac; *she* recognized the moves, even if the kids there didn't. He wasn't dancing for them, anyway; he was dancing for her, parading like the buck deer before the doe, and they both knew it, and both were delighted by the sheer *silliness* of it.

He drew a crowd anyway, a little circle of admirers, and when that piece ended and another began, *Jennie* got into the act, leaping into the circle and matching him beat for beat. He'd forgotten she used to compete in the shawl-dancing; maybe she had forgotten too, until that moment. Now it was a kind of competition between the two of them, but a competition of display, where it didn't matter who won, or even if there was a winner at all.

The band gave up before they did. But the moment the music ended, they tossed sweat-soaked hair out of their eyes, and traded a look of agreement.

This was enough for one night.

It took a little time to work through the crowd to get to the door and the parking lot. David was a little surprised when he stopped under a lot-light and looked at his watch to see that it was already midnight.

Beside him, Jennie paused to glance at her own watch. "Wow!" she said in a tone of awe. "I have more stamina than I thought!"

"Same here," he confessed, laughing. "Think we showed those cubs a thing or two?"

"Well, either they decided that we were too crazy to mess with, or we'll have started a new dance craze by morning," she replied. She stood under the light long enough to pull her hair back and braid it. That little frownline was gone, at least for the moment, and he felt a definite glow of satisfaction at how relaxed and happy she looked.

"Can I show you a good time, or what?" he asked, smugly.

"A lot better than what you used to think was a good time," she retorted. "A mug of beer, a loaf of rhetoric, and thou—"

He started to get angry, and stopped himself just in time. Things were going well. He wouldn't gain a thing by starting an argument. Besides, she had a point.

"I guess I've loosened up some, since then," he said mildly, and grinned when he saw the blank look on her face, the surprise that he *hadn't* plowed right into a fight. "You could stand to loosen up some, yourself, Jen."

She flushed, but he realized how she could take that last comment, and went on.

"What I mean is, you don't have fun enough. Take some time out, for godsake. See a movie! What was the last movie you saw?" He knew he had her then, when she had to think about it.

"Uh. *Beauty and the Beast?*" she said.

"See what I mean!" he responded triumphantly. "You haven't even gone out for a walk, or rented a horse, or *anything* unless it had something to do with your work! Right?"

She shuffled her feet a little in the gravel of the parking

lot. "I guess so. . . ."

"You need more fun in your life," he said, decisively. "If you get bleeding ulcers and wind up in the hospital, who's gonna put Calligan away? Who's gonna make sure he doesn't sell *our* people up the river? Who's gonna keep Mooncrow from living on pizza and ice cream?"

"All right, all right!" she conceded, throwing up her hands. "I surrender! If you want to be the designated maker-of-fun, go right ahead! Just remember, the work has to be done first, before we have fun."

He executed a fancy-dance step, right there in the lot, and amazingly, didn't fall on his face or turn an ankle in all that gravel. She chuckled.

He took that as a good omen.

Toni Calligan put her forehead down on the kitchen table, and fought tears. She was beginning to think she ought to pack the kids up for the summer and take them someplace *safe*.

Like maybe a maximum-security prison! There certainly didn't seem to be any safety around here!

No one, not any of the repairmen she'd called, had been able to figure just what had gone wrong with the dryer. One of them had even accused her of sabotaging it herself! He'd said it looked as if someone had just gotten in there and cut the insulation off of everything in sight. . . .

She succeeded in persuading Rod to buy a new dryer—after making certain he didn't hear *that* particular story. But that had only been the start of her problems.

A few days later, a fire started in the garage; fortunately, a neighbor saw it and put it out before it did any damage. He really *saw* it start, too; he'd been taking a break from mowing and told Toni he thought he'd seen a dog or something run into their garage. He described it perfectly; a grayish-yellow dog with pointed ears and a bushy tail, about the size of a spitz. Since he knew they didn't have a dog, and since there was a rabies scare going on, he'd gone in after it, armed with a stick, only to see the back corner of the garage go up—"like a torch," he'd said. "I couldn't believe it. One minute, everything's fine; the next, the wall's on fire!"

Funny thing, there was no dog, either, and it couldn't have gotten past him.

Rod had been livid about that. He'd been certain she'd let the kids play with matches, or that she'd stored greasy rags there, or something. And it didn't matter that the only things *in* that corner were the garden tools; it had to be her fault.

Then she'd come out into the backyard yesterday just in time to see Jill in her sandbox, about to pick up a scorpion! Thank *God* she'd come out when she did! No one could believe it, not even when they saw the crushed insect for themselves; there hadn't been scorpions around ever, for as long as this subdivision had been here.

She certainly set off a round of exterminators, though. Every house in the neighborhood had exterminators poking under it; theirs included.

And now, today—

Oh God.

Ryan came in crying not a half hour ago, bruised and scraped, claiming something had pushed him into the street, in front of a car—

And right behind him came a strange woman with a face as white as Toni's had turned, corroborating the child.

"He was just standing there, like a good boy, waiting for me to go by," she babbled, "just *standing* there, all alone. I thought, just as I got to the corner, that it was a good thing he was such a good little boy. Then, suddenly there was a man standing next to him, then the poor tyke went *flying* into the street, right in front of me, exactly like that man had shoved him from behind! Then the man was gone, and I hit the brakes—"

Ryan had only saved himself by rolling, then going flat, so that the car actually passed over him without hitting him. The driver had nearly had a heart attack before he crawled out from under her car. She had brought him home herself, quickly, at that point.

Toni was so close to hysteria herself by then that she actually felt calm.

She assured the poor woman that everything was all right, that no, there was no need to leave her name and address, that things would be fine. She was dead certain that Rod would have been on the phone to his lawyer—but she wasn't Rod, and Rod wasn't going to hear about *this*, not if she could help it.

He'd probably find a way to blame her as well as that poor woman, anyway.

After she'd somehow said the right things to the stranger, and had sent her off to her car babbling gratitude, she bathed and bandaged Ryan's scrapes and put him to bed with cartoons and a bowl of ice cream. Then she sat herself down at the kitchen table and shook.

If this kind of thing kept up, she was going to need a prescription for Valium. . . .

As soon as she stopped shaking, she was suddenly seized with the need to see that the kids were *all right*. She checked on Jill—she was still playing safely in the sandbox (checked, double-checked, and refilled with clean sand, and the exterminator had been all over the house and yard this morning). Rod Junior was at a Little League practice, and *those* were supervised. Ryan was asleep.

She went back to the kitchen, slumped in her favorite chair, and stared at the wall for a while.

That was when some of what the stranger had said—and she had dismissed—came back to her.

Ryan had been standing alone at the corner, and in this

neighborhood, there was nothing to hide behind at the corners, nothing to make it hard for a driver to see the kids. Yet—Ryan and the stranger agreed, that one moment he had been alone, but the next second, someone had jumped up behind him and pushed him out into the street.

Then, inexplicably, the attacker had vanished.

Now, the woman was hysterical, and Ryan was too. And in the few seconds it took for the woman to slam on her brakes and run to the front of her car, it was perfectly possible for a child, a bully who had gone too far, to run for the cover of one of the backyards.

Except that both Ryan and the woman agreed that it hadn't been a child. And this *adult* would have found it very difficult to hide in a normal suburban neighborhood like theirs.

For according to both the stranger—who had no reason to make up such a wild story, and Ryan—who had *never* lied, this adult had not been the kind of person you saw on the street.

In fact, he had been an Indian. In beads, mohawk, blanket, and leather pants. Everything but war-paint.

The next day, David talked Jennie into giving *him* some of the paperwork to do so that they could take in a movie. The day after, he dragged her off to Bell's Amusement Park. The day after that, he varied the routine by kidnapping her for a picnic at lunch.

It all paid off handsomely. That worry-line was becoming fainter, and she had less of a pinched look about her. And there still was no talk of him moving out of the spare room.

In the meantime, he split his time between doing that "legwork" for her—which included, to his surprise and pleasure, being granted some of the surveillance *she* had been doing—and reading the books and private notebooks that "mysteriously" turned up in his room. Some of them surprised him; stuff he would have thought was far too much along the lines of what you'd find in a so-called "occult bookstore" for Mooncrow to have any respect for. But then he remembered that business about learning things from unlikely sources, and read what had been left him without comment.

When he wasn't away from the house on one errand or another, he watched Mooncrow teaching the neighborhood kids without them ever realizing that they were learning anything. *They* just thought he told neat stories, and knew how to do excellent things. He'd even weaned them from Nintendo to real archery practice, and they *liked* it. Sometimes, David even helped the old man, when he could.

This morning, since Jennie didn't have anything for him to do, Mooncrow had asked him to help with the lessons, and he'd been pleased to discover that he hadn't lost his knack for the sport. He and Mooncrow were watching the kids practice their archery with a critical eye when the old man suddenly cleared his throat in a way that usually preceded a lesson. David gave him a glance out of the corner of his eye. Surely he couldn't intend to say anything about Medicine in front of these kids!

But when the words finally came, they were not exactly what he'd expected.

"You and Kestrel have been getting along a lot better," Mooncrow remarked, with such an expression of absolute innocence that David immediately suspected some deeper purpose in the comment.

"It didn't hurt to apologize for some things I said when we broke up—and some more I said later," he replied, very carefully. "I was out of line, both times, assuming things I had no business assuming. She overreacted, but—I can't blame her, and I'd have done the same if our positions had been reversed."

"Hmm. Kestrel has a hasty temper, like *her* spirit-animal. If you touch her nesting pole, she will scold you even before she sees whether or not you intended to climb it." Moon-crow's full attention seemed to be on the kids lined up across the yard with their handmade bows, but David knew better.

However, that was the best way he'd ever heard of describing Jennie's tendency to shoot first and sort things out later.

"She's got a lot on her mind," David replied, feeling as if he ought to defend her. "People who have bad tempers and know it can usually keep their temper under control, unless they're already handling too much. . . . I guess we both know she's a workaholic, and this Calligan thing is really getting to her. There's something going on there, a lot more than shows on the surface, but we can't seem to get past the surface. Yet. But I can't blame her for being a little short on temper, you know?"

"True." Mooncrow sighed. "I wanted to thank you. For getting her to enjoy herself a little more, and work a little less. It makes her less difficult to live with."

David had to chuckle at that. "I'm not saying a word," he replied. "Anything I say is only too likely to get me in trouble!"

He brushed some imaginary dirt off the legs of his jeans, and waited for Mooncrow's reply. There would be one. The old man wasn't finished yet; he sensed it in the way Moon-crow kept watching him without seeming to watch him.

"I don't think it would hurt if you two were more than friends," Mooncrow said at last. "I don't think it would hurt if you backtracked in some ways to when you were younger." He looked slyly at David out of the corner of his eye. "I can't say I'd mind if you didn't need that spare room for anything but storing your things."

David blinked, and licked his lips. Well, that was certainly an unexpected development! He felt rather stunned. "I can't say that I'd be unhappy about things coming around that way." He paused for a moment. "Just how would you suggest I go about doing that?"

But Mooncrow only shrugged. "I'm an old man," he replied. "Things are not the same as they were when I courted her grandmother. Jennie is a warrior in her own right; her grandmother was a simpler woman with simpler needs. I have no suggestions. If I say anything to her, she is likely to throw you out; she is just as contrary at times as she accuses me of being. So it is all in your hands, young Spotted Horse."

Thanks a lot, he thought wryly, but not with a feeling of being offended. He liked Mooncrow; more than that, he trusted the old man, far more than he had trusted Mooncrow when he had been a child. Then, the old man had just been Jennie's grandfather who told good stories. Now he was a Teacher, a Medicine Person. . . .

Hmm. I wonder if he was suggesting that as Jennie's grandfather, or as Mooncrow, Kestrel's Teacher? It would make a difference. . . .

He could even be suggesting it as both.

He would have been a lot more surprised at the oblique suggestion that he heat the situation up, if he hadn't already gotten the same "hints" from another of Jennie's relatives. Although he had *never* thought he'd hear Mooncrow suggesting he should share Jennie's bed! The other "hints" had been a lot more pedestrian. . . .

"If I didn't know better, Little Old Man," he said lightly, "I'd suspect you of being a *shoka* from Jennie's father."

"Oh?" Mooncrow replied, far too casually. "Why is that?"

David made a face. "Because I happened to 'run into him' three times in the last week—probably because he heard on the grapevine that I'm in your spare room. He dropped a few bricks—I'm sure *he* thinks they were hints."

Mooncrow chuckled at that. "My son was never known for subtlety," he told David. "Some day I must tell you how he proposed to Jennie's mother. But what were these unsubtle hints about?"

"Nothing much—just that it seems that the entire family would *really approve* if Jennie and I patched things back up again." He shook his head, ruefully. "If these were the old days, I have the horrible feeling that instead of *me* riding out to capture a bride, *I'd* be the one hog-tied and bent over Jennie's saddlebow, gift-wrapped by her loving family!"

And at that, Mooncrow broke into loud and hearty laughter, much to David's embarrassment, and the surprise of all the kids, who turned to see what on earth could be so funny.

David blushed a little, but felt impelled to tell Mooncrow all of it, however embarrassing it had been.

"He said that Jennie's mom and brothers always did like me, and that everybody wishes things would go back the way they were between us when we first started college." He sighed. "Back before we had that big fight, and I threw that stupid Huey Long quote at her, anyway. I guess she told her father about that. . . ."

"Only recently," Mooncrow said serenely. "She told me about it later, after she had brought home the Hell's Angel—"

"*What?*" David yelped, taken completely by surprise.

The kids turned to look at them again.

"Well, perhaps he was not a Hell's Angel," Mooncrow amended. "But he did have a Harley Hog, and he did belong to a bike club. At any rate, when I did not approve of the young man, she told me what you had said; to show me how much better this man treated her, I think." Mooncrow nodded thoughtfully for a moment. "He did treat her well," he admitted, "but he was too interested in the 'instant enlightenment' and not in real achievement. He did not last long."

"Oh," David said, weakly. "Well . . . ah . . . I suppose I wasn't much better. I have to admit, I even knew at the time that it was a stupid thing to say, but—"

"But you were strutting and flashing your antlers, and she was not sufficiently impressed, so you decided to turn the antlers on her." Mooncrow nodded. "Well, you were young."

"Young men do stupid things," he agreed, and sighed.

Mooncrow grinned at him. "Even not-so-young men do stupid things, David," he replied, and left him on the back steps to go and correct his young archers.

CHAPTER THIRTEEN

JENNIE LOCKED THE door of her office, turned up the radio, and buried her face in her hands. A headache had just begun in one temple. The name of her headache was—her family.

Right now, she was beginning to envy a client of hers who was an orphan.

Just once, she would like it very much if no one cared about who she was seeing or not seeing. Certainly having a family, an intelligent and curious family to boot, brought with it liabilities.

Like having a yenta for a father, she thought sourly, head in hands. *My father, the matchmaker. He could have sent a shoka in full regalia, and been less obvious. He could have trotted out the whole family with courting gifts. I feel like I'm in a damn sitcom.*

David. They all liked David. They were all making it perfectly clear to her how much they liked David, and how happy they would be if she and David would just go back to being the happy couple they'd been in college. Never mind that they really hadn't been all that happy a couple.

The worst part was, it would have been funny, if it had been happening to someone else. It would even be funny if *she* didn't like David so much.

She was getting at least three calls a day from one member of the family or another, and before the call was over, the topic of David Spotted Horse would somehow have worked its way into the conversation. How was he doing, had they gone anywhere together, did she think they might come over to Claremore for dinner some time in the next couple of days. . . . Even from her brothers; they were going fishing, would she and David like to join them—they were going to a powwow, would she and David like to come along.

Mother's bad enough, but Dad is worse. Her father thought he was being subtle; he was about as subtle as a billboard.

I don't know why he doesn't just rent a billboard. She could just see it now, out on I-44. Forty-eight feet wide, sixteen feet tall. *Jennie, when are you and David going to—?*

At least Mooncrow was keeping his mouth shut. He kept giving her *looks*, but at least he kept his mouth shut. It seemed as if everyone in the Talldeer family was trying to throw Jennie into David's bed—or vice versa—and no one was going to take "no" for an answer.

She expected that kind of thing out of David; after all, it wasn't as if he hadn't been hinting. But her own family?

I thought they were supposed to want me to preserve *my so-called honor! Not go jumping into some guy's bed!*

Well, she wasn't having any. She could be just as stubborn as any of them, and she was not, by god, going to get herded into this as if she were the prize mare and David the champion stud!

I suppose by now Dad has waylaid David at least once, telling him how nice it would be if we got back together again, she thought forlornly. *That's probably why he's been looking like a hopeful puppy these past few days.*

The worst part of it was, if she'd wanted him before, now she *really* had it bad for him. This business with finding his spiritual direction was not just for show; he'd made an enormous amount of progress, and it made him all the more attractive to her. He'd been treating her the way she suspected he *normally* treated other women; as competent equals. He, at least, had managed to unload all that old baggage and start fresh, even if she had not.

She'd forgotten, deliberately, all the things about his personality that had attracted her to him in the first place. Now all those things were coming back with a vengeance, and if *he* was frustrated as hell, sleeping all alone just down the hall from her, *she* was twice as frustrated.

"We're just working colleagues," she kept telling him. She kept trying to convince herself of that. "We need to keep a certain distance to keep this professional."

She kept repeating that to herself, like a mantra. It wasn't working.

But dammit, I will not be herded into something, no matter who thinks it would be good for me! She buried her face in her hands and massaged her temples. *You know, if the folks would just back off, it would be so much easier. He's a nice guy. He's more than a nice guy. I've got the hots for him like I've never had the hots for anyone else. I never lost the hots for him. If they'd leave me alone, I could make up my mind about him, one way or another. If I could just think about this without the pressure. . . .*

And if pigs could fly.

David finished entering the last of his data into Jennie's computer, and did a backup before turning it off. Things had been markedly less strained between them since he'd been acting more like a big brother than anything else, but they'd really improved over the past couple of days. She had stopped wincing every time the phone rang.

It looked as if her folks had gotten the message. Finally.

Mooncrow promised he'd talk to Jennie's father and get him to back off, he thought, taking a quick glance at her. *I guess he got through to them.*

He'd basically given up on getting back together with her when he'd had that little talk with Mooncrow, asking if the old man would get Jennie's family to leave her alone. He'd already cooled his own jets. Things had been getting so strained that he was afraid she was going to tell *him* to get lost just to get her family off her back. And when it all came down to it—this Calligan thing was bigger than either of them. She was the only one who had all the right connections to put it all together. He was afraid that she needed help she wouldn't get if he had to make tracks.

So in order to make sure the job got done, his own desires needed to go on the back burner. Forever, if that was what it took.

The last thing I want is to screw things up for her all over again, he had decided. *We make a good working team on this, and maybe I'm assuming too much, but I think she needs me if she's going to crack this case without breaking, herself. She needs two pairs of legs, two sets of eyes, and indirect contacts to Calligan's crew. I think she can do it alone, but it'll put her in the hospital. She needs somebody she can delegate work to, and somebody she can bounce ideas off of.*

And if he couldn't have anything else, he still wanted her as a friend and a Medicine mentor. He didn't have so many people he called "friend" that he could afford to lose any of them, much less lose one over something as stupid as her family trying to play matchmaker.

"That's it," he said, as she looked up from a pile of papers. "I've got it all in there, but I haven't spotted a pattern of artifact sales that correspond to anything that might have been taken from that gravesite. The only things positively identified as Osage are a couple of ribbon-work pieces that date to about 1890. There were some pots that could have been from the site, but they didn't seem old enough."

She sighed and rubbed her eyes. "You're getting pretty good at spotting patterns," she admitted. "If you don't see it, I don't think I would, either." She stood up and stretched. "I need the sauna. *As* the sauna. Grandfather is doing the Medicine work on this; he's so much better than I that it isn't funny."

"I'm going to call it a night," he replied. He flexed his shoulders. "I don't know how you can sit here and type for as long as you do. My eyes are tired, and I've got to meet some of Calligan's men tomorrow, the ones that are still working."

"More accidents already?" she said in surprise.

"Yeah—little ones, but a lot of them." He stood up and shoved the chair back under the desk. "Oh, Mooncrow wants us to take him somewhere tomorrow, after I talk to the guys."

Her eyes widened, and she nodded. As she had mentioned, Mooncrow had been doing *some* kind of Medicine for the past couple of days, "looking for something," she'd said. Apparently he'd found it.

"Well, go enjoy your steam, kiddo," he told her, and gave her a brotherly (he hoped) wink, and a peck on the cheek. "You've earned it. How about if tomorrow I buy you and Mooncrow some lunch?"

She laughed. "No you don't. I know damn good and well that you're on the end of your cash. I can't pay you much, but at least I can feed you."

He flushed, and shrugged. A few weeks ago he would have flatly denied he was in any financial trouble at all. A few months ago, he would have been angry at *her* for even suggesting he didn't have everything under control.

That was then. This is now. And—hey, this gives me exactly the opening I need.

"Okay. I can live with that." He leaned back against the

wall, and tilted his head to one side. "You said a while back that you needed a secretary, or at least someone to help with the routine stuff. No reason why I can't hold that particular job down for room and board. If you want."

His reply, and the suggestion, evidently caught her flat-footed. "Do you really mean that?" she asked, after a moment. "Or are you just putting me on?"

Not for a chance to stay here, I'm not.

"Call it 'assistant' instead of 'secretary' and I'd feel better, but sure, I mean it," he told her, surprised he hadn't thought of this sooner. "It's no worse than any of the other jobs I've had. Shoot, Jennie, I've worked at Mickie D's, I've pumped gas in truck stops, I've even washed cars. This is cushy, compared to those jobs, and it's sure as hell more of an intellectual stimulus. I know some about computers, and I've been a paralegal in about five states. And where else am I going to get a package that includes room, board, and Medicine training?"

She bit her lip and looked at him as if she were seeing him for the first time. "You know," she replied, slowly, "if I had an assistant, I could take on a lot more cases than I do. I could train you, help you get your P.I. license. We don't make a bad team."

He snorted. "Hell, I think we make a great team. If you're willing to make it a little more formal."

She nodded, slowly. "Tell you what; let's work out this Calligan thing and see if we can keep from killing each other, and after we get it wrapped up, whatever additional cases I can take in with you as an assistant, I'll pay you for. Deal?"

"Deal," he replied instantly. And with relief. This was something solid and settled. He'd needed "solid" for a while; he just hadn't figured it out till now.

She grinned. "You know, *you're* the one who's going to have to do all the paperwork on yourself. Quarterlies, 1099s, the whole bit!"

"Not a problem. Now go bake yourself," he told her. "We've both got early starts to make tomorrow."

She wandered off down the hall; he closed up the office and headed in the opposite direction, toward the kitchen. He got himself a quick snack; glanced into the darkened living room, and saw that Mooncrow had already retired to his room. The old man had been "working" a lot; he probably needed a good night's rest more than Jennie did at this point. *Medicine sure can take it out of you,* he thought soberly, heading back toward his own room, after making certain of all the physical locks on doors and windows and turning off the lights. *I never knew that, either. It's work, as hard as manual labor. Hell, no wonder the old man is in good shape. He has to be. Maybe that's why Jennie took Tai Chi way back when. Maybe I ought to think about some kind of martial arts class, or aerobics, or something. . . .*

As he turned off the hall lights, he saw that there was no light coming from either the sauna or from under Jennie's door. *Good,* he thought with satisfaction. *She needs the rest. I'll just do a couple of chapters in that book about the Osage and—*

But as he opened his own door and closed it again, he froze. Because he was not alone. His hand stuck to the light switch as he heard soft breathing; after a moment, he lowered it, carefully.

My .45 is tucked right on top of the Webster's. *Whoever this is—*

"Don't bother looking for your gun," came a whisper from behind him, as he stealthily reached toward the top of the bookcase by the door, where he kept his automatic. "I moved it."

A pair of hands rested on his shoulders for a moment, and turned him carefully around. "I figured your reflexes were as automatic as mine," Jennie continued, with a chuckle, "and I didn't want to get shot."

She laughed softly, deep in her throat. It was the most

incredibly sexy laugh he'd ever heard. He brought his hands up, slowly, and she fitted herself into his arms.

"Jennie, what are you doing here?" he said, finally. A stupid thing to say, but it was the only thing his stupefied brain could come up with.

"Sexual harassment," she said. "Trying to see if I can get my new secretary to go to bed with me."

"Assistant," he replied, firmly. "I'm holding out for assistant. I may be easy, but I'm not cheap."

Jennie chuckled again, and pulled him over to the bed. "All right," she agreed. "Assistant it is." She began unbuttoning his shirt, slowly, taking the initiative. "So long as it's understood that I am the one seducing you."

"Yes, boss-ma'am," he replied obediently. His fingers touched the top button of her jeans, and stopped there. "By the way, if you don't mind my asking—why now?"

"Because I don't like to be herded," she said, fiercely, then pulled his face down to hers and kissed him, licking the corners of his mouth, nibbling his lower lip. "I don't like conspiracies—especially when my own family is doing the conspiring."

"I prefer cooperative efforts, myself, boss-ma'am," he agreed, then returned the kiss with interest. Her skin tingled at the touch of his tongue; his technique had definitely improved. He pulled away just long enough to ask, "Your safe-sex, or mine?"

"Mine," she replied, rattling the little plastic packet she pulled out of the pocket of her jeans. "I'm the boss, remember?" She took the upper hand again, pulling him down onto the bed and tumbling after, pulling his shirt off and starting on his jeans. He returned the favor, slipping his hands up under her T-shirt.

After that, things only got better.

She couldn't help making then-and-now comparisons—but they all came out in favor of "now." This was a double bed, not a bunk. They didn't have to worry about being caught by the R.A., or by his or her roommate. He was a better, more considerate lover. So, she hoped, was she . . . at least she'd learned how to make putting on a condom a sensual experience.

And there was something more, now, that hadn't been there when they were in college. Something between them, a kind of energy. It wasn't passion—they'd had plenty of that, before. Probably too much. This was something that carried over into everything; made every touch of a fingertip seem doubly intense.

Whatever it was, it was wonderful.

And even when it was over, when they both collapsed in exhaustion, "it" wasn't gone.

She listened to his heartbeat slow, with her ear against his chest, and fitted herself into the curve of his arm, trying to sort it all out.

"I suppose this means asking for a Christmas bonus is out of the question," he said, conversationally.

She started to giggle; she couldn't help it. "Where the hell did you get this sense of humor?" she demanded. "All of a sudden, you can laugh at yourself—you never did that before!"

He took a deep breath, and let it out, slowly. "I had it all along, I just didn't think that—hell, I just didn't think, period." He ran a finger along the side of her face. "I don't exactly know, Jennie. Kestrel. Maybe that's it. I stopped posing with you—or when I do pose, we both know it. Does that seem logical?"

"As logical as anything," she replied, thoughtfully. "Funny; all of a sudden I feel like I'm living with my skin off."

He sighed. "So do I," he replied, slowly, sleepily. "So do I. I—have to confess something though."

"What, that your good behavior is temporary?"

He started to laugh, after a moment of silence. Quietly, but it was real laughter.

"How did you guess?" he asked. She snuggled a little closer.

"Because it happens to me, every time I have a profound Medicine experience," she confessed in turn. "I go on really good behavior for a while, then, well, I start to slip back to being a bitch. Not as big a bitch as I was before, but—still, there it is. I'm human; so are you. I guess humans can only be perfect for so long."

Her confession left him quiet for a moment.

"I'll make a deal with you," he said, finally, as she hoped he would. "If you give me a little slack when I'm being a bastard, I'll cut you some when you're being a bitch."

She smiled, into the darkness. "It's a deal," she replied softly.

Mooncrow seemed neither surprised nor displeased when they both came out of the same room in the morning. He simply greeted them both in a very preoccupied way; Jennie sobered completely, forgetting her own faint embarrassment, when she caught his mood. Whatever he expected to learn today, it was far more important than who had slept in whose bed last night, or any other night for that matter.

They all three piled into Mooncrow's car, although David was the one who drove, following the old man's brief instructions. Jennie perched in the back seat, leaning forward so she could listen to both of them. Mooncrow guided them out past the airport, following I-169 toward Catoosa, but on the local roads and not the highway. They seemed to be tracing the course of Mingo Creek. . . .

"Here—" Mooncrow said, suddenly. "Take the next turnoff."

That proved to be a graveled county road; in pretty good shape, actually, better than she had feared it might be when she saw the gravel. It looked as if the county had managed to get most of the roads graveled after the washouts of

spring. Mooncrow sat tensely on the front seat beside David
and peered ahead through the windshield. It was obvious
now why he had wanted David to drive; he was looking for
something. Or perhaps, he was watching for "landmarks"
not visible to the ordinary eye.

A crude, one-lane, timbered bridge crossed the creek
ahead of them. Jennie's guess about the creek was borne out
when the old man told David to stop at the bridge.

"We'll have to leave the car here, off to the side where it
won't obstruct anyone," Mooncrow said, finally. "No one
will be along to bother it."

David simply nodded. Intuition had told both of them to
dress for hiking, and now she was glad that they had, for
Mooncrow led them right down to the creek bed, where they
followed its path for at least a half mile. It was pretty rough
hiking. None of the flood-control projects had gotten this
far up the creek. It was full of downed trees, old tires, even
a dead car. Rocks ranging from the size of a bowling ball to
the size of that old car studded the bottom of the ravine, but
above their heads Jennie winced at the thickets of wild plum
and plenitude of blackberry vines; the going would be no
easier up there.

Finally, Mooncrow held up his hand, as they reached a
grove of ancient willows, cottonwoods, and redbuds. He
looked around, as if he was taking his bearings, and then
scrambled up the bank using the exposed roots of a willow
with a trunk that must have been two feet in diameter.

David and Jennie followed, to find him holding to the
trunk with one hand as he examined every inch of the
ground around the willow, frowning. She couldn't see anything here, and she wasn't prepared to use that inner vision
just at the moment. The willow that Mooncrow stood beneath would probably wash into the creek after a few more
big storms; fully a third of its roots were exposed. Across
from them was the silted area that *had* been the old creek
bed; now it supported a flourishing community of saplings,

weeds, and brush. Up and down the creek bed was more of the same.

But Mooncrow kept peering around, and finally looked down through the mat of willow roots. And then he blanched.

"What's wrong, Little Old Man?" Jennie asked quickly. "What have you found?"

"It is what I have not found, Kestrel," he replied, as David reached out to steady him. His voice was strong, but his hands were shaking. "It is what I have *not* found."

He sat down then, on the roots of the willow; Jennie joined him, with David on the other side. "You know that I told you how Watches-Over-The-Land had defeated an evil man," he said. Jennie nodded; this was for David's benefit, for he had not heard the story. "It was needful for him to drown that evil man, and then bury him. Needful to drown him so that his blood could not touch the earth, escape, and take his spirit with it; needful to bury him, so that his spirit could not wander, so that it would be held in place by the earth. If that man had become like the *mi-ah-luschka*, he could have found others to work through. It was here that our ancestor buried that man, with a willow planted over his body to hold him there." Mooncrow's face grew bleak. "But nothing lasts forever, and the willow did not hold him. Look—"

He pointed down below, where the creek had obviously changed its course and undercut the willow. "See, how the water came and washed everything from under the roots? The willow, I think, ate most of the bones, as Watches-Over-The-Land intended, but the evil one's spirit-bundle was buried there with him, and it—it is gone. I can feel it."

David shook his head, but Jennie felt the blood draining out of her face as well.

"These things, these spirit-bundles, can be doorways," Mooncrow explained for David's sake. "They can allow things through them. So now the bundle is loose in the world, and so is the spirit of that evil man. He can work through whoever takes up the bundle; and the longer he works through that person, the more likely it is that he will be able to take the place of anyone who touches it. This is something that he was working toward, to be able to live on this earth forever, by sending others through his spirit-door and taking their place."

David's forehead wrinkled. "But—I don't see the point—"

Mooncrow stared down at the water, as if he was demanding that it give up its secret and tell him where the bundle was now. "The point is that this evil one wanted life forever, and power, and he got his power through hate. He will make that hate grow, here and now. He will poison the earth to give him power over it. So wicked was he that he *had* no spirit-animal; he created his own, neither bird nor insect, neither animal nor serpent. He made it out of all of these things, so that it would serve him rather than guide him. And he made it corrupt, so that it would poison all that it touched. That is what made him so evil. That he would corrupt anything, so long as he had dominion over it."

David stared at the old man, his own face going pale, and Jennie wondered if he, too, had a dream like hers, of a poisoned earth, and dead eagles lying in the ashes.

"I had a dream, the night of my vision-quest," he said slowly. "I was in a place like Tulsa, but with absolutely no people, completely virgin wilderness. Everything was great—and then this—this monster came, and it was like you just described, it wasn't animal or bird, but it had pieces of all kinds of things, only twisted and distorted. Wherever it went, things just died as it passed. I was really afraid, and I hid from it."

Mooncrow nodded, listening closely, and clenched his jaw. "You are new in your Medicine, and should not have seen this spirit-thing, unless it had gotten a great deal of power. And it should not have been able to kill things in the spirit-world unless it was as powerful now as it was in our ancestor's time." Jennie felt her heart sink at his words; he saw her expression, and nodded, confirming that her feelings of danger and dread were not misplaced. The warm sunlight seemed to thin, and a chill crept over her.

"This is a bad thing, David," Mooncrow said then. "This is a very terrible thing. Somehow, we must find whoever has this spirit-bundle; we must take it away from him, and we must do what our ancestor did, so long ago."

He looked out over the creek, and his face was a mask that hid every emotion but determination. "We must catch the beast, David. Then we must take its power, and cage it. Somehow."

Rod Calligan doodled idly on the pad on his desk, and weighed out his options.

He had hoped that he'd seen the last of the Talldeer girl, when he hadn't heard or seen anything at all from her. The cops had gone off to pretend they were investigating, but there were no real leads, and he and they both knew it. The P.I. herself hadn't even set foot on the property once that he could prove. Maybe, he thought, she had taken the presence of the trap he'd left as evidence that her people *were* involved, after all, and had told the insurance company so. Or at least, she had told them she could not disprove the allegation. But it seemed that she was not going to give up, after all; Smith had just called with the bad news that she'd been put on indefinite retainer by his company. Sleighbow was higher up than Smith; there was nothing Smith could do to get her dropped.

If she'd been put on retainer, it meant that she had found something suspicious, and she'd convinced Sleighbow that more work needed to be done. Probably by telling him her suspicions, possibly by giving him her evidence. Very bad news.

So she was playing her cards very close to her chest, so close he'd had no inkling she'd found anything, and she evidently had sources he hadn't traced. Sooner or later, she was going to find something out. She had the bomb, after all, or at least he had to presume she had it; so she had at least one piece of real, hard evidence that might be traced back to him. If she could do that, she could argue convincingly that if he had planted one bomb on his own property, he could have planted more than one.

That would be more than enough to start a real investigation with him as the suspect, instead of the half-hearted investigation the cops had going now.

Then, if anyone started to look closely at the Riverside Mall project, all his layers of concealment would peel away, and it would become fairly obvious that the project was marginal at best.

Then if the insurance company—or worse, the Feds!—ordered an investigation of their own, everything would come tumbling down.

He reached into his pocket for the fetish-bundle; it had become something like a worry stone for him, and just simply handling it always calmed him. This time was no exception; as his hand closed around the leather, confidence quelled the rising panic. There was no real need to worry. After all, he had run deals along the edge of the shadow before. He hadn't ever needed to use final solutions, but he'd always had them in reserve. There was no real difference between planting a trap to get rid of the girl, and ordering her hit—other than the fact that it took control out of his own hands.

If the Talldeer girl actually had anything on him, there would be Feds crawling all over here even now. So she didn't have anything solid, only suspicions. You couldn't convict anyone on suspicions; hell, you couldn't even get an indictment on suspicion.

So, since she wouldn't fall into his traps, he was going to

have to take the direct approach to getting rid of her, even though it would be a bigger risk to delegate that task to someone else. Tulsa was a bigger city than people realized; it had its share of scum and lowlifes. If you were truly desperate, there were even punks who would fill your contract for as little as fifty bucks. But those were generally burned-out druggies, and dangerous to use; the going rate was about five thousand for a pro.

But with a pro there would be nothing leaving a trail. Not with the people Rod intended to use. Those fifty-buck punks were extremely unreliable, the five-hundred-dollar hit men would sometimes come back looking for blackmail. Rod had used the latter, now and again, but never for anything that he could be blackmailed over; most smart contractors knew muscle. Not Mafia-related, of course; that was out of his league. Just guys who, a hundred years ago, would have been rustlers and horse thieves. Rod used guys like that to strong-arm reluctant farmers or homeowners into selling at a reasonable price, or to scare tenants into moving without filing complaints with the authorities about substandard construction. He knew the right jargon, things that sounded perfectly normal on the phone.

But this time, Rod would take out his contract with a real workman; someone you saw once if at all, paid in advance, and never heard from again.

Except that the target came down with a bad case of death. And it always looked like suicide, a hit-and-run, or another tragic case of random violence. Pretty girls were raped and killed all the time. And if the pretty girl was also a P.I., well, she just had been in the wrong place, and hadn't been careful enough. It'd be good for about two nights on the local news, and wouldn't even make the nationals.

Pros didn't leave tracks. And they didn't come back after blackmail money. It was bad for repeat business.

Smith ought to know some pros in this area . . . he'd certainly hinted that he did.

Should he call Smith in on this? That was the question. He rubbed his thumb over the leather of the fetish and looked out the window, noting absently the small flock of scrawny black birds in the tree outside. Funny; they were absolutely silent, so they weren't blackbirds, starlings, or grackles. They were too thin to be ravens, and too big to be crows.

Still, weren't black birds some kind of omen of death? Maybe that was the sign he ought to move on this. Let them pick the Talldeer girl's bones, not his.

He called Smith back.

"I need someone," he said. "A reliable Tulsa mechanic. I think our equipment needs about five grand worth of work."

"I have just the right men," Smith said.

"John Smith" hung up the phone, jaw clenched, and a vein in his temple starting to throb. Not that he cared if Calligan had the chick rubbed out; in his opinion, it should have been done before this. No, the real problem was that Calligan was stupid and small-time; if things went wrong, he could implicate Smith.

No—if anything went wrong, Calligan *would* implicate Smith. He would sing so fast and so well, they'd put him in the opera.

Even if things didn't go wrong, there was no guarantee that Calligan would stay quiet. He was getting nervous; sounded a little hysterical whenever Smith said anything about Talldeer. In fact, if he'd tried something of his own to get rid of the girl, he probably left a pretty messy trail behind him.

Damned amateurs.

It might not be a bad idea to collect a little insurance of his own.

He left his desk and took a quick walk outside, to a public

telephone kiosk. Not one right outside *his* building, but one further down in the office park. He always had a roll of quarters with him, just in case.

He waited ten minutes, then called the same number he'd given Calligan.

"Fixers," said the voice on the other end.

"I need some custom work done on my car," he replied. "Something really special." That was the code that he needed a safe line to talk openly.

"Give me your number; I've got a customer. I'll call you back." Brusque, businesslike, calm. These were real professionals, probably the best in Tulsa. They should be; they'd taken care of a number of embarrassing little problems for prominent people. For instance, that evangelist with the awkward and talkative relative. . . .

Smith gave the man the number of the pay phone and hung up. A few minutes later, it rang.

"About that custom job. Yeah?" It was not the same voice. He had expected that.

"Your people just got a call from a man who wanted an Indian girl shut up," he said, quietly and calmly. "I sent him to you. We've got a deal, but he's making me nervous. His name's Rod Calligan."

"Construction." Smith's estimation of the men went up a notch. "He insisted on payment-in-person. You want some insurance on him, or do you want him shut down?"

Smith had thought about that while he made his walk and waited for the phone to ring. Calligan was still useful. "Insurance," he said. "He's got a wife and kids. Get rid of his target first, then pick up the family. Maybe get rid of the wife to prove we're serious. Make sure the Indians get the blame for all of it, so far as the cops are concerned."

"Easy, but it'll take some time to fill Calligan's contract, so it won't happen right away," the man replied. "Make your deposit, send us the spec sheet on him. That'll be fifteen. As soon as we get it, we'll open the policy for you, and fill your order as soon as we take care of Calligan's."

Send them all the details on Calligan with their fee, in cash, that meant, to their mail drop. Untraceable cash. It would take him a little work to collect the money—he had it, but he would want to get it in thousand-dollar lots, from several places, to make sure he didn't get sequential bills. "That'll do fine. Expect it in a few days," he told the man, and hung up.

So much for Rod Calligan and his little problem.

You just had to know who to call.

Toni Calligan held back tears with the last of her strength; she was just about ready to sign herself into the asylum. She was afraid to let the kids out of her sight, after the attack on Ryan. *Things* kept happening, inexplicable things, but worst of all, so far as her sanity was concerned, they never happened when Rod was home.

Rod Junior had tattled; he'd told Rod how he'd come home to find Toni crying at the kitchen table after Ryan's near accident. She had been able to keep Rod from finding out about that for maybe five minutes; after a brief session of bullying, he had the story of the near miss out of her.

Unfortunately, she had not gotten the stranger's name and phone number, so there was no one to corroborate her story but Ryan.

Now Rod was accusing her of making things up, and getting Ryan and Jill to tell the same stories. The few incidents that she had evidence of he somehow twisted around to being her fault, saying she was careless, a bad mother.

And somehow he'd found out what that one repairman had said about the dryer.

That was when he really lost his temper with her, which lately hadn't been very good, anyway. He'd taken it out on her . . . he hit her, telling her she deserved it, deserved to be punished, because she was not only unfit to be the mother of his *good* son, Rod, but was crazy and was making the other two crazy, and he was just going to have to beat the craziness out of her.

Her life had become a nightmare.

But the real nightmare was not the attacks on her children, or even the bruises that Rod's beating had left.

The real nightmare was that she was beginning to think he was right. She *was* going crazy.

She didn't know what else to think, after what had happened this afternoon when she'd been making spaghetti sauce in the pressure cooker.

She had *just* put the pot on the burner. She had turned around to pick up a pot holder, and had looked up at a sudden movement, thinking one of the kids had come in.

There was an Indian in her kitchen.

An Indian with a mohawk, some kind of shell necklace around his neck, a blanket tied around his waist, fringed leather pants—carrying a hatchet with a shiny metal blade in one hand, some kind of wooden club in the other. And his face—it had such an expression of *hate* that she shrank back with a little squeak of panic, so terrified her voice wouldn't work.

Then he was gone. Just *gone*. He didn't leave, he vanished, completely.

Just as Ryan appeared in the doorway.

It couldn't have been more than thirty seconds from the time she'd lit the flame to when the Indian vanished into thin air. She wasn't sure *what* warned her, then; some instinct, God only knew. But the moment Ryan appeared, she *knew*, something horrible was going to happen, and she just leapt on him, tackled him, and pulled him to the floor right outside the kitchen.

Just as the pressure cooker exploded.

She got both of them *just* out of the way of the shrapnel— for the pot had literally exploded, rather than having the lid blow off.

She sat there on the floor with Ryan and they both cried for a while. Then she got him calmed down, extracted a promise from him *not* to tell his daddy, and ventured into the kitchen. There was only one thing to do, if she didn't want another lecture—or worse—from Rod. She had to get the mess cleaned up, hide the damage from a cursory examination, and get some other kind of dinner going before he got home. And how she was going to explain this if he did find out, she had no idea.

Maybe she wouldn't have to. Rod never came into the kitchen if he could help it. A few hours with some plaster would take care of the holes in the walls and ceiling, and he probably wouldn't notice the dents in the fridge even if he did come in.

She set to work, frantically pulling bits of metal out of the walls, scrubbing red sauce—*like blood*—off the walls, the ceiling, the floor—trying to remember if she had told Rod what supper would be—

She had. Hell. Well, he would just have to put up with a different kind of sauce. She could say it was an experiment. She snatched tomato sauce and spices out of the cabinet, threw them at random into a pot. If it came out tasting funny, she could bury it in cheese.

But the *Indian*—she had to be going crazy. No amount of scrubbing would wipe him out of her mind. Standing there, between the table and the fridge, long hair trailing down his back, staring at her. Hating her. Telling her so, with his eyes.

And then vanishing, just like a soap bubble.

She was going crazy. She had to be.

She stopped dead at that thought, hands frozen on her scrubbing pads, hair trailing into her face.

If she was crazy, could Rod be right? Could she be doing these things *herself*? Could she have put the scorpion in the sandbox, stripped the insulation from the wires in the dryer, turned the heat up under the pressure cooker?

Was *she* trying to kill her own children?

She started crying at that, silently so as not to alert the children. Mechanically, she went back to scrubbing, tears falling to mingle with the soapy water. If *she* was doing all this—

She didn't remember doing anything!

But—people with multiple personalities didn't remember what their other "selves" did, either. Sybil, Trudi Chase, Eve . . . they had no idea what their other selves did. And they never noticed missing time, either, the places in their lives where the other personalities took over.

But then a single ray of hope came to her. The woman who had almost hit Ryan—*she* had seen the Indian too! What was more, even if this "Indian" was a personality of her own, *she* couldn't possibly have gotten into a costume, down the street, pushed Ryan in front of the car, then sprinted back to her kitchen and shed the costume before Ryan and the stranger arrived there.

She sniffed, and wiped her eyes with the back of her hand. She had to keep cleaning. No matter what, she had to keep cleaning. Cleaning up this mess, that was real reality. She *could* cope with this, even if the rest of her life was falling apart.

Even if it was the only thing left in her life that she could cope with.

CHAPTER FOURTEEN

JENNIE WRAPPED HER long hair into a French braid, and examined herself carefully in the mirror. *Hmm. A little too harsh, I think.* She added a touch of eye shadow. *Better.*

Somehow, she felt as if she were donning—well, not war-paint, but possibly bluff-paint, the colors the Osage put on when they were not taking the path of war but wanted their enemies to think that *Wah-K'on-Tah* had directed them to do just that. On the other hand, that was indirectly what she *was* doing. She was about to try to pull off a bluff.

She was still not certain of all the points in the connection between Calligan and the looted gravesite, but the little medicine-pouch proved he was involved. The presence of the *mi-ah-luschka* at the site only confirmed that. She and Mooncrow had done everything they could; she needed some kind of real-world proof that he had at least looted the gravesite. Based on that, and on the bomb she and David had taken, she might be able to convince the police and the insurance company that Calligan was running some kind of looted artifact scam, that he routinely booby-trapped his caches, and that his men had accidentally set off one of *his* bombs. It was thin, but it was better than watching him get off scot-free.

Something protected Calligan, Mooncrow said, so the Little People were going after everything "near" him. It stood to reason that they just might be attacking his family at this point. If that was the case, Calligan's wife might be willing to talk. She might know something.

So Jennie was going on the offensive. Time to talk to Antonia Calligan. There were any number of explanations for the artifacts and the Little People, including the possibility that it could be the *wife* who had looted the site and cached the artifacts. This was remote, and certainly did not fit the little Jenny knew about the woman, but still a possibility that should not be dismissed without checking.

Hence the suit and the makeup. She wanted to look like someone that Antonia would find familiar enough to talk to, possibly even confide in.

Meanwhile, Mooncrow and David had jobs of their own. Mooncrow was searching the spirit-worlds for signs of the evil spirit's work. It seemed far too coincidental for *that* spirit to have suddenly been freed at about the same time that Calligan looted the sacred ground, but whether Calligan was under the direct influence of the evil one was still in question. David was searching the papers for the same thing, going back for six months, which is about when Mooncrow thought the flood had uncovered the spirit-bundle that was missing. If they were very lucky, it was in the hands of someone who was resistant to it. If not, well, they would play that as it came.

She gave her hair another pat, and headed out.

"Would you like another cup of coffee?" Antonia ("Oh, call me Toni, please") Calligan asked. Her dark eyes pleaded with Jennie to accept, so of course, she did.

Toni's kitchen was a warm and homey place, eggshell-white and tan, but was curiously marred. The immaculate white walls showed slightly discolored patches of very fresh plaster and paint; there were odd dents in the metal cabinets and the appliances. Strange. Nothing else in the house showed that kind of abuse.

But it was fairly obvious that the kitchen was the only place where Toni felt comfortable. Jennie wasn't too surprised; you could eat off the floors in the living and dining areas, but the rooms looked like pictures in a magazine, not places where children played and people ate. Clearly the kitchen was Toni's personal domain; the only place in the house that was permitted to be less than perfect.

Rod Calligan's wife wore her dark hair in a pert Hamill-cut; despite three children, she was slender under that perky pink sweatsuit. But "pert" and "perky" were the very last adjectives that Jennie would ever apply to her, despite a petite figure and a sweet, square face.

"Hagridden," maybe. The faint circles under her eyes came from anxiety, and Jennie would have bet a year's income that the reason that the hollows under her cheekbones were there had less to do with Weight Watchers and far more to do with worry. She looked afraid, but afraid of what? She didn't exactly babble, but she spoke nervously, running on at length whenever a silence threatened, playing with her rings or combing her fingers through her hair.

What was more, Jennie had never met anyone so starved for company in her life. No, that wasn't right; not "company," but a friend. Toni Calligan acted as if she didn't have a single friend of her own, female or male, anywhere in Tulsa.

Maybe she didn't. Maybe Rod Calligan didn't permit her to have friends. After all, friends would take time away from cleaning and housekeeping. Friends might give her something to think about besides her husband.

"I just don't know that much about Rod's company, Jennie," Toni said, somewhat wistfully, as she passed over the newly filled cup. When "Antonia" became "Toni," Jennifer had, of course, become "Jennie." "I wish I did, I really don't feel as if I'm being much help to you."

Jennie had the uncanny feeling of being a mind reader, even though her Medicine talents did not lie at all in that direction; she knew *exactly* what had put that wistful tone in Toni Calligan's voice. It was simple; Toni wanted her company, wanted her to stay around. The less Toni knew, the sooner Jennie would leave, because Jennie obviously wouldn't stay just to keep Toni company.

"Actually, I'm not so much looking for hard information as you might think, Toni," Jennie assured her, feeling obscurely sorry for the woman. "Your husband told the company I'm working for that there were people making threats before and after the bombing. You've probably heard who those people were supposed to be—mostly Native American groups. What I'm looking for is a feeling of something a little off—if you remember noticing things being strange around that time period. For instance, one thing I'd like to know is if you remember any odd phone calls coming to the house this spring and summer?"

"Oh, no threats!" Toni exclaimed, immediately, brightening a little because she at least had some information, even if it was negative. "No one called here with any threats—or at least they didn't call the house line. Rod has a private line for business in his office, of course. I wouldn't know if he got any threatening calls on that line, although he didn't act as if there was anything different going on. He was tense, but not the way he'd be if there was anyone threatening him."

And how I'd love to get into that office, Jennie thought, greedily. *If there are any deep, black secrets about Rod Calligan, that's where they'll be, I'll bet.*

Grandfather was right about one thing, at least; something was protecting Rod Calligan. Here she was, mere feet away from that office, yet she might just as well have been thousands of miles away. She was unable to sense *anything* there; it was a complete blank in the middle of the otherwise ordinary house.

She would have given her hopes of ever being a pipe-bearer for the key to that office or the chance to get inside.

But the possibility of that, at least at the moment, was pretty remote.

"I wasn't thinking of threatening calls, actually," she said, slowly. "The kind of people who have been implicated in the bombing have—I suppose you'd call it a sense of honor. They would never threaten a woman or a child, so *you* would never hear any threats. No, what I was thinking was simply *strange* calls. An inordinate number of people who hang up when *you* answered the phone, people who wouldn't identify themselves or give a number for a return call. People you didn't recognize. That kind of thing."

Toni's brows creased as she thought. "Not—that I noticed," she said, hesitantly. "But—are you certain these people wouldn't consider hurting a child?"

The strange tone in her voice made Jennie's senses move to full alertness. She picked her words very carefully. "I said that the people who had been *implicated* would never consider doing such a thing, but I don't suppose it will come as any shock to you that there are some people who would consider a child a very *good* target; children are very innocent, very vulnerable." *Carefully, Kestrel. Don't say anything that could be taken as disapproval of her husband. And don't blurt out anything about the Little People.* "I'm sure you realize that your husband is in a business where people collect enemies, and it is possible that one of those people has become angry enough with him to decide to attack him personally, rather than through business channels."

Toni paled, just a little. "He's been—very tense, lately," she said. "Very on edge, and his temper has been awfully short." She laughed nervously. "Sometimes he kind of takes it out on me and the kids. Not Little Rod, but Ryan and Jill. Little Rod is a lot like his dad, but Ryan and Jill are like me."

Suddenly there was an explanation for Toni's long-sleeved sweatsuit, on a hot June day. Bruises. Welts. In other words, Rod was indulging his temper by beating his wife.

Taking it out on you, hmm? Jennie kept her anger tightly under control. She'd handled enough abuse cases to know that the women involved in an abusive relationship did *not* want anyone noticing it, much less saying something about it. They would not admit that it was abuse to themselves. They would not listen to anyone who told them it was abuse.

"This must be something new, or you wouldn't have mentioned it," she replied, after taking a sip of coffee. "Right?"

"He's always had a temper, but it's been a little worse lately," Toni said, with another nervous laugh. "Of course, we all provoke him; it's summer, so the kids are rowdy, and I can't always keep up with their messes, but it's also his busiest time of year and he doesn't have time to be patient. . . ."

She'd heard all *that* before. They always had excuses. Most of the excuses had been hand-fed to them by the very spouses who were abusing them. *Great. So now I have a classic case of spouse abuse on my hands along with everything else.*

"Everything else" was the miasma of hatred so thick in the kitchen that it was difficult for Jennie to sit there calmly sipping coffee. Only the fact that it was not directed at her made it possible for her to chat pleasantly away, and not take to her heels.

The hatred of the *mi-ah-lusćhka* hung heavily over this house. If they could not have Rod Calligan directly, then they would make him suffer through his family; that was the feeling Jennie got. Not a feeling that Toni was involved at all, but that she was as good a target as a bulldozer.

One thing Jennie was certain of; Toni Calligan was innocent of any wrongdoing. Which added yet another complication to an already complicated situation.

First, Jennie would have to get them out of the line of fire; take them away as targets for the Little People. Right now they might simply be causing the same kind of accidents that were happening at the mall site, but it was not very likely things would remain that way for much longer. Not with the blood-hunger she sensed here. The Little People wanted someone *hurt*.

Purely and simply, getting Toni and her kids into safety meant removing them from Rod Calligan's life.

"Kids sure are a handful once school closes, aren't they?" she said, changing the subject to one Toni would immediately feel more comfortable with.

This was going to take time and patience. To be certain of protection, all ties to Calligan would have to be destroyed. That could mean a mundane divorce as well as a purification ceremony. Could she talk Toni Calligan into so drastic a step?

Maybe. She did not speak as a woman who loved her husband, but rather as a woman who thought she should love her husband. There was a real and distinct difference. And if Calligan was abusing her—there was a chance.

Time, and patience, dammit. Both of which, she thought wryly, as Toni brightened and began talking about her kids, *I have always been in short supply of! It just figures. . . .*

Jennie was seeing more of Toni Calligan now than of David and Mooncrow. She began coming over after Rod Calligan had left for the day, and stayed at the house for as long as she dared. For one thing, while she was *there*, the *mi-ah-luschka* weren't playing their tricks, so at least she was keeping them from hurting anyone for several hours at a time. For another, Toni wasn't just hungry for adult companionship, she was starving for it. It made Jennie angry with Calligan all over again. How he could reduce an intelligent woman to this state. . . .

To avoid any trouble for Toni, she pitched in on the daily "decontamination" chores. She couldn't call it "cleaning"; the space shuttle went through less thorough scrubdowns! It soon became clear that all this ultracleanliness was at Rod's insistence. Only the childrens' rooms and the kitchen and laundry were allowed to look "lived-in." Everything else must look as if it was ready for a "House Beautiful" tour. At all times, regardless of anything else.

Toni's explanation was that Rod might have to bring a client in at any moment, and that client had to be impressed from the moment he walked in the door. But Jennie figured that even Toni knew better than that, just from the hesitant way in which she offered the rather lame explanation. This was just one more way that Rod controlled his wife and proved his control to others.

Only one room was off-limits; the locked office. Toni didn't even have a key to it. Every time she came, Jennie surreptitiously checked the door, but it always remained locked, and behind that door there was nothing to Medicine Senses but a black hole.

Frustrating.

Very frustrating.

Still, if she could not get into the office, she nevertheless had the mission of getting Toni and her kids out of Rod's influence so that the *mi-ah-luschka* would leave them alone. She had a foreboding feeling that the Little People were losing what little patience they possessed, and would start something soon. Toni started at every odd sound, and kept looking for something out of the corner of her eye. She might just have started to see them . . . which would mean they were preparing to work some revenge.

Slowly, she began planting hints. How "normal" husbands might lose their tempers once in a while, but they didn't blame their wives for everything that went wrong. And that adult human beings did not take out their frustrations on other humans beings. When Toni seemed, tentatively, to be receptive, she planted a few more hints, describing the Women's Shelter and some of the women she had taken there for help.

She began planting other hints as well; especially after she learned that Toni had some remote Cherokee blood in her. She told stories over coffee, about spiritual or supernatural experiences of any number of people she'd known. Harmless stories, mostly, involving brief glimpses into the Spirit Worlds and the like, and stressing how people who might think they were hallucinating could very well actually be seeing things that those with less open minds could not.

Jennie was reminded irresistibly of the winter that Mooncrow taught her how to make wild birds eat out of her hand. She had spent hours at a time, sitting in the snow, with a handful of sunflower seeds. Not daring to move, hardly daring to breathe, while the cardinals, titmice, and chickadees ventured nearer and nearer.

Eventually, her patience had paid off to the point where the birds would swoop down and perch on her hat as soon as they saw her coming.

Could she get *this* bird to come to her, too?

It might mean more than this case; it might mean the saving of a woman's sanity and the salvation of her childrens' lives. Jennie did not like the increasingly frightened look in Toni Calligan's eyes whenever she thought she heard her husband's car in the driveway.

It reminded her more and more of the look she had seen in the eyes of a trapped and helpless deer.

* * *

If the rest of her life had not been so hellish, the entrance of Jennie Talldeer into it would have been cause for celebration. For the first time since her marriage to Rod, Toni Calligan had a friend.

She used to have friends; she used to have a lot of them. But Rod had driven them away, one by one, with his sarcastic remarks and his constant badgering questions. Other women got tired of being interrogated about where they had been, where they were going, what they were going to do, and did their own husbands and fathers know about it. They didn't like the way that Rod watched them when he was home—"As if he thinks I'm going to steal the silverware or turn you into a Moonie," Frieda Miller had complained. They didn't like the remarks that one of her former girlfriends had called "sexist."

But Jennie Talldeer somehow had a sixth sense for when Rod was going to return, and she never visited when he was around, or left any signs that she had ever been there at all. Jennie was bright, fun to talk to, and didn't seem much like a private investigator at all, just like "one of the girls."

Best of all, Jennie *understood*. Even if some of the things she had to say—about husbands in general, admittedly, and never directly accusing Rod—made Toni acutely uncomfortable. Then again, maybe Jennie was simply telling Toni in a roundabout way *why* she was avoiding Rod. When Jennie was gone, and Toni sat alone over the coffee, she had to admit that what Jennie said made sense.

The things Rod did, to her and to Ryan and Jill—they just weren't right. All those cruel taunts, and the way he kept trying to frighten Ryan under the guise of "making the boy tough."

And the scolding sessions that had gone from words to blows. . . .

True, Toni's father had never been a very warm or loving man, but he had never *hit* her mother. Although he had been just as sarcastic and cutting as Rod. He'd always known what to say to just devastate a person.

So did Rod.

Well, that made sense too, from what Jennie said. Funny, she had never thought what a weapon words could be, until Jennie pointed it out. Words could hurt worse than knives, because they cut you where it didn't show.

On the outside. On the *outside*.

She had begun thinking over things, in the leisure granted her by Jennie's willingness to pitch in and help. She often had as much as an hour or two, now, when she could just sit and think, and a lot of her thoughts were very uncomfortable.

She had to admit, if only to herself, that Rod never had been the Prince Charming she'd thought. In fact, in a lot of ways, he was more like Ivan the Terrible. But she'd been so busy, what with one thing and another, that she'd never really thought about how she was less his wife and more like his housekeeper, errand-runner, and—

Admit it, Toni. Punching bag.

That was how Jennie, detached, but compassionate, had described some of her clients, women she had met at the Women's Shelter or women she had taken there. *They were punching bags for their husbands,* she'd said, sighing. *Whenever something went wrong for the man, he came home and took it out on her or the kids, or both. I mean, in a way I can almost understand it. These guys all had nowhere to go, no way to express their anger and frustration, and their wives were the only creatures they knew weaker and less powerful than they were. It's like chickens in a chicken house; the big chickens pick on the littler ones, and so on down the line, until it comes to the last chicken in the chicken house, who gets abuse from everybody. But that doesn't make it right. People aren't chickens. People know better.*

Uncomfortable thinking.

She'd asked Toni about what she'd done before she married Rod; pointed out that she could still make a living for herself, even if Rod wasn't there. That was something that hadn't occurred to her in ages, and Toni had started to wonder just what life would be like without Rod around.

Jennie was a pretty smart cookie, when it came down to it. Everything she said made sense.

She'd said other things too; things that were beginning to make Toni wonder about being crazy or not. She had a lot of funny, and sometimes not-so-funny, stories about people who'd seen what she called Spirits, things that weren't necessarily ghosts, but certainly weren't physical. And what Jennie said about the Spirits sure matched those Indians Toni kept seeing. . . .

She was seeing them, out of the corner of her eye, all the time now, half-seen shadows, or transparent ghost-images. Sometimes they even showed up when Rod was home, though never in the same area of the house as he was; they seemed to wait to try and catch her alone. The only time they weren't there was when Jennie was visiting. Toni really wished they *would* show up then, so she could find out if Jennie saw them too, but they never obliged. Like a kid, they were never there when you wanted them. They lurked around the house to the point where she saw them at least twice or three times a night, peering in the windows, grimacing at her, and disappearing when she turned to look straight at them.

They tended to show up after dark, too, which made them pretty unnerving. She hadn't told Jennie about them, but it was almost as if Jennie knew about them, just like she knew about Rod without being told anything.

Almost as if she knew—and understood.

Thunder growled, making them both look up.

"Cripes, where did that come from?" Jennie Talldeer said, glancing at her watch and then up at the growing storm outside. "I really have got to go, before this breaks.

It looks like it's going to be hell to drive in."

Toni nodded, surreptitiously rubbing her sore wrist, hoping Jennie wouldn't notice. But Jennie spotted the movement anyway, and raised an eyebrow at her.

"Arthritis?" she asked. Grateful for the "out," Toni nodded. Rod had grabbed her wrist and yanked her around last night, shaking her; the wrist had been swollen this morning. It had gone down some, but this coming storm made it twinge.

"I guess so," Toni replied, hoping her flush of guilt at lying didn't show. "It was real sore this morning. I hate to think of having arthritis already, though; it makes me feel so *old.*"

Jennie shrugged. "My brother broke his ankle fancy-dancing on uneven ground, and it gives him all kinds of hell whenever it's about to rain. And *my* fingers hurt, sometimes. Trust me, arthritis doesn't care how old you are! But I really need to go, Toni, much as I hate to."

Because the minute the rain breaks, Rod will be coming back home, Toni thought with a sigh. *Jennie knows. But she's too nice to say that. She doesn't want to run into him, I'm sure. If he knows that she's supposed to be checking him out, he'll be nice to her but take it out on me. And if he doesn't, he'll be rotten to her just to get rid of her.*

"Well thanks for coming over and giving me a hand with everything," she said, instead, and smiled. "Come on, I'll see you off."

Jennie grimaced as they got outside and saw the true magnitude of the storm on the western horizon. The window in the kitchen looked north, while this "boomer" was coming straight out of the west. Huge black thunderheads loomed thousands of feet up in the air, their tops forming the "anvil" formations that meant dangerous weather to come. The roofs of the houses hid the bottoms of the clouds, but they wouldn't for long, and the angry growl of thunder was testament enough to the amount of lightning hitting the ground at the leading edge of the storm.

"You'd better go turn on a radio," Jennie advised, as she got into her little truck. "Keep the TV off though, and stay away from the windows. This looks like it could brew up a tornado, and there's going to be a lot of lightning, for sure. You might want to get the kids ready to duck into the bathroom if we get a tornado alert."

"I'll do that," Toni said, just as the wind picked up, with three chilly gusts that sent garbage cans flying into the street and flattened her clothing against her. The air was full of rain-and-ozone-smell. "You'd better get going!" she added, over the distant growl of thunder. "This may flood the underpasses!"

Jennie pulled out, with a backward wave.

She hurried into the backyard to gather up the kids; Ryan and Jill were only too happy to come inside, but Rod sassed her. "I want to watch!" he said. "It's not here yet! You think I'm gonna melt if I get a little wet?"

Toni gave his rump a little smack for the sass. "You get in that house when I tell you to, mister," she scolded, shagging him inside after the other two. "You're not too big for me to spank; you better remember that!"

Ryan and Jill went to their rooms, and she assumed that Rod followed. She went straight to the kitchen to turn on a radio; they didn't have cable anymore, and she didn't trust the television in a thunderstorm. Jennie was right to warn her. The antenna that Rod had put up before they got cable was too high and he had never taken it down; it was on a tower that made it the tallest thing in the neighborhood, and whenever there was lightning, she was always afraid it would get hit. Rod laughed at her for her fears, but she would never allow the set on during a storm if he wasn't there to insist on it.

Outside, the sky turned black, and the kitchen went as dark as if the sun were setting. She tuned in right in the middle of a National Weather Service bulletin; they were always so scratchy and full of static she had to concentrate to make out what the man was saying. *Strong winds, damaging hail, severe thunderstorm. . . .* Not even a "watch"; this one, as any fool could see, was already here. No talk of tornadoes, though—

She caught the sound of the television from the living room, and hurried in to find young Rod messing with it in the gloom of the living room. The only light came from the screen.

"You get away from that!" she snapped. "I have *told* you and *told* you, don't use the TV in a thunderstorm!"

"I wanta see Doppler Six radar," Rod whined, defiantly. "Chill out, Ma! Nothing's gonna happen! You talk like some kind of hystric! And you act like you want me t' grow up t' be a fag!"

Now *that*—except that the word was "hysteric," not "hystric"—was straight from his father's mouth. Bad enough to hear it from Rod—but this was too much.

She saw red and was about to give him that spanking she had promised—but before she could move to give his fanny a real tanning, she saw something else instead.

The Indian.

It rose up from the shadows behind the television set, where it had either been lurking, or been *doing* something to the television set. Ryan came up behind her, and grabbed for her hand with a gasp.

This time the Indian did not disappear when she turned her full attention on it; she was looking straight at it, and although Rod didn't seem to see it, Ryan beside her did, and shrank against her, whimpering.

It grinned at her, a nasty, snide grin. *Like a wolverine,* she thought, crazily. *Like a bear trap. Like—like the Devil, just before he takes a soul!*

And it vanished.

Rod was still messing with the television. "There!" he said in triumph, as the picture came in; the Channel Six weatherman standing in front of an image of a Doppler Radar scan. "I need to tune—"

His hand was on the dial, just as lightning hit the antenna above them.

The next half hour was hell on earth.

Toni found herself on the dining room floor, Ryan beside her, with no memory of how they had gotten there. She scrambled to her feet and dashed into the living room, vaguely aware that every hair on her head was standing on end, and feeling a kind of tingle in her hands and feet, as if they'd been asleep.

Young Rod was collapsed in a heap beside the television. The back of the set had blown out, and glass shards were embedded in the wall behind the set.

Rod's outstretched hand was black and crisped. He wasn't moving.

She didn't scream; she didn't panic. "Ryan," she said, very clearly and out of some kind of unholy calm, "call 9-1-1. Tell them your brother's been hit by lightning. If our phone doesn't work, go next door and use theirs, and give them our address. If the phone does work, make the call, then go next door to Mrs. Nebles. Take Jill. Stay there."

"But Ma—" Ryan burbled, clearly terrified.

"Go *now,*" she yelled, fiercely, and then all her concentration was on the child who needed her. She ran across the living room and fell to her knees beside Rod. She put him over on his back, carefully, in case there was a spinal injury, feeling under his chin for a pulse.

No pulse. No breathing.

She had never done CPR except on a dummy, but it all came back to her now. She tilted his head back, made sure his airway was clear, covered his mouth and nose with her mouth, and breathed.

Once. Twice. Then pump his chest. She didn't need to be

too careful; he wasn't so small that she'd crack his ribs.

Breathe. Pump. Breathe. Pump. *Don't forget to breathe for yourself, or you'll pass out.*

At some point, she heard sirens over the sound of the pouring rain and the thunder outside. She ignored them as she ignored everything else.

Breathe. Pump. Breathe—

Hands pulled her away; she fought them for a moment, until she saw it was the paramedics in their bright yellow slickers, then she let them take over, surrounding Rod with their machines and their expertise.

Other people came crowding in; firemen, Mrs. Nebles, the neighbor with Ryan and Jill. She couldn't see Rod for all the bodies around him, but she heard the pure tone of a flat-lined EKG, then heard someone say "Clear!", and then everyone pulled away.

She heard the snap of the fibrillator, heard someone curse. The flat tone continued.

She collapsed into the chest of whoever was holding her, sobbing as hysterically as her two remaining children. She would never forget that horrible, unwavering tone for as long as she lived.

They tried, over and over again, to get Rod's heart started. But the tame lightning of their machines could not restart what the wild lightning had stopped.

Finally, they pronounced Rod dead on the scene, covered him up with a rubber sheet, and took him away, into the rain, in an ambulance, but one with the lights and siren dead. She rode in the back, with the paramedic holding her hand, awkwardly.

She was no longer crying, no longer screaming with the pain of her loss. She was numb, now; after the ambulance ride, after the session at the hospital with the doctors and the paperwork—how could they *bother* with paperwork at a

time like that?—after the call to Rod, missing him by minutes. They'd left a policeman at her home, the nurses told
her, patting her hand. The policeman would tell him. He
would come soon, to help her with all this.

But he never came, and she stumbled through it all alone.
Thank God Mrs. Nebles had said she would take care of
Ryan and Jill. Thank God the paramedics had reminded her
to bring her purse. What she couldn't remember was in the
papers she kept in her purse.

Insurance. *Why?* she had wanted to scream. People to
notify. Recounting it all to the police.

Still Rod did not come.

Surely he would come and take her home.

But he didn't come, and finally the nurses took pity on her
and called the neighbor who had Ryan and Jill, asked Mrs.
Nebles to keep the kids overnight, then sent her home with
another policeman rather than a taxi. They probably didn't
trust her to remember what her own address was. . . .

Rod's car was in the driveway; she walked up to the silent,
darkened house, still numb, not knowing what she was
going to say to him. Suddenly, she was afraid for him—how
could *he* be expected to bear up under this? Rod was his
image, his golden child! He must be half insane; no wonder
he hadn't come to the hospital!

She pulled open the door—and there he was, staring at
her. She opened her mouth, the tears starting again.

But as it happened, he didn't give her a chance to say
anything.

He simply dragged her inside, face full of—not the grief
she had expected, but silent fury. He dragged her into the
living room, to the spot in front of the TV, where Rod had
died. He shoved her down on her knees on the spot where
he had lain.

He screamed at her, as she knelt there, unable to move or
think. Screamed at her that this was all *her* fault—she was
a slut, a whore, an unfit mother—she had *caused* Rod's

death, to make way for her own favored brats, who were probably bastards by some fancy gigolo, conceived while *he* was hard at work, trying to make a decent life for them all—

Then, when she didn't respond except for silent tears, he hit her.

He knocked her into the wall, and she put up her hands, ineffectually, to defend herself. That seemed to infuriate him even further and he pulled her to her feet, then balled up both his fists, punching her in the face and stomach alternately, while she wept and retched, and finally dropped into merciful unconsciousness.

She woke up again, lying where she had fallen, in the dark and silent house, and crawled as far as the bathroom, using the sink to haul herself to her feet. Somehow, she got herself cleaned up, studiously avoiding looking at herself in the mirror. But she could not bear to go to the bedroom. Not to lie beside the man who had done this to her, and blamed her for her own son's death.

Instead, clutching her sore stomach, she got as far as the little bed in Ryan's room before she collapsed again, face and body throbbing with pain, onto the neatly made cotton comforter.

Eventually, she slept.

When she woke the next morning, an aching mass of misery inside and out, Rod was already gone.

The doorbell rang just as she was putting the finishing touches on a makeup job that she hoped, vaguely, would disguise the bruises, the black eye, and the swollen lip and jaw. It rang again, and she moved carefully to answer it, assuming that it must be the neighbor, Mrs. Nebles, who had taken Ryan and Jill—poor things, they must be hysterical; Rod hadn't come to get them and only God knew what they'd been told last night—

But when she opened the door, it wasn't the neighbor, it

was Jennie Talldeer, her expression one of sympathy and haunted guilt, a guilt that Toni recognized, but could not imagine the meaning of. There was a handsome, long-haired young man standing politely behind her, and Toni gulped down a surge of nausea and revulsion. Right now, she did not want to see *any* men—he would think she was to blame; he would say that Rod had been right to beat her—

"Toni, we heard on the news this morning and—*my god!*" Jennie exclaimed, her expression transforming from sympathy to shock and outrage. *"What the hell did Rod do to you?"*

Not "what happened," but *"what did Rod do to you."*

Jennie knew. It was out in the open between them. And Toni was too tired to try to hide it anymore.

"He said—" she began, then burst into tears, momentarily forgetting the presence of the young man. "He said it was my fault!" she sobbed, as Jennie took her arms and gently led her inside to the kitchen. "He said it was all my fault, and he hit me and—"

"God—how badly are you hurt? Did he touch the kids?" the young man asked, quietly, but urgently. Toni cast a quick glance at him through her tears, and to her amazement, saw that his expression was identical to Jennie's. Shock, and outrage—and concern.

"N-n-no," she replied, with surprise. Was Jennie right? Toni had thought all men must be like Rod, but— "I d-d-don't think so, I th-think they're still next door. I'll be all right, I th-th-think—"

They traded a look, and Jennie nodded. "I'll call the Women's Shelter," he said. "You take care of her." Then he turned to Toni. "Mrs. Calligan," he said, very gently, touching her hand as if it was something fragile and precious, "you stay here with Jennie. We're going to get you some help, and we're going to get you out of this place. And we won't let anyone hurt you again."

She stared after him, tears forgotten in pure shock, as Jennie led her to the kitchen table and sat her down, and began to talk to her in a voice of compassion and absolute authority.

By the time the caseworker from the Women's Shelter arrived, Jennie had buried her own feelings of guilt under a powerful load of pure and unadulterated rage. Toni Calligan's face was a mass of bruises and welts that no amount of pancake makeup could disguise. She *had* seen women beaten up worse than this—but they had not been friends.

David was just as outraged, and he was having as hard a time controlling it. "I want to go track that bastard down and beat *him* senseless," he fumed under his breath as the caseworker spoke to Toni Calligan. "That—god, he's not an animal; no animal would do something like that—"

"Stay cool," Jennie advised him, although she was feeling anything but cool herself. "If you go after him, you'll not only blow it for Toni, but you'll blow our other case for us. Remember, this is Oklahoma; everything in a wife-beating case has to be perfect for it to go through."

He nodded, jaw clenched. "I know that," he admitted, "but I don't like it."

"Neither do I." She listened with half an ear to what the caseworker was telling Toni; outlining her options, but warning her that they needed around forty-eight hours to get a space cleared for her and the kids at a safe house.

"I need to take you into the bathroom and take pictures," the caseworker said, compassionately, but firmly. "I need pictures of the bruises on your face and body, in good light, without makeup. We'll want to get a restraining order filed against your husband, and if you decide you want a divorce, we'll need evidence of this beating for both of the judges, the one for the restraining order and the one who we'll be filing the divorce papers with—"

That last had a tentative sound to it; Jennie knew why. This was the moment when fifty percent of the women who had been abused backed out. "It was just once," they'd say. "He was drunk; he's fine when he's sober." "He'll change, I know he will—"

But it wasn't just once, he never got sober, and he never changed. Not without years of therapy, anyway. And all too often, the ones who walked back into those marriages came out again on a stretcher or a slab—

Jennie more than half expected that, faced with the word *divorce*, Toni would be one of those fifty percent.

But instead, Toni's head came up a little. "I want a divorce," she said, thickly. "He doesn't like Ryan and Jill. If he can blame me for—for—" Her voice broke, for just a moment. "If he can blame me, how much longer will it be before he blames them?"

"You want the facts?" the caseworker said, with a weary sigh. "You sound like you've thought this through. My guess is maybe a couple of weeks; then he'll not only beat you, he'll start pounding them in the name of 'discipline.' The man is sick. You are not a doctor, and it's not your job to make him well."

"I want a divorce," Toni replied. "I want my babies taken where he can't hurt them, and I want a divorce."

The caseworker met Jennie's eyes for a moment, and gave her a furtive thumbs-up, before turning back to Toni Calligan. "Is your life in any immediate danger?" she asked. "Are the kids? Can you stick this out for the forty-eight hours we need?"

Toni considered this for a moment. "I think we'll be all right for that long," she replied after a moment. "I *won't* change my mind, but I think we can keep out of his way."

"Good." The caseworker took Toni into the bathroom for a brief photo session, then packed up her forms and her notes. "I'm going to go next door and talk to your neighbor, and send the kids back here to you. If she's willing, she can be the one you run to if he *does* get violent. If that happens, don't argue with him, don't stand there, just run; tell your kids that if they hear a fight starting, *they* need to run. If your neighbor agrees, she'll lock the door after you and call 9-1-1 and one of our rescue people before he has a chance to get any worse."

"I'll come get her from next door as soon as the neighbor calls me," Jennie put in hastily. "I think that will make the neighbor a little more willing."

Toni cast her a look of pure gratitude, and the caseworker stuffed all of her things into her bag and left, letting herself out the front door. Jennie reached over and patted her shoulder. "I've done this before, you know," she said, conversationally. "Toni, you're handling this as well as anyone could expect, and better than I would. I think you're going to be all right."

Toni dabbed at her eyes with a tissue. "I—I don't know if I am or not," she replied, an edge of desperation in her voice. "I just know that—that this can't go on anymore."

Jennie slid into the place that the caseworker had left vacant, and David came to stand beside her, one hand on her shoulder. She wasn't certain what to say next; guilt was replacing her outrage again, and she looked up to see that David was studying Toni's face, her frightened, haunted eyes.

"Tell her, Jen," he said, suddenly. "Tell her about the spirits, the *mi-ah-luschka.*"

"Now?" she replied, taken by surprise.

Toni Calligan stopped dabbing her eyes for a moment, to fix both of them with a troubled and puzzled look. "Spirits?" she said, falteringly, then blurted out, "You mean—like the Indian ghosts you told me about?"

David and Jennie traded another glance; then Jennie took a deep breath, and began.

"What David wants me to tell you about—involves something that your husband might have done—"

CHAPTER FIFTEEN

To Jennie's intense relief, Toni Calligan listened quietly to her halting explanation of the looted gravesite, the Little People, their burning desire for revenge, and how she and her children might have become targets for that revenge. She had been afraid that, even if Toni was in a receptive frame of mind, she still would not believe. But her words fell on ears that were ready to hear them, and the explanations met with nods and worried frowns.

"That was really what I meant, when I was talking about the people Rod Calligan"—she avoided calling Calligan Toni's "husband"—"might have gotten angry at him. The *mi-ah-luschka* have no sense of honor, since many of them died without honor. Anything and anyone is a lawful target, to them. In fact, they are sadistic enough that they might well choose to prolong the punishment they intend for him by—by hurting the things *around* Rod Calligan before they touch him."

Toni fingered her swollen lip. "What—what if Rod hurt

those things himself?" she asked, finally. "Wouldn't they think he didn't care about them?"

Jennie shrugged. "I don't know, honestly. Toni, I have to tell you, many men beat women because they look on their spouses as possessions, theirs to do with as they please. As long as Rod Calligan thinks of you as his possession, you are still a good target, so far as the *mi-ah-luschka* are concerned."

She had avoided as many of the complications as she could; eliminated the suspicion that Rod himself was to blame for many, if not all, of the "accidents" at his site. And she eliminated mentioning that Rod seemed to be protected from the direct revenge of the spirits. She concentrated instead on what she knew but could not prove; that he had looted the sacred ground, that the Little People were angry and out for blood. His, and that of anyone connected with him. "These things that have been happening are exactly the kind of things the *mi-ah-luschka* are good at. And if you've had other kinds of accidents, well—they're experts at arranging that kind of thing."

She did not mention the dead child, although the place around the television set was so full of the influence of the Little People that she was catching after-images out of the corner of her eye every time she looked through the doorway.

Toni nodded all through the narrative; hesitantly at first, then more and more eagerly. Finally, as Jennie finished, she asked another question.

"These spirits—" she said. "If you can see them, do they look like people? Real people, I mean? Solid?"

"Sometimes," David said slowly, trading a look with Jennie.

"Do they look like Indians, or like you?" Toni persisted, with an edge of desperation in her voice. "I mean, do they have ordinary clothing, or like, a mohawk haircut, leather pants, a blanket? Like modern Indians, or like ones in a movie or a book?"

"They can look like the Osage of long ago," Jennie replied. "I can't recall ever hearing of one that looked modern. Or they can look like owls, but I don't think you'd recognize them in an owl-form. Why do you ask?"

Toni Calligan shivered. "Because I've been *seeing* them, that's why!" she told them, the words tumbling out, one after the other, as if she could not stop them. "Tall men, with mohawk haircuts and wearing leather pants. Ryan has, too! Lurking around the house—and sometimes just before something horrible is going to happen—"

Explanations spilled out of her, then, a litany of accidents that were nothing of the kind, of the dryer fire, the Indian man who had pushed Ryan into the path of the car, the exploding pressure cooker—the Indians who had appeared and disappeared, the *mi-ah-luschka* who had been haunting the house at night, watching from around corners, making their presence felt.

And, finally, the Indian who had risen up out of the corner of the living room as the storm struck, young Rod playing with the TV in defiance of her orders, and the lightning strike on the television antenna, just as Rod's hand was on the dial.

Before she was finished, Toni was in tears again, recalling the horror of that moment and the fruitless attempt to revive her son. This time Jennie moved over to her side of the table to put her arm around the woman, hoping to offer some small measure of support and comfort. But this time the tears were for herself as much as for the lost child.

"I thought I was going crazy," Toni sobbed. "I thought I was seeing things, that maybe I was really the one doing all this, and I was so crazy I didn't remember any of it! I thought this morning when I woke up that maybe *I* had electrocuted Rod and I'd hallucinated the whole thing!"

"You weren't going crazy," David said, quietly. "You

saw them. They've been after you, and after your kids, and they finally hit Rod Calligan right where it hurts most by taking his eldest boy. Toni, *I've* seen them, and a meaner bunch you've never laid eyes on. And it's all Rod Calligan's fault. If anyone killed that child, he did."

"But why?" she asked, wiping her eyes. "Why would he be—robbing graves? He doesn't even *like* Indians; the whole time we've lived here, we haven't been to the Gilcrease once!"

David pursed his lips. "Our guess is that Rod Calligan has been looting gravesites and stealing artifacts, then caching them at this mall site, planning on digging them up later. Maybe he figured that if they were "found" on land he owned, he had treasure rights to them and could sell them legitimately. There are some people who are willing to pay a lot for Indian artifacts, but you can sell them for a lot more money if you can sell them legitimately."

Jennie found herself nodding with surprise and approval. Now that was something she had not thought of, but it made sense, it made perfect sense! In fact, it was the first time that all of the pieces had fallen together in this case! She gave David a brief but dazzling smile; he shrugged, but looked rather pleased with himself. As well he should be.

"Anyway, the way we have it figured, something went wrong when his own bulldozer uncovered one of the caches," David continued. "Maybe he never intended for one to get uncovered; maybe it was the fault of the *mi-ah-luschka*. Maybe they arranged things so that some of his prize loot was pulverized." His brow furrowed for a moment. "I don't exactly know how the bomb fits in there, unless Calligan booby-trapped the caches like he did the—like some of the treasure-hunters in South America do."

Jennie hadn't missed the quick rephrasing; he had almost mentioned the booby trap they had nearly sprung. Toni Calligan didn't notice anything; she was concentrating too hard on the rest of what David had said. She seemed particularly interested when David mentioned the mall site as a place where her husband had been burying looted artifacts.

"I always thought there was something funny about that place," she replied, wiping her swollen eyes. "That mall, I mean. Rod was so obsessed with it, when half the people in town told him it was going to be a disaster, because it was on a floodplain." She looked up at Jennie, her expression hardening. "What you've been basically saying, over and over, is that you really do think he brought all this on us. That you're completely certain that it's *his* fault all this has been happening."

"That's it," Jennie replied, then shrugged. "You have to take my word for it, if you're going to believe in the *mi-ah-luschka* and Medicine. It's very subjective stuff. I can't prove most of it. I can't even prove the looting. None of this would even be enough to bring charges, much less to convict him in a court. But the *mi-ah-luschka* know, they've tried and convicted him, and they're carrying out the sentence. The only problem, so far as I am concerned, is that they are also carrying it out on you and your children."

"I have one dead child, and two who had escapes so narrow it was miraculous," Toni Calligan said, the heat of anger creeping into her voice. "I know what's been happening. There is no natural explanation. I can believe it. I *saw* that Indian myself, twice. And I can believe Rod would rob graves; he'd rob his own parents' graves if he thought there was something good in them. He fooled me for a long time, and for a lot longer, I fooled myself. But I'm not going to delude myself anymore."

That might just be anger and outrage in the wake of the beating speaking, but Jennie didn't think so. This woman knew Rod Calligan as well as anyone could. This was probably experience talking, not anger. The bruised face looked determined; the hands clenched on her tissue spoke volumes about her feelings.

"It's going to take two days before I can get the kids out

of here," Toni continued. "Maria says that I should be very cool and very meek, try and stay out of his way as much as possible, and act as if I thought I deserved all this, so he doesn't suspect that we're about to run." Her jaw tightened, and tears started up again. "Anyway, I'm going to be so busy with the—taking care of—I think I can keep myself and the kids out of his way."

"Good," Jennie said, but Toni wasn't through.

"You've done so much to help," she continued. "I don't know much about what Rod's been doing, but maybe I can find out something for you in the next two days."

"Don't do *anything* that puts you at risk," Jennie warned, a little alarmed. She did not want Toni hurt worse than she already was! "You're going to be at risk enough from Rod, and then there's the *mi-ah-luschka*. I have no idea what they'll try next, or when!"

"Can't you do something for her?" David asked, his own eyes dark with concern. "You got them to leave me alone."

But she had to shake her head. "You came into their territory, and I was able to bluff them into thinking you were with me."

She turned to Toni. "I wish I could do something. If I could protect you from them, I would, but while you live in this house, under this roof, they will not believe me if I try to tell them that you are not a lawful target. It will have to wait until *you* have filed divorce papers; that act will reso- nate into the spirit world, divorcing your spirits as well as your marriage. Then I—or better still, my grandfather— can perform a purification ceremony for you that will take you completely out of Rod Calligan's sphere, so far as the spirits are concerned."

"They've already done so much—maybe they'll be satis- fied for a while," Toni replied, voice tight with unshed tears. Jennie's stomach twisted; bad enough that the poor woman had gone through losing her child—the rest of this was torture of the innocent. But the *mi-ah-luschka* had no hearts. "And maybe they've seen how much Rod thinks of me and the other two kids. Anyway, if I can, I'd like to do something." She frowned for a moment, as if she had suddenly recalled something. "You know, there *used* to be a couple of cardboard boxes full of some strange things in his office; they used to give me the creeps. . . . That was just before all this stuff, the strange accidents, started happening."

"Is the stuff there now?" Jennie asked quickly, hope rising. For that, and the chance that the "strange things" might come from Watches-Over-The-Land's grave, she'd break down the damn office door and to hell with legalities.

But Toni shook her head. "No," she replied, dashing Jennie's hopes again. "No, he took it out right about the time he started locking the door, and I haven't seen it since. I still don't know what was in those boxes. All I know is, they were really dirty, and they weren't the kind of thing I ever thought he'd have around."

"If it *was* artifacts, he's probably sold them by now," David said, sotto voce. Jennie grimaced, but he was probably right.

"Don't risk your own safety, but when it comes to information on Rod Calligan, we could use the inside help," Jennie told her, after a moment. "Every leg up we can get on this case is something we didn't have before. I'd be interested, and so would the cops. It would be nice to be able to prove he booby-trapped his own land. I'm not sure that he could be charged with manslaughter, but at the least, he could get reckless endangerment, and it would leave things wide open for civil suits by the survivors."

"I'll do what I can," Toni Calligan replied, her chin up, with a look of determination in her eyes that belied the black eye, the bruises, the swollen lip. "I promise."

* * *

David took the city bus back to the house to tell Mooncrow what had been happening; at least now they had a good theory that made all the pieces fit. If Rod Calligan were systematically robbing gravesites and caching the artifacts at the mall to be dug up in the course of excavation, it explained just about everything anomalous.

And it explained the anger of the Little People.

She asked David to write everything down and fax it to Sleighbow—with the preface that this was all very speculative, and they had no way of proving any of it. But she wanted Sleighbow to have all the information she did. Minus the Little People, of course.

She was positive that, at the least, Mr. Sleighbow would find it all very interesting. She was rather certain that using insured property for the "storage" of dubiously acquired artifacts was not covered by Calligan's policy.

Jennie thought it all the way through on her way to the offices of the Women's Shelter, following behind Maria, Toni's caseworker. The little Chevette was easy enough to follow, even though the streets were crowded as people got out for lunch. Traffic in Tulsa still was never as bad at its worst as it was in Dallas at its best.

The mall site *was* a bad one, although on the surface it might seem to be a good place to put a shopping area. Granted, there was no mall or even a decent shopping center that close to the river. This was a high-income area, heavily residential. A high-end shopping mall should have good potential.

But when you looked close, at least according to Jennie's mother, the picture changed. Existing malls still had plenty of vacancies, what with the recession and all. A smaller, high-end shopping complex associated with a hotel was not doing well, and it was very near Calligan's site. Worse yet, there wasn't nearly enough access; the streets were predominantly residential, and a plan to increase Riverside Drive to six lanes was controversial and being fought by the local residents. This site was, after all, on a floodplain, and her mother's tips from the local real estate grapevine said *that* reason alone had kept people away. He didn't even have a quarter of the shops booked. But he owned the land, free and clear, and David said just before he left that he thought Oklahoma property rights included "treasure-hunter" rights to whatever was found there.

Maria was a cautious driver; that made her easier to follow. She never ran yellow lights, much to the annoyance of those behind her. And although Jennie already knew the way, she was glad to have the excuse to go slowly; it gave her the opportunity to think this through.

David had explained the law as he understood it, cautioning that he had not looked up Oklahoma law yet. If Calligan had "treasure rights," that meant that valuable artifacts that seemed to have been *cached* there, under Oklahoma law, belonged to Calligan, unless someone could come along with proof of ownership or proof that the objects had been stolen, or both. And if that was the case, it also accounted for the fact that he'd just buried them there rather than making it look like a legitimate burial site; under Oklahoma law, *remains* had to be reburied in an appropriate place if they were dug up in the course of construction. But something that was obviously a cache site came under the heading of "treasure," even if there were bones cached with it. The bones alone would be reinterred; what was with them became simple property.

Since sacred pipes and fetish-bundles didn't exactly come with I.D. numbers or registration cards, there was no way on earth or heaven that Jennie could *prove* the artifacts Calligan had came from the looted graves.

So assume that this was what he had done; Calligan would have the right to sell them. Probably for a lot of money; if there had been a *Wah-hopeh* bundle, for instance . . . well, there weren't many of those in white hands, and none in the hands of private collectors. Selling them on the black market would get him a lot of money, but being able to claim them with the force of the law on his side would allow him to put objects up for bid openly, which would mean a lot *more* money than if he'd had to sell them privately.

So, he gets his loot and makes obvious caches on his land; now how does that fit in with the bomb? And just as importantly, how does that fit in with the stuff that was bulldozed?

That was the part that puzzled her.

Wait a minute. The more public his "discovery," the less likely it will be for someone to think he looted the stuff. So say he makes one cache of relatively worthless pieces of broken pottery and bones, and has his men dig it up. Then he fights the work stoppage so it looks as if he didn't know the stuff was there. When the archeologists say it was a cache rather than a burial site, he orders work shut down, does his own excavations, and "uncovers" more caches, these a lot more valuable than the stuff his crew ruined. He sells it all in legitimate circles, and makes back ten times what he spent on the canceled mall.

It was a beautiful scheme, and the only thing that had ruined it was the bomb. Which still didn't fit in. It was a bright red piece in the middle of the green puzzle, and it stuck out in all directions.

So why the explosion—*Well, he probably booby-trapped his caches, like David said, only the* mi-ah-luschka *moved one of the bombs. Or else the explosion was something not even he knew was going to happen. Maybe a business rival. Whatever, he decided to capitalize on it, and blame it on us.*

That way the cops wouldn't be looking for more booby traps.

The explanation for the one that nearly got David was easy enough.

He probably set that one right out in the open to get me as soon as he found out I was working on the case. He'd kill a lot of birds with one stone. He'd get me out of his hair, get another bombing he could blame on the Movement, put up more smoke and mirrors to hide what was really going on.

She nodded to herself as she pulled into the Shelter parking lot. It all made perfect sense, and it certainly explained Calligan's insistence on continuing with a project that was doomed to failure. Calligan was a lot of things, but "stupid" wasn't one of them.

But he didn't plan on the mi-ah-luschka, *and he didn't plan on me,* she thought grimly, as she got out of her car to join the Shelter caseworker who was waiting for her. *Let's just see if between us, we can bring him down.*

The office of the Women's Shelter was a madhouse; there were always a hundred kinds of crisis going on, each one worse than the last. Yet somehow, amid all the chaos, things did get done.

It took a long time to get, as Maria (Toni Calligan's caseworker) put it, "all the ducks in a row." Oklahoma was a state riddled with antique laws and outmoded assumptions. It was, for instance, a common-law state; live together with someone for seven months in such a way that everyone knew you were sharing a bed, and you were common-law spouses and liable for each other's debts under the law. For that matter, check into the same motel room and you were automatically common-law spouses, if one of you wasn't already married!

This was not such a good thing, so far as spousal abuse was concerned. In Maria's words, "In Oklahoma, unless you can get witnesses and documentation that the abuse went past simply 'slappin' her around to larn her,' you don't get protection *or* a divorce." Judges, especially older male judges, were not inclined to take abuse seriously if there was nothing but one woman's word against a man. They were too inclined to believe that "the little woman" was just angry with her hubbie and trying to get a little attention for herself.

So the neighbor's testimony had to be taken, then Jennie's, as well as Maria's and Toni's; Jennie had to swear that the pictures Maria had taken were undoctored and had been taken exactly the way Maria said they were.

David had to come in long enough to make a statement, which was good news as far as Jennie was concerned. She got a chance to tell him *her* speculations, and to warn him she thought that she was going to be here for a while. He got a chance to tell her that the assumptions he had made about Oklahoma "treasure" law were correct.

Once all the documentation was in order, they still weren't done. A lawyer had to draw up the preliminary papers. A judge had to review them, and the evidence—

And besides all that, the safe house had to be located and room made for Toni and the kids. Maria's guess of forty-eight hours was based not on the fact that she knew they *had* a place but that it would take that long to locate one for her.

All that took time, and it was well after ten when the last of the "ducks" were properly lined up, and Jennie could go home. She was exhausted, but it didn't stop her mind from working.

Another rather nasty thought had occurred to her, after David had gone back to Mooncrow to make sure he didn't gorge himself on pizza.

All this time they had been assuming that the appearance of the Evil One had nothing to do with Rod Calligan. But what if they were wrong?

What if *Rod Calligan* had taken the Evil One's spirit-bundle? What if it had been the Evil One who had been behind the looting of Watches-Over-The-Land's grave-goods?

She had put the thought out of her mind while she and Maria worked on the more mundane matter of getting Toni Calligan out of her husband's hands, but it came back to her as she walked out to her truck.

The lighting was very good here, in a place where mostly women worked, and where angry men might want to come after them. Still, although the shadows were small, they seemed all the darker for that. She thought she saw vague, bird-shaped things watching her from the trees. Not owls—something more like starved crows, except their legs and necks were all wrong. And not *mi-ah-luschka*, either; she would have *seen* them, while if there really was something there, it was doing its best to make sure she couldn't see it.

The back of her neck crawled, and she was very happy to get to the Brat. She got in and locked the doors, quickly, and started the engine. The familiar surroundings made her jitters seem silly, and she shook her head at herself, frowning as she worked through all the implications of that last speculation.

What if Calligan had gotten the spirit-bundle with some other loot? Or—what if he had even picked it up, all by itself, after it washed down Mingo Creek? The Evil One would certainly have known where Jennie's ancestor was, just as Mooncrow had pointed out. He would have been delighted to assist in the desecration! What if *Calligan* was the instrument through which the Evil One was working?

What if all this was *because* of the Evil One, and not just Calligan's own greed?

A nasty thought; a very nasty thought. But it would explain the bomb, because the Evil One wouldn't care if Calligan's own people died. He thrived on creating the maximum harm to everyone, no matter whose side they were on. He had no allies, not really, and anyone who thought he was an ally was deluding himself.

She pulled out of the lot and headed down the relatively deserted street, her frown deepening. The Evil One would find a ready enough instrument in Rod Calligan, that was for sure. The man purely didn't give a shit about anyone but himself. He was positioned very well to do an incredible amount of damage to the Native American population of the area right now. Her hands tightened on the steering wheel, and she drove paying only scant attention to the road, taking backstreets to avoid the lights. Calligan already had some people convinced it was the Indians who'd blown up his dozer. It wouldn't take much to get another good chunk of the previously uncommitted population on his side. Convincing one decent journalist would do that.

He could undo everything any of the tribal leaders had done in this state. He could get at the Oklahoma legislature easily enough and get them to try to restrict Native sovereignty. That would mean that Indian-run gaming could be shut down, for instance, something that the fundamentalist groups were already agitating for. Any forms of tribal income other than arts and crafts could and *would* be shut down. That would cut off a lot of funding for all kinds of education and health-care projects, and plenty more. Say good-bye to tribal police, for instance. . . .

He could, by playing this whole situation right, set Indian rights back by fifty years or more. Or, at the very least, he could see that it all got tied up until it had to go in front of the Supreme Court. That would take years to settle, if it ever got settled at all.

And meanwhile, even if they won before the Court, they would still lose in terms of public opinion. It hadn't been that long ago that a kid had to hide the fact that he was an Indian if he didn't want trouble, if he wanted decent treatment and a decent job. If Calligan and the Evil One were really working together, pretty soon it wouldn't just be yellow journalists like Anger who were bad-mouthing Native Americans. . . .

She was so wrapped up in these unpleasant speculations that she didn't even realize she was being followed until she pulled onto Pine, and finally noticed that the car behind her had been there since she'd left the Women's Shelter parking lot.

A chill ran down her back, and she clenched the steering wheel.

It could just be a coincidence—

But why not check?

She made a couple of really odd turns, and felt another thread of cold fear trickle down her spine when the car behind her did the same. Her gut tightened, and she looked at the darkened houses around her, knowing there was no help coming from them. Not in this neighborhood.

They *were* following her, whoever, whatever they were, and they didn't care if she knew it. Someone from Calligan, trying to scare her off by roughing her up? Possibly. Not car-jackers; her Brat wasn't worth taking. But for a woman alone, there were other possibilities, all of them nasty. Sure, she knew martial arts, but that wouldn't help her much against two men, bigger than she was.

Now she wished she'd had the three thousand for that evasive-driving course!

Shit. She would be on the side of town where there wasn't a police station! And in North Tulsa, sadly, the only time the cops came was if shots were fired. This wasn't the worst neighborhood in town, but it wasn't the kind where anybody paid any attention when someone yelled for help.

And I didn't bring my gun, because I thought we were calling on a bereaved mother. I didn't plan on being out this late. I didn't plan on being alone!

Too late now. There was only one thing to do; try to lose them. Speed, and hope a cop stopped her! She'd *gladly* risk a ticket—

Then, just as her foot came down on the accelerator and she passed the limit by five miles per hour, a red light popped up from the dash of that sinister dark car behind her.

And all her adrenaline flowed away in a rush of mingled relief and disgust.

Oh hell. An unmarked car, cruising for easy fish and quick tickets for the monthly quota! And I fell right into it! I should have known better than to go through this area at the end of the month. She didn't know whether to laugh or curse. She pulled the Brat over to the side of the road, stopped as the car behind her followed her like a shark following the scent of blood, turned off the ignition, and rolled down her window just enough to pass her license through. The car behind her stopped just behind her rear bumper by a couple of feet; the light on the dash went out, although they left their headlights on, and a bulky figure in a uniform and hat got out of the driver's side. She squinted at him through the back window, trying to make out what he looked like against the light.

Odd. That was an awfully large car for a cruiser. That didn't look exactly like the Tulsa P.D. uniform—there was something wrong with the shape of the shoulder patch. And why weren't there extra lights behind the grill?

The driver paused, just short of her door, as she tried to identify the make of the car.

She handed out her license, but the cop did not take it. "Get out of the car, please, miss," the man said, in a calm and neutral voice.

Alarm threaded her nerves all over again. *Wait a minute. They don't ask you to get out of the car on a routine traffic stop!*

She glanced back again, and got a better look at the car; it was a Lincoln.

There wasn't a city in the country that could afford Lincoln Town Cars for unmarked units!

Too late. Her moment of hesitation gave her away.

The last thing she saw as she reached for the keys to start the car and get *out* of there was the club swinging at her window; the last thing she remembered was throwing up her hands to protect her face from the club and the shower of safety-glass fragments.

The last thing she felt was a blow to the side of her head, followed by an explosion of stars, and oblivion.

"Think this'll do?" "Jim" asked, as "Bob" slowed the car at the top of the dam at Lake Keystone.

"Bob" squinted down through the darkness at the little spit of park below Keystone Dam. "You sure they're planning on opening the gates around two?" he asked his partner.

"Absolutely," "Jim" said. "They're going to do a major water release; it was on all the news programs. It'll send all the garbage that's been collecting under the dam downriver. By the time they find her, she'll be under the Twenty-first Street bridge, if they find her at all. Fred's leaving the truck at Riverside Park. They'll never know where she went, unless she floats up."

"Tom" grunted in the backseat. "Let's get this over with," he said, in a calm and dispassionate voice. "I don't like doing a job in the open like this. Too big a chance somebody'll come by."

"Bob" took the Lincoln down past the dam, then made the unmarked turnoff that led to the tiny park. After they made the turn, there was a small sign that advised that the park was closed after nine in the evening, but he ignored it. There was no gate, and with the economy as bad around here as it was, there was no money to spare for cops to patrol this area.

That made it a good place to do a job.

If he'd had more time, he would have gotten a four-wheel drive vehicle and taken the mark down a little further, to an access road and the sand and gravel works. It would have been just as easy to get rid of her there, with less chance of discovery. But beggars couldn't be choosers.

Besides, "Tom" still had on his uniform; they still had the dashlight. If anyone came by, they could claim to be police looking for pushers. That would get kids to clear out fast. And kids looking to neck or score would be all that would show up out here, this time of night.

The parking lot at the foot of the dam was completely in shadow. He pulled the Lincoln in under the shelter of some trees, just in case, and the three of them got out.

The mark moved a little when they opened the trunk, but "Tom" was good with that club. She was still pretty much out, and her facial cuts had all been superficial enough that paper towels they'd put over her face and under her head had blotted up all the blood. Those would go into the river with her. Calligan, the pervert, had wanted them to rape her before they got rid of her. Asshole. Didn't he know that semen samples were as good as fingerprints for catching somebody? And what if they got blood on themselves? They had to think of these things. You never knew what a body was going to do; sometimes things got screwed up, and some kid found a stiff while it was still fresh. You just didn't leave anything of yourself behind; that was the rule. That was why all three of them wore surgical gloves, crewcuts, common shoes a size bigger than they usually wore, and brand new clothing.

Besides, "Bob" didn't screw stiffs, and this one was the next thing to being a stiff.

Well, this was going to be quick, clean and professional, and screw Calligan. None of the three got any jollies out of pain or terror. With luck, she wouldn't even fight them.

"Tom" rolled up his sleeves and pants, picked her up, wrapped in the garbage bag they'd lined the trunk with. She whimpered a little; he ignored her, carrying her like a roll of carpet over one shoulder. There was a good place down at the end of the parking lot; all gravel, no sand to hold tracks. The other two didn't bother with saving their clothing; it came from K-Mart, and it would all be thrown in the Goodwill bin as soon as they got back to Tulsa. There was a gym bag with jeans, sneakers, and T-shirts in the backseat.

She started to come to just as they reached the water; she really woke up when they put her in. The water was a lot colder than he'd thought it would be, hardly much above freezing. Strange. It shouldn't have been that cold. The cold water woke her up, and that was when she put up as much of a fight as she could. Not much of one, really; she was tiny, and there were three of them to hold her down.

They held her under until she stopped struggling and stopped bubbling. Then "Tom" noticed the lights of a car on the other side of the dam.

"No point in taking chances," he observed. "Bob" agreed.

Quick, clean, professional. Get out before anyone sees you. Leave nothing that can be traced.

They got into the Lincoln and left; "Bob" noticed the lights of a car pulling into the access road in his rearview mirror, and congratulated himself on a clean getaway.

So, dying wasn't really that bad, after all. Curiously, after the lungs stopped straining for air, there was no pain. Only weariness, and complete detachment.

Kestrel perched in a tree high above Keystone Dam, and watched her murderers with a dispassionate eye, as if she were watching a movie that she knew she would not see the end of. No doubt about it, they were professional. She hadn't even *guessed* that they weren't cops until it was too late; they had the light, the uniform, even the regulation billy club. Not that it was particularly hard to buy any of that stuff through catalogs, but if you wanted to get rid of a mark without a fight, that was the way to do it.

Funny, though, that they brought her all the way here, just above the eagle nesting grounds, to finish the job. Ironic, in fact.

They probably would never even be implicated. She was certain that the car would undergo a complete cleaning and vacuuming as soon as they took it back to Tulsa. They had been careful not to let so much as a thread of theirs adhere to her, or anything of hers touch the car, wrapping her in a common industrial-sized garbage bag, which they left in the river. In a way, she could even admire them, as one admired any professional. They were good. Probably the best in the area. And the solution to a number of deaths which had always seemed rather odd to *her* suddenly presented itself, as the three men got into their car and drove away with the lights still off.

She flipped her wings a little to settle them, and continued to watch. There didn't seem to be any urgency in going anywhere, anymore. She might as well watch and see what happened next.

Mostly, she was tired, and rather numb. The flood of complete fear that had taken her over at the end seemed to have exhausted every other emotion.

But to her mild surprise, another car came screaming down the access road at a rather dangerous speed, not more than a minute after the Lincoln left. It was hard to tell cars in the dark, and from above, but this one looked rather familiar.

Then, as the doors flew open and David flung himself out of the driver's side, she recognized it as her grandfather's.

Poor David; just a little too late. . . .

She felt as if she should be angry that they hadn't come sooner, but—it just didn't seem important anymore. In fact, there wasn't much that was important anymore, when you came right down to it. Kestrel yawned a little, and blinked, feeling vaguely restless.

Shouldn't I be going somewhere?

David went right to the spot where she'd been left, as if she were iron and he was a magnet, with Mooncrow right behind him. He pulled her out, limp and dripping, and began frantic CPR. It would make a lovely dramatic scene in a movie.

She sighed. *Too late, love.* She knew. She'd been under too long; nothing, not even a miracle, would revive her now. If he'd had her in the light, she'd have been blue.

At first she thought that Mooncrow was simply frozen with shock, but then she realized as she saw his spirit-shape forming over his head that he had gone into a Medicine trance. *He* stood like a statue, while a misty shape wisped upward, becoming more and more solid, until at last there was a glistening bird hovering just above his head. He was wearing his white crow-self, and when he looked up and saw her in the treetops, he arrowed up toward her.

But something was holding him away; his wings pumped furiously, but he made no progress toward her. He changed to a raven, and the results were no better. His wingbeats slowed; his wings seemed to get heavier, and he dropped back toward the ground, back to his body. . . .

She shifted from foot to foot, restively, with growing unhappiness. Surely she should be going somewhere! She didn't want to stay here anymore, watching Mooncrow try to reach her, watching David crying and trying to force life back into a lifeless body—

Huge wings shadowed the moon for a moment. The tree shook as something landed just above her. She turned her head sharply, and Eagle peered down at her, his great beak gaping in greeting. Immediately her unrest settled. This must be what she had been waiting for, a guide to the Summer Country.

Well, little sister, he said.

She thrilled at the sound of his voice in her mind, the first real emotion she had felt since she found herself perching here. She bobbed her head, modestly. *Greeting to you, Great One. Do you come to guide me?*

He turned his head, to peer at her from his other eye. *Do you wish guidance?* he replied, watching her closely. *You have much still to do, here.* Ta-hah-ka-he *cannot deal with the tangle of the Evil One, nor can your grandfather, not alone.*

At first she was confused by the Osage name, Deer-With-Branching-Horns, until she remembered David's spirit-quest, and what his spirit-animal had proved to be. Of course, Eagle would not use anything but David's Osage Spirit Name, and David would not know what it was in Osage. It was too bad she could not give it to him, now.

She felt a vague regret, and a dim sorrow, as she saw how David was weeping over her, even as he continued to blow futile air into lungs that would get no use from it, and tried to force life into a heart that had ceased to beat.

But Eagle's point needed to be addressed. *Great One, I fear that the time for action is gone for this one. The spirit-house below is beyond repair; there will be brain damage after so much time without heart beating and lungs breathing.*

Again, she felt a vague emotion, this time anger. If *Wah-K'on-Tah* wanted *her* to do something about Calligan and the Evil One, shouldn't he have brought help a little sooner?

But Eagle laughed, silently, his beak open and his thin tongue showing. *Would I have come to remind you of your duty if the spirit-house were unusable?* he asked. *You know how chill the water is. I need not explain it to you. And whatever else is wrong, I will see it taken care of.*

As he spoke, a warm golden glow haloed him, a hint of the sunlight in the midst of the night.

She bowed her head down to her toes at that, humbly, overcome with deep awe. There was no doubt in her mind that she was in the presence of one of the Great Spirits; a messenger of *Wah-K'on-Tah,* as she had named him. What he pledged would come to be, for he had the authority to make it so.

He turned his head to look down below, and sighed. *There is the small matter of* Ta-hah-ka-he, *as well,* he observed. David was clearly at the end of his rope; she had never imagined him losing control to anything but anger, and to see him in hysteria was something of a shock. *Small, perhaps, in the larger view, but if you are gone from his life—he may lose his way, and he will surely lose his focus. He loves you; you love him. Together, you form a balanced whole. Should this not count for something? But there is a larger matter at hand, as well—*

He spread his wings, and in their shadow she saw What-Might-Be.

She saw Toni Calligan, dead, and dumped into an oil pit by the same men who had murdered her. She saw Rod Calligan galvanizing opinion against the Native Americans, as she had already imagined. She saw Calligan and another man turning the abandoned mall site into a dumping ground for toxic waste; saw the entire ecosystem along the Arkansas River destroyed, poisoned, with the first to go being the bald eagles nesting here. She saw the toxins spreading all through the ground water, until even the local wells were poisoned, and wildlife vanished. But then she saw what was behind it all.

The Evil One, who had grown powerful enough that he had the ability to split small bits of himself into the independent forms of his choosing. And what he had chosen were three Black Birds, birds that even appeared in the waking world, to act as his eyes and ears there. He intended to infuse Rod, Ryan, and Jill Calligan with the spirits of his Black Birds. Using them, he would destroy the Native Americans he hated, the whites he despised. He had studied Rod Calligan, and he would gain power through the accumulation of money and influence, specializing in the destruction and poisoning of the Earth, of the lives of humans who had no idea he even existed. He would reduce "life" to the misery all too often depicted in fiction; he had seen and read that fiction, and it had amused him. He planned to use it as his pattern, to make it into a reality.

It would be all too easy to do; people were accustomed to being miserable, and would not notice one more increment of misery. They were used to the mediocre. They were already doing what they were told.

He would gain control so gradually that no one would notice in the general population. And those who *would* take note, he would destroy, through Rod Calligan for as long as the man lasted, and then through his children.

Eagle folded his wings, and she came back to the present, but found herself looking deeply into his golden eye.

Where she saw herself, reflected, without distortion.

Kestrel, who had cut herself off from her emotions, living her life totally by reason and logic—until David came back and led her into the habit of *feeling* again. Who had concentrated all of her life on *the job*, as if simply living wasn't as important as *the job*. Who had, most of all, been unwilling to give up control, and let outside forces and purposes take it, even for the briefest of periods. As if, by always being in control, she would always be able to do exactly the right thing and would never, ever, make a mistake.

And all because she was afraid to lose control, afraid to make those mistakes that had to be made if you were going to be a person and not a machine.

Eagle blinked, and she found herself looking into his eye again, seeing the laughter there.

Laughter that suddenly became too much to resist.

Well, little sister? Eagle said, mildly. *Have you seen at last the lesson that held you back for so long? Are you ready to take a new path, and perhaps share it with the Young Male Deer?*

Well, staying in control sure hasn't worked! she laughed. *And how I could have been* afraid *to make mistakes*—

Eagle grinned. *Then you will return?*

She laughed even harder at her own absurdity. *Of course!* she agreed—

And suddenly, she was freezingly cold, with stones biting into her back, ribs and head aching horribly, lungs afire. Coughing up water—

And laughing, even as her lungs burned and her heart pounded.

"Jennie!" David caught her up in his arms, babbling, crying, holding her and pounding her back to help her cough up the rest of Lake Keystone, all at the same time. She managed to get her arms around him, still alternately laughing and coughing. He stopped pounding just long enough to kiss her, and she tasted the salt of his tears mixed with the river water.

Mooncrow covered her with a blanket, wiped her face and hair with a towel, saying nothing, but grinning with tears on *his* face.

And David just held her, as if he wanted to keep her there forever, his shoulders shaking with fear and cold and grief-turned-joy.

And she—she let him.

She and Mooncrow kept glancing at each other all during the ride home, and giggling. *I'll have to explain it to poor David,* she thought, more than once; he obviously thought they were both still hysterical. He just drove; he had no intention of stopping until he got them both home, and he kept his eyes on the road and both hands on the wheel, even though he clearly would much have preferred to trade places with Mooncrow in the backseat.

But Jennie shared a joke with her grandfather that would be very hard to explain; it wasn't so much a *joke* as it was a state-of-mind. Relief, for one thing. A knowledge shared; the absurdity of how she had been blocking *herself*, and how easy it had been once she saw what Mooncrow had been trying to tell her.

"Heyoka," she would say to him, and they'd both break up. *"Heyoka* yourself," he would reply, and it would start all over again. In fact, they really didn't stop laughing until they got home, which was just as well, since as long as she was laughing, her head didn't hurt quite so much.

David insisted on carrying her into the house, still

wrapped in Mooncrow's prize blanket. Her grandfather followed, as David carried her to her room and laid her gently on the bed.

"Take these," he ordered, handing her pills and a bottle of orange juice.

"What are these? Time-release contrary-capsules?" she asked, and set him snickering again.

"No," he replied, through the little snorts. "Vitamins, aspirin, and antibiotics."

She raised a rebellious eyebrow at that, but David took them from Mooncrow and sat down on the bed beside her, holding out the juice. "You either take them, or I give them to you," he said sternly. "Mooncrow is right; you don't need pneumonia on top of everything else. And when you get done taking the pills, you go to sleep—"

But Mooncrow waved that off, before Jennie could object. "No, first she must tell us what happened to her," he said. "All that she learned. You and I know only what my vision told us, that she had been attacked and taken to the dam. Not who, and what, and why."

There was something about the inflection of his voice that made even David sigh, but bow to his will. And Jennie took the pills.

She told them all that had happened, or all that she could, at any rate. Most of her experience with Eagle simply didn't translate well into words, especially the parts about the Evil One and his plans. So she left that part out, said simply that she had been *there*, watching, and stuck to what she knew about the hit men—

Especially that Toni Calligan was next on their list. David looked skeptical at first, but after a while he began nodding—

It helped that she was able to describe in detail everything that *he* had been doing.

"I won't pretend to understand half of this," he said finally, then glanced over at Mooncrow. "I guess it's enough that the Little Old Man does."

"It is enough, for now," Mooncrow murmured.

Jennie leaned back against the pillows they had heaped up behind her, and sighed. Now that it was all out—she felt absolutely spent. And very much as if someone had hit her on the head, drowned her, and left her for dead.

"You need rest," Mooncrow said, and got up to leave. "We will speak of this in the morning."

But his eyes said something else entirely.

We will meet in the Spirit Worlds, she read there. *I see that there are things you cannot tell me here. Things that he would not understand.*

She nodded; at least in *that* place her head and body would not be bruised and aching!

He smiled, winked once with another meaning entirely, and left the two of them alone.

David started to leave; her hand on his wrist prevented him. "Don't go," she said, softly. "I've had enough of being alone to last for the rest of my life."

"Good," he replied, and stayed.

CHAPTER SIXTEEN

"I HOPE YOU know what you're doing," David murmured, two days later.

"I hope I do too," she replied, quite seriously. "I'm sorry, my love; it isn't much of a plan, but it's all we have. This time I have daylight on my side, and I know the countryside, the back roads."

He shook his head, but leaned down and kissed her through the newly repaired window of her Brat. "I'd like to keep you wrapped up safe—but you're Kestrel, and you have to fly and hunt. You wouldn't be Kestrel if you didn't do that. You wouldn't be Jennie if you didn't do your job. Break a leg," he said, and went back to Mooncrow's car.

The only obvious souvenirs of her death and revival were a few cuts on her face, already healing. The bruises under her clothing were more extensive, but they were healing too.

Now she was back on the job. It was not nearly over yet.

But she did not want David to know *how* dangerous what she planned to do was.

She pulled her truck out of the parking lot of the fast-food joint six blocks from the Calligans' place.

She glanced down at the remains of her meal; the wrapper from a sandwich, an empty fry carton, a soft-drink cup and a half-finished frozen yogurt cone.

The condemned ate a hearty meal. Not.

The hit men were watching the Calligans' house; David had spotted them when he went to check on Toni. He was afraid that if the goons knew that Toni was bailing out on Rod, they'd move in to pick her and the kids up. Once she got to a safe house, she would no longer work as a bargaining chip against her husband. In fact, once she got to a safe house, the thugs might not be able to locate her any more than Rod could!

Jennie didn't *think* those things, she knew them. If Toni was in their hands, she was dead. If the kids were in their hands, Rod would do anything their employer wanted.

Toni, Ryan and Jill were innocent, as innocent as any of the slaughtered women and children at Claremore Mound. Jennie had been born far too late to save those innocents, but these three, at least, she could, and would, rescue.

So they would somehow have to lure the goons away— and while they were gone, David and Mooncrow would pick up Toni and the kids as scheduled, and take them to the offices of Women's Shelter. Once Toni signed the divorce papers and request for a restraining order, Mooncrow would sever all ties to Rod in a special ceremony of purification. Then, thugs thrown off the track, mundane *and* spiritual connections to Rod Calligan parted, she and her kids should be safe from Rod, the hit men, the Evil One, and the *mi-ah-luschka* as well.

Jennie still was not entirely certain how the hit men figured in all this—who had brought them in to take Toni and her kids, not why Rod had hired them to take care of *her*. There was some part of the picture still missing; some mundane connection she had not seen in her Eagle-guided vision. Somewhere there was someone who wanted a handle on Rod Calligan; she guessed it was some kind of silent business partner who was as deeply into this thing as Rod, if not more so. Well, fine. That was one thing she could try to track down *later*.

Meanwhile, it was time to play hare and hounds.

Or perhaps, Kestrel and Black Birds. . . .

She drove slowly past the Calligan house, paused as if to stop, and then pretended to spot the Lincoln on the corner.

She was near enough to see the faces of two of the three men through the windshield of their car, and it was one of those moments when she wished she had a camera. The expressions on their faces were absolutely priceless. She had never seen anyone quite so stunned in her life—unless, perhaps, it had been a deer caught in the headlights of an oncoming car.

A sudden impulse hit her to thumb her nose and cross her eyes at them. She fought it down, although it was *terribly* tempting. She *had* to make them think she was as startled to see them as they were to see her; had to make her "rabbit" attractive enough that they would leave the target they had staked out in order to finish the job on her.

So she pretended to gasp, threw the truck in reverse to spin it around, and took off.

And as she had hoped, they reacted to the bait she had thrown out; acting with atypical impulse, they came right after her.

And as she fled, the remains of her meal bumped her leg. She looked down, and the half-eaten cone caught her eye.

This, she could not resist.

She reached down and grabbed the cone; she slowed, just a little, swerved, just a little—

—and tossed it out the back window.

The white yogurt hit the middle of the windshield of the

Lincoln with a hearty *spack*.

She couldn't help it; the gesture had been so *heyoka* that she burst out laughing. The yogurt looked like a huge bird-dropping in the middle of their windshield.

Surprise!

The men slowed abruptly, reacting to the sudden impact; slowed just enough to give her an edge as she sped off. *Now* she certainly had their attention! And given the care that they had taken so far that their vehicle take *no* damage, this would surely ensure that they followed her!

This time she had a route planned. *This* time they were not ready with their police gear.

This time it was broad daylight.

The first thing she had to do was to get onto country roads that she knew, and they (hopefully) didn't—get them out where there wouldn't be civilians in the line of fire. And onto roads where that big, heavy Lincoln town car would be at a disadvantage and her light Brat would have the upper hand. This was a fine line she had to follow; she had to keep them close enough that they would not give up. Yet she had to make certain they didn't catch her.

This time she was not unarmed; her .38 and five speed-loaders were on the dashboard just under the steering wheel, in a special tear-away Velcro holder she'd designed herself. If a gun battle started, she was ready for it. If they cornered her, she was ready for them. She hoped.

But the plan called for nothing so violent; in fact, the plan called for her to lead them straight into the speed trap at Catoosa. She was fairly certain they had a number of things in that car that the cops would find very interesting. And even if they didn't, well, she had filed assault charges while her bruises and injuries were still fresh, creating mug por-traits of all three for the Tulsa P.D., and pointing out these three had committed assault and impersonated police offi-cers. So—with any luck, they would at least spend *some* time cooling their heels in a holding tank.

And with no luck—she had enough connections in the department to find out where they lived; even though a check on their license number had revealed a post office box, there were other ways to get their addresses. A professional hit man did not want himself exposed. Chances were that a discreet visit by, say, three of her large and muscled occasional employees would persuade them that Tulsa was no longer a good place to operate.

All that means I have to survive this *though,* she reminded herself, as she sped down a series of turns that would take her out into farm country and two-lane gravel roads. She took a quick look in the rearview mirror. They were right on her tail, and from the look of it, they were perfectly well aware that the safest way to get rid of someone in Oklahoma was to run him down, then refuse to take the sobriety test. *So they're going to see if they can't crash me, then act drunk. Right. I just hope they didn't pony up the three grand for the evasive driving course! And I hope that they are still as worried about scratches on their pretty Town Car as they are about catching me. If they actually decide to ram me off the road—they outweigh this little Brat by about twice.*

Rod Calligan stood in the shade of his office, a frown on his face, arms crossed over his chest, watching work progressing on the mall site. And it *was* progressing; that was why he was frowning.

All of the Indians had come back to work yesterday, with no explanations. *All* of them. By law, since they'd been out sick, he had to take them back. And the "accidents" had stopped, at least yesterday and today. So it was business as usual; better than usual, since they seemed to be determined to make up for the "sick time" off by working twice as hard. If they kept working like this, he was going to have a difficult time finding a rationale for shutting work down unless he blew up another dozer. . . .

He was so busy watching his industrious crew that he didn't notice the commotion in the air above the site until more than half of the workers stopped what they were doing and began pointing up at something in the sky. He squinted, shaded his eyes with one hand, the other hand going automatically to the fetish in his pocket, and looked in the direction they were pointing.

By the time he spotted what they were looking at, virtually everyone else on the crew was already intent on it—

"It" was an aerial battle, a kind of dogfight, with three scrawny black birds chasing something else, a swift little brown bird about the size of a blue jay or a robin.

What the hell? he thought, fuming, fingering the fetish in his pocket. Work had completely ground to a halt while the men watched, the Indians among them cheering the bird being chased as if it were their personal friend.

It swooped low enough to the ground, and near enough to him, that he saw it was a hawk or falcon, though smaller than he'd thought hawks were supposed to be, with brown and gray feathers, a speckled breast, and black markings around its eyes.

He should have been pleased; this was throwing delay into the work again, and that was what he *wanted*. But he wasn't; the very sight of that bird escaping the black ones over and over sent him into an unthinking rage.

If the Indians seemed to think that the hawk was their friend, *he* felt the same about the other birds. Hawks were vermin; they took game that rightfully belonged to human hunters. The black birds were probably protecting their own nests from a bird that would kill their young! And just when it looked as if the black birds finally had the little hawk cornered—

A *raven* flew up out of nowhere, croaking alarm and flapping wildly, distracting the black birds enough that they missed their strike! The Indians cheered wildly as the hawk arrowed right between a couple of pieces of equipment, did a wingover, and climbed past her pursuers.

Damn them! Calligan thought, his stomach sour with anger. *Damn them, damn them!*

Without any idea of who he was damning, or even why. . . .

Jennie wiped sweat out of her eyes, and clutched the wheel until her knuckles ached. Her stomach was in knots; her shoulder and back muscles tighter than banjo strings. She was in trouble; trouble she hadn't anticipated.

A few moments ago she had narrowly missed getting forced over, and only got away by hitting the brakes, doing a bootlegger turn, and shooting off in the opposite direction she *intended* to go. Now she was going the wrong way to hit that speed trap in Catoosa. She needed another plan.

And another route! This was a bad road for the Brat and a good one for the Lincoln. Lots of straightaways—

Highway 20, she decided. *It's all curves, all those little crossroads where traffic comes up out of nowhere—and there's that climb up from the Verdigris River that's all switchbacks! That's it!*

If she could just get there—the bluff rose a good two hundred feet up, maybe three, offering one of the most spectacular views in this part of Oklahoma. No way that boat of a Lincoln was going to be able to keep up with the Brat on those switchbacks!

And then—then straight on 20 until she got to Lynn Lane—then Lynn Lane to Eleventh Street—

Did these guys know there was a major copshop on Eleventh? If they did, they might not realize how close to Lynn Lane it was, especially not if they never came at it going south. She *might* be able to lead them right up to the door—certainly she could trick them into something stupid, like speeding along there.

Right now, she didn't care if she got caught and they

didn't! Right now, she was more concerned with escape.

The Lincoln loomed up in her mirror. She floored it. *First, get to 20!*

That damn bird kept getting away! Rod wished passionately he had a gun, he'd have *shot* the damn thing! And his crew was acting like the spectators at a horse race; in no way was he going to get them back to work while this was going on. His hand was clenched so tightly on the fetish that it ached; his eyes burned and watered from staring into the bright sky.

Larry Bushyhead watched the young female kestrel slipping just ahead of the talons of her pursuers with his hands clenched tight, and a knot in his stomach. When she twisted out of their clutches yet again, he cheered her wildly, as if by his cheering he could give her the strength and the spirit to keep going.

There was more to this than some strange birds chasing a little falcon; he knew it in his bones. This *meant* something, something important.

These weren't just birds. This was an omen—or a reflection of something else, some deadly hunt elsewhere. Those birds were like nothing he had ever seen before, and he knew his birdlife. There was a sinister, not quite natural air about them. If only he knew what it was—

But since he didn't, he did what he could; he stared at the little dot of a bird and *willed* her strength, speed, stamina. *Willed* her all the power he could. If only he knew enough about Medicine, so that he could help her with Medicine power!

And beside him, he sensed every other Indian on the site doing the same thing.

Fly! he told her, prayed for her. *Fly, little girl! You can do it!*

But he knew by her faltering wingbeats that she was in trouble.

Jennie was definitely in trouble. Her guts were filled with the ice of pure fear; she bit her lip and tasted blood.

She hadn't reckoned on the fact that she would be going *uphill.* All the advantages of her smaller car were outweighed by the fact that the engine was smaller too.

The bad guys were catching up to her, and there was still about a half mile of switchbacks yet to go.

Come on, she begged her laboring engine. *Come on! Just a little farther—*

The Lincoln loomed up in her rearview mirror again, filling it.

Fear closed a cold hand around her throat.

Come on, you can do it—

The man driving was smiling.

And he vanished from her mirror as he pulled into the left-hand lane.

He's gonna force me off the road—

And right here, "off the road" meant down. About a hundred and fifty feet worth of "down." No one could survive a drop like that.

They turned, together, and he was right at her rear bumper; he nudged the accelerator and came right alongside. A blind corner, a left-hand switchback, loomed right up ahead—the last turn before the top—if she could just keep him from forcing her off there—

Then, a flash of inspiration.

There's two pedals, stupid! she screamed at herself just as he pulled alongside, grinning at her across his partner in the front seat. *Use the other one!*

No more than a hundred feet from the corner, she

jammed on the brakes.

He went sailing by, staring at her, mouth agape with shock—

Just as a bus rounded the corner up ahead. In his lane.

He had just enough time to react; he jerked the wheel wildly to the right—

At the same instant that the bus driver, in a panic, jerked his to the left to avoid the oncoming car.

Jennie could only watch, hand stuffed into her mouth, as the bus tried to swerve back into its own lane, and hit the Lincoln a glancing blow along the driver's side, just in front of the rear wheel.

Just enough to send it spinning right over the edge, tumbling over the side of the bluff.

The kestrel went into another dive, but this one had the feeling of desperation about it. The Black Birds were right on her tail, and she was either going to plow into the dirt of the Arkansas bluffs, or fly right up into their claws. *Do something!* Larry Bushyhead told the white eye of the sun, fiercely. *Help her! Do something!*

And at that precise moment, someone *did* do something.

The kestrel skimmed the surface of the river, the Black Birds following—so intent on her that they paid no attention to anything else.

Like the pair of Bald Eagles that suddenly dove down out of the sun, straight for them.

Larry watched in stunned joy. He remembered something a falconer friend had once told him. *"If you want to really know what the fastest bird alive is, ask someone who just had their prize peregrine falcon taken by an eagle."*

The Eagles were like twin thunderbolts—and evidently no one had ever told *them* that Bald Eagles were fish and carrion eaters, because they were obviously after those

Black Birds, and the Black Birds didn't even know they were there!

A second later, they knew all right—but by then it was too late.

It happened so quickly that Larry could hardly believe it. Just the two plummeting Eagles, and three little explosions of black feathers as the Eagles fisted their prey, knocking the birds out of the sky and into the river.

They fanned their wings and tails to brake down, then made a graceful, leisurely circle to land on the sandbar beside the skinny black bodies. Larry found himself cheering like a madman as they made their fly-by, and it seemed to him that they bowed once, like star performers for an appreciative audience, before bending to dine.

The kestrel soared wearily up into the air, and was lost in the blue of the sky.

Larry cheered himself hoarse, then turned—

And found himself staring into the face of his boss, Rod Calligan.

A face that was transfixed with such rage and hate that for a moment, Larry didn't even recognize him.

The bus bounced off the wall of the bluff and skidded along it to a halt, the white-faced driver fighting the wheel and the momentum of multiple tons of steel and plastic and passengers. The passengers themselves screamed loudly enough to be heard over the shrieking of air brakes, the scrape of metal on rock, and the dull thud of an explosion as flame blossomed over the edge of the curve.

The bus slid to a stop mere inches away, just off her bumper. The driver stared down at her through his windshield, statuelike, whiter than marble.

Jennie just sat, frozen, her hands clutching her steering wheel, her heart trying to beat its way out of her rib cage.

It was the shrieking of the passengers that finally galvanized her into movement. She slammed the Brat's door open and sprinted for the bus, certain from all the noise that there were people sprawled in various states of *broken* all over the interior.

But miraculously, no one was hurt.

The driver was in a complete state of shock, as well he might be, but Jennie and a couple of the passengers who had their wits about them began helping the others out of the bus. Within a few moments, more cars appeared on both sides of the road, some of whose drivers had seen the plume of flame and smoke from the Lincoln. One driver had a cellular phone, and two had C.B. radios; all three called police and ambulances.

Jennie stayed there anyway, as the only witness to the entire "accident." She told the police, when they finally arrived, that the driver of the Lincoln had been trying to pass her on the blind curve, and that the bus driver had pulled off the best "save" she had ever seen in her life.

Since no one in the Lincoln survived to dispute her version of the story, and the driver honestly did not remember much besides seeing the Lincoln on the wrong side of the road and swerving to avoid it, the cops were perfectly willing to believe her.

It was only when she finally pulled her Brat away from the scene that she saw what was written on the side of the bus.

Eagle Tours.

David gritted his teeth and went on with *his* part of the "plan," even though he wanted to go chasing right after the three guys in the Lincoln as it sped off after Jennie's Brat. This whole thing depended on everyone doing *his* part, doing it right, and doing it without interfering with the rest of the plan. He wouldn't help either her or Toni Calligan by rushing off and doing something stupid.

Toni was not even aware of what *else* was going on. But the dual threat of her soon-to-be-ex husband and the *mi-ah-luschka* was probably more than enough for her. She was white as a sheet under her makeup and healing bruises, and the two kids, poor little mites, were clearly just as terrified when David came to the door. He wondered what had been going on in that house in the past forty-eight hours—

—then decided that maybe he really didn't want to know, after all. It would only make him madder. And he *might* lose his temper, go down to Calligan's construction site, and beat the bastard's face in. He was only heartbeats from doing that as it was; only his promise to Jennie had kept him from dashing out to kill the man when he realized *Calligan* had sent those goons to drown her.

But David had promised. She would not respect him for breaking a promise. She would never forgive him for messing up the case by breaking Calligan's head. Logically, he knew that. Emotionally, though, countless generations of warrior ancestry told him to go collect some blood.

He hustled all three of his charges into the backseat of Mooncrow's car and threw their luggage into the trunk; the sooner they got out of this neighborhood, the less chance there was of getting caught. Mrs. Nebles waved good-bye from her front window, and gave Toni the high-sign as they pulled away. Toni smiled weakly and returned it.

Everything was ready and waiting at the office; a small and private room, the Shelter lawyer, the papers, the ride to a safe-house. The lawyer coached Toni through the procedure with sublime disregard for Mooncrow, who smudged Toni, the kids, the lawyer, and the papers impartially, chanting and drumming with his other hand.

Then again, this probably wasn't the strangest ceremony these offices had ever seen. Hadn't Jennie said something about being part of the dedication ceremonies?

Yes, she had told him about it. She'd offered an Osage purification and blessing, along with a female rabbi, a female Episcopalian priest, a female minister, a voodoo priestess, and some kind of witch. . . .

No wonder the lawyer wasn't fazed. *On the other hand, given what they're doing here, they probably figured they needed all the blessings they could get,* he decided.

Mooncrow and the lawyer were equally efficient; they finished at about the same time, and both stood aside to let Maria herd up Toni and her kids like a faithful sheepdog and whisk them off to somewhere a lot safer.

"Wait," Toni said, just before Maria herded them out the door. Maria paused, and Toni looked back at David. "Before we go off—I didn't get a chance to tell you this. I want you to get hold of the cops that are investigating the bombing," she said, firmly. "Tell them that I have things they need to know, things I found out over the past couple of days. I want to testify against Rod. And I found a *lot* of papers and tapes in the safe in his office when I got in there this morning. He had them in a box marked 'Insurance.' I guess he thought that was clever; they're all in my suitcase."

David nodded, and looked at Maria, who grimaced. "Actually, Toni, if you have things you think might put you in danger, I'll take you downtown before I take you to the shelter. You might qualify for the witness protection program, and that would free up a little more space for another woman who doesn't."

"I thought about that," Toni replied, and licked her lips nervously. "With what I overheard on the phone—I think I would qualify, and I'd feel a lot safer with the cops watching us. No insult meant, Maria, but your people don't know Rod, and I do. I—think he might try something really drastic when he realizes we're gone."

"You're on." Maria waved her out the door, and David relaxed a little, then joined the lawyer in opening windows and fanning smoke out of the room.

"Sorry about this—" he began, apologetically. The lawyer laughed.

"Don't worry about it," she assured him. "I've seen weirder, believe me. The worst was the time we got some poor little Haitian girl in here who was so terrified of a curse that she wouldn't even pick up a pen until we brought in the woman that helped at the dedication. A little smoke is nothing—the *obeah* brought in chickens, a goat—I thought we were never going to get the goat smell out, and we're still finding feathers in odd corners!"

David laughed as they chased the last of the smoke out the windows and opened the door to the rest of the office. Then he borrowed the office phone long enough to call in a progress report to Sleighbow and Romulus Insurance. And Mr. Sleighbow was very interested in what Toni Calligan had said before she left. *Very* interested.

"Thank you, Mr. Horse," he said, gravely. "I'll get in touch with the Tulsa P.D. and have them call me as soon as they've taken Mrs. Calligan's statement. If she is that concerned—" he hesitated for a moment"—*please* remind Ms. Talldeer that she told *me* she was not Nancy Drew. Urge her to take extreme caution."

Well, it's a little too late for that, David thought, with heavy irony. But Sleighbow didn't know about the past three days; the attack was the one thing that Jennie had insisted on keeping from him. She had pointed out that she could not prove that her attackers had been sent by Calligan. If, however, she could get the thugs picked up, they would very probably sing some fascinating tunes.

At least Sleighbow was concerned for Jennie's safety. David had to respect that and the man himself. Sleighbow didn't know Jennie personally; she was just a "hired hand."

So David made sure to thank the man, and promised him another update as soon as they had any information at all.

The rest of the Shelter volunteers were clustered around a television set as he came out of the little office, and it did not look as if they were watching soaps. Not with the expressions of shock on their faces. "My God!" said one,

"Isn't that Jennie Talldeer?"

"What?" he exclaimed, sudden images of Jennie lying hurt or worse flashing into his mind. He practically leapt the desk to try and get a look at the screen himself.

He got a brief glimpse of Jennie—*Alive, all right, oh thank god!*—before the station went to a commercial. The woman who had made the exclamation spotted him crowding in, and said, "Aren't you Jennie's boyfriend?" Then, before he could answer, she reached for the channel changer. "Hang on, I'll bet they'll have this on another channel!"

This time they apparently came in right at the beginning of the newsbreak; a different reporter was on the scene of some kind of accident. . . .

He recognized the spot immediately; near the top of the bluff above the Verdigris River on Highway 20. The camera panned down the bluff to the smoking remains of some kind of vehicle far below, before turning to the road, and showing a bus and Jennie's Brat, practically nose-to-nose.

A different reporter was interviewing Jennie, who looked remarkably composed. Unless you knew her, and knew that it was nothing but a mask.

The woman turned up the sound.

"—acted like they'd been drinking, and tried to pass me just in front of the blind curve," Jennie was saying. "I slammed on the brakes just as the bus came around the other side. That poor bus driver didn't have a prayer of missing them, and the only reason I didn't end up in the wreck was because I had already stopped. The driver should get a medal for keeping that bus under control and on the road!"

The reporter thanked her, and went on to interview one of the passengers on the bus. The cameraman panned down on the wrecked car again.

Was it a Lincoln? It sure could have been.

David looked over at Mooncrow, who only nodded.

Nodded? Wait a minute—Mooncrow looked a lot more

tired than he should be for the simple ceremony he'd just completed. Unless, of course, he had been doing Other Things at the same time!

David got the old man aside while the attention of the women was still on the television, and hissed, "You knew about this, didn't you? You knew she was in trouble!"

Mooncrow shrugged. "What good would it have done to tell you? I did what I could, and you could have done nothing."

David scowled and gritted his teeth. The old man might be right about that—but still!

When Jennie came in about an hour later, the entire volunteer staff had cycled through and no one knew of her involvement in the bus accident. David got to her first.

"I don't know whether to hold you or hit you," he said under his breath, as he caught her in a tight embrace.

"Hold me," she advised. "I have enough people trying to hit me."

She looked as gray as Mooncrow, and about as tired. The old man came up beside them, and David watched them trade significant looks with a sense of frustration.

I hope to hell they get around to telling me about what's been going on, he thought, grinding his teeth a little. But there was no point in taking out his frustration on her. Did those close to all Medicine People feel left out like this?

"Toni's in police custody," he told her, instead of snapping at her. "She found something out, something big enough that she wants to testify."

Jennie's head came up at that, alertly. "Damn!" she swore softly. "In that case—we'd better get those papers served on Rod Calligan, before he gets wind of that and goes into hiding. If we can't serve the protective order and the divorce papers on him, that's only going to complicate the state's case. Did you call Sleighbow for me?"

"Already taken care of; I figured he'd want to hear that," David said, pleased that he'd thought of it. "My only question is, are you up to this paper thing?"

"You need me along," she replied, staunchly. "Or actually, to be completely truthful, we need each other. If he's going to try anything, we'll be two against one. I don't think that he'll try anything with a witness around."

David grimaced, but she was right. And given Rod Calligan's recent history, he wasn't going to bet on the man reacting sanely to the papers being served.

"All right," he said. "Let's rock."

"I will come," Mooncrow said suddenly. They both turned to look at him. The old man had regained most of his color, but he still looked exhausted. Nevertheless, he was adamant, David could tell from his expression of stubborn will. "I will come," he repeated. "I will stay in the car, but I will come."

Jennie nodded, slowly. "I think he's right," she said. "I think he'd better."

David shrugged. "The more the merrier," he replied philosophically, and gathered up the papers he was going to serve on Calligan. "Shall we?"

Jennie remained very quiet all the way to the mall site, but her hand crept into David's and she settled her head on his shoulder with a sigh. He squeezed the hand, and turned his head just enough to kiss the top of her hair, but kept his attention on traffic. This was not the time to get into an accident.

Mooncrow did stay in the car when they reached the site; it was just past quitting time, but Calligan's Beemer was still there, and there was a light on in the office.

"Bingo," David said, softly. Jennie nodded, and let go of his hand; they climbed out of the car and headed for the portable building housing Calligan's remote office.

The door wasn't locked; David simply walked right in. The secretary's desk just inside was unoccupied, but David spotted Rod Calligan sitting at a second desk just inside a door on the left, at the back of a larger office. Calligan looked up as they both entered, frowning, but he either didn't see Jennie or simply dismissed her as unimportant.

"I'm not hiring," he began, but Jennie wasn't paying any attention to him. She was concentrating on the artifacts on Calligan's blotter.

They were all old, earth-stained, fragile-looking. A medicine bag of some kind, a pipe, a fetish-bundle wrapped in ancient, handwoven grass-cloth—

"I'm not here for a job, Mr. Calligan," David said, formally. "You *are* Rod Calligan, aren't you?"

Calligan nodded, looking annoyed.

"Good." David held out the papers, and Calligan took them, reflexively. "This is a protective order forbidding you to come within one hundred yards of Antonia Calligan, Ryan Calligan, and Jill Calligan, and a preliminary divorce decree. Thank you for accepting them."

He stepped back from the desk; Rod Calligan stared at him for a moment in stunned shock. Then his face began to turn purple-red with anger.

"By the way, Mr. Calligan," Jennie said, from behind David, "I'm Jennifer Talldeer, an investigator hired by Mark Sleighbow at Romulus Insurance. I've got a few questions I'd like to ask you. About your three friends who drove the black Lincoln—"

Jennie realized as soon as she entered the office that Calligan didn't recognize her. In fact, he probably had no idea who she was or what she looked like. So even though she was certain the hit men had told him she was dead, he showed no surprise as she followed David in through the door.

Until she told him who she was, that is.

It had been hard to concentrate on quick strategy—hard to concentrate on much of anything, once she saw what was spread out across his desk.

Calligan had an entire array of stolen artifacts from

Watches-Over-The-Land's gravegoods, and others. Jennie could not imagine how he had managed to keep their presence hidden from her; she should have been able to sense them the moment they got near the site!

Unless whatever had been protecting Calligan was also hiding his stolen treasures. . . .

He had been about to launch into some kind of display of anger, verbally or possibly physically, against David, and men who were angry didn't think about what they were saying.

She knew he had hired those three thugs, but she didn't know if he had actually seen or met them. But he had to know that there were three of them, and he might assume whatever car they drove was dark.

The minute she spoke her own name, he went white.

But when she said the words "black Lincoln," he went berserk.

He leapt up out of his chair, his face suffused with rage—

And his hand clenched around something, something that pulsed with an evil dark power, power that oozed thick and blackly poisonous as crude oil. A power she had sensed before.

The Evil One!

Now it all made sense; the grave-robbing, the bomb, and her visions! *Now* the pieces all fell together and she saw the shape of what she had been facing!

She had only just enough time to recognize the fetish-bundle for what it was, and to make that sudden realization, when Calligan lunged at her.

She backpedaled, frantic to avoid the touch of that bundle; he came up over the desk at her, equally determined to touch her with it. There was no room to escape; he body-slammed her into the filing cabinets behind her, and as she flailed to avoid further contact, she did the very last thing she wanted to do—

She accidentally touched the hand holding the spirit-bundle.

This time, there was no gradual transition; something seized her, shook her like a dog shook a rag, and flung her away.

She was—not in the Waking World.

Not any longer.

CHAPTER SEVENTEEN

KESTREL STOOD IN the heart of the Spirit World, but in a part of it she did not recognize, at least, not at first. This was a bleak and barren landscape, where nothing grew and nothing lived. The sky was the color of ashes, the ground under her feet cracked and lifeless. Nothing broke the arid horizon but the occasional dead stick of what had once been a tree, now withered and sere. A thin and bitter wind sighed mournfully across this land, full of acrid, burning stenches and the sick-sweet smell of decay.

She wore her human form, in her full regalia as *Hunkah* and *Tzi-sho,* as Warrior and Medicine Person.

Before her stood another human; someone she did not recognize at all. By his costume, he was Osage of long ago; his hair was cut in the Warrior's roach, and he wore the deerskin leggings of a hunter, but he had no eagle feathers in his hair, and no shell torque about his neck. Instead, he had the feathers of some sooty black bird braided into his hair; a soft down plume on the *right* side, and the hard tail-feather on the *left*. The very opposite positioning of the two eagle plumes she wore. Around his neck, he had a collar of hard black talons, of no bird or animal that she could recognize, centered with a disk of shiny black flint. And his face was painted, not with war-paint, nor with bluff-paint, but with jagged lightning bolts of ebony-black.

And he was one with this terrible landscape she found herself in. He stood here with the full confidence and comfort of one who belonged to this place, was familiar with it. The predator in the heart of his territory. . . .

That was when she recognized it as the place of her dream, before this all began. The terrible place where the eagles died.

The man before her was neither old nor young, and his expression was so completely blank that he might have been a department-store mannequin. But his eyes held an evil and a hatred so intense that she instinctively stepped back a pace or two from him.

He reached toward her, and she backed up again; she sensed that if she let him touch her—

He'll drain me, she thought with growing horror. *He'll take everything worth having from me. I'll still be alive, but there won't be anything left of what makes me what I am. No spirit, no heart, no energy, no laughter, no creativity, no hope. No love. That's what he did here. . . .*

And that was what made him so horrifying. *This* was why Watches-Over-The-Land had to stop him! He devoured people, things, from within, and left nothing behind but the dregs.

He makes them into something worse than nothing, worse than killing them outright, because they know what he's done to them, and he's left them despair. Despair is all his victims have left.

And now, with no physical body to limit him, nothing to confine him, and all the protections that had been put around his spirit-bundle gone, he was more dangerous than he had ever been in her ancestor's time.

He reached toward her again; slowly, as if he was toying with her. She evaded him, but not easily. It felt as if she were moving through mud; was he mustering the resources of this place against her? She tried to summon up some sort of protection, and failed.

He laughed at her, his voice ringing with scorn.

"You may have conquered my Black Birds, Little Hawk," he told her, sneering, "but now you meet the De-vourer. I am Hunger, and you cannot escape me."

She didn't reply; she could only wish, desperately and profoundly, that there was some way to invoke Watches-Over-The-Land, to bring him back from the Summerlands. He defeated this Evil One before; her ancestor *Moh-shon-ah-ke-ta* was the one who *knew* how to deal with him, what worked against him the first time—

But she was on her own.

She was more frightened now than when she had been struggling to keep from drowning; more frightened than a few hours ago, facing her murderers for a second time. That had only been a physical death that she risked. This was more—the death of all that made her whole.

She had never, ever, felt so helpless in all of her life.

What was worse, she watched the Evil One's eyes, and knew that *he* knew all of this by the sly smile creeping onto his thin lips; knew that he read her every thought, and could play on all her weaknesses and exploit them.

You have to deal with the enemy inside yourself before you can take on the enemy that faces you. . . .

Like I have the leisure for a psychological review right now! What should I do, ask him to wait for a minute while I bring in my analyst?

His smile widened, just a little more, while the bitter wind of *his* place, called by *his* power, whipped her hair around her face, stinging her eyes and calling up tears of pain and pure unadulterated fear.

He licked his lips, as if he tasted and relished those tears.

David was not prepared for Calligan to come lunging over the desk; he stepped back, instinctively. That was a mistake; he cleared the way for the man to body-slam Jennie into the wall of filing cabinets opposite the desk.

Then he reacted, leaping to Jennie's defense, but it was too late; Jennie was out cold, and Calligan was backing away, toward the door. Quickly, he positioned himself between Jennie and Calligan, taking a defensive stance over her prone body. He glanced down briefly, desperate to determine how badly she was hurt, but afraid to take his eyes off Calligan for long.

But Calligan relaxed, and gifted David with the *nastiest* smile he'd ever seen. David tensed. If something made Calligan smile, he had a pretty good idea that *he* wasn't going to like it.

Then the contractor reached around behind his own back and locked the door of his office.

"I told Romulus, I told Sleighbow, over and over, that they couldn't trust you savages," he said, pulling a clasp knife from his pocket. "Now—let's see if I can come up with a good story." His eyes focused just past David's shoulder for a moment. "Got it. That primitive little tart must have decided to use you as her way to bring me down." Calligan eyed David as if he were some kind of lower form of life, a bug or a worm. "I can see why; you must make a lot of money as a gigolo. So. First you seduce and steal my wife, then persuade her to file against me; then you use serving those papers on me as an excuse to get in here to try and murder me." He shook his head and *tsk*ed. "Barbarians. There isn't a judge and jury in Oklahoma who'd blame me for killing you and your bimbo. Temporary insanity, that's what they'd say."

Strange; Calligan spoke as if he was reciting something; as if someone were coaching him with a hidden mike. But his eyes were alert enough, so he wasn't on drugs or anything.

David tensed, his eyes on Calligan's, regretting profoundly that he had left his gun at home and his knives in the car with Mooncrow. But Jennie had sworn that he couldn't risk going armed when he was serving legal papers. And he really hadn't thought that Calligan would try anything stupid in a place as public as his office.

Calligan handled that knife as if he knew how to use it. A very bad sign.

Calligan saw his eyes flick briefly to the knife, and his smile widened. "I was a Navy SEAL, did you know that?" he asked conversationally. "They train the SEALs right. Missed 'Nam, though. I always felt kind of cheated. I'd have enjoyed it."

He circled a little, and made a brief feint to the right. David saw immediately what he was up to; he wanted to get David away from Jennie.

So instead of moving, he simply pivoted, watching Calligan's eyes, and trying to think if there was anything within reach that *he* could use for a weapon.

Kestrel backed up another pace, but she didn't think a simple tactic like that was going to work for much longer. It might look as if she could back up forever across this wasteland, but this was *his* wasteland, and he could manipulate it in any way he chose. Sooner or later he was going to get tired of this.

Oh, Ancestor, if only I could call you back to me!

"*Daughter—*" said a deep voice just behind her, suddenly; so suddenly that it made her jump. Something materialized at her side, a bright presence in the darkness. She glanced to her right, and almost sobbed with relief.

Another Osage stood beside her, his costume dating from the same ancient days as the Evil One. Like his, all the decorations on it were non-European; shells, quills, claws, teeth—but *this* man wore proper war-paint, a mussel-shell torque. And like Kestrel, he wore eagle feathers; both the under-tail covert of the *Tzi-sho*, on the left, and the hard tail-feather of the *Hunkah*, on the right.

There was no doubt whatsoever in her mind who this was, not when she sensed an immense power and strength in him, and an enormous confidence.

"Moh-shon-ah-ke-ta," she said, with a little nod of respect, and a smile of relief. "Ancestor. You are very welcome here!"

As she spoke, she moved back and to the side, instinctively placing herself shoulder-to-shoulder with him. He smiled back at her, and some of that power and strength flowed into her, erasing some of her blind terror.

But when she looked back at their enemy, the Evil One did not seem to be any less confident. He looked *Moh-shon-ah-ke-ta* up and down, contemptuously. "One, old and brittle," he said with scorn, "and one, green and with no experience. Hardly a challenge at all."

"So?" Watches-Over-The-Land said mildly. "But you are hardly younger than I."

Kestrel felt a third presence join her and *Moh-shon-ah-ke-ta*; a moment later, Mooncrow stood at her left shoulder. He looked very much like Watches-Over-The-Land, except that the decorations on his ritual clothing, like hers, boasted the additions of ribbon- and beadwork.

The Evil One snorted. "Even three-to-one you cannot defeat me!" he laughed. "You, old fool—" he continued, pointing at Kestrel's Ancestor, "—should have warned them! You had the Little Old Men of all the gentes beside you when you bested me last! You have only these two at your side now! And I—"

He seemed to loom larger—no, he *was* growing larger,

looming over all three of them!

"—I have no limits upon my power *now*!"

He spread his arms, gathering his power to him, and lightning flickered about his head as he prepared to strike them.

But Watches-Over-The-Land was not going to stand there and wait for him to act!

"Follow!" he ordered, and fled.

Kestrel followed him, as he somehow twisted the very fabric of this place, and escaped from the Evil One's land into another level of the Spirit World.

Her sight distorted, then cleared; she gasped for a moment, trying to breathe air that was suddenly heavy.

No, it was not *air* at all.

Kestrel found herself wearing the form of a fish, the swift and clever trout, arrowing through the sparkling water of a clear river. Ahead of her was a great salmon, which must be *Moh-shon-ah-ke-ta*; beside her, a black bass, which was surely Mooncrow.

The river darkened, as something passed overhead. Kestrel gathered herself and leapt, high—

The Evil One was there, waiting for her, fishing spear in hand. He had already stretched a net across the river ahead of them! They were trapped!

He struck at her leaping body; she writhed as she fell, and the head of the spear just skimmed past her sleek flank. This time it was her turn to cry *"Follow!"* as she fell back into the river and gulped life-giving water, then twisted the fabric of the river and—

Ran on four hooves across a grassy plain, in the shape of an Appaloosa mare. Her unshod hooves thudded dully beneath her, cushioned by grass that had never seen a blade. This grassland stretched from horizon to horizon, dotted only with a bush or two, with a hint of thin darkness to the east where there might be trees following a watercourse. Overhead, the sky was a blue bowl, the sun a white-hot disk in the midst of it. Two stallions raced behind her, a Medicine Hat pony, and a tall palomino; and she pulled herself up, not wanting to run blindly into a new trap. She stood warily sniffing the wind that whipped her mane and tail, head up, looking for the Evil One. The stallions followed her lead, each facing in a different direction.

She wondered how the Evil One would counter *this* shape; there wasn't much that could take on three mustangs and win, not on the plains—

Then the palomino whinnied sharply, and she and Watches-Over-The-Land pivoted in his direction.

Fire!

Fire sprang up in a long line stretching from horizon to horizon, racing toward them, eating its way across the landscape. Kestrel fought her horse-instinct to run in a blind panic, as more fires cut across the horizon, until they were ringed with flame.

"Follow!" whinnied Mooncrow, and reared, and leapt—

She followed, and found herself—

Fluttering through air that tasted thick and grainy. In bird shape. But not the familiar bird-shape of Kestrel, but black, speckled, stub-tailed.

A starling? She faltered for a moment, then picked up her wingbeats again, moving easily among the—

High-rise apartment buildings?

Fumes drifted up from the traffic below, but they didn't seem to bother her in this shape. Car horns blared, sirens screamed, construction equipment rattled and pounded, and the noise of uncounted engines battered her ears.

Beside her flapped an English sparrow and a pigeon.

The air behind them *popped.* And the Evil One, in his form of Black Bird, hovered there for a moment, confused by the terrific noise.

That moment was all that Kestrel needed. It was time to stop running and give *him* a taste of being the prey! Calling a starling alarm, she dove on the Black Bird, certain of what would follow.

Her alarm call swiftly summoned a cloud of starlings from all directions, which followed her lead and proceeded to mob the Black Bird mercilessly. Individually, the Evil One was more than a match for them—and in fact, he lashed out with beak and claws, and sent several of his tormentors tumbling dead out of the sky. But that only made the rest of the starlings angrier, and they pecked at his head and pulled at his feathers until he began to falter and lose height. And he could not tell *which* of the starlings was really Kestrel; he could only strike blindly and hope that luck would put her into his reach.

He could not win this one, and so *he* changed the setting, shattering the air with a terrible cry that wrenched the fabric of time and space, sending them all hurtling—

Into the white of a landscape of nothing but snow and ice. Wind ate at her; snow whipped around her, driving itself into her eyes and nose. The sky was white, the ground was an undulating white; *everything* was white.

Kestrel shivered, despite the thick coat of fur she wore, encased as she was in the body of an arctic fox; beside her were a white wolf and a snowy owl. She had barely time to take in what form she now had, when what she had thought was a snowdrift heaved upward on two hind legs, roaring, and came at them with monstrous paws spread wide to crush them all.

But they were not there when the polar bear's foreclaws hit the snow. Kestrel had gone to the right, the white wolf to the left, and the owl straight up. This time *they* attacked the bear; the fox nipping at its hind end, the wolf tearing at its flanks, and the owl battering its face and eyes with its wings.

The bear roared with frustration, and knocked the owl out of the air. Instantly, both Kestrel and Mooncrow leapt

in, each snatching a wing, and pulling it away from the
bear's claws.

This is nothing but stalemate, she thought to herself, as she
panted, her sides heaving, her lungs aching. *He can wear us
down like this—we have to find some way to bottle him up!*

"Put me down and follow!" commanded *Moh-shon-ah-ke-
ta,* and she obeyed unthinkingly, opening her jaws, then
followed as the owl plunged forward into—

The cool, green depths of the forest.

A very, very *large* forest—

No, she was simply very small.

She scampered instinctively into the shelter of a leaf-filled
cranny beneath the trunk of a fallen forest giant. She was a
deermouse; beside her was a chipmunk, and beside him, a
vole. She peered out at the forest outside; it was as silent as
the city had been noisy, with one lone bird calling off in the
distance, and not even a faint breeze rustling the trees.
Sunlight lanced down through the branches, making shafts
of gold among the green.

"Kestrel, will you trust me?" asked her ancestor, twitching
his whiskers with agitation. Nearby, a black wolverine
snuffled through the dead leaves, and she knew that this was
the Evil One, looking for them. But for the moment, they
were safely hidden in the hollow beneath the fallen tree.

"Yes," she answered simply.

*"Then when you find yourself as a swallow, fly into the first
cave that you see."*

Fly *into* a cave? But even though swallows were clever
flyers, and often nested in caves, how would that help?

She never got a chance to ask that question, for at that
moment the black wolverine caught their scent, and began
to dig at the entrance to their shelter.

"Follow!" cried Mooncrow.

And once again she darted through the air, this time
above a landscape she recognized. It was the area around

Carlsbad, New Mexico, and she was, indeed, in the shape of a swallow.

Unfortunately, she was entirely alone.

And behind her was a Cooper's hawk, talons outstretched to snatch her out of the sky.

The Cooper's was the deadliest predator of birds that flew; Kestrel had seen them take starlings and crows before their prey even knew there was a danger. With a squeak of panic, Kestrel twisted and dipped and turned, trying to outmaneuver her enemy.

But she was tired, and the Evil One wasn't even missing a wingbeat!

She looked down, hoping for some kind of brush to dive into to shake her pursuer. But there was nothing down there but rocks and cactus—

And the mouth of a small cave.

She folded her wings and dove. The hawk followed, but as she looked back, she heard him laugh, and saw him transform in midair from a hawk to a great black owl!

Too late for her to change direction—

She shot through the mouth of the cave into echoing semidarkness. *"How kind of you to be so stupid as to go into a place where I have the advantage!"* he mocked, as she banked frantically, just in time to avoid the back wall of the cave. Then she had to bank again, as her flight took her too near the entrance he was guarding, evading his talons by so little that she squeaked with pain as he grabbed one of her primaries and yanked it out.

He lunged at her—

And as soon as he passed into the cave itself, he flew directly into the web of an enormous spider!

It confused him, and he flapped in place, angrily shaking his head to try and rid himself of the clinging fibers. But before he could, a huge bat dropped down on his back from the ceiling above, knocking him into the floor of the cave so hard that he hit his head. And for the moment, he lay stunned.

Kestrel seized the opportunity and darted outside, followed by the bat.

The bat transformed into *Moh-shon-ah-ke-ta* as soon as both of them were outside; Mooncrow rose up from out of the rocks, and Kestrel dropped down beside him and took her human form again.

"Now!" cried her Ancestor.

They joined power, calling on the ancient rocks, calling on the Earth and Air, the Sky and Lightning—

And all the ancient spirits answered them.

The earth shook itself, knocking them off their feet; the Sky sent down Lightning all around them, blinding them, deafening them, hemming them in—

Rocks tumbled down the slope of the hill, blocking the entrance of the cave, and before the Evil One could find a shape to escape the trap, Lightning struck the hillside again and again until the sand smoked and fused, sealing him inside for all time.

David dodged a swipe of Calligan's knife, and stumbled into the side of the desk, sending everything that was not already on the floor flying. He grabbed an ashtray and flung it at the man, who dodged it, laughing wildly, and slashed at him again.

The window's too small to get out of, even if Jennie were conscious. The only chair is on the other side of the desk. The filing cabinets are too heavy to tip over—

He ducked another knife strike, frantically running through his limited options.

The phone is on the floor, and I don't think he's gonna give me a minute to call 9-1-1—

Was that smoke?

He glanced to the side and swore. The lamp that *had* been

on the desk had gone into the wastepaper basket; smoke wisped up from the trash. Calligan followed his glance, and grinned even more as flames licked up from the paper and the bulb exploded with a pop.

Oh shit. Isn't the other side of this trailer where they keep the explosives' shed?

To put it out, he'd have to leave Jennie—which was exactly what Calligan wanted. The minute he left her unprotected, Calligan would kill her.

Calligan laughed, and David snarled as the flames licked up a little higher from the wastebasket.

This guy is effin' crazy! Where the hell is Mooncrow? Can't he see the fire from here? Mooncrow might not be able to get through the locked door, but if he called the fire department—

Calligan lunged, and David skidded out of reach, the blade actually ripping his shirt in passing. Calligan was as fast as a striking snake; he recovered and lunged again, as the flames caught the chair next to the desk and dense black smoke mingled with the flames—

If the fire didn't get them, the smoke *surely* would!

Where was Mooncrow?

Calligan's got him. Or he's had a stroke. He'd looked awfully gray back there at the office.

Calligan lunged again, trying to drive David away from Jennie, and cackled insanely. *And this joker doesn't care if we all die so long as he gets me and Jennie!*

Screw this. There's only one way to deal with this maniac.

He knew he was going to get hurt, but he didn't think that Calligan would anticipate his next move, and he remembered something one of his Lakotah buddies told him about going up against a knife-fighter.

You can always take the knife out of the picture if you're willing to get hurt doing it. Just force the target on him; don't let him pick where he's going to stick you.

And the flames were climbing the wall beside him, now.

They didn't have more than a minute or two if they were going to get out of there alive!

Calligan lunged—and David charged into the lunge.

He took the knife in his shoulder, but his adrenaline was up now, and he didn't even feel it. He body-slammed Calligan into the wall; grabbed both his shoulders and slammed his head up sideways into the filing cabinets. Calligan's eyes rolled up into his head, and David let him fall.

He pulled the knife out of his shoulder with one hand while he kicked the door open. The flimsy lock didn't hold past the second kick.

Now the flames covered the back wall entirely.

He took the two steps he needed to reach Jennie, thanking all the gods that she was tiny, then slung her fireman-style across his good shoulder, as blood poured from the wound in his other shoulder, soaking his shirt.

As he turned, he took a fraction of a second to look for the artifacts, knowing that Jennie would ask after them, remembering that she had said they were important. But there wasn't anything anywhere in sight, and he had no time, no time left at all—

He plunged through the door, stumbled down the stairs, and staggered across the bare, sandy ground—the office was going to go up at any moment, and they needed some cover, *quick*—

There. He spotted a pile of bags of sand for concrete and tumbled around in back of them, dropping Jennie as soon as they were behind them and falling to his knees—

He pulled her further into safety, then took a quick, nervous peek around the edge.

Just as that whole corner of the lot went up.

Jee-ZUS!

He fell back as the ground beneath him shook, momentarily blinded and deafened.

But by the time he could see again, the fire department,

half the cops in Tulsa, and everyone in the neighborhood were converging on the site, sirens and people screaming.

"No, sir," Jennie said politely to the cop, while the paramedic bandaged David's shoulder. "We don't know what happened. David and I were delivering the divorce and protective orders from my client, Toni Calligan. You can check that with the Women's Shelter yourself. Mr. Calligan wasn't happy about it, but—" she shrugged. "He threw us out."

David had stalled the cops just long enough to think of a story they might believe. "She's being polite, officer," David put in, grimacing a little with pain. "Mr. Calligan told us to go to hell and went berserk, and threw us out of the office. Threw Jennie, literally, and she landed on the steps and got knocked out cold. Then for some reason he assaulted me with a letter opener. You get a look at Mrs. Calligan, you'll see what I mean; that bastard was a psycho. That poor lady's black and blue."

"It all checks, lieutenant," one of the other cops said, radio to his ear. "His wife's got a protective order on him *and* she's turning in evidence on him in the bomb case out here." The lieutenant gave David a sharp look; he returned one as bland and innocent as a baby calf.

"Honest to god, I don't know what the hell happened after he went after me," David said, still wide-eyed. "I got out after he stabbed me and he locked the door; I figured he might be going after a gun or something, so I picked up Jennie off the steps, slung her over my shoulder, and got the hell out. I got just past that pile of sandbags, when the whole place went up."

Not too bad a story for one built as hastily as this one; it accounted for his stab wound and Jennie's goose egg.

Right now all he wanted was for the cops to let them loose. He had the feeling that by the time Toni Calligan finished making her statements and the cops finished searching Calligan's home office, they'd find more than enough to make them overlook a few minor discrepancies in his story.

He wanted to get to a hospital and get a pain-scrip for this shoulder. Then he wanted to go home.

He *didn't* want to think about what he'd seen, in the moment before the office went up like a demo from Industrial Light and Magic. . . .

A whole swarm of the Little People, grinning like fiends, dragging Calligan, kicking and screaming, behind them.

Jennie listened to David's improvised story with a feeling of awe. *Damn! If he can make up things like that out of nowhere, he's going to be a hell of a partner! I never could do convincing fibs!*

The police lieutenant gave them another one of those looks, after spending a good ten minutes trying to shake their story, but finally sighed. "All right," he said. "You and Ms. Talldeer can go. Just don't leave town."

David visibly summoned the rags of his dignity. "Officer," he said, earnestly, "Ms. Talldeer is making me her partner. The *last* thing I want to do is leave town!"

He dragged himself to his feet with the sympathetic help of the paramedic. Jennie stood up with care for her aching head, and they both headed for the car where Mooncrow waited for them. *Thank god he's all right.*

Apparently the fire hadn't actually been visible from outside; Mooncrow told David and the police that he hadn't known there was anything wrong until the explosion itself. David evidently believed him.

Good thing, too. He wasn't anywhere near ready to hear what had really happened.

"I don't suppose you saved the artifacts, did you?" Jennie asked, sotto voce, as they neared the car. She was wistful, but not at all hopeful.

" 'Fraid not, babe," he replied, apologetically. "I didn't see anything, and I didn't have time to look. Getting you out was a lot more important."

She sighed. "Well, it's better destroyed than in a museum, in Calligan's hands, or with some private collector." Then she brightened. "I just realized—we *did* this! We took care of everything! Calligan—he had the Evil One's spirit-bundle, and with that gone, we even took care of *that* part of the mess!"

No point in getting any more elaborate than that. Not yet, anyway.

She stopped, just at the car door, and turned toward him. She felt a glow of pride and happiness that not even the headache from her concussion could dim. "*We* did this, David! I could never have done this without you and Mooncrow!"

He flushed with pleasure, and flushed even more when she stood on tiptoe to kiss him, a kiss that lasted so long that Mooncrow finally called them back to their surroundings by clearing his throat ostentatiously.

"Much as I enjoy seeing you two enjoy yourselves. . . ."

They separated, reluctantly, and climbed into the car. "Your turn to drive, Little Old Man," David said, getting into the backseat with Jennie and putting his good arm around her shoulders. "We're walking wounded, remember?"

"Certainly, sah," Mooncrow drawled, in an excellent imitation of an impeccably English chauffeur. "And what are your directions?"

"We need a doc to look at us both—" Jennie began. "The paramedic said we needed to go to the emergency room—"

Mooncrow turned to glare at her. "I have enough friends at the Indian Hospital to get someone to do a house call," he said acidly. "What kind of a grandfather do you think I am?"

David laughed. "A contrary Little Old Man," he replied.

"All right, I know what you're waiting for. 'Home, James, and don't spare the horses!' "

"Veddy good, sah," Mooncrow replied with immense dignity and a twinkle in his eye, once more assuming his chauffeur persona. "Veddy, veddy good."

But he didn't immediately put the car in motion. Instead, he reached over the back of the seat and dropped a long bundle across Jennie's knees.

"A friend of ours wanted you to have this," he said, as the wrappings fell open.

David raised an eyebrow in surprise. It was a pipe, a very old pipe. It could have been the twin of the one lost in Calligan's office.

And Jennie, cool, unflappable Jennie, just stared at it, looking as stunned as if someone had just hit her in the back of the head with a two-by-four.

AUTHOR'S NOTE

I am not an expert on Native American religions. I hope that I have not offended any Native Americans with my depiction of Jennie Talldeer and her grandfather. This book was intended as entertainment; I have an extensive library and many trustworthy sources to ensure that it is as accurate as may be, but it is not to be taken seriously, not to be taken as reality. I am not portraying reality, or attempting to.

I have tried to be as accurate and honest as I can, within the realm of storytelling. My chief source for this story was *The Osages: Children of the Middle Waters,* by John Joseph Mathews, himself an Osage and a graduate of both the Universities of Oklahoma and Oxford, England. This book and many more in the "Civilization of the American Indian" series are available from the University of Oklahoma Press. I highly recommend them.

I am not a guru, shaman, Grand High Pooh-Bah, Guardian, Mistress of the Martian Arts, Avatar, Cosmic Earth Mother, or any incarnation of the same. I have no lock on Immortal Wisdom, and in my experience, anyone who claims to, has his eye on your money (granted, I do too, but only insofar as entertaining you enough to buy my next book). To confuse me with what I write is as fallacious as confusing a truck driver with his Peterbilt.